Jamie and The Lion's Gate The First Key

By, A. L. Barker

Jamie and The Lion's Gate
Is dedicated to my children, my heart.

A special thank you to all my readers.

To those who supported me through this process.
Thank you,
Mom, Sally, Odin, Piper, Phoebe, Rachel and Gypsy.
Thank you to my Models
Piper, Katy, Phoebe and Cavalier

Chapter One, An Off-Kilter Day

I awoke in the middle of the night, frozen in my bed. I tried to move but could only manage to shift my eyes. I looked around my room. Everything was in place, but this was of little comfort, as I was overwhelmed with a sense of dread. I soon realized there was a good reason for my apprehension. As I scanned the room, I noticed my bedroom door start to open very slowly. I tried to call out, but I couldn't speak. I looked to my little brother's crib, which sat on the other side of the room. I could see he was asleep, peacefully unaware of our current impending doom. I looked back to the door and was in shock at what I saw. Filling the space of my doorway, like a shroud of pure darkness, was an enormous, cloaked figure. The panic I felt seemed to wrap around my entire body. I tried to scream but couldn't manage a single gasp. I struggled harder and harder to move. The man stepped closer. My heart pounded inside my chest, and terror flooded my every thought. He peered from under his cloak, his glowing yellow eyes the only feature that broke the blackness of his silhouette. I started to panic, now struggling harder than I've ever before. His hand reached for me, and just as I thought this was the end, my throat finally cleared, and I unleashed a scream, "AHHHHHHHH!!!!" My Dad tore into my room with his gun in his hands. "Are you OK, Jamie? What's going on?" He looked at me, confused. The figure was gone.

"Dad, there was a giant man in here with yellow eyes. He reached for me!" I sobbed.

He set his gun down. "Jamie, you had a bad dream. I know moving has been tough on you. That's probably what triggered it." He walked to me and hugged me. I wrapped my arms around his shoulders.

"No, Dad, I wasn't asleep. I saw it in my room. It was real standing just there!" I pointed next to him.

"Dreams can feel real," he said, trying to reassure me. "It's just a trick of the mind. Look around. You're safe. Now go back to sleep." My Dad tucked me in and closed the door as he left the room, just as he had earlier that night.

"The door was opened when my Dad came in just now. I know it wasn't a dream." I thought, only half believing it myself. I turned in my bed to face away from the door, trembling as I stared at the wall until I fell back to sleep.

I skipped breakfast with my family the next morning, choosing to sit outside to draw in the dirt. One week ago today, my parents moved us here to Boise, Idaho. The betrayal seemingly magnified by the fact that my birthday was just a week earlier. I've just turned 11, and the last thing I wanted for my birthday was to leave my family and friends to live in the potato state. I am trying to make the best of things, but it hasn't been easy. The rain here is icy cold, no matter how hot it is outside. If that wasn't bad enough, these terrible thorns are all over the ground, which the locals refer to as "goat heads." I can tell you that they are brutal! I hate wearing shoes, but it is impossible to go without them. I learned that the hard way, and my feet still hurt. I miss the rolling, plush fields of green and the woods where I would dance with fireflies as the sunset. I miss the thunderstorms and catching toads and turtles. I miss having my aunts and uncles close to me, my grandma and my Great grandma, the creeks and swimming holes, but I miss having friends most of all.

My Dad greatly exaggerated how "great" it would be living in Boise. He claimed that this would be a "city among trees, a forest," so much that its very name means "The City of Trees." Compared to the outskirts Columbia, Missouri, it looks and feels like a desert. Not even a cool desert, like The Painted Desert in Arizona, we once visited during our family road trip. More like a sea of dirt, cheatgrass, and spiny plants. It's so hot here all the time, and to top it off, I hear that the winters get equally as cold. But that's not it. There is something off about the people too. They are distant, rude, and angry. The previous owner of our house showed up and wanted to fistfight my Dad for having the house painted a new color. So, I wonder, is this what everyone is like here? Is this how people are raised, or did something horrible happen to make them like this? I have a bad feeling all around about this area. To top it all off, school is starting in about a month. How could things possibly get any worse?

"Jamie, come here," my Mom called from the house. I ran inside to see what she wanted, leaving behind my newly formed piles of dirt I created while brooding. I found her in the laundry room, pulling clothes out of the dryer and placing them neatly in a hamper.

"What's up?" I asked.

"Can you please take Evan and go exploring or find something to do? I need him out of my hair, and you could use this as an opportunity to become familiar with the area. Take water bottles, and don't come home until supper," she ordered, posing this as a question, but I knew full well it was a demand.

"But mom, I don't want to." I could hardly stand my little brother. He eats his boogers and is always cold and clammy. Not to mention he is "the favorite child." The first-born son who left me the forgotten middle child.

"No buts!" My Mom barked while giving me that "mom look." You know the one. The look that meant another word, and the wooden spoon would come out of the kitchen drawer, and I would be on the receiving end of a paddling. Even if I were to get a spanking, I would still have to do what she asked, or worse, she'd tell my father.

So, with no other options, "fine, Mom. Evan, let's go!" I yelled down the hall. As if on cue, he came out of his room with his finger digging in his nose. I gaged at the sight of it, and my contentment for him swelled. I swallowed my pride and headed to the kitchen to fill my water bottle as my Mom commanded. After tying Evan's shoes, we headed out the front door and down the street together.

Evan didn't bother to ask me where we were going because he knew as well as I did that I had no idea. We reached the end of our road and turned onto another, and began walking up a hill. We hadn't made it very far when I was startled by the sound of a blaring horn coming from behind us. I turned quickly towards the sound and was confused to see a Jeep speeding in our direction. I pulled Evan to the side of the road as it slowed down alongside us. As it passed, to my shock, the driver shouted out profanities. I jumped while tugging Evan away from the street. "What is going on," I thought, half confused and half frightened by the driver's actions. The driver extended his arm out the window and threw a pile of half-finished food at us. As the items showered onto us, and I could hear the driver laughing as he sped off.

A crumpled-up paper bag with dirty napkins and a half-full paper cup struck me, causing orange soda to splatter all over my clothes and into my eyes. Evan was hit with a partially eaten hamburger, and the bun stuck to his face. My head began spinning with disgust and anger. "WHAT THE?! NASTY! WHY! WHO DOES THIS? JERK!" I spat incoherently with shock and confusion. Evan was only six, "what kind of monster tries to hurt a six-year-old?" I thought." I can't believe this is how people behave here! What a jerk!" I growled while peeling the bun from my brother's face.

"What did I do to deserve this?" Evan said while sobbing. I licked my thumb and wiped the remaining ketchup from his cheek.

"That was random. You didn't do anything. That man was a pig. Are you OK?" I tried to reassure him. Evan nodded and wiped his eyes. Although I could still see he was shaken by the incident.

"Why did we have to move here? People are mean here."

"I don't know. I think it's because Dad hates us," I remarked quietly as if my Dad could somehow hear me. I finished pulling a few chunks of meat from Evan's hair and was satisfied that he was clean. We continued walking up the hill, the recent series of events still weighing heavily on our minds. When we reached the top, we found a large meadow.

"Let's cut through the field, to avoid another run-in with jerks on the road." He agreed, and I searched for a way through. I looked over the landscape. The field had tall unkept dry grass, and there were little footpaths, which meant we could walk through it without getting the cheatgrass stuck in our shoes.

"Maybe we can find frogs like we did in Missouri," Evan added, his voice sounding a little more hopeful.

"I don't think there are frogs here. I don't see water," I sighed.

"Aw shucks," Evan moaned in disappointment. We continued walking slowly while searching for any rocks or random items. Then the sound of Evan whimpering echoed across the field.

"What now?" Assuming he had a splinter or a stubbed toe, I turned to view him, and he looked at me confused.

"That wasn't me," he raised his hands and shrugged. I looked across the sea of grass, a shiver ran up my spine, and I got the feeling someone was watching us.

"There's no one else there. You heard that, right?" I checked, not trusting my instincts, and feeling like I was overreacting.

"Yes, I heard that," Evan nodded suspiciously. We both stilled ourselves to listen for any other sounds or to see if anything moved.

"Maybe, it was, just the wind?" I whispered, trying to make sense of it, as everything seemed to be normal.

"Just the wind?" Evan looked at me with an eyebrow

raised.

I shrugged it off, "I don't know?" We refocused our attention away from the sound and started exploring, turning over stones, and looking for hidden treasures. After a while, the hot sun became unbearable, my feet started burning through my shoes, and all the rocks became too hot to hold. So, I glanced around, attempting to find another place for us to go. In the distance to our left, I spotted some trees near a road where we could sit and maybe have some relief from the sweltering heat. "Hey Evan, let's go towards those trees so we can take a break and rest our feet for a bit." I pointed towards a grove of trees as I spoke.

"OK, but can't we just go home?" Evan groaned, his face sweaty and red.

"Sorry bud, mom said not until supper time," but I felt his pain. I took a sip from my water bottle, handed it to Evan, and we moved towards the tree line.

We made it a few steps then another whimper carried to us on the wind. We both stilled ourselves. "I defiantly heard that! There's something out there. Let's go. We should try and find it," I felt something inside of me tugging me to it.

"WHY!?" Even protested and started stomping behind me as I turned and led the way.

"Because we don't have anything else important to do, and something out there might need our help," we shifted again to the right and started to push our way through the tall grass.

"This is stupid, and the grass is itching my feet!" Evan groaned.

"You'll be fine," I argued as we advanced to the area the sound had come from.

"Literally anything would be better than this," Evan spat, but I had stopped listening.

We kept walking until we found ourselves on another footpath. "That sound had to have come from around here," I considered while stopping to remove rocks and grass from my shoes.

"What do you think it was?" Evan asked.

"I'm not sure," I acknowledged and began scratching my legs. Everything itched, and I had a few cuts from the grass, and our shoes looked ruined.

"Should we really be trying to find it? You know, it could be a mountain lion," Evan insinuated while pulling out the stickers from his own shoes. I was about to explain that mountain lions wouldn't be this far into town, but before I could, I was cut off by the same unknown whimpering as before. We both jumped up and quickly rushed towards the sound. My heart started to pulsate with excitement and a trace of fear. It was louder this time which meant we were getting close. We continued onto another footpath. "What if it's a weirdo doing weirdo things," My brother puzzled with fear in his voice.

"What weirdo things, Evan? Anyways, even if it was a weirdo, they would take one look at you and be grossed out," I snickered, trying to mask my own concern. I glanced over my shoulder at him and stuck my tongue out, and he kicked dirt at me to retaliate.

"Hey!" I spun to face him, to return the gesture when my foot slipped off the path catching loose rocks, and I began falling; in an instant, I realized I wasn't falling down a hill; I was falling straight down. "Ah!" I screamed, then landed with a thud onto my back. Dirt showed onto me and filled my mouth.

"Where am I?" I looked around as I spat; I had landed in some sort of crevasse. "Yuck," I tried to assemble words as mud and dirt poured out of my mouth. I looked up, trying to assess my situation. There was a small crack just over my head with light coming through.

"Ahhh, Ahhh!" My brother screamed, and my

concentration shattered with it. I quickly sat upright with concern. Thoughts of mountain lions eating my little brother flooded my mind. Followed by more thoughts rushing through my head about how I would possibly be able to save him from the jaws of a mountain lion, and my gut twisted.

"Jamie, Jamie, are you dead?" Evan hollered to me, his voice shrill and squeaky. I tried to respond but couldn't with my mouth was full of dirt and gravel.

I managed to sigh with relief, "he's not being eaten." Then I became annoyed at him for making me think he was being eaten.

"I'm so sorry Jamie, I didn't mean to kill you," he sobbed.

I whisked away mud from my mouth with my fingers and hollered, "shut up." I looked up, and Evan's face peered down into the hole at me.

"Oh, you're alive. Oh good, I was really scared. I don't know how to get home from here. I was afraid that I was lost," he sniffled, sounding relieved. I rolled my eyes and got ready to stand up when the whimper sounded again, this time from right next to me. Startled, I let out a yell, and, in an instant, I turned on impulse and found myself nose to nose with a pair of desperate eyes staring at me! I lunged and pulled myself out of the crevasse, then in an instant, turned and eased back into it and began throwing rocks out of the hole.

"What's in there?" Evan's voice shook.

"It's a dog, it's stuck, the poor thing, its legs are trapped in dried dirt. It must have gotten caught in here, then it rained. I am trying to get it free! Stand back so I can throw the big rocks out," I dug and dug, clawing at the earth with my fingernails as fast as I could as if something was telling me to hurry, it wasn't safe here. Still, I figured that was just me and my need to free this dog.

"Evan, hand me my water bottle," I yelled up to him. Thump, it landed right on my head.

"Ouch! Really? You little jerk," I rubbed at the spot it hit to soothe the pain.

"Sorry, I don't want to fall in; you're all dirty. I don't want to be dirty," Evan called back. I rolled my eyes. I poured water into my hand, and the dog lapped it up.

"How long have you been down here?" I asked the poor animal, not really expecting a response. I removed a few more rocks, and the dog was freed. Laying on my back, I pushed her out of the hole first. Then I rolled to push myself up. I faced the spot where the dog had been. Something shiny flashed and sparked my curiosity. I scooted closer to it and started wiping the dirt off of it.

"Um, Jamie, is this dog nice?" Evan's voice shook. I realized I didn't know. I turned my attention away from the object and quickly got up and climbed out. I positioned myself between the dog and my brother and extended my fist in a gesture of friendship. The pup began licking my hand with a pathetically dry tongue. I assumed at this point that the dog was safe and began wiping the dirt from its nose. "She's nice," I smiled, and Evan joined in, and we did our best to remove matted clumps from her fur.

"Ah, can we keep her?" Evan asked.

"I wish, but you know as well as I do Dad wouldn't like it," I sighed, feeling connected to the animal after the ordeal we had just experienced. "Come on lets, get out of this grass and try to find a hose. We need more water," I turned, and we began to walk with the dog following close behind. We continued across the field in the opposite direction of our home. My instincts pulling me, urging me on. A row of houses came into view down a slight incline, and we hurried towards them. We entered a yard. I filled my water bottle and gave the dog another drink. Then we all continued past the yard onto a road. We followed it with no destination in mind.

"Why are we going this way?" Evan questioned.

"I don't know. I feel like we need to, I guess. It's not supper time, and Mom said to explore, so why not?" I struggled to come up with an explanation. To my relief, Evan didn't argue, which was weird for him. I wondered if it was because he felt guilty about the water bottle hitting me in the head, the fall, or maybe he felt the pull to keep moving forward as well. We turned another corner and headed down another road when the dog suddenly bolted past us, running straight into a house about ten houses down." Um, bye, dog. Evan run!" I demanded and grabbed his hand. We turned around and raced back the way we came. I didn't know whose house the dog ran into and didn't want to be associated with it anymore, especially if it was stealing someone's dinner.

We scrambled off as fast as we could, running back the way we came. When out of nowhere, the same dang Jeep from earlier started speeding up the road behind us, blaring its horn at us again. "Really," I gasped. Evan and I raced to turn through the same yard we crossed through before and back into the field. "Hurry, Evan." I pushed. The Jeep went past the row of houses and further down the street, and we started to slow down. I dared to look, hoping our pursuer had lost interest. Then, suddenly the Jeep turned sharply, veered off the road, and started driving through the field straight for us.

"Oh, no, no, Evan, run faster!" I pushed, panicking. He was crying while we ran, neither of us wanting to be alone in a giant field with whatever monster was coming for us. We were nearing the other side, closing in on the road that led to our house, when the Jeep reached us. "Dang it! Dang it," I cursed to myself for not being able to outrun it. I jumped between the vehicle and my brother and stared the driver in the eyes. I looked at the adult, and I knew I wouldn't be able to protect Evan from whatever horrors a man like this might bring, but I would fight, even though I knew I wouldn't win. "Keep running, Evan," I growled. Winded and tired from the chase and unsure of what I could do, but I had to try. I raised my fists and stood my ground. Instead of the diver opening his door, the strange man began rolling his window down, my face contorted in anger and terror, "What, do you have more garbage to throw at my six-year-old brother and me? What do you want from us?!" I yelled, my voice quivering with defeat, fear, and rage.

"I'm, I'm sorry," the man apologized. I studied him. He looked to be about twenty-three and wore a ball cap with a nice blue t-shirt.

"What?" I questioned, fists still raised and tears rolling down my dirty cheeks.

"Where did you find my dog? I've been looking for her for the last four days now?" The man asked.

"The dog? Oh right, the dog," I had forgotten about the dog. My full attention had been focused on fleeing from him. "I dug her out of a hole. Just over there, her legs were stuck in hard dirt and under rocks," I rasped as I pointed in the direction of the hole.

"Well, thank you, this dog means the world to me. I put up posters and offered a reward for whoever found her. Do you want it?" He asked with sincerity in his voice and extended a hand with two twenties in it out his window. I could see the shame on his face. I thought about it, but I still didn't trust him, and I didn't want to be anywhere near him.

"No, I don't want the reward, "I refused. I felt my little brother's hand pulling at my shirt while remaining hidden behind me. "Instead of giving me cash, just promise not to throw garbage at little kids anymore," I glared at him, then quickly turned and put my arm around Evan, and we ran towards home. To my relief, the Jeep turned around and headed back the way it came, and I sighed.

"Why didn't you take the money?" Evan asked after a

couple of moments.

"I didn't want his money," I uttered softly.

"You were really brave, but you're still all dirty," Evan commented.

"I know, I'm telling Mom it's your fault too," I teased and placed my hand on Evan's shoulder and pulled him closer to me, "I'm really glad we are alright," I softly said.

"Me too. If you tell Mom, I got you dirty. I'm going to tell her you tried to feed me to a stray dog." Evan attempted a comeback.

"You wouldn't dare," I pretended to worry. We approached our house with the sun setting behind us, both of us exhausted. The smell of dinner greeted us. I looked at my Mom through the kitchen window, and my tummy growled. I was starving, and she always made the best food, unless it was green beans. I hate green beans. I couldn't wait to devour whatever I was smelling. Her eyes met mine through the window, and her jaw dropped. She came running out the front door.

"Don't you even think for a moment about setting foot in my clean house looking like that! My word, child, you are worse than a hot pig in a mud hole! Evan, get me the hose," my Mom Demanded.

"But Mom," I started to protest.

"I'll just stop you right there! You can explain after you're clean, and it better be a good story. Oh, look at your shoes. That cheatgrass is not easy to remove, you know. You'll spend the day doing that tomorrow. I swear I'm raising a neanderthal," She scolded, then sighed. Her face was contorted in what I could only assume to be a mix of horror and frustration. Evan handed her the hose and began to laugh uncontrollably while I got doused.

Chapter Two, Making Friends is Tricky

<u>Trigger warnings, this chapter highlights issues</u>

<u>regarding the racism and violence of the era.</u>

I started school yesterday, and as I suspected, it's already a disaster, to put it politely. The first day was a nightmare. My Dad made me wear an awful floral brown pilgrim era dress with fluffy sleeves for the first school day! Why, you ask? I have no clue. All I was missing was a bonnet on my head and a pilgrim I would've been. In the morning, I had tried to sneak off to the bathroom before the school bell rang to change into something less embarrassing when the door opened, and I got caught by my new teacher. Who in turn called my Dad, who now says; I have to wear this monstrosity of a dress every day for the next two weeks! As if that wasn't enough, I received ten lashings with his leather belt, which I had to count aloud without tears, or I would get ten more. He says the two weeks is for the dress and the lashings for the scene I caused on my first day of school. I say, "what a load." Not to mention, what was the teacher doing in the kid's bathroom anyhow, and why did she feel the need to rush and call my Dad and tell on me? I hate her; this is going to be a long year.

It's day two in this dress now, and I am officially the biggest loser ever. No one will talk to me other than to point or yell, "white trash. Hey, look the poor kid, or look at the kid from the freak family." Even my older sister is pretending to not know me. So, let's just say it has not been a good start to things. Most of the kids here made their friendships at birth and have no interest in making new ones. The whole atmosphere at this school is deranged. The students spend more time hiding from the staff and each other than they do playing. I miss Missouri so much. The icing on the cake was my run-in with one of the popular girls that I named Mean Girl One, who travels in a pack with two other girls that I have subsequently named Mean Girl Two and three. They had the nerve to cornered me at recess, call me "white trash," then slapped me in the middle of the playground. I was surprised that not one of the adults even blinked at it. I was also mad at myself for not punching her on the spot, but I'm the weird one here. So, I'm sure if I lifted a finger in retaliation, I would've been the one who got into trouble. That seems to be the mentality here. I can't stop thinking about it all, I'm so mad. Who does she think she is?

The bell rang, and I began to tidy up my desk. My head was spinning with rage. My legs and rear still stung from the whipping, then having to sit on them all day made it worse, and to top it off, some bimbo decided to slap me? I grabbed my backpack and stormed out the door, walking across the playground towards the school field, anger fueling my stride. I saw my brother ahead walking home with my sister in the distance, so I knew I didn't have to worry about him. I headed in the same direction for the road that led to my house. "I wish I could disappear. I have a gut feeling that when I get home, I will have to face consequences and will likely get slapped for getting slapped for "causing a scene." That somehow, it will be my fault." I reached the road just off the school property. My brain stewing and churning with the events of the past two school days and having to face two more weeks in this dreadful dress. I got snapped out of brooding with the sound of a girl pleading for help,"help me, please." My attention adverted. I stopped and listened. I could hear the voices of the popular three mean girls, the ones that cornered me and the same one that hit me earlier.

"I have a bone to pick with them," I thought while dropping my bag I cracked my knuckles. Their yells echoed and the profanities were hard to hear and who ever they are hurting must be really hurt. However, I paused for a moment stunned that the other kids from school continued on their ways, without so much as a lick of concern, like this was just a normal Tuesday. I pushed that out of my mind and surveyed the tall wooden fence between me and the mean three. I knew they were just on the other side from all the noise they made. "I'm in the mood for a fight," I convinced myself, so I reached for the top of the fence and pulled myself over.

I examined the scene to plot my attack and was shaken at the horror of what I was witnessing. It was worse than It had sounded, though it sounded horrible too. Mean Girl One was sitting on another girl, the one I assumed called for help. The girl on the bottom had a bloodied nose, a swollen lip, and swollen eye. I knew by the look of it the lip and the eye would turn black soon. She was pinned down on her back and had her hands trapped under the knees of Mean Girl One. Mean Girl One was in the act of spitting lumps of phlegm on her face then forcefully spreading it around. The other two, standing faced away from me, were both kicking the girl on the ground. Mean Girl Two kicked her in the legs, while Mean Girl Three kicked her in the shoulder and neck, the two simultaneously chanting, "die, trash, die."

While Mean Girl One spewed, "Stop being so ugly, savage you belong in the ground with the rest of your kind."

Something in me snapped, and I raced forward. I grabbed the two Mean girls that were viciously throwing their kicks by their hair, and with all my strength, I threw them to the ground. Both crashed forcefully into the dirt. I spun and kicked one in the face and then spun again, kicking the other in the face before they could react. I didn't waste any compassion on the blows I took either they weren't worth the thought. Both their noses were instantly bloodied, and they had looks of terror as I quietly and with a cruel voice said, "run." They struggled to their feet, holding their noses, and took off, clawing their way over the fence while choking on their sobs.

I bolted towards Mean Girl One, who was still on top of the other girl. She hadn't noticed that anything had happened, completely fixated on her hate and cruelty, the one who slapped me. I unleashed my rage and revenge, and I swooped in and grabbed her by the throat and shoulder and threw her off of the other girl. She landed with a thud on her butt and quickly rose her feet. I moved towards Mean Girl One, placing myself between her and the victim, making it clear with my posture and locked gaze that this would be a fight.

"Look, little prairie girl, come to save the little Indian girl. How sweet," Mean Girl One hissed maliciously and spat in my direction.

"I already kicked your friend's butts, and they ran away. I don't think you will be much of a problem inbreed," I clamored, looking her straight in the eyes.

She looked around to verify what I said was true. "I don't need them anyway," she snarled at me.

"You sure about that? From where I'm standing, it seems it took all three of you just to beat up one girl, so you're either weak or a bunch of cowards," I retorted, knowing I wasn't great at comebacks. I took another step in her direction to avoid having to think of another witty word, and she kicked me hard right in the gut. I rocked back a few steps and gasped for air.

"Looks like I get to kill two dirty savages," her vile struck a chord. I swallowed my pain.

"Learn a new line already," I rolled my eyes pretending it

didn't bother me as I spoke. I lunged again, making sure to avoid her legs this time, and elbowed her right in the chest; she fell off balance and slapped me again while falling back to the ground. The rage tore through me, and I jumped on her. She started throwing her hands around, trying to make contact. I successfully blocked thwarting her attempts while throwing punches of my own; we rolled back and forth in a struggle. Then I grabbed her head and rolled her underneath me. Tears began welling up in my eyes, but I pushed them back. My fists started to rain down on her. Punch after punch kept making their mark. Her nails clawed at me, shredding, and tearing at my skin. I could feel the warmth of my blood running down my arms. I didn't care. I was nowhere near being done.

Then a hand gently landed on my shoulder, and a soft voice said, "That's enough. You have done enough." I stopped. In the heat of it all, I had completely forgotten that anyone else was there. Then I felt instant guilt, "what kind of heroin forgets about the victim."

I stood up, and Mean Girl One scrambled away from me and rose. She screamed in a shrill voice, "You freak, I'll kill you!" I turned my gaze from the ground to her again and lifted my fists, and fear washed over her face; she quickly turned on her heels and scrambled for the fence.

"You can try, but you're the one running away. I'll be here when you're ready for more." I threatened. I held my ground until she was gone, then I took a deep breath in and slowly turned to face the girl with a soft voice. The one they hurt way worse than me and had kindness enough to help the meanest one of the pack. I was nervous about what she might say or think of me. I slowly lifted my gaze, and her eyes met mine. She was beautiful. She had long dark hair, piercing eyes the color of honey. They seemed to glow against her perfect complexion. She was petite, slightly taller than me. Even with her shiner fully blackened now, she was far prettier than her attackers. "What's your name?" I asked, stunned by her beauty.

"Onacona," she answered as blood streamed from her nose.

"I'm Jamie. You can use my dress to wipe your face off. If you get blood on it, maybe I won't have to wear it anymore. You'd be doing me a favor," I offered. I couldn't come up with anything else to say. Also, I was trying to cover up the guilt I felt for deciding to forget compassion in my fight. With it being the only thing, I had to offer, that's what I went with.

Onacona choked out a laugh, and that pretty face became even lovelier, filled with light. She accepted my gesture and wiped her face off with my dress. When she was done, she asked me, "Why do you have to wear this dress? Are you Amish?" Then it was my turn to laugh.

"No, I'm not Amish. My Dad has a sick sense of humor and said I have to wear it for two weeks because I embarrassed him on the first day of school by trying to not wear it," I answered with as little disgust as I could manage.

Sadness swept over Onacona's face. "My Stepmom is like that too," her eyes drifted to the ground, and I could see the sorrow in them was soul-destroying.

"Hey, do you want to walk home together?" I offered as a shiver went up my spine.

"Sure," Onacona smiled, hiding away whatever image was haunting her. I looked around the yard and didn't see a gate, just the tall fence and an abandoned house sitting on the opposite side of the property. The place seemed to be watching us. I blinked and refocused on the situation, ignoring the thought.

"How did the mean girls get you in here?" I asked, confused about how they could force her over such a tall fence with no gate.

"Jessica was chasing me, so I climbed in here in hopes of getting away, but it was a trap. When I got over it," she paused and glanced at the fence, "Gina and Lisa were waiting for me. It went downhill from there. I saw your feet through the hole at the gap over there," she pointed at a small hole at the bottom of the boards and continued. "Then I hoped whomever you were that you would stop and help me."

"So that's their names. I was calling them Mean Girl one, two, and three. Which one was the one sitting on you?" I questioned.

"That's Gina, she's the worst, she's the leader of their pack, and I don't get it. She's mean to everyone, yet everyone adores her, including the teachers," Onacona took a breath and continued. "She acts like she's perfect and that her life is perfect, but it's all just an act. Her parents are as mean as the next, and she mows lawns all summer to get those nice clothes she wears." She paused, and her eyes dropped; the world felt still as if all things were listening, allowing her story to be told. She continued. "Gina, Lisa, and Jessica started beating me up last year, and it happens just about every day after school unless I can outrun her. No one has ever stopped to help. At least not until now. How did you learn to fight like that? I've never seen Gina so defeated,"

Onacona looked at me.

"Every day for a year! Well, there it is. The guilt's gone. This was long overdue," I thought, attempting to hide my horror. "I had to, I have an older sister, and she's mean, and my Dad," I choked. "Well, he's mean sometimes too," I wasn't proud of it, but it was the truth. "Let's get out of here," I shivered again. The sun was lowering, and I couldn't hear any other kids on the road, so I knew it was getting late. When Onacona lifted her bag off the ground. I saw it had flecks of blood sprayed across it, and I felt rage brewing in me again. We climbed the fence and started walking towards home. I was happy to find out that Onacona and I were practically neighbors as I dropped her off at her yard and went just two more houses further to my place.

"Mom, I'm home," I called through the noise of my family as I entered my house.

"I'm back here," she answered loudly from the opposite end of the house. I made my way to her, stopping briefly to kiss my three-year-old brother Neil on the head. I found her breastfeeding my baby brother, whom I affectionately call Waddles, on the couch in our family room. Waddles at just two months old and shares my room. My job is to feed and change Waddles at night, so my Mom can get sleep, and I don't mind he is so cute. My sister, who is the oldest, shares her room with Neil. When my sister and I are being civil, we joke that instead of pets, we got brothers. Of course, Evan being the favorite, got his own room. I had another sibling, another brother, who had died shortly after his birth. He would've been older the Evan. My Mom was so heartbroken that she made it her mission to have as many babies as possible to ease the pain. At least, that is the story I tell myself.

"Did you just get home?" My Mom asked while eyeballing me suspiciously.

"Yes, I took a detour, and guess what, I made a friend," I smiled, keeping my response as short as possible.

"You did! That's wonderful!" She said a little too enthusiastically. "Tell me all about her, or is it a, him?" She lifted her eyebrows at me twice.

"Yuck, Mom, of course, it's a girl. Her name is Onacona. She lives just two houses down," I smiled, proud.

"Oh, that's a pretty name. Do you know what it means?" Mom asked.

"No idea. I'll ask her for you," I responded and started to turn. My Mom had ignored the blood on my dress, so my plans to be rid of it had failed.

"Jamie, there's something I need to talk to you about. Come take a seat." My Mom said a bit more serious.

"Dang it, dang, she knows," I thought to myself. I gathered myself, ready to receive a verbal lashing for getting slapped on the playground. "Ooookaaaay, am I in trouble?" I whimpered cautiously.

"Not that I'm aware of, should you be?" She lifted an eyebrow and stared into my soul.

"No," I squeaked and sat down.

"Your father was in a good mood today since he got word that he needs to spend two weeks in Greece for a work conference, and I told him I need extra help. So, we agreed that every day, you make dinner, and this can start today. You won't have to wear that dress to school. Just no more nonsense, agreed?" She said matter-a-factually.

"Yes! Of course, I will, Thank you, Mom! Thank you!" I grinned, overjoyed. "I'll start right now," I responded enthusiastically.

"OK, just clean yourself up first. I have a chicken thawed. You can roast it and check frequently it to make sure it cooks evenly," My Mom instructed. I gave my Mom a careful hug and made sure not to bother Waddles, who was happily eating and I ran to do what she asked.

Onacona and I walked to school together in the morning with Evan and my older sister Noora in tow. In class, I worked on math. I struggled with it having been diagnosed with dyslexia. With little research in the field, the teachers often felt hopeless when it came to me. In math, all it took was one number moving, and the whole problem was thrown off. My teachers assumed I was just writing random answers when I fully understood how the equation worked. I just did it with the incorrect placement of numbers. When the bell rang, I was relieved to run outside and play with my new friend.

Onacona and I grabbed a large jump rope and headed to the field. Upon getting there, we realized we needed more people to make our plan of skip dancing a reality. We both started scanning the schoolyard, searching for other kids to join us. "Onacona, do you know anyone that might want to hang out with us," I asked.

Onacona responded grimly, "not really. Everyone here avoids me like I have pinkeye."

My gaze landed on Gina and her posse. They had found

new marks and were walking straight for them. A husky girl with long strawberry blond hair and a skinny, tall girl with long brown hair had faces contorted in fear, waiting for whatever horrors Gina was going to unleash on them. "Onacona, do you know those two girls, the ones Gina has cornered?" I pointed while I watched the scene unfolding.

"Yes, that's Shelly and Connie," Onacona answered.

"Are they good people?" I checked as a plan formed in my head.

"They have never said anything mean to me but have never really talked to me before, so I suppose," Onacona wisped with a tinge of jealousy in her tone.

"You realize we need more people in our group, and there's safety in numbers," I reminded.

"Yea, I know," she responded while kicking at the grass.

"So, let's go make their obviously horrible day a little better," I pushed, trying to convince her, and I gave her a sly grin.

"Fine," she sighed, accepting my proposal. I whispered my plan to Onacona as we made our way straight for the mean girls. We stopped just behind them.

"Well, well, Onacona lookie here, the three rats are at it again," I blustered loudly. The three startled spun around to find me nose to nose with Gina. Onacona began swirling the jump rope around like a whip, far enough away that the teachers couldn't construe it as a threat but close enough that she was steps away and could attack if needed. The mean girls understood that was the intent. "Really, Gina, is being a jerk all you have in life? You're even more pathetic than you look." I scoffed loudly, then quickly dropped my voice to a low growl. "Take your friends and leave now, or you and I are going to have a problem, and everyone here will see how easy it is to take you and your friends down. You will lose whatever this is, for good."

Gina's eyes scanned the scene, and she realized she was beaten. "Give me something," she whispered back.

"No. This is the offer. You are wasting my recess, and unless you want your bruises to have bruises walk away now," I hissed while examining her black eye.

"Hum, you and I could be friends. We are a lot alike," Gina whispered a proposal.

"I would rather eat dog droppings. You're a bigot and a bully. I am nothing like you. Now go," I snapped my fingers next to her face, and she flinched.

"Fine, you're going to regret not taking my offer. Come on, Jessica, Lisa, let's go. This trash isn't worth our time,"

Gina commented, sounding bored, and they all charged off. I stepped back to let them pass.

I approached Shelly and Connie. "Hi, I'm Jaimie. Do you two want to hang out with us?" I greeted as Onacona fell into place next to me.

"You realize everyone is staring at you right," Shelly responded. I turned to look. Sure enough, everyone was watching in complete silence, the whole lot of them looking dumbfounded. Not knowing what to do, I took a bow, and everyone quickly looked away and pretended not to notice. "So, we wanted to jump rope dance, want to join us?" I posed the question again.

"Sure," they nodded in agreement, and we headed back to the field. We jumped and spun, kicked our legs, and laughed until the bell sounded. We started running back to class.

On our way, Connie grabbed my arm and halted me, "I like you, but something you need to know is Gina is clever and cunning, and she will find a way to hurt you for standing up to her. To be honest, I am a little scared for us all for defying her," She warned with apprehension in her tone.

"Don't worry, I've had to deal with girls like her before, and I doubt it will be the last time. I'm not afraid of getting hit.

I can hit too," I boasted, feeling full of myself.

"Just watch your back, your teacher is her Mom, and she is mean to," Connie finished as she ran for her classroom.

"Oh no," I thought to myself. I never considered Gina's Mom was working here, but now my teacher's behavior on the first day made sense. She was looking for a reason to humiliate me. She was a bully, and Gina was just like her. I walked into class feeling especially vulnerable. I slid into my seat with my head down, avoiding eye contact with my teacher.

The whole class was silent. No one passed notes. No one whispered to each other, and no one looked at me. "Students go to the library and select a book on of your favorite historical figure. You are going to write a monologue on the said figure and perform it at the end of the week." My teacher instructed. I felt a whisper of comfort and quickly lined up with the rest of my classmates and headed down the hall to the library. I instantly had a figure in mind. Virginia Hall.

I had been drawn to Virginia since I first learned of her plight when I was younger. I had recurring dreams after that. Where I, too, was a spy. The only difference was I was living in a home with many passageways hidden in vents, and people would show up needing help. I had to lead those people to a river to be secured by boat and taken to safety. Virginia was way more fascinating than that. She was the most successful spy during WWII and my instant hero. She was responsible for more sabotaged missions, leaking inside information on the Nazis, and accountable for more jailbreaks than any other spy. It took me longer than expected to find my book. I took it to the counter to check it out. Then as a class, we headed back to our room.

Upon entering our classroom, the teacher announced. "Children, I hope you all selected your person wisely. Now, I am going to do a random bag check to look for paraphernalia. Whoever's name I pull from this bowl, will you please collect your bag and bring it to me." I didn't think much of it, they did this in Missouri as well, and I realized you had to be an idiot to bring anything off-limits to school. Mrs., Reeves stirred the bowl with her hand and pulled a small piece of paper from it. "Jamie Eriksen," She announced. Her eyes instantly fell on me, and everyone fell silent.

I went and collected my bag. "Here you are, Mrs. Reeves," I offered respectfully as I handed it to her. I knew the only things in it were my lunch box and raincoat. I had nothing to worry about. She pulled my raincoat out and set it on a desk, then my lunch box.

"OK, this all looks to be in order," Mrs. Reeves approved. Then she picked up my raincoat to put it back into my bag and to my horror, a pack of cigarettes fell out of it onto the floor.

My heart dropped to my stomach. "Those are not mine," I blurted out as I watched her pick the pack of cigarettes up.

"Well, it doesn't matter whom they belong to; you are not allowed to have these at school. So, before you tell me they are your Mom's or Dad's, I'll save you the energy and let you know this is very unacceptable. The principal and I will be having a meeting with your parents after school. The rest of the class is dismissed," Mrs. Reeves scolded with an odd look of pleasure on her face. Everyone rushed to collect their bags, with their heads down and without a single word, as if they all knew that this was a setup, but what could they do? "Take your seat Jamie and don't move! I have a call to make," My teacher demanded as she headed out the door towards the school's office. Leaving me there to stew in my own dread.

It felt like an hour had gone by before my Mom made her appearance. She peered into the room from the door. I couldn't bring myself to look her in the eyes with tears rolling down my cheeks. I spoke first. "They weren't mine," my voice quivered with defeat.

She walked over to me and knelt down next to my desk. "What wasn't yours?" My Mom asked.

"You haven't talked to the principal?" I whimpered.

"No, I demanded to see you first. It took me so long to get here because I had to wait for your sister to get home to watch the boys while I came. Your sister is the one that said I should talk to you first, so tell me what's going on?" She questioned. I looked at her, and between sobs, I told her the whole story from start to finish. I told her about getting slapped during recess, how I found Onacona being beaten, the conversations, what happened on the playground earlier, about the teacher being Gina's Mom, and how the cigarettes fell from my raincoat during a random bag check.

The tears washed down my face and puddled onto my desk. When I was done, I waited for my Mom to speak in complete silence. The classroom felt like a tomb ready to swallow me. I raised my eyes to look at my Mom's face, waiting for the scolding to start. I wasn't surprised when I examined the anger in my Mom's blue eyes. She didn't yell or strike me. She just inquired, "Is that the bowl your teacher picked your name from?" While pointing at the teacher's desk.

"Yes, Ma'am," I said on my best behavior as if trying to win some points. My Mom stepped to the teacher's desk, pulled out a piece of paper from the bowl, and read it. Then she made a choking sound and stormed in the direction of the principal's office.

Moments later, my Mom's voice yelling at the top of her lungs filled the entire school. Teachers ran from their classrooms and assembled in the halls. Confused by it, I, too, made my way from my desk to the door that led to the hallway. I only caught bits and pieces of what was being said as her voice would roar then soften. Something about my Dad being a lawyer that she was a charge nurse by trade "I have dealt with many, manipulative, lying, power-hungry." Her voice trailed off. "Don't you think for an instant that my daughter would ever bring anything of such nature to school! I have proof she was set up by this." Her voice went too soft to hear. "Don't you Ma-am me, principal Jacobs!" Her voice lowered again, and then the door to the principal's office swung open. The teachers scattered back to their classrooms, and here came my Mom dragging the principal by the arm. He looked baffled and unnerved as they stormed down the hall towards me. Mrs. Reeves followed right behind with a look of bewilderment strewn across her face.

"Shoot, shoot, here they come, oh, no," I hurried back to my seat, unsure what to do.

My Mom, principal Jacobs, and Mrs. Reeves rushed into the classroom, and I braced. They didn't stop at my desk but went straight past me to Mrs. Reeves's desk. My Mom picked up the bowl. "Here is my proof Mr. Jacobs," My Mom snapped while practically throwing the bowl at him.

He lifted a piece of paper from it, then another. "Oh, I see," he looked surprised but managed to speak clearly. "Mrs. Reeves, can I see you alone in my office? Mrs. Eriksen, it was a pleasure to meet you. You and your lovely daughter are free to go home," he finished cordially.

"OK, Jamie, let's get out of here," my Mom ordered. I grabbed my bag and bolted for the door to outside.

When we got to the car, I climbed into the front seat and fastened my safety belt. My Mom climbed in next to me, closed the door, put her hands on the wheel, leaned forward, and released a sigh. With her forehead between her hands, she spoke, "I am so mad." The words were forced out through gritted teeth.

"I'm so sorry!" I pled, and she cut me off.

"Not at you, at those pathetic jerks at your school, and at myself for not noticing how hard it has been for you," She explained.

"Oh, I'm sorry too," I whimpered, gobsmacked, and not knowing what else to say.

"Jamie, look at me," my Mom asked, and I obeyed. "You stood up for your friends against impossible odds and got set up by a trusted adult. You have nothing to be sorry about. I'm proud of you. If more people were like you, the world would be a kind place. Just trust me enough to tell me when you're struggling like this," she said softly.

"OK, I promise. You shouted at the principal," I teased, still surprised by what had just happened, and my Mom barked out a laugh.

"Yes, I did. Let's keep this between us, not a word to your father, or he'll have both our heads," She smiled.

"Agreed," I accepted with a nod.

"Hey, I have an idea. How about this weekend you invite your friends for a sleepover? You all can sleep in the camper van since it's not too cold yet," My Mom suggested.

"Really! Awesome, thanks, Mom!" I agreed and threw my arms around her neck, and we hugged. The following morning just after class started, the principal introduced a new teacher.

"Good Morning class, this is Mrs. Skipper. She will be your teacher for the rest of the year. Mrs. Reeves has decided to take a sabbatical and won't be back until the new school year. I expect you all to show Mrs. Skipper the same respect you have shown to Mrs. Reeves." With that, Mr. Jacobs exited the room, and the new teacher began.

Chapter Three, The Ghostly Games

It was already a busy day for me, having vacuumed, swept, mopped, dusted, and polished furniture around the house. Honestly, I was happy too. I was preparing for my friends to come over. I hurried outside to the camper van with bedding tucked into my arms to set up before my friend's arrival. Once I climbed inside, I gathered some support bars from a compartment above the couches, locked them in place, then slid the two sofas over them, and then laid them flat, making one large bed. I neatly rolled out sheets and blankets over it, and when I finished, I looked around with pride. "This is going to be great,"

I had attempted to host sleepovers in the past. Things would be going well. We would run through fields, play in the creeks, catch fireflies, crawdads, and build forts in the woods, then my Mom would call us in for supper, and my friends would meet my Dad, then ask to go home. Everyone was scared of my Dad even though he was always on his best behavior around any company. So, I couldn't put my finger on it. Maybe it's his height. He is a giant of a man standing at 6' 5 with very broad shoulders. He keeps a tidy beard with shoulder-length hair pulled neatly back in a ponytail, or perhaps it's his Dad jokes. Either way, he is gone for another thirteen and a half days, so all was well.

My Mom had mentioned in passing that she called the other parents earlier and confirmed times. Also, that the other adults seemed nice. My older sister set up a play pin in her room to watch Waddles and made it clear that I owed her for taking him. My Mom gave my other brothers specific instructions to provide my friends and I with space and to mind their manners. "We'll see how that goes."

It was just after four pm when the doorbell sounded. I went running to answer it. I swung the door open and was overjoyed at the sight of all three of my friends standing there, arms filled with bags and pillows. "Come in, let me help you with your things," I offered. I led them through the living room, to the dining room, and out the side door towards the campervan.

"Your house is bigger than it looks from the outside,"

Connie complemented politely.

"Thanks, we have a sauna just there," I pointed to a door to my left. "If you all want to sit in it later, we can? Though it's not much fun, it gets really hot, and other than that, there's nothing to do in it. I guess adults like that. The last time I sat in it, I got a bloody nose because it was so dry," I didn't see the point of it but thought I'd offer.

"Neat," Shelly looked at it approvingly as she opened the door to peek in, then closed it.

"Want to know what else? I used my allowance to rent Swamp-Watcher. It's a scary movie but rated P.G., so my Mom said it was alright for us to watch it; want to see it later?" I asked no one in particular.

"I do! That sounds better than sitting in a sweaty sauna. I've been meaning to see that," Connie answered.

"I've wanted to watch that too!" Onacona chimed in, and Shelly gave me a thumbs up.

My friends and I climbed inside the R.V. and began glanced around. "This is wicked cool," Onacona said.

"So cool. I'm totally stoked we get to stay in here," Connie agreed.

"Thanks," I responded politely. The R.V. was older, with a small kitchen and the two couches on either side that pulled out to make the bed. The front was two car seats, a C.B. radio, and everything else you would expect to see in any vehicle. We crawled onto the bed and began placing our pillows where we wanted our spot to be. Then everyone started unpacking their bags. Shelly pulled a two-liter of caffeinated soda out of her bag and lifted it in the air. My eyes widened in excitement; I rarely got soda let alone one with caffeine.

My parents considered it to be just as bad as alcohol and just as forbidden. "Anyone want some?" Shelly asked, holding it up proudly.

"Yes!" we all responded in unison. She twisted off the lid, and the fizz rose to the top, making its glorious Shh sound, and she took a big gulp then passed it to me. Then we each took turns gulping it down.

After we finished it, we began laughing hysterically, teasing each other, enjoying being drunk on caffeine and high on sugar. We lept out of the R.V., ran through the yard and started playing a game of tag, and then crack the whip. We continued running wild until the pizza delivery man pulled into the driveway. I ran inside with my friends barreling in behind me. I yelled, "Mom, pizza's here," across the house.

"Coming," My Mom answered as she made her way to

the front door, with her checkbook in hand. We passed out paper plates and started sitting down at the kitchen table.

"You girls can eat that in the family room while you watch your movie," my Mom offered. "Cool, thanks, Mom. Noora, do you want to watch it with us?" I offered.

"Gross, no way," Noora responded, looking insulted at the mere thought of it.

My Mom lightly slapped her arm and told her, "Watch your manners."

We weren't bothered by it, though, and with plates loaded with pizza, my friends settled into the couches, and I pushed the tape in the VCR and joined them. "That was so good! It blew my mind. I totally thought Jessica was a ghost!" Connie roared at the end of the movie and made a booming motion with her hands.

Onacona chimed in, "Who knew there could be such a good horror film for kids."

"I know, right," Shelly agreed. "I especially love the part where the ghosts pop up in the mirrors," Connie added.

"I loved the abandoned church where it all began and ended," I paused. "I love anything abandoned. The history always makes it so interesting, and you always have to wonder where the people went and why they left all their things behind," I finished.

"You know there are three abandoned houses around our school. If you draw a line connecting them, it will make a triangle. It's like if anything gets too close to that school, it rots and disappears. We should explore them sometime," Onacona suggested.

"Ya, imagine what treasures could be in there or secret passageways. Maybe we can find some rare stamps, coins, or jewelry," Shelly eagerly said.

"Oh, I'm in," I added. We looked at Connie who remained still.

"You know the one with the fence with no gate," Connie shuddered, and the color from her face started to drain. We gave a silent nod. "I heard the notorious River Killer lived in that house and used to take his victims, mostly young women, girls, and then two little boys there. He would take them from around the school and do terrible things to them before he'd murder them, then send their body parts floating in the in local rivers," She gulped and continued. "I heard the killer was drug out of his home after one of the little boys escaped. Story goes the killer was beaten to death by the boy's Dad, Uncles, Police, and a few other parents then buried on that property," She paused, then continued. "Since he dumped his victims into different rivers, there was no evidence left for the police to take him to court, so they all decided to take the law into their own hands. People were scared, and since women were going missing left, right, and center at the time, they agreed it was best to finish it then and there. Story has it, that the cries of all his victims pleading for help can be heard at night, and they built the fence with no gate to keep his evil in, but I wonder if that gate keeps his victims in as well," Connie's face had lost all color, and her hands trembled as she finished.

Silence filled the room, and I thought about Onacona pinned down on that lawn. The image of a deranged man with bull horns flashed in my mind as if his energy was somehow fueling Gina's actions. The victims, the women, and the children crying out for help were just as ignored by the passer byers as Onacona had ignored when she cried out for help. "If people can still hear them, the bad guy must still be there hurting them. The victims must be trapped. We need to help them," I said, unable to shake the feeling that something was still wrong in that house.

My Mom entered the room. "Help whom?" She asked.

"Oh, we're just telling ghost stories about the abandoned houses near the school," I quickly answered.

"Oh well, I don't want you, girls, to go near those houses. Who knows what kind of state they are in? A wrong step could send you through a floor or make the roofs cave in on you, trust me, whatever trash is left in there is not worth the risk," Mom stipulated.

"But Mom, I want to chase ghosts," I teased and batted my eyes.

My Mom rolled her eyes and changed the subject, "Instead of chasing ghosts, what if I teach you a ghostly game instead. Will that take your mind off of sneaking into condemned houses?" She asked.

"Yes," I answered, eager to learn a new game. Onacona, Shelly and Connie nodded in excitement too.

"Alright, so my grandma taught me this when I was about your ages, and it really works," she said with a tinge of excitement in her voice. We all nodded to let her know we were paying attention.

"It's called Light as Feather Stiff as a Board. The way you play is you have one person lie down with their arms at their sides. One person kneels at the head and the other two on either side. Each of you will need to slide four fingers under the person lying down. Two fingers if you have more people. The person at the head tells a scary story but doesn't finish it. Then you say, "light as a feather stiff as a bored," then the next person chants it with you, then the third. Once you all have said it together, lift straight up, and the person laying down will be light as a feather and stiff as a board," my Mom finished, Then added. "I need you, girls, to keep it down now. I'm putting the boys to bed, so have your fun quietly," She leaned over and kissed me on the mouth, then disappeared into the hall, and I could hear her rounding up my siblings for their evening rituals.

Excited to play, I asked, "So, who wants to lay down first? I can tell the story." Onacona responded, "I will." With that, Connie and Shelly took their places, one on each side of her. We all slipped four fingers each under Onacona, and I began, "It's a cold, dark night, and you are lying awake worried in your bed. The wind is howling outside your window; you try to ignore it, but the constant moaning keeps you from relaxing. You begin to question if the noise is only wind or something else. Are you really alone? You close your eyes to try and sleep, but there's a tapping at your window. Your eyes burst open wide, and you turn to look. Light as a feather stiff as a board."

Then Connie joined in, "light as feather stiff as a board."

Then Shelly joined us, "light as feather stiff as a board."

We lifted, and to our amazement, Onacona rose with ease as if there was no weight to her. We lifted her above our heads, fully extending our arms, and began to stand.

Then Onacona broke the silence and asked, "Are you going to lift me? Ahhh," she screamed as she crashed to the floor.

"I guess you aren't supposed to lose concentration, or you get heavy again," I said, looking down at her.

"I didn't even realize I was being lifted," Onacona snapped in her defense, and we all burst into laughter. Then we rotated our positions in the game, and we each took turns filling different roles as we played. Each of us coming up with our own stories and thrilled by the results. After we had finally had our fill, we loaded up with chip bags and headed to the R.V.

Once safely inside with the doors locked. Connie asked, "Can we talk to people on the C.B. radio and see who answers."

"That sounds great," I moved forward to turn it on. I clicked through the channels until I found one without people already talking on it. I turned to my friends and started explaining the rules of talking on a C.B. radio. Having heard my Dad speak on it during past trips, I was familiar with a bit of the lingo. "So, girls, you have to have talk slowly and clearly, you have to have a code name, don't talk too loudly, you can't talk on the same channel for more than five minutes at a time, most importantly, don't tell anyone where we are. Kojak with Kodiak means theirs a cop with radar, negatory means no, organ donor means motorcyclist with no helmet," I was interrupted.

"OK, we get it!" Connie blurted out, and we all laughed.

I collected the microphone from the hook where it hung and spoke, "Anyone awake out there, this is little roamer looking for conversations, over and out." We eagerly waited in silence for a response.

Then a voice answered us, "This is Jack of spades. You're coming through loud and clear." We all giggled with excitement. "What now?" I asked the other girls.

"Oh, ask if he has kids our age," Shelly suggested.

"What? no. That would make it obvious that we are kids. Tell him there's a cop on Overland Road," Connie insisted.

I held the button on the mike and said, "I wanted to warn you that there's a yogi on Overland and Meridian road over and out," I released the button.

"Ten-four. Thanks for the heads up. Over and out," Jack of Spades responded.

"What does that mean?" Shelly whispered.

"You don't have to whisper! He can't hear you when she's not holding the button down on the microphone," Connie snickered.

"It means state police, in trucker talk," I taunted. "Most welcome, over and out," I finished conversating with Jack of Spades. Then I turned the dial to another channel.

"We should come up with a plan before we talk to the next person," Onacona suggested. So, we started to scheme; we made call after call, got the truckers talking, then dropped a joke and quickly turned the channel after the punch line, while laughing hysterically at ourselves.

"OK, let's do one more, then get some sleep," I suggested feeling the day had taken its toll. Everyone agreed.

"Oh, we should try asking the radio if there are any ghosts out there that want to talk," Shelly suggested.

"Awe, yes. Now there's a good idea, finally," Connie quipped with a sly half-grin.

I picked up the microphone and brought it to my lips. "Are there any spirits out there that would like to communicate with us tonight?" I asked the void. The RV. was dead silent, all of us on edge waiting for one of our lost loved ones to come on. We waited and waited. Nothing happened.

I began to lift the mike to my mouth to ask the question again, but before I could, a scream roared throughout the R.V., fracturing the silence! I dropped the mike and jolted backward in shock. My friends all scrambled in panic. I covered my ears as the scream continued. I tried to make sense of what was happening, but I couldn't.

A deep booming voice took over, and I froze. All the speakers throughout the R.V switched on simultaneously without explanation, and the horrible voice surrounded us. The screaming became muffled as if a hand was coving a person's or a ghost's mouth, trying to forcefully silence it.

The sinister voice bellowing from speakers its jargon in another language, "Khnum sa'utalib ruhak, Neter." It began chanting it. The noise was horrible and inescapable. Everything around us began shaking, the doors rattled, and the curtains moved. I feared the creature doing this would come through the speakers and poison us, turn us dark and twisted. My friends and I all started screaming in unison. The voice continued to assault us with its words murmuring its vile intent. I looked around in sheer terror and began trying to find a spot to flee and hide, to get away from the shaking and darkness. Then Connie flung her body forward and switched off the box.

The camper fell silent again, and the rattling stopped. I gaped at my friends with my eyes wide and my mouth open. My head was racing, and my heart felt as if it was going to pound out of my chest. I wanted to thank Connie for having her wits about her and making it stop, but Shelly spoke before I could. "What the H. E. double hockey sticks was that!?" We all flinched again; intrepidity being long gone. None of us knew how to answer that, so we just shook our heads.

"Um, Jamie, can we sleep inside the house instead?" Onacona asked.

"Yes, of course, we need to plan our escape," I paused, and everyone agreed. None of us wanting to spend another minute outside alone in the campervan. "OK, when I open the door, we will run for the house," was all I could manage, and everyone nodded. We gathered all our belongings and went to the door, all of us practically piled on top of each other, no one wanting to be left alone and ready to make a mad dash towards the house. I gulped then carefully opened the door; the pitch black of night met my gaze.

Slowly I began sticking my foot out of the R.V., getting ready to exit and run. When a noise echoed through the dark streets. It sounded like footsteps coming up our driveway. I quickly pulled my foot in and slammed the door shut, then shoved the bolt into place, securing the door. "Did you hear that?" I asked my friends. They all nodded. We climbed back onto the bed and drew all the curtains closed. Then huddled in a pile together as close as humanly possible.

Connie whispered, "Who do you think is out there?" We all silently listened for any further noises, on high alert.

"I don't know," I whispered back after I felt it was safe enough to do so. We continued listening in silence for any signs that we weren't alone.

After a while, my eyelids grew heavy. The next thing I knew, I found myself waking up to the dim light of early dawn. My left arm hurt. I tried to move it without success. Onacona was passed out on top of it. Shelly was leaning into my other side with Connie leaning into her, both also fast asleep. I realized we all had fallen asleep sitting up and hadn't moved the rest of the night. I smiled at the dim light of dawn, and felt relief, and knew it was too early to wake anyone up. So, I shifted Onacona onto her side in a laying position, then slid the other two off and laid down, and drifted back into slumber.

I woke to my Mom's voice saying. "Alright, you lazy bunch of heathens, up and at-um. I have pancakes and bacon ready in the kitchen." She was poking her head through the driver's side door of the R.V.

"I guess we forgot to lock that door," I thought silently. She didn't have to tell us twice. We all got up and dressed then went barreling towards the house.

Chapter Four, The Ghost and The Storm

I looked at the calendar to see whose day it was to do the dishes. When I looked at the date, I thought, "I can't believe it's already been a month since I last had a sleepover." My friends and I hadn't done much outside of school together due to family life and responsibilities. I've been helping around the house because my Mom has been sick, and my Dad's working on a big case. Noora has been temperamental, so I have been stuck caring for Neal as well. Onacona and I try to steal time when able to hang out, but rarely with success.

"Noora, it's your turn to do dishes!" I yelled across the house.

"Screw you!" Noora yelled back.

"Whatever, I'm going to bed," I hollered and left to my room. I wanted to get to bed early because Waddles wasn't sleeping well lately, and it was wearing me out. My Mom doesn't sleep with Waddles at night because she takes medicine that knocks her out. So, we make do, and I mostly don't mind. It's just been a bit much since Waddle's first tooth has started to come in.

I woke up to the sound of my alarm and saw that my Mom had slipped in sometime before and collected Waddles. It was an average morning at my house. I got dressed and ready, put on my coat and grabbed my bag, then slipped out the front door to school. I met Onacona at her house, and her Dad gave me a friendly nod while her Stepmom scowled from behind him. I had only ever talked to her Dad a few times. He liked to smoke a tobacco pipe on his porch. He was serious and respectable by appearances but seemed kind. Her Stepmom never spoke to me, and she gave me the willies, so I didn't mind. Onacona and I waved to them then trotted towards school.

"I asked my Dad if you, Shelly, and Connie could come over after school, and he said it's fine. I got my hands on some old newspapers about the girls that went missing, and I thought we could each read a couple, then compare notes to try and figure out what happened," Onacona suggested.

"That sounds great. I'll have to ask after school, but I am

owed some time to myself, so it shouldn't be a problem," I answered. Onacona, Shelly, and Connie had been trying to look into the abandoned house's history where all the murders supposedly happened. Connie had gathered a few details from gossip at the local barbershop while her Dad got his hair cut. The house was in ill repair, and no one knew who the previous owner was, or at least they didn't admit to knowing. None of our parents wanted to take us to county record, saying that looking into such things was morbid and not something young women should be doing. If they, had it their way, we would be practicing cross-stitch and making dolls. I couldn't help but roll my eyes at the thought.

I hadn't been inside Onacona's house yet, either. So, her offer also sparked my curiosity. "So, will your Mom and Dad be there?" I asked.

"Yes, but they don't know that we are looking into the murders. They think we need all the papers for a school project," Onacona looked at me sternly.

"Understood," I responded, then started to think up a project we could use as our cover story. "I know, we could tell them that we are working on a project about writing articles for a paper, if they ask," I suggested.

"That will work. I'll let Connie and Shelly Know

sometime during class today. I called them earlier, and they are both aloud to come," Onacona mentioned.

A strong cold gust of air hit us, and we stopped to zip up our coats. Then a harder blast hit us, and we both rocked back, and a soft, almost inaudible voice carried to us on the wind and said what sounded like the word "gate." We both turned and looked down the road to see if someone was talking to us, but all the other kids were carrying on to school as normal. "Did you hear that?" I asked Onacona.

"It sounded like the word, Gate," she shivered. I turned to look the other way, and we were at the fence that wrapped around the abandoned house. I turned again to look at Onacona, and she looked pale, having just made the same realization herself.

"Well, that was weird," I said jokingly to try and make light of the situation. We both swallowed then quickened our pace to school.

Later that morning, the wind outside my classroom started to whistle, and the school creaked. Little flecks of snow began to fall to the ground and melt once touching the earth. I watched them through the window. I had been assigned to do a project on how the law works, and it was boring. The title of my project was Mitigate. So, I watched the snow lost in thought, then the heater kicked on, and some of my papers blew from my desk blew to the floor. I turned in my seat and bent down to collect them. I looked over the mess and was instantly snapped out of my daydream with surprise. All my papers had landed upside down except for one.

"This cannot be an accident." I thought. Every word on my title page was covered up by other fallen sheets of paper. Even the Miti portion of the title itself was gone. All that was left uncovered stared me blatantly in the face was the word. "Gate." I continued staring at it, hoping to find some other clues, and I wondered, "Is there a ghost out there that wants me to put a gate in the fence at the abandoned house since it doesn't have one? But why? Shouldn't they be able to just float through a fence?" I tried to make sense of it while I silently fixated on the word "Gate." The sound of a fart broke my train of thought, and the class erupted in laughter. I scooped up my papers and put them back on my desk. I turned to look at my classmate Tom who sat next to me on my right. Was blushing from ear to ear, then my nose was struck by what smelt like rotten fish, and I gagged.

After the final school bell rang and my teacher let us go, I bundled up and stepped out of my classroom's door into whipping winds. I shielded my eyes and looked out over the snow-covered landscape. I spotted Noora and Evan off in the distance, quickly running towards home. I didn't blame them. It was snowing harder now and had begun to pile up. Little bits of ice stung my cheeks like tiny needles. I made my way to Onacona's class, and she stepped out. "Let's get out of here," I said. Connie and Shelly joined us at the door, and we started walking across the school field towards Onacona's house.

"This blows, pun intended," Connie barked.

"You're not kidding," I scowled while pulling my hands inside my sleeves and tucking my chin to my chest to protect my eyes. The deep snow made it difficult to walk.

All four of us had barely made it off the field onto the road, and the storm began to roar violently around us. Everything became blindingly white, making me lose my depth perceptions, and the world around us vanished. I tried to push forward against heavy gusts of wind. Only able to see short distances in front of me. I took another step forward, and Connie, who was standing next to me, lost her footing and fell face-first into right into a snowdrift. Onacona, Shelly, and I ran to her. We grabbed her by her clothes and backpack, and pulled her upright, then helped her get the snow off her face. After that, we tried to collect ourselves to continue, but thick blankets of icy winds were consuming us, and snow piled up to our knees.

I desperately tried to see a landmark, a house, anything that would indicate where we were. "Um, which way is your house, Onacona?" Shelly asked nervously, her voice raised to be heard over the roar of the wind. Onacona looked around, but she was just as lost as the rest of us. None of us could tell which way led us home or even which way led back to the school.

"Hold hands, everyone, so we don't lose each other," I barked. We gripped firmly one to the other and chose a direction to walk. One step, two steps. We pushed forward and slammed right into a barrier. We lost our footing on impact and fell on our butts.

"What was that?" Shelly bellowed through the wind, her voice scarcely audible.

Onacona yelled back, "It's a fence. Everyone grab hands, and we can walk along it feeling our way home." We locked hands again.

A siren began to sound over the storm. "This can't be good," Connie yelled out.

Onacona hollered, "Change of plans, we need to get

over the fence and take cover! We'll push each other over one at a time, and the third one will straddle the top of the fence and pull the last one up. The siren means that we need to shelter now!" None of us argued, and we tossed Connie over first. Then, Shelly, I hoisted Onacona up, and she helped lift me. We hoped down the other side.

"Is everyone here?" I cried out. The wind was thrashing at us, and it was hard to maintain my balance. Hands reached out, and we all locked again.

"Which way do we head now?" I shouted.

"I don't know, I can't see a house," Connie yelled back. Fear started to creep in, but I knew I had had to keep my wits about me. Because panicking In this situation could get me or, worse, my friends killed.

Then just a few feet in front of me, I could make out the outline of a woman. She was barely visible through the dense wall of white and wind. I hoped I wasn't hallucinating, I called out. "Can you help us?" I couldn't make out any discernible features, just her outline, but none of that mattered.

"This way," the woman's voice carried to me on the wind as if she couldn't be silenced by the storm. Not in a position to question what I saw, I stepped forward and pulled my friends with me as I followed her. She moved with unnatural ease just beyond us. While we struggled to keep up behind her, unable to lift our legs out of the deep snow that was up to our thighs now, we pushed through it on and on. My feet were freezing, with snow packed in my shoes. My face and my hands were numb, but I didn't stop or let my friends stop. I kept my focus on the women to keep us from getting lost. In my heart, I hoped she was leading us somewhere we could be safe.

The shape of a house started to come into view, and we were just a few steps shy from the corner of it. The woman guiding us picked up her pace and walked faster as we approached the house. Unable to keep up with her in these conditions, she disappeared from my view. I hoped she would be waiting for us inside and that I could thank her for coming to help. However, my gut was telling me that something was off. We climbed up some creaky stairs and stomped to get the snow off our bodies. I looked at the house from the front porch. It was completely dark. "The power must be out," I yelled, pointing at the windows, the wind gusted, and I moved to the door. I was shivering and needed to get inside.

I entered the house first then quickly found a spot out of

the way. I promptly sat on the floor and pried my frozen shoes from my feet. I cupped my hands around my toes and blew warm air on them. "Ouch, my feet hurt," I wined while rubbing them. I looked around. "Hello, Hello," I called out while waiting for my eyes to adjust to the dim light. No one answered.

"I don't think anyone is here," Connie moaned in pain.

"No. There's a woman. I think she came in just before us," I said, unsure and confused.

"What Woman?" Shelly asked, sounding puzzled.

"The one that showed us how to get here," Onacona replied slowly.

"She told us to follow her and led us here," I explained, a knot forming in my gut.

"There was no lady. You two pulled us here. How did you really know where to go?" Connie responded through her chattering teeth.

The inside of the house had taken shape; items were strewn across the floors and on furniture. There were boards randomly fixed over the windows. I figured someone put them there to prevent the glass from breaking. The gaps in the wooden panels only allowed for little streams of light to enter the rooms. The room to the left of us had a couch sitting in the middle of it facing an old TV, with a coffee table between them, a bookshelf stood in the corner of the room, and the walls were stained where pictures once hung. To my right was what looked to be a once-working refrigerator, a kitchen and in front of us was a table and four chairs. The thought of being stranded here alone made my heart pound, and my hands started to shake.

"Oh no, are we." I gulped "in the murder house?" My mouth went dry. The door shook with the wind, and I jumped.

"Of course, we are! Of course, this is where you brought us," Connie scowled fear and anger in her voice. "You know I never got caught in a storm or believed in ghosts before you came barreling into my life like a wrecking ball. You don't even like it here, and now, you got us stuck in the murder house! For who knows how long. Great job!" She threw her hands in the air, then crossed them over her chest. I found myself thinking of what to say. I wanted to apologize, but before I could.

Shelly started in, "Ya Connie, well, you have lived in a tiny world with me as your only friend for too long! You do nothing but put everyone else down. You experience nothing; I planned to ditch you as soon as I found other friends because you're so boring. Now we actually have a life, and if you mess this up, you will be alone. Who cares how long we have to stay here? Jamie may be new, but she's a heck of a lot better friend than you are. At least she led us to shelter. What did you do? You fell down and got us all lost. We could've died out there! At least she did something!" Shelly coughed with disgust, her hands rolled into fists at her side.

Not wanting to see a fight break out, I attempted to ease the tension. "Hey, you don't happen to have a bowl of popcorn, do you? I need one, so I can enjoy this more thoroughly," I teased while shifting my finger from Shelly to Connie. Neither looked amused by it. But hey, I thought it was worth a try.

"I'm cold," Onacona shivered and rubbed her arms.

"I'll look for blankets. If we cuddle up on the couch together, we can share our body heat to warm each other up. While we wait for the storm to pass," I suggested, and I began walking briskly towards a hall past the living room. The hallway led to four doors. I opened the first door, and behind it was a bathroom with an old green tub, a matching green sink, and floral wallpaper. "Who puts wallpaper in a bathroom?" I thought to myself. I moved on to the next room and scanned it for anything useful, but it was empty aside from a turned-over dresser and old clothing piled up in the middle of the floor. My eyes drifted down. "hum, that's odd," I thought to myself. I walked forward and knelt. The floor was covered in weird dents and scratches, too big to be human, but I couldn't place them. The sound of the others settling down onto the couch caught my attention, and I headed back into the hall.

I opened the third door and entered. It was darker than the other rooms, but I could make out a big bed in the dim light, with side tables and a dresser. I walked over to the bed and smiled. It had two thick blankets on it. "I found blankets," I yelled down the hall. I lifted them and gave them a couple good shakes, and dust went flying. I coughed and sneezed, then rolled the blankets around my arms. I glanced down at the bed before leaving, and odd markings on the sheet made me pause. It seemed to have a shape or faded stain on it. "I wonder what it is?" I debated, moving closer for a better look.

"Are you coming? I'm freezing," Onacona yelled from the front room. I turned on my heels and headed back to the couch. I stretched the blanket out evenly across everyone and sat next to Onacona and curled up with her under it. "Ewe, these blankets are gross and smell old. I wonder if they have lice?" Connie said with disgust while looking at them. Shelly shot her a glare, and Connie rolled her eyes and shivered, then hesitantly slid deeper under the blankets.

The storm continued to rage outside as we sat, the wind pounded against the house, and the sound of it was almost deafening. The boards creaked and groaned from the strain of it. I leaned forward and picked up a dusty old newspaper. It felt stiff to the touch, but I needed a distraction anything to get my Mom's words out of my mind. They played over and over in my head, "One wrong step and the roof may cave in." The eves in the ceiling moaned, and I became jittery with the fear. I wanted to leave, but it wasn't an option. The situation felt daunting, and the lack of conversation was awkward. So, I lifted the paper to my face and strained my eyes in the darkness to try and read it.

"Can you read that out loud, please," Shelly asked, her voice shrill with fear. I figured my Mom's words were running through her head too.

"Sure," My voice squeaked. I could only make out one word at a time in the darkness, but slowly I began to read:

"Another missing girl has been found dead. Layla Frost 20 disappeared May 16, 1981, while biking home from work." I stopped, not wanting to scare anyone. Things were bad enough as it was. "Of course, it couldn't be a paper about puppies or rainbows. Dang, it, I'd settle for a car wreck," I thought to myself. What were the chances?

"What else does it say?" Connie asked, and I looked at her, stunned.

"Really?" I double-checked, caught off guard by her interest. "Well, we are in the murder house, and we are stuck here. So, we might as well," She shrugged.

I looked at the other two, and they nodded their heads for me to continue. I started to read again, one word at a time. "Layla worked at the Dollar Store on Crook Road. Her remains were recovered on 9 June 1981 in the River. Almost exactly one year since Leilah Valdez, 12, disappeared on her way home from a friend's house. She, too, was on her bike. The body of Leilah has never been found. Authorities believe these two cases are linked. If anyone has any information that could help with the investigations of these two girls, please call the Idaho Police." I took a breath. "What, that's it? That is all they had. Why did they think these two cases were linked? Because they both rode bikes?" I scowled, disappointed.

"No. They have to have more. Something they aren't saying," Onacona sounded let down.

"They both have the same names just different spelling; maybe that's why they think they are linked?" Connie proposed.

"Maybe they both lived near each other?" Shelly suggested.

"Or maybe someone left this paper in here, and that is how the rumors began about the house." Connie mumbled.

"Are there any more papers in here?" I asked while trying to spot another paper in the darkness.

I stood up to have a better look around, and the other girls stood up to help search. We sifted through garbage around the room. We all wanted answers. The storm was still hard at work just beyond the front door, and it felt like this was a much-needed distraction. I began to collect random items around the table. Connie was searching under the couch, and Shelly was looking through the cupboard in the kitchen. Onacona started sifting through piles on the bookshelf. "Jamie, did you see any papers in the bedrooms?" Shelly asked.

"I didn't notice anything, but I wasn't looking, and I didn't even go into the fourth room," I answered casually while putting a glass on the table.

"Maybe we should check those rooms more thoroughly,"

Shelly recommended.

"No luck here," Onacona chimed in after looking behind the TV.

"Shelly's right. There's nothing else here. We should check the rooms," Connie advised a bit too enthusiastically. But hey, she was trying, so I wasn't going to call her on it.

"Let's all look together, so we don't miss anything," Onacona added while clapping the dust off her hands.

"AHH! look what I found!" Shelly squealed. I looked and a smile instantly formed on my face.

"You found candles!" I couldn't contain the joy in my voice. This was better than finding gold, considering our current circumstances. "And matches!" She giggled. We all huddled around Shelly as she struck a match and the sound of it catching fire was the most beautiful sound I had ever heard, as the candle-lit relief washed over me.

"This will make looking around so much easier, and this place doesn't seem so scary now," Connie said with hope ringing in her voice. We placed a couple of candles on plates and placed two on the kitchen table and another two on the living room's coffee table. Then each of us put one in a cup to use as our own personal flashlights.

We huddled together and slowly moved down the hall,

our candles in hand. The floorboards moaned against our weight while the rest of the house creaked with the howling winds. I opened the door to the bathroom.

"Did you check in the mirror or under the sink?" Connie asked.

"To look for blankets, no," I responded sarcastically, then we all crammed ourselves into the bathroom and began looking around.

"There's toilet paper, an old rusty shaving blade, a can of shaving cream, and a comb under the sink," Onacona reported.

"No soap? Typical of a man," Connie spat. Onacona opened the mirror to look through the shelf, while Connie avoided touching anything. I was pinned between the toilet and the window myself, so I decided to look at things closer. I turned to the window and slid the curtains to one side and looked at the windowpane. I spotted a small bracelet with two charms, a puppy charm, and a four-leaf clover charm.

"Look at this," I held up the bracelet over my candle so everyone could see it.

"Oh, that's pretty. I bet it was Leilah's. It looks like a little girl's bracelet," Connie said.

"Can I have a look at it?" Shelly asked while standing in

the empty tub, and I handed it to her.

"There's a stamp on the back that says, 24K, that means its real gold. Who gives their kid real gold?" Shelly paused and examined it closer, then continued. "The stamp also has the initials SJ on it that's probably short for the Jeweler. If we can find SJ, maybe we can get a name for who this belongs to. Can I hang onto this; I think I'd like to follow up on it?" Shelly proposed.

"All yours," I answered. There was no way my parents would take me to jewelry stores. They didn't have the time for that.

"Hey, look what I found," Onacona said, pulling a prescription bottle out of the mirror. We all huddled in.

"The bottle is prescribed for a Cynthia Bard, 1984," she said, perplexed. "So, the sink has man items in it, but the pill bottle is for a woman and theirs a girl's bracelet. Yet the paper is about the murdered girls. I don't get it," I wanted an answer.

Onacona slipped the bottle into her pocket. "I'll check the phone book for a Cynthia Bard when I get home," Onacona said. Being satisfied with our two new clues, we left the bathroom and headed to the next bedroom.

I opened the door, and we all stepped in. "This isn't much

of a bedroom," Shelly said while looking around.

"I thought the same thing the first time I came in here," I sighed. "Look at the marks all over the ground," I pointed at the floor. Everyone's eyes dropped, and Onacona moved forward and knelt next to them, letting her candle illuminate them.

"Those are strange. I wonder what kind of object made those? They are too thin for a bed to have made them, but bigger than the marks our desks leave all over the floors at school. Also, it doesn't look like drag marks, like someone would make scooting something around. More like something heavy was dropped repeatedly," Onacona postulated while kneeling next to the marks and running her fingers gently over them.

"You got all that from looking at them for maybe a minute?" I smirked. She stood up slowly to keep her candle from snuffing out.

"Well, my dad takes me hunting, and his hawk often drops its smaller prey from the sky, and they leave these kinds of impressions on the ground," She explained.

"Wait, you have a hawk? That's so cool. I didn't know you could own a hawk. What's its name, how did you train it to hunt, does it sleep with you, what kind of hawk, can I hold it? I have so many questions," I said excited and in utter surprise.

"Her name is Talon, she's a red-tailed hawk, most people can't own them, but my Dad has a special native permit to keep her, you can hold her with my Dad's supervision, I don't sleep with her, she sleeps in a shed out back at my place," Onacona expelled.

"Can I holder her too?" Shelly asked, looking just as excited.

"Of course," Onacona nodded with a big smile.

We looked at Connie. "I'm going to pass on this one; red-tailed hawks are huge, and that sounds terrifying, but I'll wave at you all from a safe distance," Connie gave a half-smile, and we all laughed.

We spread out. Shelly began digging through the clothing on the floor with one hand. Connie started looking through the dresser, I moved to the closet, and Onacona searched the corners and window in the room. "Well, there's nothing here," I said bleakly, looking at empty shelves. The others nodded in agreement, having found nothing themselves. "To the next room," I cheered while shrugging my shoulders. The wind gusted outside again, and the house shook. We all froze for a second, looking around, questioning its stability in our minds. When the house settled, we began moving slowly to the door while shielding our candles as we continued down the hall.

We opened the third door and stepped inside. "Now, this is a proper room," Connie said, her eyes sparkling in the candlelight. She began making her way to the dresser. Shelly went to the closet. I started sifting through items on the floor while Onacona moved to the bed and started looking under it. I glanced over the mess and looked for anything that could be a clue to this mystery. I lifted an old towel and put it aside; under it was a pair of jeans. I reached into the pocket and pulled out a folded envelope. I carefully flattened it and gently pulled open the top. I examined the contents. It was a handwritten letter signed with the same name as on the medicine bottle. "Hey everyone, I found a letter, listen to this," I read the letter to the room.

My Dearest Jacob,

It's been three months since I last saw you. This distance is almost unbearable. I whispered your name to the wind under the full moon last night. My heart hopes it carried it to you, and you could hear my voice. Jenny misses you too and can't wait for you to join us. Please, Jacob, we are safe now, and this is a good place. Please come home to us. You have done enough.

My Love forever,

Cynthia

I turned the envelope around to see where the letter came from, but there wasn't a return address, and the postmark had been torn off. My heart hurt for this woman. Whatever situation this family was in, it was obviously dire. "I don't think we can call this the murder house anymore," I said, feeling guilty that we had assumed the worst even if the previous occupants didn't know. Everyone went silent and still. The mood in the room dropped. Onacona stood up from where she had been sitting while going over the items under the bed. I could tell by her lightly lit face she was hurting too.

Onacona glanced down at the bed. "Wait, look at this." She moved her candle closer to the bed.

"Oh ya, I noticed a stain earlier but couldn't see it very well," I said softly, placing the letter in my pocket. I walked to her and put my hand on her shoulder, and she put her hand on mine. Then I looked down, and what I couldn't see before was now blatantly clear. My bottom lip began to tremble.

Shelly and Connie held hands and walked to us. "If that's a pee stain, Onacona, and you're pulling a fast one on us. I'll pinch you." Connie joked sarcastically, she reached us, and her mouth fell open.

"It's not Pee," Onacona said. We all gathered tightly together and took a step back.

"Is that blood?" Shelly puzzled.

"Obviously," Connie asserted, fear rising in her voice. Onacona and I were still too shocked to join the conversation. The stain wasn't just a stain, and it wasn't "just" blood either it was a word written in blood. "Why does it say, Gate?" Connie asked, her voice squeaked.

I mustered the courage to talk, "I don't know why it says, gate, but this isn't the first time this word has come up today." I turned around, and we shifted into a circle, each of us facing each other, the candles lighting our faces. I explained how Onacona, and I had heard a voice earlier when walking to school and that all it said was: gate. How my papers fell off my desk, and the only word left facing up was the word, gate.

Everyone's faces were grim, Onacona sighed, "when I was in PE, The teacher asked me to get a ball from the bin of balls. When I reached into it, I noticed all the balls were turned, and the part that said North was covered up. All that was showing was the word "gate" over and over again. Every single ball." For a moment, we all went silent and listened, listened to the sounds of the house creaking and the storm raging.

"What does this all mean?" Connie asked softly. I tried to respond, but my voice had stopped working.

My head started to spin, and the room went black. After what felt like an hour of staring into the darkness, my throat cleared, and I yelled into the blackness, "Hello! Hello!" No one answered. I screamed, "Where are you, Onacona, Connie, Shelly!" Fear washed over me like a tidal wave over a rowing boat. I heard footsteps coming towards me in the dark. I tried to turn, to run, but my legs wouldn't move. My heart pounded in my chest, my body began to shake. The steps came closer and closer. I was terrified of what I might see or what might happen to me. My thoughts raced through my head, incoherent and dizzy. I thought I was going to faint; every fiber of my being screamed, this is wrong. A large shape began to take form just a few feet from me. "This is it. I'm going to die!" I thought. The thing came into view. Its eyes glowed gray under a hooded cloak made of shadows and gloom. The figure reached its hand towards me and moaned, its fingers unraveled, extending its palm as if it wanted me to take it.

I recoiled, and the room began to spin. Silver ribbons of light began streaming from me, carrying me into the endless sky. I didn't have time to think, just experience. The room vanished, and I was on a beach. All the fear was gone, all my pain was gone, all my weariness was gone. It was absolute freedom. I tried to remember my life, but it was like a distant memory, a story I told myself long ago. A woman walked up to me. She was beautiful, graceful, completely at peace, and I felt whole. I looked at her and somehow knew she was me, and I was her. This place felt more tangible and real than anything I had ever felt before.

She looked at me and spoke. Her words fell on me like warm, gentle rain. "You are doing beautifully. You are becoming who you are meant to be. Every drop in this ocean is a life you have lived, don't be afraid." She lightly touched my palm, "find your power," she urged me softly, and the world began to fall away. I didn't want to leave. My life felt like a sad dream. Wasn't it just a dream? This place was everything, and I longed for it. My heart began to break as it all fell away.

I found myself standing on a cliffside overlooking a vast canyon. A naked man with wings was perched kneeling on a rock. He looked at me, confused. No words needed to be exchanged. I knew what he was thinking. "What are you doing here?" Our eyes locked. I stared at him in wonder. Then shifted my gaze down through the never-ending canyon. I beheld many worlds with different forms of life and many realms for each planet, layers of beings. I gasped, and this place too fell away, and I was in the darkroom again. This time unafraid. In my heart, I knew now that there were beings much more significant watching me, and fear was unnecessary. I looked at the figure again. This time, I knew that it was a manifestation of my own fears and that it drew from my energy to take form. The cloak of smoke fell away, and I allowed the truth to take shape, and it revealed a woman. Her face was kind, with gentle yet sad eyes. She was middle-aged, with a slim build, long dark hair, and wore a golden chain around her neck with a rose-shaped locket. She stood before me, as plain as any real person could. She began to speak, and I recognized her voice. It was the voice I had heard in the wind.

"You have to find The Gate. You must close it. Jacob tried and," Her voice trailed off. "Close The Gate, find the missing pieces, and set him free. Be careful if they find out you're seeking them." A green hand reached out of the darkness and yanked her back into it. I felt the fear spreading through my body again like cancer as if just now, I fully came back into myself. My hand burned as another hand thrust out the dark at me, and I tucked my head while raising my hand to shield myself. The darkness repelled back at a light. I looked, and my hand was beaming in the spot my other self, touched it. A shape formed where the light expelled, and the symbol seemed familiar, but I couldn't place it.

I relinquished my fear and yelled, "Go!" and the darkness fled, and I was thrust back into my body.

"Jamie, Jamie, wake up, please wake up." I heard Onacona's voice whimpering.

"She's dead, isn't she" Connie sobbed.

I heard a door shut, "The storm is still too strong, I can't, I can't get help," Shelly cried.

I blinked my eyes open, "What are you all going on about? I'm not dead." I smiled. My voice was raspy. "What happened?" I was surprised to find myself lying on the couch and began moving into a seated position.

"She's OK!" Connie cheered. Onacona's head dropped, and she sighed in relief. Then they all rushed to me and threw their arms around me.

"You were just standing there, then your head fell back, and you hit the floor. We tried to wake you, but you were so cold, deadly cold. So, we rushed you in here and covered you up." Connie explained while sniffling.

"We were so afraid," Shelly swallowed. "We thought you died." She choked while tears ran down her face.

Then Onacona spoke, "tell us what happened to you, I heard other voices around you, but they were too quiet to make out what was being said." I stopped and looked at her in all her beauty. I loved that she said it like it was. I understood her and she me. I sat up and patted the seat next to me.

"You're all going to need to sit down for this," I said softly. Onacona, Connie, and Shelly all cuddled into me, and we wrapped ourselves in the blankets. Then I told them everything.

"You know how I know you are telling the truth?" Shelly paused a gleam sparkled in her eye.

"You glowed while you spoke. Light radiated from you as if you brought it back with you," Shelly smiled.

"I saw it too," Connie chimed in.

"Me too. And I felt it," Onacona added. The room went

silent. No one tried to tell me it was a fever dream or tried to make sense of it. They just excepted it as the truth.

"Jamie, Do you think you saw an Angel?" Connie asked hopefully.

"That would be my first guess, but he was naked, and there wasn't a halo. So, I don't want to assume anything. I'll talk to my Grandpa. He's from Norway and is always telling me stories of different beings. I'll ask my great grandma on my Mom's side too. She used to be a medium. Maybe they know," I considered. I couldn't help but be curious about him too. "I, however, do know two things though, one we need to look in the fourth room, and two, we need to decide where we want to sleep tonight. It's late, the storm isn't finished, and we are not walking home in five feet of snow in the dark. We can figure out The Gate thing another day," I yawned, feeling the day had taken its toll.

We gathered together and made our way down the hall. We passed the first door, then the second, then the third. I grabbed the knob and twisted. Holding my breath, I pushed the door open. At first glance, the room seemed tidy and untouched, unlike the rest of the house. A desk sat near a boarded-up window, with a journal and some papers atop it. A bookshelf stood to the right of the desk, a filing cabinet to the left, and another bed against the wall, next to the door. The only thing out of place in this room was a giant mural of a lion sitting on a gate in front of a star system.

"What does that mean?" I wondered. I didn't even have to point it was staring us all in the face.

"Maybe The Gate that needs to be closed has a lion on it?" Connie suggested.

"Huh, maybe," Shelly yawned halfway through her sentence.

"Let's just put the papers and journal from the desk in our bags, and look at it later, then go to sleep," Onacona suggested, rubbing her eyes with her free hand.

"Maybe we sleep in here tonight. Theirs more blankets on this bed, and we will all fit if we sleep sideways on it. We can pile on the other blankets as well. That way, maybe we can all stay warm," I proposed, barely able to hold my own eyes open. Everyone nodded. Shelly headed to the living room to grab her backpack. Connie followed behind her to grab the other blankets while Onacona gathered up the contents on the desk, and I made the bed and checked it too; I didn't want to sleep on anybody's bloody message. After we all had completed our tasks, we climbed under the covers and laid down.

"I'm really sorry about what I said earlier. I'm still not happy about being stuck here, but I'm really glad I'm not stuck in here alone, that it's you all I'm here with," Connie whispered.

"I'm sorry too. I wasn't really going to ditch you, Connie. I love you. I love you all," Shelly whispered back.

"I love you all too," Onacona stifled, and she wrapped her hand around mine.

"Me too," I smiled in the darkness and let sleep take me.

I woke up to the sun shining through the boards over the windows and to silence. No Wind! I felt elated. "Wake up, Wake Up! We can get out of here!" I buzzed enthusiastically. We all tumbled out of bed, like a stampede of wild horses, throwing our shoes and backpacks on. We crashed through the front door and ran as fast as we could manage through waist-high snow. I was starving and thirsty. We all were. We got to the fence, and I heard a familiar sound. A whistle that was so loud it echoed from ocean to ocean, and I only knew one person who could whistle like that.

"THAT'S MY MOM!" I said to the other girls.

"MOM! MOM!" I yelled and tossed my bag over the fence.

Then a Man's voice yelled out, "Onacona!"

"DAD! I'M HERE!" Onacona roared back. The volume of it caught me off guard. I didn't know she could scream that loud. "That's My Dad!" She said, grinning. I locked my fingers together and gave her a boost over the fence.

"OVER THERE!" I heard a woman cry.

Then a man hollered, "IS SHELLY WITH YOU?!" The sound of feet running toward us in the snow was a relief.

"That's my Dad," Shelly said smiling, and she threw her bag over the fence, and I boosted her over.

"OH, MY GOODNESS, SHELLY! PLEASE SAY CONNIE IS WITH YOU!" Another Woman yelled with desperation in her voice.

"I'M HERE, MOM," Connie bellowed, then tossed her bag over the fence. It was a bit of a struggle, but I managed to push her over too. Then I reached for the top of the fence, and a set of large hands took mine and lifted me over. It was my Dad. I worried for a split second that I would be in trouble when I saw his face, but he took me in his arms and cried. I'd never seen him cry before. Then it struck me, "he loves me." I began crying too. My Mom reached us and threw her arms around me and sobbed.

The hugging was nice for a minute, but now, they were suffocating me. I tilted my head back to try and breathe. "I'm hungry," I said while gasping for air and both of my parents cracked up laughing.

They eased up. "Let's get you home then," My Mom smiled while she carefully examined me for any injuries.

"I'll make you a steak. While you tell us how your night went," My Dad offered while looking at me with pride.

"This is weird. He never listens to me." I thought.

"OK, that sounds great!" I practically drooled. The thought of a steak made my dry mouth water. I looked at my friends, and they, too, looked like they were being smothered by their parents. Connie's parents were both heavy-set like her, and Shelly's Dad was skinny like her. We all turned and walked home with our parent's hands placed on our shoulders as if they were afraid if they let go, we might vanish again.

Chapter Five, The Unimaginable

<u>Trigger warnings, topics in this chapter highlights issues regarding the racism and violence of the era.</u>

It was nice to wake up warm in my own bed and even better, I don't have to go to school today! Snow Day! School is out for the rest of the week. I overheard my siblings cheering about it when the call came in earlier this morning. Last night, I had asked my Dad if I could call my Grandpa and Great Grandma today. He said yes, as long as the conversations don't last more than ten minutes each, to avoid out of control long-distance fees. I'm so excited to hear their voices.

When I got home yesterday morning, I spent hours telling my parents about our stay in the abandoned house. Minus the ghostly stuff, and I left the part where I passed out for last. Knowing my Mom, The Nurse. It was a good thing I did, too, because she did a full medical workup on me. She took my blood pressure, blood sugar, temperature from my butt. She says," it's more accurate that way." She listened to my lungs and inspected me for infection. Then she gave me a pile of pills to take for good measure. After was ordered to drink a gallon of water, eat a pile of food, take a hot bath, and go to bed. I didn't mind going to bed early; I was exhausted and ended up sleeping the rest of the day and through the night, but today is a new day, and I look forward to taking full advantage of it. I stretched my arms and sat up in bed.

"Knock, Knock," Noora said while opening my door.

Then Neil and Evan ran past her and plopped onto my bed. "Hi, boys," I smiled and gave them a tight squeeze.

"The storm was really scary, and the lights wouldn't turn on, and we had a party, and Mom and Dad were freaking out. Dad lit a fire in the fireplace, and the whole house filled up with smoke, and they said it had a flue." Neal attempted to explain his evening before anyone else had a chance.

"No, Neal, they forgot to open the chimney flue. That's what the vent is called. The fireplace didn't have the flue," Noora corrected him while rolling her eyes. She then walked over to me and gave me a very awkward hug.

"Hey, I'm glad you're OK. Evan and I barely made it home ourselves. We couldn't see anything by the time we reached our street. I had to carry Evan most of the way to keep him from getting separated from me. It got intense, but Mom was doing her sonic whistling from the house, so I just followed that horrible sound until we got home. So did a bunch of other kids. She stayed out there doing that for like two hours, and kids kept turning up. So that's why Neil thought we were having a party. The storm picked up even more just after Evan, and I had made it inside. Dad kept trying to find you in the storm with Onacona's Dad, but they kept getting turned around and had to follow Mom's whistles to get back. However, they did get a bunch of the other kids to their homes, and other parents showed up every now and again following that sound and claimed their kids too. The phones were down, so Dad contacted the police on the C.B. radio. The police told him that even the snowplows were inoperable in those conditions and ordered him to stay inside. After everyone else went home, Mom cried and prayed for another hour while Dad screamed for you outside. Sorry, we didn't wait for you," Noora said genuinely.

I felt guilty for not considering how this affected everyone else and for not trying harder myself to get others inside. I didn't think about how this would affect my parents and how it must have felt, having kids show up repeatedly, but not your own kid. I sniffled, "You don't have to be sorry. If you waited, you and Evan would have been stuck in that cold house with us. That wouldn't have made it any better for Mom and Dad or Evan. My friends and I got inside right after the sirens started to sound because we couldn't see anything. In fact, we barely made it to that house. I'm really glad you are alright too. I wonder how often this happens here?" I tensed, concerned.

"Actually, the news is calling it the worst storm in fifty years, so hopefully, not for another fifty years. People all over town were stranded where they were. People slept in the stores, bars, cars, and strangers' homes. It was a mess. Anyhow, you now owe me for taking care of Waddles. You get Neil tonight, so I can get some sleep. He's going through a growth spurt and is a pain at night. So, enjoy," Noora finished and left the room. Neil and Even followed behind her.

I grabbed my journal from my bedside table and wrote all the events from my night in the abandoned house in it so I wouldn't forget anything. After I was satisfied, I had every last word spoken written down. I headed to the kitchen for breakfast and to use the phone. I found my Dad reading an old newspaper at the table. "Did the paperboy get a snow day too?" I asked my Dad as I sat down next to him and Waddles, who sat in a highchair next to the table.

"Seems so, now I have to wait for the five-o-clock news to get more details about the storm," he grumbled, annoyed.

"Can I have the comics?" I asked him, and he turned the pages of the paper and handed me the section with the comics, and my Mom gave me a plate of scrambled eggs and asked me to feed Waddles while she made mine. Just like that, everything had gone back to normal, and I was glad.

I decided to postpone making my calls until I could have some privacy and play in the snow outside. "Evan, snowsuit up, kiddo, we are going on an adventure. Neil, come here so I can get you dressed." I yelled down the hall, and the sound of little feet hitting hardwood floors echoed throughout the house. I pulled Neil and Evan in the sled around the yard as fast as possible, back, and forth. The snow was deeper than I expected but light and fluffy. The boys were thrilled that I was their willing sled dog.

"Mush, Mush," Evan yelled while cracking an invisible whip.

"Aruuu aruuu." I howled at the sky while I pulled them

gleefully through the snow.

I looked down the road, and I saw a boy about my age watching from a few houses down. I recognized him from school but couldn't remember his name. I waved him over to join in the fun, but he got an embarrassed look on his face and ran to his house. "Ha, boys are weirdos," I thought to myself. I spun around and splashed snow at my brother while laughing wildly.

"Hey! That's cold," Evan snarled at me, and I did it again. He growled, then burst into laughter and started splashing snow at me in retaliation. Neil, who was not happy about getting caught in the crossfire, started crying. I swooped him up and lifted him above my head and spun him around and ran him to the house. I placed him gently on the floor.

"Jamie, Great Grandma will be heading to the doctor soon. You better make your call now, or it will be too late," My Mom yelled from the family room.

"OK, Mom," I hollered back to her a then turned back to the door and yelled to Evan, "Evan, time to come in. I have to make a call."

"Oh, man!" Evan wined, disappointed, and stomped towards the door with a scowl across his face.

I grabbed the phone from the wall and stretched its cord all the way across the living room. I checked around corners to ensure that I was alone. Satisfied that I was, I sat down and dialed. "Hello, who's calling?" My Great grandma answered.

"It's Jamie. GG," I responded cheerfully. I call her GG for short since Great Grandma is a mouthful and makes her feel old.

"Who's calling?" GG asked again.

"IT'S JAMIE," I bayed even louder.

"Who's calling?" GG repeated yet again.

"My word, this is going to take up my ten minutes," I thought to myself and yelled, "PUT YOUR HEARING AID IN GG!"

I heard my Mom burst into laughter from the family room. "Hold on, toots, I need to put my hearing aids in," she responded.

"finally," I whispered.

"Hey, I heard that you," GG said sarcastically.

"Well, one can only tolerate so much GG," I said tauntingly back.

"Your Mom told me this morning that you all had quite the ordeal out there in the wild west, and my Bluestockings tell me you took a trip to your higher self and another realm and that you might be getting in over your head in the spirit realm. Let's talk about that," She insisted. Getting to the point is her style and always has been. She used to be a medium by trade, so I wasn't surprised that she caught a whiff of my situation.

"Yes, GG, a ghost woman, who I think is named Cynthia, told me I need to find a way to close a gate. When my friends and I were stuck in the abandoned house, we saw a giant mural painted on the wall of a lion sitting on a gate with a bunch of stars behind it. I think it's linked. Do you know what it means?" I asked.

"Well, toots, I reckon that would be the Lion's Gate. Get some books on stars and signs that should point you in the right direction. I don't know how to close The Gate or why it's open, but this isn't mine to know. My Bluestocking is telling me, you ought to proceed with caution and not rely on the words of spirits about the gate. They have their own agendas. You can't fully trust them. Just follow your Bluestocking doll. She'll cut out some of the hubbub. I always knew you had the gift, girl, and your Mom marring your Dad was no coincidence either. Even if he is a scumbag for moving you all out there, away from me. You need to tap into that Viking blood of yours. That line is powerful. Odin will have a direct link to you and give you wisdom. That Frigga lady is a good lady too, but don't forget to call on my roots as well sugar, the goddess Asteria she's the goddess of the stars, I have an inkling she'll be more precious to you than gold. Make tools; you can't fully ward off the dark forces without them. Feel the wind and follow the call. Let your heart lead you," GG paused, and I could hear her chomping on her dentures while she thought, and they made a sucking sound with a click, then a pop, and I cringed. "You are going to face some ugliness Hun, you be careful now. You got that child?" She asked.

"How am I supposed to have all that? How do I connect to these bluestockings, and what tools?" I wondered as a shiver went down my spine.

"I see battles coming in your life some sooner than you think, as well as in this undertaking, your friends will make good allies for your spirit and for battle. Help them purge what is no longer useful to make room for magic, help them shed their darkness. You keep them close to your heart. Before you worry about goddesses and gods, first, you connect to your Bluestocking. You hear me?" GG said sternly,

"How on earth do I do that?" I asked. This was getting a bit kooky, even for me. I could hear her chattering to herself. I always wondered if she was really just talking to herself, or a ghost, or if she was crazy when she did that, but if she is crazy, then what does that make me? I saw a naked guy with wings.

"Don't get sassy with me, Darlin. I know it seems like a lot, and change is scary, but a life worth living isn't lived without risks taken. The alternative is worse. You could be boring and normal and fail at life. You know when your Great Granddaddy died and left me with four babes to fend for during the depression. I had to risk everything to ensure their safety, a roof over their heads, a meal on the table, books for school, and clothing for their backs. Trust me, it wasn't easy; folks didn't give ladies work back then. I had to put my pain, vulnerability, and fear aside, which hurt more than you know. I had to call on my own power to raise my family up against all odds, and I ran the best speakeasy in town, and I talked to the ghosts for people and turned a good penny. While the normal people watched their babes starve, yet they still turned up their noses to us. Even if I offered them a meal, they wouldn't accept it. They let their pride kill off their kin. It was the hard truth of the time, and yes, what I did was illegal but look at my family thriving, and what I did well it didn't harm a soul. I don't question my decisions for a moment. You choose your path Hun, you can be a fool and do what folks tell you is right, or you can do what is right." She paused for a moment.

So, I spoke, "GG, I come from strong women, don't I? I want to be like you." That is all I could think of to say.

"You do, Darlin, and if you could've met my Momma," she paused and sniffled. "Well, she was stronger than me, now hush child, I have more to say, and I have done gone off-topic," GG bade softly with a tinge of sorrow in her raspy voice.

"If you want to hear your Bluestocking, you must first learn to listen. To see them, you must look through water and earth," she coached.

"Oh, come on, that doesn't make sense," I mumbled sarcastically to lighten the mood, and she perked up.

"Sugar, you know as well as I do somethings have to be earned, now put that fire of yours to use. That's my ten minutes, right? You tell that fine-looking Viking Grandpa of yours I say, he-ya toots, for me, won't ya?" GG chuckled. I glanced at the grandfather clock then cringed when that last sentence sank in.

"Gross GG, you're nasty," I sneered, repulsed. I couldn't think of anything more disturbing than my GG putting the moves on my Grandpa, and she laughed. Her crackle made me laugh in turn. "I love you, GG. Unfortunately, the ten minutes are up," I groaned, not wanting to say goodbye, but it was time.

"Oh, sweet cakes, don't be sad. I'm not going anywhere for a few more years. Remember to keep lavender on hand and salt. Oh, and tell that Muyaay'an girl her Momma says she loves her, to stay strong, and to talk to her Daddy. She will know what that means. I'll let you go, for now. Write me. I love you. By now, Jamie," GG finished talking and hung up.

"Who the heck is the Muyaay'an girl? Maybe she's had too much moonshine," I thought. I hung up the phone and headed to my room to write our conversation down. I knew the conversation with my Grandpa would be weird too, but, in another way, and I didn't want to forget any of it. Words from my GG were always special to me, and I thanked my lucky stars for her.

I sat on my bed and opened my journal, and began writing it all, word for word, trying not to forget a thing. I thought to myself, if I have children someday, I want them to know this woman. I want them to be like her. So, I wrote and wrote. I had just finished the sentence about the Muyaay'an girl, and I heard a knock at the front door. "I'll get it," I roared and ran to the front door. It was Onacona, to my delight. "Hi, Onacona, come in," I welcomed, excited to see her.

"Who's there?" My Mom yelled from across the house.

"It's Onacona. Can she hang out for a while?" I hollered back.

"That's fine by me. Just don't make any messes." My Mom bellowed.

"Understood, Mom," I agreed. "Want to come to my room?" I asked Onacona.

"Ya. Sure." She said mundanely with a shrug. Once we both entered my bedroom, I motioned for her to sit next to me on my bed.

"So, what have you been up to? It's pretty neat we get three days off from school, huh?" I beamed while trying to spark up a conversation.

"I haven't been up to much, and I wish we had school, or we were back in the abandoned house!" Onacona snapped, and it took me by surprise.

My gut dropped. I knew something had to be really bad for her to dismiss time off school. "You want to talk about it?" I asked carefully.

"No. There's nothing to talk about," she rasped, but from the sorrow in her eyes, I knew she had lied and having had that same look in my eyes before. I knew it involved suffering, whatever it was. "I don't want to talk. I want to sit here and think," Onacona demanded.

I started feeling that this was worse than I previously thought, so I gently responded, "OK, we will just sit here then. For as long as you want." I stacked my pillows against the walls, and we leaned on them. I switched my radio on, so we didn't have to make sitting in silence any more awkward. After a few commercials, a song by a woman country singer came on, and I listened to the words.

"Momma said, open up to me now, tell me what's hurting you child, and don't lie to me. I know when something is wrong.

I haven't seen you leave the house in a few days now, and you haven't spoken a word since the cows got out, and that's been three days ago this evening.

Honey, you got sorrow written all over your face, your eyes are swollen, and you haven't changed out of your P.J.s. Now daughter tell me what's going on?

Then I burst into tears, and I poured my heart out to my Momma."

Onacona jumped out of bed and hit the off button on my radio.

"You have to know I didn't plan that; I was hoping for R&B." I rationalized with my eyes wide, knowing that seemed like too much of a coincidence to be random.

"I know you didn't plan that! I'm not stupid," she scolded me.

"Onacona, I'm sorry. Also, you are the smartest person I know," I sucked up, worried, and unsure how this was going to play out.

"I can't talk to my Mother! My Mom is dead. She was killed by her so-called doctor when she was being sterilized after giving birth to me. Because she was an Indian like me, and we are just "stupid trash," and we aren't supposed to make babies!" Onacona grieved and fell to her knees and cried into her hands. "They kill off the Mothers and leave the children to be raised by cruel, evil women. We were researching the deaths of a couple women when we should've been looking into the thousands of missing Native American women and kids. But no, we aren't supposed to speak about that!" She vented while sobbing. I moved to the floor next to her, put my arm around her, and felt helpless with her. She shifted and tucked her head into my shoulder and continued to sob.

"You can talk to me about it, and I will listen every day for the rest of my life if that is what it takes. We can forget everything else and focus fully on this if you want us to. Anything you need, You are my best friend, and what affects you, and hurts you, and what you need to heal is the only thing I care about. Look at me, Onacona," I took her face in my hands. "You are not trash; you are not stupid. You are kind, the most beautiful person I have ever met, inside and out. You are going to make beautiful babies, and you are worthy of love. If your stupid Stepmom can't see that she is blind and ignorant," I protested while trying my best to comfort her. I wrapped my arms around her, and we sat crying together and holding each other for several moments longer.

Onacona moved to face me and slowly removed her jacket. While keeping her eyes locked on mine, she then started to roll up her sleeves and exposed her arms. I examined them and dry heaved. I flew into a rage at what I was seeing. I rallied to my feet and stormed to the door, "I'm going to get my Dad's gun, and I'm going to kill her," I raged in dead resolve. I opened the door, and Onacona ran to me and slammed it shut.

"You don't need to fix this," She pled, looking me in the eyes.

I looked away, "No! I have to! It can't let this go, not until you are safe!" I growled through gritted teeth, unable to breathe. I was mad at myself for not noticing that she always wore long sleeves; I was angry at Connie and Shelly for never telling me she always covered her arms in gym class because anyone who saw what I saw would've called the police.

"Jamie, if you say anything, she will blame it on my Dad, and since he is Native American and she is white, the police will believe her, and then I will lose him too," she pleads with me.

"Not if I kill her myself. I'll go to juvie, but it will put a stop to this. Juvie is only until I turn eighteen, and this is worth that," I argued, unafraid, needing to do what is right.

Onacona burst into tears and began reprimanding me.

"No, Jamie, if you do this, you are doing it for you! To make you feel better, and it has nothing to do with me. If you walk through this door, you will be throwing away our friendship, and everything you said to me will mean nothing. It won't heal anything. It will hurt me more than what has been done to me. If you do this, you are selfish and a coward," she said her piece and let up on the door.

I dropped my hands from the doorknob, turned, and took hers. I looked at the cigarette burns covering Onacona's arms, the ones that had healed and left scars. The ones where the cigarettes had been drug down her arms, the ones that were blistered than re-burned on top of the blisters, the infected ones, the healing ones, and the mess of scars covering every inch of the flesh she bore to me. Then finally the fresh ones made earlier today. I closed my eyes and swallowed. Both her arms were mutilated beyond anything I had witnessed before, and I felt that any person who did this wasn't worth the air they breathed. "How am I supposed to handle this? What do you need from me? I can't keep this secret. I can keep any other secret but not this," I swore, feeling like I failed her and was betraying her with every word. I couldn't look her in the eyes, knowing that if I did, I'd lose my nerve and give in, and she would continue to suffer.

"Let's talk about this," Onacona bade softly, and we went back to my bed and sat down. "Maybe we can catch her by videoing her in the act. You can hide in the closet with a camcorder, and we could get it on film, and then they wouldn't blame my Dad," Onacona puzzled.

"That won't work the camcorder is too loud and big; I'd have to leave the closet door wide open, and she would know what we are up to. Plus, I'd have to watch without reacting, and we all know that's impossible," I countered.

"Maybe we can just record the sounds of her doing it. I can record every time she does it until it's enough for the police to realize it's her," She posed.

"Absolutely not!" I was horrified at the idea that we just kept letting it continue. "This is never going to happen, not ever again! You hear me!" I exhorted, disgusted.

"You are unreasonable!" Onacona spat.

"Well, you want me to sit by and keep quiet!" I rebutted.

"Well, your Dad hit's you," she snapped back.

"Well, hitting isn't illegal, but burning is, and he has never done anything like this. You have to see this is far worse than what I have to deal with," I insisted, not wanting to lose this fight, knowing the cost was too high.

"Well, I wish I didn't show you!" Onacona blustered.

"Well, good thing I'm not a genie, and you can't wish it away!" I snarled back at her.

"Well, I'm going to get something on you then, and you will have to keep your mouth shut!" Onacona grabbed my diary and started to read it.

"Go ahead and try. I have nothing to hide!" I crossed my arms over my chest and stared out my window. "Oh boy, she looks determined, and I can't let her win. I hope I don't have anything in my journal she can use against me. I don't, right? Nothing equal to this at least," I thought to myself. I started glancing over her shoulder to see what she was reading. She was concentrated on the conversation I had with my great grandma earlier, and I felt my face blush. "Uh-oh, if she gives this to anyone, I will be sent to a funny farm with my Great-grandma in tow. We will be put in straight coats and forced to live on a Jell-O diet! This was a bad idea," My head was dizzy with thoughts. I started squirming, and she glared at me out of the corners of her eyes, and I froze, pretending to be uninterested. "I could say everything I wrote was made up or run away forever, but it's really cold outside. Dang, it," my head spun away with me again, but I had to keep my resolve. Onacona dropped the diary and began to cry. "Oh no, now she's going start pleading again. We are going to be at this all day." I swallowed but kept my mouth shut.

Onacona spoke. "I'm originally from southern California; my Dad moved us here a few years after I was born and after my Mom died. We lived with our tribe down there. We moved here because he said it was too painful to stay there." She gasped for air and continued. "I never told you what tribe I'm from because, well, you never asked, and saying I have a tribe makes me stick out more than I already do." She paused again and wiped her eyes, I steadied myself for a blow, but I was also confused about how any of this could be used against me. "My tribe is the Muyaay Tribe, and your GG talked to my Mom." She burst into sobs, and my heart broke even more for her. I couldn't move or come up with anything to say. I was too stunned.

Onacona swallowed a wiped her eyes, and, in a squeaky voice, asked me, "What is a; "My GG"?" Then sniffled again. I barked out a laugh, on accident, and straightened myself up.

Then answered, "My GG is my Great Grandma the medium. I use "GG" only as her nickname with my family." I began to wonder if my GG knew this would happen today and when it would because if I didn't call her when I had, I wouldn't have had time to write it before Onacona came over. I was certainly not going to bring this up, though. "So, what do you want to do?" I asked, really hoping for a different outcome but not expecting it. We sat in silence. I started contemplating ways to tell her Dad and was sure she was doing the same. I waited for her to talk first, not wanting to force anything else. I knew I was stressing her out enough already.

"I guess I should tell him if my Mom suggested it, it has to be OK. I don't know how; my Stepmom is always around and never lets us have time alone, and I can't do it in front of her," Onacona puzzled with fear in her tone.

"I have an idea about that," I divulged, and I whispered it to her as if her Stepmom was listening. Luckily and to my relief, she agreed. With her permission, we started enacting it.

Chapter Six, The First Phase

Trigger warnings, topics in this chapter highlights issues regarding the racism and violence of the era.

I walked to the room next to mine, Noora's room. "Noora, can you please watch the boys. I did something really awful, and I need to confess to Mom and Dad. I don't want the boys to have to see this," I lied while attempting to look as guilty as possible. It was the only way I could think of to get her to take the boys and not ask questions.

Noora rolled her eyes and grunted. "I swear, you are so stupid. Can't you just behave?! Fine, BOYS! Come to my room!" She roared, and she went to the family room and collected waddles from my Mom. My Mom was instantly suspicious of me when Noora scooped up waddles, walked away, and began eyeballing me.

My Dad lifted an eyebrow as I stood in the doorway of

the family room, looking guilty. I waited silently until I heard Noora shut her door, and I had my parent's full attention. "Um, Mom, Dad, I have something I need to talk to you about. Can we go to the living room? It's just that I would like to have some privacy?" I asked and instantly ran to the living room before they could protest. I could hear my Dad stomping towards me and my Mom walking softer behind him. As my parents entered the living room from the opposite door, I positioned myself near the front door. Onacona was sitting on one of the two fancy couches with her back to them. "Please take a seat," I extended, motioning to the empty couch.

"Jamie, what is going on?" My Dad questioned sternly as he made his way to the couch.

"Hold that thought. I'll be right back." I stated and turned and ran out the front door and two houses down to Onacona's house. When I reached Onacona's home, I pounded urgently on the front door. Her Dad answered it with her Stepmom right behind him. "Hi Dawn, My Dad was trying to replace a hose on the toilet because it burst during the storm and has now melted and sprung a leak. Unfortunately, he's not very handy, and water is going everywhere. It's a huge mess, the floor stinks, and he broke his wrench and asked me to run over here and get a wrench from you, and maybe for our sake, if you could, come to help him?" I pled, and halfway through "Big mess," Onacona's Stepmom had lost interest and walked towards the TV. Just like I wanted. Dawn, being the good man he is, ran, grabbed his coat and tools from a closet, and we set off to my house.

I opened the front door, and everyone in the Living room was staring at us with blank expressions. My Mom and Dad, and Dawn looked dumbfounded. "Um, hi everyone." Is all I said. "Oh no, I didn't plan past this point." I thought to myself.

"What's going on here?" Dawn pried with a look of confusion and set his tools down next to the door.

"Well, Jamie, explain yourself, and tell us what all this drama is about." My Dad chimed in with less irritation in his voice than I expected.

"Um, Dawn, I lied to you about the toilet, but I needed to get you here, alone," I explained.

"Why, what?" Dawn started to look worried.

"Please sit down." I motioned towards Onacona. She looked like she was about to faint and was avoiding eye contact with everyone. Dawn cautiously moved towards his daughter. I assumed he was expecting some sort of prank. He sat down gently next to her, and I sat next to him.

"OK, can we get on with it already?" My Dad urged sternly. Onacona reached out her arms, her hands shaking, and slowly started to roll up her sleeves and exposed the truth. Shock and horror washed over all the parents. Dawn flew to the ground, pounded his fists into the floor, and began weeping. Onacona and I jumped back, startled by his reaction. I looked at my Dad, and he had a pale greenish look on his face, and his head bobbed. I worried that he was going to be sick. My Mom jumped up and ran past me to the kitchen, and I could hear her rifling through cupboards.

Dawn had his hands in his hair and groaned violently aloud, "WHY! How could this happen? Why!"

My Dad put his hand on Dawn's shoulder. "Come on, Dawn, She showed us her story. Now we need to hear it too. Do you mind if I ask some questions? I'm a lawyer, and I will help you with this in any way I can." My Dad softly reassured him and offered his other hand to help him up. Dawn stayed still for another second, then slowly nodded, took my Dad's hand, and stood up. My Mom came running back into the room with her medical bag in hand, sat on the floor in front of Onacona, and started examining her arms. I could tell she had cried but was trying not to show it now. That was the nurse in her and why I wanted her here for this.

I curled up in my spot on the couch. "Onacona, can you tell us who did this to you?" My Dad asked as gently as a giant can. He already knew but needed to hear it so everyone present could be a witness, and that was the lawyer in him, and that is why I needed him here for this. "My," Onacona choked out a cough. "My Stepmom did," she finished.

"How long has your Stepmom been burning you?" He asked in his professional voice to try and mask his sorrow.

"Since about a month after her and my Dad got married." She said, looking down, and I wanted to hug her, but everyone was in the way. Dawn's hands began to shake, and his face was a burning red, and I wondered if that is how I looked when I was ready to kill Sheryl.

I put my hand on his, and I whispered ever so quietly, "She needs you." and his face softened a tiny bit, and he blinked in acknowledgment.

My Dad cleared his throat, I could tell he was nervous now, but he asked his question despite it. "Why didn't you tell your Dad the first time it happened?" Onacona started to cry, and her. Dad put his hand on her back to avoid touching her arms. My Mom was busy cleaning the fresh wounds and putting gobs of different ointments on the blisters and infected open sores. Onacona looked up at her Dad, and Dawn gave her a nod to continue.

Onacona started to talk, this time through gritted teeth, and her eyes hollowed. "She said that Dad would call the police, and she would say that he did it. That Dad and I were lying. That the police would believe her since she is white. Then Dad would go to prison, and I would go to an orphanage where I would get killed because nobody would want a filthy little brown girl. I believe her," Onacona finished. I looked around the room, and everyone looked like they were about to erupt. I braced.

"That filthy mutt," my Mom spat, and everyone looked surprised as if they had forgotten she was there.

My Dad cleared his throat again and spoke, "thank you, Onacona. You are very brave, and I promise you, Sheryl is the only person going anywhere. Dawn, Tracy, can you two come with me? Girls, we will only be gone for a few minutes, don't go anywhere." The three adults went to my parent's bedroom and shut the door.

"I'm going to listen in," I whispered to Onacona, and she nodded, "me too." We began creeping down the hall, I knew every board to avoid as we made our way, and Onacona stepped where I stepped. I gently put my ear to the door, and so did she.

"Dawn, this is going to be a hard pill to swallow, but Onacona is right. The police are more likely to take Sheryl's word as truth, and if Sheryl is capable of doing that to a little girl. She will likely tell every lie in the book to save herself and place the blame on you. I've witnessed it a million times before. We need to make a plan." My Dad advised.

"Are you suggesting we kill her?" Dawn questioned approvingly.

"No, we can't. That would be too obvious, Onacona needs skin grafts, or she will lose the use of her arms. Her injuries are more severe than any I've ever seen from cigarette burns, and I worked in the ER for years. There are wounds on wounds, some are infected, and the doctors will file a report. If Sheryl is conveniently missing, well, it won't take the police long to figure out what happened." My Mom was interrupted before she could say any more.

"I wasn't suggesting murder!" My Dad sounded both

shocked and disturbed that My Mom and Dawn were both contemplating it.

"I have an idea for working around the prejudice when it comes to the police. It's awkward, but to start, Dawn, we need to make you look influential and, for lack of better terms, wealthy." My Dad said, sounding disgusted at his own words, and the other two gasped.

"Come again, Shawn. I think I misunderstood you!" Dawn said aggressively, and my Dad quickly responded sternly. "Listen, I'm not trying to be insensitive, but if we are going to make this work so Onacona can have a father, we have to get messy and uncomfortable. American history has proven time and again that anything less than white is completely dismissed, especially in when it comes to legal proceedings." He took a breath and cooled his tone. "Let me tell you a story, so you know why I'm suggesting this. My granddad came to the USA during WWII to fight against the Nazis since Norway wasn't in the fight yet, and my Grandpa knew the land like the back of his hand from his travels and wanted to help. The Military was more than happy to have him fight for them. However, they never listened to his years of advice and knowledge of the terrain, not even when it mattered most, and it was to their own detriment. My

Grandpa had to watch countless lives get lost due to their willful ignorance. When the war was over, he was treated like a pariah for being foreign, even though he had served and was awarded medals of honor and had saved lives where he could. Not a person here treated him with respect. He got fed up, he moved back to Norway.

My Dad moved here when he was twenty to fight in the Korean war, and he is whiter than most, but he was treated the same during his service. After the war, no one would consider him for a job, not even sweeping sidewalks. He only stayed in America because he met my Mom and had me. Otherwise, or he would've left too. He only got a job once he learned to fake an American accent. He didn't want to, but he did it for my Mom and me so he could support us. Now if two, white war heroes faced that amount of discrimination over an accent. I can only imagine how you would be treated under the current circumstances that your wife has planned for you. It is the sick reality of this country, and I'd love to fight it, but those types of changes won't be made in the next few days. So, if we want a fighting chance, we must try and work around it.

We have a step up, knowing Sheryl is already planning to take advantage of their discrimination, so let's turn the tables on her give her a taste of her own medicine. Let's expose her for the white trash hillbilly she is. I'm not asking you to do it for me. I would rather not be having this conversation. I'm also not asking you to do it for you. I'm asking you to do it for Onacona." My Dad finished. They all were quiet. I looked at Onacona, and there was fear written across her face.

"OK, Shawn, I'll do what is needed for my daughter, but you should've led with the part about exposing Sheryl as a white trash hillbilly. It would've made the pill easier to swallow. What are we going to do?" Dawn asked my Dad.

"Where do you work, and what is your role?" My Dad asked.

"The Birds of Prey Rescue for Wildlife in Flight Center, and I rehabilitate and train birds," Dawn answered.

"OK, So we will call you a Veterinarian Specialist for Endangered Avian Wildlife. Do you own a suit?" My Dad asked.

"I like that title better than the one I have now. I do own a suit, but if I wear it, Sheryl will notice. I can go buy one and hide it in my car," Dawn answered.

"No, we don't want to accidentally raise any suspicion, and a large sum of money missing will do that. Tracey, get my best suit. Try on one of mine, Dawn." My Dad suggested, and I could hear hangers moving around.

"There's no way he's going to fit into any of my Dad's suits," I thought to myself. My Dad had a good foot on him. "Tracy, can you make this fit him?" My Dad asked.

"Let me get my pins. I'll have to cut and sow it, but it's doable." She determined.

"That's fine." My Dad acknowledged, "Now we are going to need the girls to help." My Dad was interrupted by My Mom before he could continue.

"Absolutely not, Shawn! Don't you dare put those two in danger! You have a big brain in that head of yours. You make another plan. One that leaves them out of this. They have done enough!" My Mom scolded.

I burst through the door with Onacona. "I want to help!" We both yelled. Before she could talk him out of it, and they all turned to look at us.

Then Noora walked in after us and spoke, "I want to help too." We all looked at her dumbfounded "What? I can hear everything that happens in this house through the vent. It works better than a phone." Noora conveyed while she successfully looking uninterested and focused on her nails. Then continued, "Now, let's sink this hillbilly. Well, stop staring and get talking. I don't know how much longer the boys will be asleep." She rolled her hands, motioning for us to hurry up.

"Noora, don't be so rude!" My Mom snapped.

"You called her a mutt." Noora retorted, and my Mom rolled her eye. My Dad laid out the plan. Then Dawn headed home to tell Sheryl that they fixed the pipe and that he gave Onacona permission to stay the next two nights since the school was out and wanted to give his loving wife a break.

Chapter Seven, The Reckoning

<u>Trigger warnings, topics in this chapter highlights issues regarding the racism and violence of the era.</u>

Today was game day. The tension in my house was so high you couldn't chop through it with an Axe, and it felt heavy. Onacona sat at the dining table wringing her hands; Noora, unable to conceal her worry, was sitting next to her. My Dad had left for work early and said he had some business to take care of before everything went down. Dawn left for work about an hour earlier. "It's time." My Mom said calmly with uncertainty in her pitch as she looked out the kitchen window, lost in thought. She turned and started walking down the hall. "Boys, Nap-time." She called out and stopped to picked up Waddles from his baby swing. He was already nodding off, then headed to my room to put him in bed.

"But Mom, I'm too old for a nap," Evan protested while following behind her. "Not this week, you're not. Let's discuss it again next week. Now off to bed and take your brother with you," my Mom insisted in her "I mean business tone." I swallowed my fear and replaced it with rage because it was what I needed to fulfill my task. I focused on the years of pain that Onacona had suffered. The pain she will have to face to correct the damage done, I thought about the consequences if it didn't work, or we backed down, and I readied myself. I swallowed, and my belly started to burn with fire. A fire needed to bring this evil down. I looked to Onacona and said, "let's be done with this once and for all."

Onacona walked to me, grabbed my hand, and spoke, "I'm ready." I saw the hollowness enter her eyes, and I thought to myself, "good."

Noora stood up and dialed the police. She then held the phone face up so everyone could listen. "This is the police. What's your emergence?"

"Hi, I can hear my sister screaming for help from our neighbor's house! My Mom is trying to get in to help her, but the door is locked; I think my sister's friend's Mom has gone crazy! I think she is hurting them! Please Help!" My sister said with a perfected tone of panic.

"Ma'am, can you give me the address to where they are located?" The emergency operator asked.

"Yes, it's 0000 Dusty Meadows drive. Please hurry!" My sister pleaded.

"What is the name of the person you suspect to be harming your sister and her friend? The Operator asked. That was our cue, and Onacona and I headed for the front door and to her house.

In the distance, I could hear Noora say, "Sheryl Matuwir."

We entered Onacona's house, where Sheryl's presence haunted its very fabric. Everything smelt like her, and it felt ill. I shut the front door and locked it behind us, and we went up the stairs to the kitchen, and I unlocked the balcony door that had stairs leading to the lawn below. Then Onacona and I entered her room. There were cigarettes randomly placed throughout it. Putting them there was supposed to be one of our tasks, but since we didn't return after the first near failure, the task had fallen to Dawn. My Dad had warned us not to lift them without a cloth to keep our fingerprints and DNA off of them in his original plan. I picked up a shirt off the floor, lifted one of the cigarettes, and pulled a lighter out of my pocket.

"What are you doing?" Onacona asked with her eyes wide.

"I'm sealing the deal," I said disengaged.

"You can't! It's not in the plan," Onacona tried to plea with me, but it was too late.

I lit it and drove it into my arm. "SHARYL, YOU'RE AN UGLY, STUPID RATBAG!" I screamed as it burned my flesh. Onacona looked terrified.

"Hide," I told her, and she turned to run, then steadied herself.

"No," She replied, resolve in her tone. She instead walked to me and locked her hand in mine, and we listened to Sheryl storm up the stairs.

The door flew open with Sheryl in a rage. "You stupid, little, rotten fools, who do you think you are?" Sheryl snarled at us.

"Screw you," Onacona said, and Sheryl lifted her arm to slap her, and I spun around and back kicked Sheryl in the shin.

"YOU LITTLE BRAT!" Sheryl wailed at me and grabbed me by the hair, her fingernails dragging across my scalp. I screamed melodramatically, and Onacona slipped behind her, shut her bedroom, and locked it. "Sheryl didn't notice. whew," I thought, and I stomped down on Sheryl's foot and elbowed her in the gut to loosen her grip while continuing to scream. "What the heck is wrong with you? You freak!" Sheryl lashed out as she forced me to the floor by my hair and sat on me. I glanced at Onacona, and she was sitting in the corner of the room next to her bed, rolling up her sleeves.

I spat in Sheryl's open fowl mouth, and she slapped me. My ears rang, my cheek burned, and I knew there would be a bruise. "HELP!" I screamed, and Sharyl lifted her arm to beat me again. I took the opportunity, and I slipped my lighter into her underwear. I braced for the blow, and the bedroom door burst open, and three police officers rushed in and grabbed Sheryl and drug her off of me and out the door. She started to scream profanities, and my lighter dropped out of her underwear.

One of the Officers, dragging her, yelled, "Are you hiding anything else in your drawers?" I heard Sheryl hit the ground with a thump. I smiled inside while keeping a look of horror on my face. Knowing my plan worked better than my Dad's would've.

His plan was for us to start screaming. Then, when Sheryl walked in to see what was wrong, one of us would casually lock the door behind her while she was distracted. At the same time, the other would carry on about seeing the spider to keep her occupied. "As if I could ever pretend to be afraid of a spider," I thought. He has said, "having an adult locked in a room with screaming children would automatically make her look guilty when the police arrive. In addition, she would lose credibility with her appearance." Then we were to claim that she was hurting us, and Onacona would show them her arms. "Oh yes, this is far better," I thought to myself. I had been beaten up worse, so it really didn't feel like a big deal to me, but it would be a big deal to the cops.

A fourth officer walked in to assess the scene. "Hi, I'm Office Pirit. You are safe now. I am here to help you. Are you OK to stand up?" She asked, concerned, and knelt down next to me while I cried hysterically. "Can we sit and talk for a moment?" Officer Pirit asked. I nodded while wailing, pretending I was too upset to vocalize anything. I stood up with Officer Pirit's help and sat on Onacona's bed. Officer Pirit sat next to me. "May I have your Names, please?" Officer Pirit asked politely while pulling an audio recorder out of her pocket. "My Name is Jamie Ericksen, and this is Onacona Matuwir, and this is her home." I choked out while forcing myself to shake.

Officer Pirit turned to look at Onacona and immediately lifted her walkie-talkie to her lips. "This is Officer Pirit requesting to know if a bus is enroute to my location? I have two minor females with me. One requires urgent medical assistance, the other has minor injuries, Over." Officer Pirit let up on the button.

"This is dispatch. I can confirm a bus is enroute, approximately ten minutes from your location. Over." Officer Pirit took a deep breath and asked us, "can one of you please tell me what happened here?" Onacona lifted herself from the floor to the bed and sat next to me.

"I've been staying at Jamie's house the past two days because my Dad wanted to let my Stepmom have time alone. Well, I ran out of clothes, so Jamie and I came here to get some, and My Stepmom got really mad that we came here and said we weren't supposed to be here. She grabbed me, and" Onacona stifled and started to cry, and I couldn't tell if it was an act.

The officer looked at me. "Well, I couldn't believe what I was seeing, she was going to burn Onacona, and I don't know why but I threw my arm in the way to stop it, and Sheryl burned me instead, and it hurt really badly. So," I paused and looked down, pretending that I felt shame, "I know it was wrong, but I couldn't help it. I called her a ratbag, and she grabbed me by the hair, and I started to scream. She threw me to the floor. I tried to crawl away until Sheryl said she would really hurt Onacona now because of me and that I had to watch and do nothing. Then she demanded that Onacona rolled up her sleeves. Then I saw Onacona's arms and was shocked! I had no idea," I paused. Took a breath and resumed,

"I don't know why but it really scared me. I thought Sheryl might try to kill Onacona. So, not really thinking about it, I donkey kicked Sheryl in the shin to try and stop her, and she pushed me back down and sat on me, then slapped me! I thought she was going to do to me what she did to Onacona. Then you showed up." I finished talking, and fake sobbed into my hands.

Officer Pirit put her hand on my shoulder, and I was startled at the touch and flinched. "It's OK, you are safe now. You were very brave protecting your friend," Officer Pirit reassured me softly. Then turned her attention to Onacona.

"Onacona, I have some questions to ask you regarding your injuries. Would you prefer that Jamie leave before we continue?" Officer Pirit analyzed.

"No, please don't make Jamie leave," Onacona said,

fear in her tone, and she tightened her grip on my hand. "OK, Jamie can stay if that is OK with you, Jamie?" Officer Pirit asked.

"Yes." I nodded.

"Then we will proceed. Onacona, can you give me the full name of the person or persons who did this to your arms, and how?" Officer Pirit asked.

"My Stepmom Sheryl Matuwir did by burning me with her cigarettes," Onacona answered.

"Can you please call your Stepmom by her first name for the rest of the questioning? Will you tell me the length of time this has been going on, Your father's full name, and why your Dad didn't stop it?" Officer Pirit asked.

"Sheryl has been burning me almost every day since a month after she married my Dad in 1988. My Dad is named Dawn Matuwir, and he didn't stop it because I never let him know. I always wear long-sleeved shirts," Onacona continued answering a series of questions and made sure to be thorough, giving a word-for-word account of the four years of abuse she had suffered at the hands of Sheryl and the way Sheryl had intimidated her into silence.

The officer looked sad for a moment then put her professional face back on. "Can you confirm one more time for me that your Dad has no knowledge of you being harmed by Sheryl?" Officer Pirit inquired.

"I Onacona Matuwir now confirm that my Dad Dawn Matuwir has no knowledge of Sheryl Matuwir burning me for the last four years and a half years. Is that good?" Onacona asked with fury in her tone.

"Yes, that was perfect. You did really well." Officer Pirit said and turned the recorder off.

There was a knock at the door, and an EMT entered the room. He looked at us and then hurried to Onacona. "Hi, I'm Cody. I am going transport you to the hospital," He informed the room, looking over Onacona's arms and then looked at the officer. "Both girls need to come so we can collect DNA samples from their wounds and take pictures of all their injuries. I also need the fingernail scrapings and clippings from the suspected attacker to be collected and sent to the lab. Is it OK to move them out of here now?" Cody asked the officer.

She lifted her walkie-talkie and spoke, "This is Officer Pirit asking for the all-clear to move the victims? Over."

I heard shuffling around the house, and someone responded. "You are clear to exit. Over."

Then she responded to the EMT, "Yes, you exit first and

proceed to the stairs, then head straight to the front exit without stopping. I need you, girls, to follow close behind him and not stop. You keep your eyes on him, got it," Office Pirit detailed, and we all nodded in understanding. We left the room. I followed her instructions despite my own curiosity telling me to look around.

When we got outside, I could see Dawn's truck and my Dad's car parked out front, but I couldn't see them. Anxiety was coursing through me, but I kept my brave face on. My Dad had explained this whole scenario to Onacona, almost to perfection, thinking it would only be her needing to go to the hospital, but I was plotting even then. I soaked in every word he said. Everything the Officers would ask and even how they would walk us out of the house, shielding us from seeing what was happening. They wouldn't let her touch or hug her Dad to avoid contamination of DNA. He had told her that they would likely allow her to be picked up from the hospital four hours after she got there. It had been comforting to know how this part of it would play out. I then thought of Dawn and worried about how his part of the plan was playing out, but we had done our bit, and now it was a waiting game.

Once we arrived at the hospital, we had a series of

pictures taken of our wounds. The nurses had us change our clothes into open back gowns to take more photos. Onacona and I had a huge laugh at that. It was so funny moving around with our butts hanging out. We started to play tag, and the nurses didn't look pleased. Then when I did a cartwheel, a nurse said, "oh my lord," and demanded we stay still until they were done with all the tests, or they wouldn't give us desert with our dinners. So, when it was my turn for pictures, I pretended to be made of cement, and they tried to nudge me forward, but I couldn't move. I was cement. It was hilarious until a giant nurse came in and gave me "that look," the one that meant you do what I say, or you'll die. So, I strengthened up real fast and struck my best supermodel pose for the photographer. Onacona burst out laughing, and so did a couple of the nurses. Then the big nurse came over and sat me down. I obeyed after that. After she walked us to our room, and I plopped on a bed, and Onacona took the other, and we laughed about the events that just took place.

After a minute or two, a forensic nurse entered our room to take samples, drug a cotton swab through Sheryl's fingernail gashes in my head, shoved a q-tip into my burn, cut a chunk of my hair from my head, and put everything into little baggies that had my name on them and big red stickers that said evidence. Onacona had to get x-rays and a cat scan. That took hours, and she told me the cat scan was loud and scary, though I don't know how anything with the word "cat" in it could be. All this was quite the ordeal. After a few more jabs and pokes, A nurse bandaged Onacona's arms carefully. Then came over to me and put a band-aid on my burn, some iodine on my head, and it stung. Then gave me an ice pack for my face. I felt a little embarrassed that I was at the hospital, and all I needed was a band-aid and an icepack, however at the same time, I was glad it wasn't worse. We sat reeling from the day's events for what felt like forever. At one point, we got into an ice tossing battle, and a nurse ran in, scolded us, and took the ice cubes away. We climbed back into our beds and sat silently. The events of the past few days started to take their toll. I looked at Onacona, and she was asleep, so I closed my eyes.

The next thing I knew, my Mom was taping me gently. I looked at her confused a quickly looked around the room. I saw Dawn standing by Onacona, still dressed in his nice suit, and everything came rushing back, and I remembered where I was. "Hi, Mom," I said.

"I hear you gave the nurses a run for their money today," My Mom eyeballed me.

"Nothing you couldn't handle, Mom. Maybe you should work here and teach them a thing or two," I winked at her.

"Very funny." She leaned forward to kiss my neck, then she whispered into my ear, "Jamie, what did you do?" With a pleased tone. Then lifted a finger to shush me. There was a camera in our room behind her, and I blushed. "Come on, get up. It's time to go home," My Mom handed me a change of clothes.

"Thank goodness," I thought to myself. I didn't want to wear this revealing gown home. Noora would have a field day if she saw me walking around with my rear hanging out. I got changed and instantly felt much better.

"OK, Hun, let's get going," my Mom insisted and started to shuffle me out the door.

"Wait, Mom, didn't you and Dawn drive together? Onacona isn't ready yet." I froze in my tracks and felt instant confusion and fear.

"No, Onacona has to stay to see a specialist about her arms," my Mom explained sympathetically.

"What?! No, she has to come home, or I have to stay. I'm not leaving her. What is a specialist?! Is she going to be, OK? You were just going to take me and leave her alone?!" I was unhinged, horrified, and feeling betrayed.

"Jamie, no one is leaving her alone. Dawn will be with her, and she is going to be fine." My Mom promised, trying to reassure me.

"No, that's not good enough. What is a specialist?!" I demanded. My Mom started to explain again, but Dawn put his hand on her shoulder.

"Tracey, may I?" He asked, and she motioned to go ahead. I folded my arms across my chest and turned away from them. "I'd be damned if I was going to abandon her now." I thought to myself.

Dawn knelt next to me and whispered. "Thank you, Jamie, if you didn't befriend Onacona." He coughed, and I sneaked a peek out of the corner of my eye and saw he was fighting back tears, and I softened. He continued, "If it wasn't for you, Sheryl would still be harming her, and I would be in the dark about it or worse. If I found out what Sharyl did and called the police and Sheryl had her way, and I was arrested. Then Onacona would've been left to Sheryl's wickedness. My daughter was brave enough to go to you for help, and you helped. Not only that, but you managed to rally your whole family to help. I promise you, I will protect Onacona from here and won't let anything else happen to her." Dawn said sincerely.

I looked at my Mom, and she had her hands over her heart and looked in awe of his words. I rolled my eyes and said, "No! I'm not leaving!" I stiffened up again. I turned my head just in time to get hit right in the face with a plastic cup.

Onacona yelling at me from her bed, "Get out of here, Jamie or I will march myself over there, and your other cheek will need an ice pack!"

I looked at her, pointing to the door. "oh boy, she not kidding around," I thought. "Fine, Mom, we better go," I agreed and grabbed my shoes.

"I'll call you tomorrow at 3:00 pm," Onacona yelled as I power walked out the door.

"OK!" I acknowledged back, already halfway down the hall with my Mom following behind me.

Once I got home, my Dad scolded me for not following his plan, and I got a spanking, only four lashings with the belt since my heart was in the right place. I felt lucky it wasn't more. Then I was ordered to my room. After sitting for a bit, I could hear my Dad talking to my Mom in their room, so I put my ear to the vent like Noora had suggested.

"I know she did a good thing, Tracey, but I had to spank her. She can't think it's OK to ignore me like that. She could've ended up getting into serious trouble. She should've listened to me." My Dad insisted.

"She's a little girl Shawn, and she showed tremendous courage. That behavior should be rewarded, not punished. She made this a closed case and kept Onacona from further torture," my Mom retorted.

"I know that's why I went easy on her," My Dad defended. Then resumed, "Look, I'll go talk to her, and tomorrow I'll go take her to get one of those silly witchy objects I know she loves," he compromised.

"Good, then you can't get mad at her when she plays with it," my Mom demanded angrily.

"I know, but I blame your family for this silly obsession," my Dad responded, and I heard his door open. I scurried back to my bed before he caught me eavesdropping.

There was a knock at my door. "Come in," I called out, and my Dad walked in.

"Jamie, Can I for a moment there's something we need to discuss?" My Dad asked.

"Sure," I agreed and moved my legs to make room. He took up nearly half of my bed when he sat down, and it creaked under him.

"So, I wanted to tell you how it went today. After the police arrived, while you were upstairs. Your Mom tipped them off to the back door, "possibly" being unlocked so they could sneak in and do a surprise attack. They charged Sheryl with intent to do harm and kidnapping for locking you two in. Like I wanted. I was surprised that they had to pull Sheryl off of you, though, but we already talked about that. The police called Dawn and me at work to tell us what was happening, and they didn't catch on that we knew. Dawn Kept his cool, so Sheryl couldn't pretend she was afraid of him. However, she tried to say Dawn made her punish Onacona that way, but the police looked at him and then told her to save it for court. They let her grab clothes for court; when she gathered them from the floor, they had stunk to high heaven from the cigarette water. Ha, we can thank Noora for that part. One of the officers gaged at the putrid stench. I overheard another say they wondered how someone that filthy ever landed a respectable man like Dawn. I'm sure the judge will think the same thing. Speaking of Dawn, did you know he has a pet hawk?" My Dad concluded.

I was pink with joy. "Yes, I know they have a hawk. I can't wait to hold it some time," I grinned at the thought." Then I asked, "what else is she being charged with?" Knowing full well there would be more than just the two.

My Dad started to list the charges. "Sixty-four accounts of assault against a minor, which is worse than regular assault. They counted as many burns as they could and charged her accordingly. Sixty-four charges of aggravated assault against a minor for using a weapon, in this case, a cigarette, and two counts of child abuse. The judge will throw the book at her with all the evidence and being caught in the act. She's likely to get 15 years in prison," he smiled.

"Awesome!" I reveled.

" Jamie, I know I'm hard on you, but I was mortified when I arrived, and I heard that Sheryl attacked you. I said Dawn kept his cool, well I didn't, and about six officers had to keep me from attacking Sheryl. You can't do that to your poor old Dad. Anyhow for being brave, even though it was against your better judgment. I thought maybe you and I could go out tomorrow and do some shopping and go to lunch or something. Does that sound good to you?" My Dad finished.

"That sounds great, thanks, Dad," I smiled, and he patted my head and left the room.

I shifted in my bed, collected a piece of paper and a pen from my nightstand, and started writing a letter to GG to tell her that her little warning, "some battles will be sooner than you think." Was not much of a warning. When I was done, I figured I would write in my journal as well. I licked the tip of my pen to get the ink going, and there was another knock.

"Come in," I called, and my Mom entered with a plate of food.

"I thought you might be hungry," She offered kindly and made her way to me.

"I am, thank you," I responded and took the food and started to stuff my face.

"Jamie, I wanted to tell you that I'm proud of you, and I'm sorry your Dad spanked you. I didn't agree with that. I wish he would learn another way to discipline you and your sister, but he is stuck in his ways. However, he is a good provider, and we owe him a lot, so I guess we have to deal with it. On a similar note, you haven't told me what you did to get Sheryl to attack you, so?" She posed the question and raised an eyebrow in anticipation.

I swallowed my food and said, "Well, I actually burned myself." I braced, unsure how she would take that.

"You did not," my Mom interrupted me, her face bewildered.

"Yup, and then I screamed, Sharyl is a stupid ugly ratbag, and she came storming up the stairs. Then I elbowed her, and she pulled my hair, then I back kicked her in the shin, oh and I spit in her mouth, and she slapped me." I said nonchalantly.

My Mom's eyes were wide, and her hands covering her mouth. "Well, that defiantly explains why she attacked you!" Mom looked baffled, then laughed. "Well, good, she deserved every bit of that and what she has yet to come. Let me know when you're ready to sleep, and I'll bring Waddles in for the night. Tell GG hi for me in your letter. I bet that old bat knew every single thing that happened before it did. She always said people don't really want to know what's coming because it takes the experience of it away. Well, in this situation, I would've liked to know," my Mom gasped and stood up, kissed me on my head, and left the room. I started to write again while I chewed, and there was another knock. I jumped in fright this knock didn't come from my door but from my window.

Chapter Eight, Shared Magic

I quickly shifted everything from my lap and moved towards the window. I had the curtains drawn. "Really," I thought to myself. "Tonight, of all nights? What's a girl need to do to get some rest around here?" I mumbled as I reached for the curtain and slowly pulled it to one side. I jumped back at the sight of movement and the sound of another knock. I couldn't make out what it was on the other side of my window due to the reflection my light made against the black of night. I ran to my light switch and turned it off. Then in the darkness, I crept cautiously to my window. I cupped my hands around my eyes, placed my face to the glass, and waited for my sight to adjust. Once the blur started to clear, I saw a face looking right at me. I jumped back and let out a startled scream. Then gazed at the creature before me.

The fear subsided, and a feeling of peace and calm filled

me. I whispered to the window, "Hello, what are you doing here?" The raven tapped again, and I heard my Dad enter my room behind me.

"What's happening?" He asked with an alert tone. I pointed at the window, and he looked. He swallowed. "A raven came to visit you today of all days. After a battle of sorts. If you were my Dad, he would take this as a sign that his Gods took notice of your brave deeds and that they will be praising your name tonight. He would say that you honored them, but that is just superstition," my Dad said and moved closer to me and put a hand on my shoulder.

"He must really be touched by this to be saying these things." I thought.

"This is really neat though, it will make a fine story. Look at it. It's huge and stunning. Have you called your Grandpa yet?" My Dad asked.

"No, not yet" I answered calmly, fixated on the raven.

"Call him tomorrow, after we go out. He will love this. I'll let you have 20 minutes with him since you have two big stories to tell him about now, and he loves stories." My Dad said, and I swear I heard a little spark of excitement in his tone.

"Maybe, just maybe, he does believe. Deep down, and

he just can't or won't dig deep enough to find it." I thought to myself.

"I'm going to go get your Mom. She has to see this." My Dad said and swiftly walked off.

I moved to the window and placed my hand on the glass. The raven tapped the other side of the window. I saw a light flicker in and out. Then the symbol I had seen that night in the abandoned house reflected in the glass and vanished again. "Thank you," I said to raven reverently. I didn't know I could have the light in my physical form. I heard my parents enter the room behind me. My Mom gasped. The bird tapped at my hand again, but nothing flickered. The raven cawed then took flight. I didn't move, hoping it would return and teach me all the secrets of the earth and sky.

My Mom came over to me and whispered in my ear. "Tell GG about that in your letter; this is true magic," She kissed my cheek and turned to leave with my Dad, who for once looked at peace.

"Mom," I breathed before she stepped into the hall.

"Yes," She paused. I ran to my parents and hugged them both.

I looked at them and spoke, "I think I'm going to go to sleep now. I love you both."

They smiled and responded, "I love you too." Then I returned to my bed and cleared it off, and I tucked myself in. I left the curtains open and stared into the night sky in wonder as I drifted off into dreamland.

I was standing on a dock overlooking the sea. The wind surrounded me like a blanket. I opened my arms and let it lift me, I twirled slowly, and everything was as it should be. I landed softly on the beach, and the waves washed in out. Bits of earth washing in and out. I knelt on the sand and looked through the earth and water, and it sang to me, the song of my spirit. I touched it with my light. The light that resides inside me. The sand and the water stilled, and I gazed through it. The ground below it slipped away, and the depths beneath it were endless. The darkness rose and tied itself to my light in a perfect balance. I vanished through the earth and water.

I evolved in perfect light and darkness, and in this place, I knew that light and dark were equal. One not being superior to the other. Then I heard a voice say, "babies grow in the darkness of their mother's wombs, as seeds germinate in the night of the earth, do not fear the darkness. Light gives us our sight and warmth. We thrive in the light. Don't fear the light. "I accepted the message and rose, I lifted through the water and earth, and I awoke.

The sun was peeking through my window. For a moment, I was confused about where I was. I looked around and remembered. "My room, I'm in my room." I looked into Waddle's crib. "It must be really early, waddles is still in bed," I thought to myself. I sat up and peered out the window. Everything was so still and peaceful. I changed and walked to the kitchen. It, too, was quiet. "Everyone must still be asleep." I thought to myself. I poured myself a glass of water and quietly stepped outside. The cold air struck me, and I could see my breath, and I hugged myself. I walked to the edge of the deck and looked down at the ice formed over the ground.

"Look through water and earth! That's what GG had said. To hear, I must first listen!" I ran back inside all the way to my room, grabbed my blanket from my bed, ran outside and curled up on the porch, and starred at the ice, and listened.

I sat until I couldn't feel my toes. Thoughts started to fill my head, "ice has bits of earth, right? I'm listening! Maybe if I look through some glass, it's made of sand, that's earth, I just need to get it wet." I stood up and dumped what was left in my cup on the sliding glass door, it froze, and I tried to gaze through it, nothing. "Oh wait, I see something! Oh, that's Neil." I thought to myself. Neil came running to the window, giggled, and waved. I opened the sliding door and stepped back into the warm house. "Hi Neil, how are you doing, little buddy?" I smiled, and he poked at me then pointed to the kitchen. "Whatcha want? Are you hungry?" I asked, and he shook his head yes. So I went to the counter, pulled out a bowl, and poured him some cereal. Then retreated to my room.

I sat on my bed and finished my letter to GG. I told her about all the events that took place the past couple of days, about the raven last night, and about my dream. I made sure to write extra-large for her and in black ink. The letter ended up being four whole pieces of paper, front and back completely filled. I neatly folded the letter, slipped it into my envelope, licked a stamp, and started towards my bedroom door, and I ran into my Mom.

"Oh, Jamie, you surprised me. Are you alright? You're sure up early, excited to go out with your father today?" My Mom asked, startled. "I'm fine, thank you. I just finished writing my letter to GG. Is Dad awake? I asked eagerly.

"Yes, he just got up. He'll want to read his paper before he's ready to leave, so don't be pushy," my Mom bade.

"OK, I'll wait," I said impatiently. I walked past my Mom and headed for the front door. I slipped on her shoes and made my way to the mailbox. When I was done, I sat at the table next to my Dad, who was trying to read his paper over the sound of my tapping finger.

He set the paper down and looked at me, annoyed "fine, we can go." He grumbled. "Yes!" I cheered enthusiastically and ran to put my shoes on.

On our drive to the store, my Dad stopped for gas, then stopped at his work to show me his office, the bank, a furniture store, a bakery, a car parts store. I couldn't say, "let's get on with it," because he didn't know I knew where we were really heading. I half wondered if he was working up his nerve. Then finally I could see the magic store. We stopped a block away, and I thought to myself "What now." We got out of the car and started walking towards the store.

I started speed walking, and my Dad stopped me. "Hey Jamie, I have to make a call. I'll just be in that cafe," He pointed across the street. "I think they have a payphone. Do you want to go pick something out in the?" He stopped and looked at the sign and turned three shades of red. "The Pondering Pixie? Here's some money. I might be a while, so don't rush." My Dad shoved some money at me, then hurried off.

"I knew it. He was afraid to go in," I thought as I watched him practically run away. I organized the money and counted it. "THIRTY BUCKS WHOA! I'M RICH." I cheered silently and put it in my pocket, then ran to the store.

I opened the door, and the smell of incents filled my nostrils, and I instantly felt at home. The store displayed pictures of various deities throughout it, covering the walls. There were shelves upon shelves of magical items, rocks, books, and a clothing section. It was a sight to behold. I started to look at the various things. Trying to find something that called to me, then a boy my age approached me. "Are you going to the scrying circle too?" He asked anxiously.

"What's a scrying circle?" I asked.

"I don't know, but my Mom said it's fun and only takes a few minutes. I thought it would be neat if there was another kid there," He mentioned plainly.

"My Dad said I can take my time, so sure," I shrugged.

"Neat, I'm Oden. What's your name?" Oden asked.

"I'm Jamie. Oden, huh, so you're named after the Allfather, God of wisdom?" I asked, and he looked surprised.

"You know about the God Odin? Most people think he

is the God of war, but if they read about it, they would know that's Tyr," he explained as if he had to every time, he introduced himself. "Yes, I know all about the God Odin. My Grandpa's from Norway," I noted.

"Neat, oh, we better go to the scrying circle. My Mom is waving at us to come now," Oden turned while looking towards the back of the shop. I followed him towards a woman in a loose-fitting dress with long blond hair who stood next to an open door. She smiled kindly at us and motioned for us to step into a large room. The room was beautifully decorated with a ring of petals on the ground encircling the entirety of the inside of the room. Pillows were placed on the floor around the inner edge of half of the circle. Large candelabras stood in the corners of the room and were lit with different colors of candles. In the center of the ring was a small table with a single candle placed on it and a pillow on the opposite side of the table. A woman with a cloak on motioned for us to sit. Oden and I chose pillows in front next to one another.

After everyone sat, the woman in the black cloak began to speak. "Merry meet, my fairy folk. I'm so glad you could join me today and learn how to scry for past lives. I am Priestess Singing Rock. With formalities aside, I'd like to jump straight into it. I will start by cleansing away any negative energy from you and this sacred space." She pulled a green bundle from her pocket and lit it. I knew from the smell that it was sage. She walked around the room and whisked the smoke over us. I felt my worries melt away and coughed. I felt safe.

"We all come from the great mother. Her water sustains us, and her lands feed us; our bodies return to her when we pass. In this, we are all connected. We are connected to all living creatures, the trees, the rocks. We all share the same DNA. This is why nature gives us peace. We are all brothers and sisters. To lose love for one another is to lose ourselves. Our spirits are timeless and endless. We have lived many lives as our soul's journey to seek wisdom. Today I will share with you how to glimpse into your past. May I have a volunteer?" The Priestess looked around the room, and no one stood up. "This will be done without judgment as we are each on a sacred journey, and you will be safe. The ring will protect us." The Priestess added due to the lack of volunteers. Feeling awkward for her, I raised my hand.

"I will. What do I do?" I volunteered, unsure but willing.

"What's your name, sacred sister." The Priestess asked me.

"Jamie." I stood awkwardly.

"Welcome, Jamie. All you have to do is sit over there in the center of the room and look into the candle's flame." The Priestess answered, motioning towards the small table.

"OK," I nodded and walked to the center of the room and sat facing the rest of the group of about eleven people. The flame of the candle flickered in front of my face, and I looked into the fire.

"Now the rest of you need to stare at her face, and it will begin to change. Allow your mind to accept these changes, and don't break your concentration, for you will lose the shape it takes. After a new form can be glimpsed, speak what you see. After you acknowledge one shape, it will shift onto another past life and continue on that way. Don't be surprised if you see a man or a creature. Our soul doesn't take just take a single form. We are made of energy, and energy changes shape. It doesn't care about gender, It doesn't care about color; it cares about experience and courage, kindness, and knowledge. Now clear your minds and gaze." The Priestess instructed. I felt awkward knowing that everyone was asked to stare at me, but at the same time, I was really curious about what everyone might see. So, I sat still staring into the light.

"I see an ancient being, skin dark as night with stars for eyes," One person announced.

"I see that too," A few others agreed. It went quiet for a moment, and I reflected on what kind of alien I must have been.

Then someone else divulged, "I see an old witch spinning a silver thread." Others agreed, then it fell quiet again. "Now I see a Man weathered and warn like a warrior or a farmer." Someone else reported, and again, everyone agreed, then paused again.

"I see a woman with long golden hair who is dedicated to helping children," another acknowledged, and again others agreed. Then everyone gasped in awe.

"What is it? It's too beautiful to describe," someone expressed.

"That would be a higher being, say, Valkyrie or a goddess, and it looks like our time is up for the day. Thank you, Jamie, for letting us experience your past lives. Next week we will learn to scry with dark mirrors. I hope to see you all then. Love and light," The Priestess closed the circle, stood, and walked to me while everyone else exited. Oden stood by the door and waited for me.

"Jamie, it was a pleasure to meet you. I wanted to let you

know I saw much more than the shapes of your past lives. You are in this world for more than knowledge. You have a great quest, so to speak about to unravel before you. From the purity of your heart, I am guessing you volunteered when you were in the waiting realm. That's where spirits wait to be born. You have a direct link to magic and wisdom. You have to be careful. Lower beings will look to use that power for their own ambitions." Priestess Singing Rock warned.

"Thank you," I smiled politely and started to walk away, then paused. "Ma'am, how do I look through earth and water?" I asked. I figured if anyone knew, she would, and since my GG wouldn't say.

"Precious one, You are earth and water and so much more. Look inside yourself." She smiled at me. I began walking towards Oden when she spoke to me again. "Don't you have something else you need to ask me?"

"Well, if it's not too much to ask, how do I close the Lion's Gate?" I queried, and she walked to me and knelt to my height.

"Are you sure that's the question you need to ask?" She paused, and I shrugged my shoulders and thought.

"I guess I first need to know what The Lion's Gate is," I asked.

"That's better. The Lion's Gate is open every year between the end of July to the middle of August. When the brightest sun of Leo aligns with Sirius, known as the spiral sun. It pours out psychic energy into the universe. Inspiring beings to be courageous, strong, and creative. It opens the third eye. The veils between worlds thins and spirits can pass through and choose where they want to live their next life and travel freely to do so. All planets and universes depend on that magic. If something, say evil energy or beings, were to force it to stay open, then the whole of all universes would be thrown out of balance. All worlds would become vulnerable to intruders. The Lion's Gate's magic would be tainted, and newborns may enter earth with corruption already inside them. Now that is all I can say now. I have an appointment to attend too, but before you leave, take one of my business cards and call me if the need arises. Love and Light." The Priestess walked off, and I stood still thinking about what she had just told me.

"Hey, that was pretty neat, wasn't it?" Oden noted.

"What?" I asked. "The scrying for past lives. My Mom said when we get home, we can try it on each other." Oden smiled happily.

"Oh, ya, that was neat. I think I love this place." I smiled.

"Ya, it's OK, I guess. Hey, do you want to exchange numbers? It's just no one else ever brings their kids here, and well, it was cool talking to you today. Maybe we can hang out again sometime. I'd like to talk more, but my Mom says it's time to go." Oden explained.

"Ya, that would be great." I agreed, and we left the circle and entered the store area again. I wrote my number down for Oden and gave it to him, and he gave me his number, then went.

I started to quickly look around the store. I didn't want my Dad to get impatient, or he would use it as an excuse to never bring me back here. I grabbed a bundle of sage, a bundle of lavender since GG had suggested it. Then I picked up a jeweled pen and headed to a necklace that hung on a rack near me. It was stunning. Its chain was braided leather, with a large orange spiraled fossil, and it was fixed into a clay design with flowers and vines. A card attached to it read: Ammonite, A fossilized prehistoric animal; the shape represents the ram's horn. The spiral helps the wearer to find their way when lost. It helps to protect one from negative energy.

I looked at the price. "Dang, I have to put the pen back to get this. Do I really want it? It's nice, but the pen is beautiful and has glitter and is useful?" I thought to myself while comparing the two objects side by side.

"I'd choose the amulet if I were you." a little voice whispered, and I turned to see who was talking to me, but no one was there. I stood for a second in disbelief.

"Well, I guess I'm getting the necklace," I said aloud.

"That's great. Just bring it over here, and I'll get you rung up," The teller said loudly from across the store. I put the pen up and purchased my three items. I slipped a business card into my pocket and left.

When I got to the cafe, I found my Dad sipping on a coffee while enjoying the newspaper. It dawned on me that I could've been in there all day, and he would've been more than happy to sit in the quiet and enjoy his coffee without interruption.

"Hi, Dad," I greeted and took a seat across from him.

"Oh, Jamie, I didn't see you come in. That was fast; did you find something you like?" He said pleasantly.

"Yes, I found a necklace I like," I answered and pulled it from the bag to show him.

"Now that's pretty, I like fossils too, and here I was worried you would come back with a crystal ball," Dad said jokingly.

"Oh, I didn't think of that. Can I have some more money?" I teased back.

"Well, it's 11:30. Where would you like to go to lunch?" My Dad offered as he looked at his wristwatch.

"Can we get pizza?" I requested.

"Sure, that sounds good." My Dad agreed, and we got up and left.

We had a pleasant time eating. When we got home, I went to my room and wrote about the morning in my journal. Then I called Connie, who would call Shelly, and told her what I had learned about The Lion's Gate. I didn't mention what happened with Onacona. That would be her story to share if she wanted too and I respect that. I still needed to discuss with Onacona what she wanted to do when it came to our investigation. I made a promise, and I always kept my promises. I was still worried sick about her and couldn't wait to hear how she was doing. I looked at my alarm clock, and it read 2:05 pm. I still have a while until she calls me. I better call my Grandpa." I thought to myself and headed to the phone

I settled into a quiet corner and dialed my Grandpa's

number. "Hello, who's calling?" My Grandpa answered.

"Ya buddy, this is Under World Insurance company, and man, do I have a deal for you," I lied in my best adult voice.

If there was anything my Grandpa hated worse than a coward, it was a solicitor. "Let me stop you right there. Who do, "My Grandpa started to speak, then I interrupted him.

"Now, hold on before you get started, buddy. I am going to save you so much money. I'm talking about a deal of a lifetime you are going to want to listen to this!" I paused on purpose.

"I am not your buddy! What makes you think I have to talk to you?" My Grandpa growled.

"Because you looovee me," I said slyly. Then there was Silence.

"Now this has just gotten ridiculous! What kind of person tells a stranger that?" My Grandpa had a mix of amusement and anger in his voice now.

"Barnebarnet dit." I spoke 'your granddaughter' in Norwegian. My Grandpa erupted with laughter, and I started laughing with him.

"Jamie, you really had me going! how are you?" He said gleefully.

"Oh Grandpa, I have a lot to say. How about you go

first. How are you doing?"

"Eisa, I don't have much going on. I won at poker last night. Other than that, I don't have anything else to report," my Grandpa hummed.

Eisa was the nickname he gave me at birth. "Well, it all started when my courageous friend shared," I began. Then continued telling him everything that happened with Onacona and how I got Sheryl to attack me, and how the police caught her in the act, and about the hospital. I told him everything.

"Well, that is quite the story. Ha-ha, ha-ha, you really showed that nasty piece of work, didn't you? You are definitely my blood." My Grandpa roared with pride, and it made my heart smile. "So, how much time do you have left before you have to go?" My Grandpa asked.

"I have 16 minutes left and two more stories to tell you," I detailed.

"Really, you have more? You better loan me 30 seconds to grab a drink. This is the most excitement I've had in a long time. The fellas at the barbershop are going to enjoy this tomorrow morning when we have our coffee." Grandpa informed.

"What kind of barbershop has coffee?" I asked.

"The kind where all men go to hide from their wives," my Grandpas joked. He set the phoned down, and I could hear him cracking an ice tray in the background, then the sound of ice landing in a glass. "Alright, Eisa, I'm settled down now. Tell me your stories." My Grandpa offered.

"Last Tuesday, my friends and I were walking to Onacona's house after school, and a blizzard struck, and it turned into a full-on white out!" I told him the story of the night we spent in the abandoned house.

When I finished, he gasped and spoke. "Eisa, I definitely have some things to discuss with you, but first, you must finish your next story with me. That way, I can form a proper opinion and share my wisdom on the matters." I could hear his accent creeping through, which meant he was caught off guard.

"OK, Grandpa, the evening after we all got Onacona's Stepmom arrested, a Raven came to my window," I began and told him the story of the raven, the dream that followed, and what the Priestess had said.

"Alright, Eisa, I am going to have to be straight with you if I'm going to be able to fit in everything I need to say before we end this call. So just listen and try not to interrupt. First off, everything started of slowly but is picking up pace.

Before you know it, things are going to start happening very fast. That tells me this is not something you can ignore and have go away. You have a lot of wisdom you will need to find. Your experience yesterday may have been more than a lessen but a test. To see if you would face up to the challenge and see how well you performed under stress. To see if you are the right person for the job. The raven coming to your window was an acknowledgment that you are. Ericksen's don't back down from a noble fight. Now, do you know why I call you Eisa?" My Grandpa asked.

"No?" I answered.

"I gave you that nickname because, at birth, you had a mark on your hand in the shape of a rune. Baldur's rune, Sowilo. This rune has been long associated with our family. It is said that my father's, father's mother, all the way back through our line to the first mother. Whom was a walkurjas or better known as a forest maiden. Still, she wasn't just any forest maiden but a Wotan, a powerful witch, and she took some of the seed from Balder and put it in her blood. There it would remain hidden until another powerful Wotan Witch was born, and this child would have a direct link to the Gods. If this is the case, the Priestess you speak of was right to acknowledge goddess attributes in you, but you are not a goddess. At least not yet.

Who's to say at the end of your life if your deeds are found to be deserving enough for such a title? Now what I'm getting at your nickname, Eisa means ember of light. You carry the seed of light. A powerful weapon and powerful magic. Who thought my Son would be the one to sire a Wotan Witch?" My Grandpa said and was silent.

"Well, Grandpa, that was all very interesting but gross," I teased, awkwardly, and he laughed.

"Well, my Eisa, I better go. I just had a knock at my door. You take care of yourself and be smart." My Grandpa said affectionately.

"I will try. I love you too. Bye, Grandpa." I hung up and sighed.

"A Wotan Witch. I wonder what this all means for me. What does it mean for Onacona, who too can hear and sense the other side? What does it mean for Connie and Shelly? It seems like the more I talk to people about it, the more confusing it gets. Yes, I have a lot of good information from everyone, and I know what the Lion's Gate is. However, I still don't know how on earth I am supposed to close it. How I am supposed to use my light. I feel like this is a task for an adult. How am I supposed to take all this on?" I debated, feeling heavy again despite all that was already achieved. I put the phone on the receiver and decided to go to the family room and play blocks with Neil before Onacona rang. Just to take my mind off all these tasks and what was to come.

Three O clock came and went without my anticipated phone call. I began pacing up and down the dining room. "I should've stayed. I should've fought her on this. What am I to do?" I panicked. I ran to the front door and down the street to Onacona's house and began pounding on her door, then I rang the doorbell repeatedly. "Dang it." I cursed with thoughts of her disappearing into foster care, filling me with dread. I raced back to my house. "I will demand my parents take me back to the hospital right this instance!" I started practicing my serious tone.

I burst into the house and marched into the kitchen and found my Mom on the phone. "Mom, I need to ask you something, no, I need to tell you something!" I demanded.

"Shush, Jamie, can't you see I'm on the phone?" My Mom snapped.

"Mom, Mom. Mom, Mom, Mom." I repeated.

"Can you hold one for one moment, please? My daughter is obnoxious. OK, thank you, Dawn. Jamie, what is so important you feel the need to interrupt me?!" My Mom scowled.

"That's Dawn? I need to talk to Onacona now!" I insisted.

"You're going to have to wait. Now sort yourself out, or you won't be talking to anyone! Sorry about that, Dawn. What method was used? Did they use autograft, heterologous graft, or xenograft? Aha, aha." She kept going.

"This is a nightmare. What the heck is an xtreoaro whatever?" I thought to myself. My Mom kept going,

"OK, and is she on adequate pain meds? If not, I can make a call to the hospital, and I know exactly whom I could complain to." My Mom was still rambling on.

"For the love! Shut up already." I wanted to blurt out but kept my mouth shut and started tapping my foot instead.

"Yea, OK, Ya, that will be fine. Jamie can do that no problem." My Mom drawled.

"Jamie can do what?" I asked. I actually wanted to know, instead of giving me an answer, she shooed me with her hand. I was about to lose my mind when my Mom looked at me.

"OK, Dawn, I have Jamie here. Before I hand you the phone, Jamie, I need you to know Onacona is heavily medicated, so she might sound strange. I told Dawn, you can feed their hawk for them tonight. He'll let you know how." My Mom finally finished and handed me the phone.

"Hi Dawn, I get to feed your hawk?" I said awkwardly.

"If you would please, I'd like to stay here with Onacona tonight. I have skinned rabbits in the freezer under the back porch. Next to the freezer, you will see a table with a large cleaver. I'll need you to chop one of the legs off." I interrupted Dawn.

"Ewe gross, I have to chop off a bunny's leg?" I shuttered. I looked at my Mom to protest.

Even she looked grossed out, then she whispered. "Just do it. You'll be fine."

"Alright, what do I with the leg?" I asked Dawn.

"I need you to cube the leg so Talon can swallow it easily. Then when you get to the shed, knock three times, and you'll hear Talon fly to the back of the shed. Enter foot first, so Talon doesn't attack you." I cut Dawn off mid-sentence again.

"Attack me! Is Talon like an attack dog but instead of a

dog, an attack hawk?" I worried.

"No, I trained Talon this way to keep her from getting stolen," Dawn explained and paused.

"OK, foot first got it," I remarked. "This is an awesome bird," I thought.

"So, after you get in, shut the door behind you, place the meat on the tray, you'll see it. Make sure she has water in her bowl. Then make sure you shut the door again after you leave. Do you have all that?" Dawn asked politely.

"Yes, I'll be careful," I began to worry.

"OK, thank you so much. I'll hand you over to Onacona now." Dawn concluded.

"Helllllloooo," Onacona rasped in a tired but playful tone.

"Hi Onacona, oh my gosh, I'm so glad to hear from you. How are you?" I sighed, thrilled to finally hear from her.

"You're going to eat bunny leg? That's not going to taste good. I can make you some pie if you're hungry. Yup, I make a good mud pie. Do you want me to feed you?" Onacona offered, sounding woozy.

"Um, No. I'm not going to eat bunny leg or pie. In fact, I'm not hungry at all. Thank you for asking, though." I said, amused.

"You know what?" Onacona asked.

"No, what?" I answered. "I got new arms today yup, they cut off my old arms, and I got new ones. They are man arms," Onacona said, and my stomach dropped!

"Mom! They cut off Onacona's arms! Those monsters! How could this happen! I thought they were going to draw grafts on them!" I yelled in horror. My Mom jolted at my cry and flicked contents out of the pot she was stirring.

"No, Jamie, she's fine. She got new skin, not new arms. I'll explain after you get off the phone. "My Mom snapped and started wiping up the splattered bits of stew from around the stove.

"Ha-ha, you just screamed, you scream a lot, Jamie. Did you know I am the granddaughter of a Chief? That makes me a princess." Onacona said.

"I didn't know that, but that explains why you are so pretty. How do you feel?" I asked.

"I feel great! I think I can fly now. I think my man arms grew wings." Onacona declared, and in the background, I could hear Dawn say, "OK sweetie, I think that's enough talking for one day you need to sleep. Say goodbye and hand me the phone without hanging up."

"My Dad says I need to say goodbye. Don't tell my Dad, but instead of sleeping, I'm going to fly to you when he isn't looking, and I'll show you my man arms." Onacona said, and the phone made a loud crashing sound, and I would bet money that was the sound of the phone hitting the ground. I could hear Dawn telling Onacona to sit that she can't really fly, and I started to laugh at the thought of her in one of those butt gowns flapping her man arms around. After a minute, I could hear the phone being picked up.

"Jamie, don't pay attention to anything Onacona just said. She's on a lot of meds at the moment. I'll have her call you tomorrow evening. Hopefully, she will feel better by then." Dawn announced quickly and hung up.

"Well, that was fun." I thought. Then I asked my Mom. "Mom, now, can you tell me why Onacona has man arms?" She looked at me, confused.

"I don't know what she said, but a skin graft is when they take excess skin from your own body or someone else and replace your ruined skin with it," my Mom said as if it was no big deal.

I felt instantly sick. "They skinned her alive?!" I said in horror.

"It's not like that, Jamie. Her arms were damaged beyond repair. There was no way her skin would heal on its own. It had to be done." My Mom explained.

"This is going to take me some time. I need to think about this," I said.

"OK, honey but think about it while you feed their hawk." My Mom insisted. "Fine," I said. It never turned out to be a pleasant experience when my Mom volunteered me to do things. "One time, she made me help an old lady plant a garden, and she said, "it would be good for me." The old lady was nice and grateful, but I got stung by a bee! A bee! Why do our parents make us do these things?" I grabbed my coat, slipped my Mom's shoes on, and headed towards Onacona's house.

I felt excited to finally meet the hawk. I just didn't expect it to be like this. I had imagined being in a forest with the wind blowing through my hair and a magnificent hawk sitting on my arm. The both of us looking majestic and wild. Having to hack off a rabbit leg was not what I pictured. I climbed the fence into Onacona's backyard and headed to the freezer Dawn had described. I opened it and got an eye full. It looked worse than I imagined. I felt bile coming up my throat and swallowed it. "Come on, Jamie, you can do this," I sneered. I closed the lid then looked around for gloves or tongs, anything to not have to touch one of those monstrosities that lay dead in the freezer. There wasn't a baroque, but they did have an oven made from rocks but still no tongs near it. I heard the bird moving around it the shed then, it made an extremely loud screech. I began to get nervous. My visions of beauty were completely shattered at that sound, and now I was picturing a manticore with lion's claws and a foul beast ready to attack me.

"Um, Hi Talon, I'm getting your food, just a minute," I called through the closed door and ran back to the freezer. I opened the top, closed my eyes, and plunged my hand in, and pulled out a stiff, red veiny looking thing in the shape of a rabbit. I tossed it at the table, not wanting to touch it longer than need. I swallowed as my eyes fell on the cleaver. "Sure, Jamie can do it. Just do it, Jamie. It's not a big deal." I mocked my Mom. "If it's no big deal, she should do it herself." I thought aloud.

I picked up the cleaver and moved the rabbit with it. I positioned the mutilated beast where I needed it to make a clean cut. I raised the knife and thrust it down, and the leg came flying off and smacked me in the face. "Oh yuck! Dang, it all! that's so nasty!" I practically screamed while extensively wiping at my face. I sat in the dirt angrily. "Man, that was so awful," I said to myself, and the bird screeched again. "You owe me for this, you disgusting foul," I yelled at the shed. I got up and tossed the bulk of the bunny back into the freezer and put the leg onto the table to dice it. I cut it slower this time, flinching with every slice forbid another chunk come flying at me again. I scooped the frozen bits into my hand and walked to the shed.

I looked at the door. "How on earth am I supposed to knock?" I thought while looking at my hands full of dead rabbit bits. "Come on," I wined to myself. Then put the meat into my jean pockets. I started gathering myself to knock and face the manticore. I rapped at the door three times and heard the beast move to the back of the shed. "OK good, foot first." I reminded myself, then opened the door slowly and extended my leg into the shed. I stretched it as far in as humanly possible. "You see my foot right, Talon? Please don't attack me!" I said loudly while using the door as a shield for the rest of my body. I wiggled my foot through the gap. Talon didn't make a sound.

"Good." I thought and stood upright and peeked through the crack. I saw Talon sitting at the back of her pin, with her head tilted to the side. "Don't you judge me," I stepped in and closed the door behind me. The floor was covered in straw, and cut trees stood throughout the shed fastened to the walls. Talon perched on one in the back. "You really do look majestic," I walked to a tray and emptied my pockets of the meat atop it. The bowl of water was full, and I was relieved. I started picking bits of lint from the flesh, and the bird screeched and started to fly towards me. I flung myself back and rolled to my feet, and rushed to the door, terrified she was going to attack me. I opened the door and threw my body out of it, and kicked it shut behind me. After a few moments, I carefully cracked it open and peeked back in. Talon was happily eating her raw bunny ice cubes. "Whew, that was scary," my heart pounding. I made sure to lock the door and headed home to change and take a long hot shower with as much soap as we owned.

Chapter Nine, The Fairy Realm

I began mulling over the lack of events since last Sunday as I sat bored in class and thought, "it was nice to have some normality back in my life." My teacher kept going on about the tea party, and I thought to myself, "It must be a mandated ritual for every school in America to talk about the tea party every single year. Ugh, I'm so over it, blah blah they sunk a boat, blah taxes blah. Sure, it was interesting the first couple of years, but now it makes me want to rip my ears off. I may save Onacona the agony and just do this lesson for her if her teacher is lecturing on it too." I sighed. Since I take her homework to her Dad every day anyhow.

The doctors say Onacona can home on Thursday after the threat of infection is gone. Also, to make sure her body doesn't reject the new skin. I find the whole process of skin swapping very interesting. She says her arms look mostly normal now except for bruising and small scars around her wrists and more around her shoulders. She's excited to wear short sleeves in the summer. I can just imagine how good it must feel to not wear long sleeves constantly after such a long time. Connie and Shelly have been curious about Onacona. They know something is up. Onacona still hasn't said anything to them. She may never, and I'm fine with that. I thought about it a lot, and I don't know if I would. She has new arms now, so no one ever has to know. Whatever she decides, I am happy for her.

On another note, I have been trying to think of more ways to connect with my Bluestocking. "I have to look deep inside myself," The Priestess had said. Well, that is harder than it sounds. Every time I try to meditate, I start thinking of random things. Last time it ended up being a sandwich. If it's not thoughts intruding, it's my little brothers. I got up at midnight the other night to try and concentrate alone, and then here comes Evan. He wanted to talk after I got him back to bed and situated myself. Waddles woke up hungry and poopy.

In defeat, I checked a book out from the library written in the 1960s on deep meditation. It had a lot of useful tips. I just had to ignore a lot of text about how "sex frees the mind." My Mom's generation is full of sickos. I may try some of the more useful tips like I need to inhale peppermint, pretend I'm in a room with nothing but a chair, and every time a thought creeps in, I send it out the window. "I can do that." I think I found the perfect place to try it too.

I took Evan on a walk while exiled from home and saw a grove of trees in a pasture with lamas, so we snuck into it. In the little circle of trees, they have a neat little pond. I thought that would be the perfect place to get some quiet. The snow melted Monday, and everything since has been a gross soupy mess. It's getting warmer each day, though. So, I thought, "Friday night, I'll sneak out of my window after everyone is in bed and try it again. I guess it's normal for the weather to teeter-totter here until mid to late November. People say if they make warm Halloween costumes, it will be too hot for them. If they get thin ones, it ends up snowing. So, I guess when it comes time to make my costume, I'll have to figure something out that can be comfortable either way." The bell rang. "Finally, lunchtime." I rushed to my backpack and outside.

"Connie, Shelly," I yelled across the schoolyard as I ran to them.

"Hey Jamie, what's up?" Connie asked.

"Not much. Want to jump rope after we eat?" I suggested, and they nodded as we settled down and opened out lunch boxes.

"So, what did your Mom pack for you? I got a soggy peanut butter and jelly sandwich. I swear if I wasn't starving, I would toss it right out." Shelly moaned while looking gloomily into her lunch pail.

Connie and I looked into our lunch boxes. "Yuck, I got a bologna sandwich," I shuttered.

Connie followed. "I got egg salad." We all held our noses and ate our lunches. We choked down our soggy sandwiches and ran for the jump ropes. After picking the least warn one that was still available, we headed to a free spot on the pavement and began jumping. When we had our fill, we headed to a bench and sat down.

"So, when is Onacona coming back?" Connie asked.

"Maybe Friday?" I said casually.

"I tried to call her last night, and no one answered if she is homesick how come, she isn't home?" Shelly inquired.

"I don't know. I'm not her babysitter." I snapped back. "Oh, sorry about that. I didn't mean to sound rude." I quickly apologized.

"It's fine. I just don't like her Stepmom, so I worry about

her being away so long." Shelly explained, and I began to feel a bit guilty and didn't want to lie, so I just nodded in agreement.

"Well, hopefully, she's back soon. Class isn't the same without her," Connie added.

"So has anything else happened, you know, anything supernatural?" Connie said in a whisper.

"Not since Raven and my dream. Are you two trying to connect with your Bluestockings? I asked.

"Us? I thought it was just you who has one." Connie sounded confused at the idea.

"No, everyone has a Bluestocking or guide, realm walker, teacher, or guardian. In Norse mythology, they called them Fylgja. The Celts called them Nemausicae. Ancient Greeks called them Daimon or Genius, in ancient China Tu Di Gong. Of course, Native Americans have deep knowledge and bonds with Spirit Guides. My Great Grandma says some are likely to be family passed or yet to come. My Grandpa says they are beings that are going through rites of passage to get to where they want to go, and this is just a stop along the way. The hippy book I have says they are cosmic energy. So, if we meet ours, let's make sure to ask them which one they are." I smiled.

"Wow, that was an information overload," Connie said, unimpressed.

"Well, my Great Grandma and Grandpa talk a lot. I'm going to try and meet mine Friday. I'm sneaking out and heading to a pond I found to try and meditate." I said nonchalantly.

"Can we come, My parents never check on me on a Friday that's their fun night?" Shelly asked.

"I don't see why not. If it doesn't work, we can all try alone again Saturday." I agreed.

"Connie, you have to come too," Shelly demanded.

"I don't know. What if something crazy happens again like the other two times we were together at night. Plus, if I get caught, I'll be grounded." Connie hesitated.

"Well, we live two streets away, and I'm not walking to Jamie's house alone in the dark." Shelly paused to think. "I know, come spend the night at my house. In fact, you too, Jamie and Onacona too if she is well enough by then. My parents get super drunk with their friends while playing cards on Fridays, their friends get taxis to get home. It's a whole thing, and they will be none the wiser." Shelly entailed, then looked at Connie. Silence. Shelly smacked Connie's arm and gave her a stern look.

"I guess; if your parents say it's OK then, fine. I will."
Connie finally agreed, and we all giggled.

"OK, so if Shelly's parents say it alright, then we all have
to make sure to bundle up really warm and bring plastic bags
to sit on, it's warmer now, but the nights are still cold,"
Connie deliberated.

"I will wear my new necklace too. It's supposed to have
protective powers," I noted.

"I will wear my bracelet my Mom gave me. It makes me
feel safe like her love is around me when I wear it." Shelly
added.

"Really, jewelry is going to protect us, well I don't have
any. How about we bring a baseball bat and a slingshot."
Connie murmured, not impressed.

"We'll bring those as well, and I have a hunting knife my
Grandpa gave me that I bring. I suggested the jewelry only
because that's what witches wear for protection against bad
ghosts and stuff." I explained.

"Come on, Connie, Oh, I know you can wear the SJ
bracelet we found last week in the abandoned house," Shelly
grinned enthusiastically.

"Are you out of your mind! There is no way I am ever
going to wear a ghost's bracelet, especially when we are

going to be outside in the dark!" Connie rebutted.

"You need to bring something. Oh, I have another idea. You can wear that beaded necklace your little sister gave you for Christmas last year!" Shelly teased, and Connie turned red with embarrassment.

"You know very well those aren't beads, it's macaroni, and I wouldn't be caught dead in that thing," Connie said with disgust.

"Well, then ask your Mom for something. I'm sure she has unwanted jewelry she can give you." Shelly demanded.

"Fine! I'll try." Connie growled through gritted teeth.

The bell rang, and we all stood up. "Shelly, call me at about four-thirty tonight and let me know if we can stay. That way, I can give my parents time to decide since they have to plan around Waddles, and I don't want Noora to make plans first." I scheduled. What I said was truthful, but the real reason was to talk to Onacona after and see if she could come, and she calls at Six.

"OK, no worries," Shelly smiled and trotted off to her class with Connie, and I ran to mine.

The rest of the day went normally. Noora was already on the phone when I walked in, so I eavesdropped on her to make sure she wasn't making plans for the weekend already.

She hangs with the popular kids at school now. I wondered what horrors she had to participate in to make that happen. Whatever it was, it worked since they call her all the time. I've had to reserve my spot for the phone. I listened in again. "Whew, they are just talking about boys. I know nothing of interest will come from that conversation." I thought to myself.

I went to the kitchen to help my Mom make after-school snacks for my brothers. I started to pull saucers from the cupboard when my Mom said, "Jamie, I wanted to let you know something. Noora will probably begin her period soon. I can smell it on her. So, I'm making plans to move Neil into Even's room to give her space when that happens. He mostly sleeps through the nights now and is growing out of his crib, so it should be fine." She finished.

"Oh, well, great, Noora can have fun with that," I commented, uninterested. Noora hung up the phone then headed back to her room.

Then worry crept in, and I asked about Waddles, and my Mom informed me that he still has a couple more years before we need to worry about another room for him. I was actually relieved to hear that. It means we don't have to move for at least two more years. When my parents decided to move, it was never just to a bigger house, they moved us to another state or town, and everything had to start all over again. I should be used to that by now, but somehow every move still manages to shatter my heart.

The phone began ringing, and I ran to it. "Hello, this is Jamie," I answered.

"Hi Jamie, It's Shelly." She replied.

"Who's on the phone?" Noora yelled from her room.

"It's a solicitor," I hollered so she wouldn't come running to my Mom to secure her plans first. "Sorry about that, so what did your parents say?" I asked Shelly and watched my Mom walk to the family room to check on Waddles.

"They said it's fine, as long as we keep quiet and out of the way. So, I promised that we would be so quiet, they wouldn't even know we were there. Since we won't be there anyhow." Shelly chuckled.

"OK, cool. I'll go ask right now and let you know, so hold on for a moment," I said. I walked into the living room then heard my Mom's purse spill onto the floor.

"Dang it." My Mom and I said at the same time. I ran back to the phone.

"On second thought, I will tell you tomorrow, something came up. I have to go. Bye," I panicked and hung up. I ran back into the family room as quickly as possible, so I could help her clean it up before. It was too late. All my siblings were there circling my Mom like vultures. There was no way I could make it to her to help.

"Oh look, five dollars, I can have that right," Noora demanded as she continued grabbing at my Mom's belongings.

My Mom spoke, "No, I was saving that for." She got interrupted by Noora.

"But I really need it. I never have money. You're an adult. You can just get more. It's only five dollars, Mom. Don't you love me?" She manipulated in a disgusting tone. I watched Neil shoving old gum into his mouth. I knew it tasted like crusty perfume and dust, but still, he filled his mouth, piece after piece.

"Fine, whatever, Noora." My Mom snapped, unable to think. The grabbing of coins, candy, and attacks continued on. Evan started grabbing quarters and dimes and pennies, putting them in his pockets.

"STOP IT, YOU ANIMALS! LEAVE MOM ALONE. STOP STEALING FROM HER!" I screamed as I couldn't bear to watch it continue.

"Shut up, Jamie. This is none of your business." Noora

sneered as she grabbed my Mom's chapstick.

"Noora, don't take that." My Mom pleaded in defeat. Noora started to walk off with it despite my Mom's request.

"Give it back now, Noora!" I moved into Noora's path as she tried to flee with it.

"GO AWAY, YOU STUPID, UGLY COW! "She screamed in my face then threw a punch that landed on my cheek. I shoved her, and she fell, and I jumped on her and started to wrestle it out of her hands, and she lifted her head and bit me.

"Ouch! What is wrong with you?" I shrieked as I got the chapstick free.

"Screw you!" Noora yelled at me and slapped me with her free hand. I grabbed her ear and rolled her onto her tummy as she kicked, wiggled, and bite at me. I quickly reached into her pocket, grabbed the five dollars, a pair of earrings, and a little mirror jumped off her and ran to my Mom. I shoved the items into my Mom's hand and raced for the door. Noora chased behind my, nipping at my heels. I made it outside, and I knew I was in the clear as I could easily outrun her here. She gave up halfway down the driveway and turned back to the house. I continued down the street a little further. Then when I could no longer see her,

I turned to walk back home.

When I neared the house, I spotted my Dad driving down the street towards us. I waved then ran into the house, but the chaos was still continuing. I heard my Dad's car door slam, and I knew it was too late.

"STOP IT, ALL OF YOU!" My Mom Yelled at the top of her lungs just as my Dad entered the house. He dropped his briefcase and stormed into the family room, and everyone froze.

"WHAT IS GOING ON IN HERE?!" My Dad yelled. No one moved or spoke. "Well, someone explain to me right this instant! Why did your Mother have to raise her voice and why you all are touching her things!" My Dad demanded.

"Oh, Shawn, it's not as bad as it looks." My Mom lied, trying to defuse what was to come.

"All of you kids to my room now! You too, Jamie. I saw you running from your sister, so I know you are a part of this mess as well." My Dad scolded and demanded. I knew better than to talk back, and so did my siblings. We lined up and waited for our turns. The boy got the hand, while us girls got the belt. Then we all silently went to our rooms to brood.

About a half-hour passed when the sound of the phone broke the silence. I carefully crept from my room to the phone. I answered softly. "Hello, this is Jamie," I greeted.

"Hey Jamie, it's Onacona," she said.

"Oh no, I forgot I was supposed to ask about the sleepover before she called." I was reminded by the sound of her voice. "Hold on just a minute," I requested, and I nervously walked to the family room. "Um, Dad, Mom," I spoke softly.

They both looked at me, and I read the room, and it seemed the hostility was gone. "Yes?" My Dad asked.

"Shelly invited Connie, Onacona, and me for a sleepover on Friday. I was wondering if I could please go?" I whispered as if a louder tone would create more drama.

"I'm fine with that, are you, Tracey?" My Dad checked and looked at my Mom. She gave a single nod, yes, and my fear was replaced with excitement. I ran back to the phone.

"Thanks for waiting for Onacona. Shelly wanted me to ask you if you could come for a sleepover at her place this Friday? Connie and I will be there." I walked into the living room for privacy and slid into a corner.

"I'll ask my Dad when he gets here with dinner. It should be any minute now." She sounded pleased, then paused. "What have you told everyone, about you know. Why I'm not at school?" Onacona asked nervously.

"I told them you have been off sick. I figure the rest was for you to say or not say. It has to do with your family. It's not my place to tell them." I answered softly.

"Really, you haven't said a thing?" She sounded surprised.

"Well, with your new skin and all, I figured you could decide to go either way. I don't mind if you tell them or if you choose not to. I want you to do what you want." I roused.

"Wow, it's just, since you were there, I thought you would say something," Onacona was caught off guard. "It's just," She cried.

"Do you want me to tell them?" I asked, confused by her tone.

"No, I mean yes, Wait, I don't know. I figured you did already, so I didn't realize I had a choice. I have to think about it. Thank you." Onacona said sincerely. We paused for a moment.

"Onacona, there is something I have meant to ask you, and I feel like this is going to be an awkward conversation so," I paused.

"What is it, Jamie?" Onacona sounded worried.

"Well, we talked about putting The Lion's Gate on hold to investigate the missing Native American women and children. I am still happy to do that, I gave you my word, and I always keep my promises. However, some other things came up about The Lion's Gate, and I needed to ask you if we can do that too, you know, split our time fifty-fifty or do one then the other? It's just The Lion's Gate is still pulling me to it, and I need to know why?" I rambled on, trying to convince her without dismissing another important journey.

"Jamie, it's OK. I made you promise out of my own anger and pain. Also, I am pretty sure my Dad won't let us travel to every tribe in America and poke around to get names. Maybe we do that when we are older." Onacona suggested.

"Well, we can at least write letters to a few tribes and see if we get any names? I would love to travel together all over America when we grow up, though. Also, I thought you were really courageous through everything, and thank you for trusting me enough to share," I said, feeling shame and helpless, not knowing what else we could do.

"Thank you for saying that" Onacona said sweetly. "Oh, hold on, my Dad is here. Dad, can I go for a sleepover at Shelly's this Friday to catch up on Schoolwork? Connie and Jamie will be there too?" Onacona pled with her Dad.

"I don't know. We will have to see what the Doctor

says. If she says it's OK, it will be OK with me as long as there is no nonsense or roughhousing. We don't want you to reinjure your wounds and end up back in here. I have dinner." I overheard Dawn say to Onacona.

"Hey Jamie, I have to go. Let's talk again tomorrow." Onacona said.

"OK, cool. Bye." I agreed, and we both hung up.

I quickly called Shelly back and let her know I could come to her house. Then headed to the kitchen to start prepping dinner, and my Mom joined me. I didn't mind cooking. It was relaxing. After everything was ready, we sat and ate as a family.

After washing the dishes, I headed to my room, grabbed my necklace, and placed it in the window. I didn't know why but it just felt right. When I was about to fall asleep for the night, my sister barged into my room.

"I can't believe you swooped in and stole Friday night! I wanted to hang out with my friends on Friday." Noora growled at me.

"Then invite them over here, and you all can take turns watching Waddles." I snapped back.

"I told you last week I wanted this Friday." She snarled at me.

"I don't remember that" I argued, and it was true I didn't.

"I don't care if you don't remember I did, and now you need to stay home!" Noora demanded.

"No, Noora. You should've asked Mom first if you wanted it, and you need to learn the word, no, anyways." I spat back.

"You're going to regret this." She yelled as she slammed the door on her way out. I rolled my eyes then laid down to sleep.

I stirred at the sounds of fluttering wings and the tickle of tender nudges on my cheek. I opened my eyes, and my room was lit softly. My sleepy brain's first thought was, "oh, how nice someone lit some candles in my room. Then no, that's not right," and my consciousness slipped in. A little voice whispered in my ear, "time is like a fairy tale. I share with you. My jaw dropped, and I gazed at the little green, purple, pink, and red lights that danced back and forth. I laid still and watched as I didn't want to frighten the little creatures away. "What am I seeing? It's so beautiful," I thought to myself.

Even in my mind, I whispered as if it too didn't want to frighten the delicate lights away. A white light drifted into the room. It was bigger than the others. It floated gracefully towards me, stopping over my face for a brief moment as if to say hello. Then floated to the window. It landed on my necklace, and the spiral in the Ammonite lit up and glowed a brilliant orange. Then all the little lights streamed to the window, and they started to spiral upwards in the orange glow and rose to where the ceiling was supposed to be. "Wait, there's no ceiling." I thought to myself and looked up through a canopy of trees overhead, where the stars were the brightest, I had ever seen, and the moon cast its silver streams of light through the branches and leaves. The little lights continued to spiral up into the night, and I laid there watching them until they vanished. I blinked, and it was all gone. The ceiling had closed, and my room was as it had always been. I looked at the window where my necklace lay, and I reached for it. I slipped it around my neck, and I fell back to sleep with my heart full.

The next morning, I awoke to the sound of my Alarm. I slapped at the clock aimlessly and whispered to it, "shut up you filthy animal." I wiped my eyes then scratched my chest and find my necklace there. "Wait, didn't I put this in the window?" I questioned myself. "No, that couldn't have been real. I was dreaming, right? Wait, I put my necklace on after all that happened." I examined the large Ammonite closely, and it was still the same as it was the day, I bought it. "What on earth was that? I sat thinking in bed. After a few moments, I stood up on my mattress and reached for the ceiling. I stretched but couldn't quite touch it, so I climbed onto my headboard and extended my arm and slammed my hand into the roof. "Yup, it's solid." I thought to myself and that was affirmation enough for me that it did indeed happed. I climbed back down and began to get ready for school and for once I was excited to go.

I had just finished morning arithmetic, and the school bell rang. I put my pencil down and headed to the playground. It didn't take me long to find Connie and Shelly.

"You'll never believe what happened to me last night," We all said in unison.

"Wait, you go first, no, you go first." We all talked over each other.

"I'll go first," Connie said. Shelly and I quickly went mute, excited to tell our own stories. "I asked my Mom for some jewelry, and she gave me this locket," Connie explained and showed it to us with pride. It was an old ornate locket with little swirls attached to vines. It had faded gold with silver showing through the worn parts of it. "It was my Grandma's, then she gave it to my Mom because she never wore it. It felt special from the moment I saw it. When it was time to go to bed, I placed it in the window for some reason. I just thought maybe moonlight would make it feel even more special. I fell asleep, and at some point, in the night, I woke up too little lights." Connie continued to tell us how she had a vision of creatures entering her room and going to the locket. I quickly realized it was the same story. "After the ceiling closed, I put the locket around my neck, and when I awoke this morning, it was still there! So, it had to be true!" She said, absolutely glowing.

"That's exactly what happened to me, word for word only with my bracelets!" Shelly was elated, and they both began to giggle. Then they looked at me.

"Me too!" I smiled then I felt a bit guilty because I just remembered that I forgot to tell Onacona to bring a piece of jewelry. "Do either of you have a quarter?" I asked, and they looked confused.

"Yes, I do in my backpack. Why?" Shelly questioned.

"I want to call Onacona to see if she had this experience too. I forgot to tell her to bring a piece of jewelry with her tomorrow. So, I want to make sure I give her a chance to place something in the window too." I stuttered.

"OK, I'll go grab it," Shelly smiled and ran for her classroom. When she got back, we headed to the payphone in front of the school.

I made sure to get there first to position myself in front of the numbers so they couldn't see what I dialed. "Hold the phone, so we can all hear," Shelly requested, and I did.

"Hello, Onacona answered." Her voice was stale, as if she had just woken up.

"Hi Onacona, it's me, Jamie, and I have Shelly and Connie here with me," I talked quickly, so I wouldn't give away where she really was.

"Hey, everyone!" She greeted happily, then cleared her throat.

"Hi, we really miss you. How come we haven't been able to get you on the line before?" Connie asked.

"I've been too sick to get out of bed, but I'm feeling a lot better today," Onacona said convincingly.

"That's so great! That you're feeling better, not that you were too sick to get out of bed before." Connie clarified.

"We wanted to call you to tell you to bring a piece of jewelry with you tomorrow." I cut in to avoid any more questions about her health.

"You know it's crazy that you are mentioning that

because my Dad gave me my Mom's old medicine bag last night. It's so beautiful it has a leather strap with a little black fox fur satchel on it. The fir spirals, you know, a cowlick and has some herbs in the pouch. It was hers, that's the best part. Anyways I set it in the window last night, and the most wonderful thing happened." Onacona began, and Shelly cut in.

"You saw fairies, and the bag lit up, then you saw a forest?" "Well, ya, kind of there was more. How did you know?" Onacona asked.

"The same thing happened to all of us last night," I replied.

"Whoa!" She gasped.

"You said your bag has a swirl on it?" I spoke.

"Yes, in the fir, but when it began to glow, it created a spiral up into the sky," Onacona answered.

"Shelly, can I see your bracelet. Shelly lifted her wrist, and at the points where the bracelet met, a little spiral clasp completed the loop. "All of our jewelry has some sort of spiral. I wonder what it means?" I pondered, and we all continued to debate it and enthusiastically chat about how beautiful our experiences were until the bell rang and lunch break was over.

Chapter Ten, Bluestockings

I woke up before my alarm even went off. Excited to start this new day and eager to walk to school with Onacona and see her! It felt like forever since I saw her last. I packed my bag for the sleepover and added four rolls of toilet paper. In case meditating near the pond didn't work. We could make use of being out and about by decorating someone's yard. I also added some snacks, a pillow, and a blanket. Then dressed overly warmly, with my knitted hat, mittens, and a waterproof coat.

I walked into the kitchen to tell my Mom goodbye, and she got a worried look on her face then spoke. "Sweetie, I know the last time you and the girls were all together, you got trapped in that awful house. I checked the weather, and it's not going to snow again anytime soon."

I was confused for a moment, then realized she was

referencing how I looked. "I know, Mom. I just want to be prepared. You know, just in case," I explained, so she wouldn't ask me to change.

"Alright, well, come give me a hug," she requested, and I wrapped my arms around her.

"I love you," I smiled and started to walk towards the door.

"Jamie, call me when you get to Shelly's house, so I know you are safe," my Mom called after me.

I hollered my replied back, "I will, bye Mom," and I left for Onacona's house.

When I arrived at Onacona's house, I was thrilled to find her there waiting for me. She looked even more beautiful than I remembered.

"Can I hug you?" I asked.

"Yes, of course, get in here, just avoid touching my arms," she bade.

So, I grabbed her around the waist and squeezed. I soaked her in like a new mother soaks in their baby. "I missed you. You look so gorgeous." I smiled.

"Um, Jaimie?" Onacona raised an eyebrow.

"Yes?" I replied while holding on to her tightly.

"Why are you dressed like this?" She questioned.

"Oh ya, you need to get some warm clothes for tonight," I answered as I finally released her.

"Oh right," She sighed and ran back into her house to collect some items. I stood in the doorway, and what I could see of the house looked new and inviting. All evidence of Sharyl was gone. Onacona came around the corner from the stairs. "OK, I'm ready." She determined, and we left.

The school day was going on as normal. I turned in all of my homework for the week and then lined up at the door to go with my class to the library. When we got there, the Librarian was pleased to announce that the school's first computer was up and active. It was amazing! I was about the size and shape of a large microwave, and you could type on it like a typewriter. The Librarian explained that one could use it to look up where to find books. Or input keywords to find a specific type of book. It could also order books from other schools if ours didn't have them. The Librarian showed us how to type in the codes for the different search options, and I quickly lined up to have a turn.

While I was waiting, I could overhear the office staff sneering at it, saying it is just a phase and won't be around long.

So, when I stepped up to the keyboard, I whispered to the machine, "I hope you stick around. You're pretty neat," Then I typed in the code for keywords and input "magic jewelry." To my delight, it came up with two options, one being a thesaurus. So, I wrote down the book numbers and made my way to section AB-03. I selected a thesaurus. I opened it and scrolled through the pages until my eyes landed on one that read. "Jewelry infused with power is referred to as amulets." I paused, thinking I've heard that word before.

Then the Liberian walked up to me and spoke so the whole class could hear. "I forgot to mention before that all the thesauruses and dictionaries are loaded onto the computer as well. So, if you want to look up something simple, and you can search by typing in a short description of what you want." The whole class and I gasped in amazement. "

So, you don't need to use this," The Librarian said and tapped the thesaurus.

"How does all that information fit into such a small box?" I asked, completely mystified by the magic of it.

"Oh, I don't know, maybe the same way a TV works?" The Librarian answered. Then I wondered how a TV works, but she was gone before I could ask.

I touched my necklace and remembered why I was

there. I got up and went to the computer and typed in, "Amulet." Sure enough, the computer was able to produce some information for me. It read, "Amulets, Jewelry, Normally a necklace with a distinctive or ornate pendant. Or other Jewelry. Believed to protect its wearer against evil, danger, or disease. Amulets are often beloved by their wearers and sometimes named after them." I touched my amulet again, and in my head, I called it "The amulet of Jamie." The teacher snapped her fingers, and I knew it was time to head back to class. It felt good to get so much information so easily. When we got back to class, we had a short discussion about the computer, then the bell rang, and school was out for the weekend.

I piled my warm clothes on, and everyone looked at me like I was crazy. The temperature outside was in the high sixties. I ignored their sideways looks and slipped out the door. Onacona, Shelly, and Connie were already waiting for me next to their classroom. Shelly and Connie lived just two streets over from me, but they normally took a different route home. Instead of crossing through the field, they left the school's front and took the main road to a side street.

"Hey, you ready to go, woolly mammoth?" Shelly teased in a sassy tone.

"Ha-ha, ya, I'm ready," I smirked, and we took off. I started to sweat before we even cleared the school parking lot, and I wiped at my face. "I'm going to suffocate in this," I groaned.

"Well, you could've packed two bags," Connie snaked.

"Then my hands wouldn't be free." I wined. We were just about thirty paces down the main road, and we were lost in conversation over a new hit song. When I got a tingle up my spine, and all of a sudden felt cold, then in danger.

"Everyone stop," I demanded so I could assess what was going on, and everyone froze. I looked at my friends and asked, "Do you feel that?" Everyone's faces went pale, but they weren't looking at me. They were looking past me, behind me. I turned slowly, and in the field next to us stood an abandoned house. The school was in the center of three abandoned houses. I knew that already, but I had never come this way or looked into this one.

"I feel that every day when I walk past this place," Connie said wearily.

"Ya, but it feels worse right now for some reason," Shelly added. Onacona didn't say anything. She was just still. I stared at the house and could swear I saw a shadow move under the door. "I think I just saw something move," I shuttered.

"Ya, I think I did too," Shelly confirmed. Then the sound of a growl hit our ears.

"I think we should go now," I insisted, not wanting to find out what made that sound. Then the door slid open and the man with yellow eyes from my dream flashed in my mind.

"Run!" I cried out, and we all took off as fast as we could. None of us looking back. We turned down the side street and kept going until the feeling of danger subsided, and I said, "I think we are safe now." as I slowed my pace.

"What the H. E. double hockey sticks was that?!" Shelly growled.

"I have no idea, but whatever it was, I don't think it's following us," I remarked.

"That was too frightening for my taste. I will never step foot into that house." Connie added.

"Jamie, can you carry my bag, please. I wouldn't ask, but I'm still a bit weak from being sick, and the running really exhausted me." Onacona explained, and I could tell she was hurting.

"Oh gosh, of course. Are you OK?" I asked, concerned.

"Yes, I'm not hurt or anything, just tired." She murmured. I nodded in fear if I spoke, I would say the wrong thing. I took her bag, and we continued walking.

"Can you imagine if that was the Abandoned house, we got stuck in a couple weeks ago?" Shelly mentioned.

"I didn't think our situation could've been any worse. I guess I was wrong." Connie shook her head. We walked the rest of the way in silence, working out what just happened, and I wondered if we would eventually have to face whatever was in that house

Formally meeting Shelly's parents was nice, even if our visit with them was brief. They ordered us pizza then sent us downstairs for the rest of the night. We played Light as Feather Stiff as a Board, then relentlessly rang the radio station and dedicated songs to one another. When it started to get late, we snuck upstairs, ensuring not to disturb the group of adults, and slipped into the kitchen. Made a pot of coffee and tip-toed it back down to where our bed was made up. Shelly poured us all a cup, and I took a sip then said. "This," I pointed at my cup, "is disgusting." I took another sip and nearly gagged.

"I don't get why adults like this," Onacona spat, trying to choke hers down.

"Did you know hundreds of years ago coffee was so essential to the Turkish people that women were OK to leave their husbands if they didn't provide them with enough of it?" Connie added.

"Really divorce by coffee," Shelly laughed. After we heard everyone upstairs say their goodbyes and Shelly's parents stumble to bed, knocking into things on their way, we knew it was time.

We started slipping into our warm clothes and placed all our folded blankets into one bag. Onacona and Shelly passed out flashlights. "Alright, ladies, are you ready?" Shelly smiled wildly, and we all nodded. Then she slid open the window, and we popped the screen out and climbed into the darkness.

"What's the quickest way to get to my street?" I questioned.

"This way," Connie turned, and we followed her past a few houses, then cut through some stranger's yards. Hopped fences an irrigation creek and then made it to my road. We moved quickly in silence, keeping to people's front yards so we could hide behind shrubs if a car were to pass. Once we made it about halfway down the road, I motioned, "over here," and we cut through another yard, hopped a fence, and landed into the pasture. Once in the field, we turned on our flashlights and made our way to the grove of trees and the pond.

After we reached the pond's edge, Connie asked, "Now what?"

"Let's set up places to sit," I replied. We picked our spot and sat side by side and faced the pond. Onacona sat to my right, Shelly to my left, and Connie to her left. I passed the blankets out, and we bundled up in them.

"OK, what do we do now?" Shelly asked.

"I'll walk us through a meditation. Everyone close your eyes. Pretend you are alone in a room, you feel safe, and your heart is filled with love." I began, and Shelly giggled at the words. Then Connie shushed her and spoke.

"Sorry, Jamie, hold on for just a moment. Shelly, I let you talk me into coming out here. I would rather be home safe in my own bed, thank you very much. So, you better sort yourself out and take this seriously, or you can leave now."

"Fine, I'm sorry. Go ahead, Jamie." Shelly apologized, and I began again.

"You are in an empty room with nothing but a chair and a window. You sit down in the chair and make yourself comfortable. You take a deep breath in, hold one, two, three, and release. You clear your mind. If any thoughts come in, you send them flying out the window. You feel yourself relaxing deeper and deeper. You feel warm and safe. Take another deep breath in, hold one, two, three, and release. You open your eyes and stare over the water. Take a deep breath in hold, one, two, three, and release. You see a white fog drifting over the water. Continue breathing and look into the fog." I stopped talking and gazed into the white fog focusing on my breath. Watching the still waters. We sat silently, letting time pass while maintaining our concentration.

The water began to ripple, and I looked into the fog, and in the dim light, I could see the outlines of four people walking across the water. Side by side, the silver moonlight caught their shoulders, and their shapes became clear. Four women walked towards us. I felt joy filling my heart and felt safe and secure. The one directly in front of me came into view and the other three faded from my sight. "I am yours, and you are mine." The words rang in my ears though no sound was made, and my instinct told me that the others weren't for me to fully see that they belonged to my friends. I beheld her in all her beauty and glory. She was perfectly petite, not much taller than me, with long flowing brown hair. She wore a silver fir across her shoulders, with a sword hanging at her side. Her face was kind, stunning, and gentle.

"Jamie, do not fear me. I have been with you all your life and know all your secrets. You need not confess any past deeds to me. You are worthy, wise, and strong. I will be with you for the rest of your life. I am your Bluestocking." She spoke to me, her voice in my head, and her words filled my soul.

"What's your name?" I asked without saying a word.

"Sally," She spoke.

"How did you become my Bluestocking?" I wondered.

"We have been friends for many lives. When we are not walking a world together, You are a torchbearer for me in my lives, and I am a torchbearer for you in yours." Sally answered. I stood to meet her, my gaze locked to hers.

"So, have we walked different worlds together? I pondered. "Why do you carry a sword? Is your life dangerous?" I questioned out of curiosity.

"I am a Valkyrie in training, as are you training to become a Wotan Witch. It takes many lives and many deeds to obtain enough knowledge to become either. You are a warrior, teacher, and leader. As am I. We are drawn to protect and join to others who are courageous. We see nobility by deeds, not status. We are sensitive to all the worlds, we wield our magic with honor, and when we fulfill our goals, we will be mighty, and our true lives will begin." Sally proclaimed.

"Our true lives?" I asked, remembering how the other world felt more real than this one.

Sally grinned and said, "Yes." I paused, overcome with joy.

Then asked the next question that popped into my head, "How do you have the time to watch everything I do and train?"

"Time is slower in the human mind. Does a stream ask what time it is? Does the wind or wild beast? When you sleep, you let go of the constraints of time and can travel through many lives. All things are happening at once and separately, ending and beginning, over and over again simultaneously. That is the truth of the universal flow. We are all infinite and only bridled by our own doubts and beliefs." Sally answered.

"How can I hear you in my mind without sound, and how do we close The Lion's Gate?" I asked with another thousand questions dancing in my head.

"Our souls are interlocked by a pact we made at our first spark into existence. The Lion's gate is your journey with your friends. I will beseech you that you must claim all the keys before you can fully close The Gate. Each will come at a cost. I will help protect you when it's time, and I will illuminate you where I can. Trust your instincts and listen for my voice, don't dismiss me as a mere thought." Sally counseled as she started to fade from my vision.

"Wait, how do I summon you? Or do I come here every time we are meant to meet?" I pressed, needing to know.

"Scry for me in water. A bowl of water will do. Or in black mirrors." Sally instructed, and she turned and walked away across the water, the other three Bluestockings falling into stride with her, together they vanished in the mist just as they had come.

I wanted to ask her about the fairies, my amulet, how to find the keys, how many keys there were. What the light in my hand could do. "I guess all that will have to happen later," I sat down again to contemplate what just happened. I ran my fingers over the soft earth and wondered if it too was watching me. I looked at my friends, and I could tell they were reeling from what they had seen.

We sat for a good while longer, then Shelly spoke, breaking the silence. "That was totally awesome!" We all burst into laughter.

"We better head back now. Who knows what time it is?

We can share when we get back to Shelly's place." Connie ordered. We quickly gathered up our belonging and headed back to Shelly's house.

When we got back to the house, we slipped back through the window without so much as a peep. We looked around. Nothing had been bothered, then we tip-toed up the stairs to get some drinks. All was quiet and well. No one noticed that we had left. Shelly passed out cups, and I looked at the clock on the oven and whispered.

"Look at the time. How on earth were we only gone for twenty-five minutes? It felt like we were gone for hours, but it was just minutes. The only time that passed was what it took us to get there, meditate and get back. No time passed when we were actually talking to our Bluestockings." I finished. This time issue was going to break my brain. By the look on my friend's faces, I could tell they were equally confused. We went back to our room and positioned ourselves into a circle. I opened the snacks I brought, and we started to share our experiences.

I started first and told them everything, About Sally and her beauty and features. Everything we had discussed, needing to "Claim the keys at a cost," about how contacting them further meant learning to scry in water or back mirrors.

How my Bluestocking was my soul mate, a Valkyrie in training, and I was a Wotan Witch in training.

Shelly began talking next. "My Bluestocking is named Vega. It means shooting star. She is an astral being and is made of starlight. She can walk on stars and direct the power of a supernova into creating new worlds. She travels through all the solar systems. She said that stars are seeds in the gardens of the universe and that even we are made of stardust therefore connected to all life. Her light can ignite our connections, making it possible for us to travel to her plane of existence. Since not all worlds are made up of air and water, that could come in handy.

She also said that I would be unable to withstand seeing her in her true form. Until I fully yield myself, which would mean training in another realm. So, she takes the shape that is the least threatening for me to see. I kind of wonder how scary she looks in her real body when she doesn't look like a glittery supermodel. She told me that I can channel cosmic energy, move the unmovable, and project great power where it needs to be directed. That these skills will follow me into my next level of existence, but seriously, my mind is blown right now." Shelly took a breath and tapped Onacona. "What about you? She asked.

Onacona started, "My Bluestocking is named Catori. She is beautiful with long dark hair, striking brown eyes and wears leaves, flowers, and herbs as clothing. Catori was carrying a bow. She is a realm walker. Her job is to find lost souls and helps them heal so they can find peace. She also retrieves the missing pieces of people's souls. When someone or some creature has been traumatized, the innocent part of their soul sometimes detaches and becomes lost. It often won't return to them in fear it will happen again. Soul retrieval Is when you find that piece and make it strong enough to return. The good souls are called Obvojen Dusa.

If a bad person chooses to act on their impulses, they too lose a piece of their soul, and that piece becomes more and more deranged and unable to grow and connect. She calls those devoroc. When they become so twisted and have lost all humanity, she hunts them. Then sends them to be trapped and recycled into the Eccotomb, a plain that she said she would tell me more about later. Her work, though, is mostly healing, and she can guide us when we communicate with spirits because she can see their energy and know if they are good or evil. She also said she can heal people and animals physically as well." Onacona stopped and looked at me with a glimmer in her eyes, and I knew there was more she wanted to tell me when we were alone. Then she continued, "She said I hold power to heal, and I am to develop that gift through herbs and magic that when I ascend, I too will be a realm walker. We all gasped amazed then turned and looked to Connie next.

"Well, first off, mine didn't worry about appearing in a form I was comfortable with because she kept changing shapes and clothing. She was young and wild-looking in one form. Next, she transformed into a woman our Mom's age with a baby in her belly and blood on her legs. If that wasn't bad enough, she would then shift into a horrifyingly ugly old dirty woman in a cloak. I didn't know what to say, so I asked her if she had split personalities, and she told me she was a Volva, better known as a Wyrd witch. I thought she said, "Weird witch." Because I didn't know what Wyrd was. Then I said, "I could see that," and she tossed a spider at me! It crawled into my ear!

She said it would help me learn magic. She laughed when I screamed. I still think it's gross. She then told me I have been her understudy for a thousand lifetimes, and this life is my final rite of passage to becoming a Volva witch myself! She told me that I am currently a Stitch Witch. I thought that was 'witch code' for the 'B' word with the way she spat it out. So, I told her to put a toad in it, and then she tossed a toad at me and told me to be silent and listen. She said a Stitch Witch is a seer and powerful earthly witch that can wield both light and dark magic. That being one is a steppingstone for gaining higher powers. That eventually, I would oversee the fates of a different worlds. She told me I could see people's destinies by reading spiderwebs. That I need to "learn spells to bind, protect, cast away, and set free. To help us claim the keys?" I asked her how I do that, and she told me, "The way would become clear." She also said it would be best if you all learned with me.

She then touched my locket and told me the fay have blessed us, and now our amulets will act as shields as long as we wear them. Nothing that wants to harm us can touch us with magic. However, she warned me that it doesn't mean they can't trap us, physically attack us, or find other ways to hurt us. Then she told me to be brave and never stop questioning. To dance in the rain, sit in the mud, and welcome adventure. She told me I was beautiful and to follow my heart. Then I felt a tight bond between us that I don't fully understand, and I think I saw a tear in her eye as we said our goodbyes." Connie finished.

I thought to myself, "She just rhymed. Maybe she's

already casting spells." Then I teased, "I finally feel a lot better. I know where to start, and now I don't feel like it is all on me. I think it is all on Connie now." Connie tossed a chip at my face, and I laughed. "See, there's the witch again throwing things. I'm just glad it didn't crawl into my ear." I chuckled.

"Well, what kind of Bluestocking is named Sally? Does she sell seashells in her free time?" Connie joked back, and I tossed a chip at her, and Shelly laughed a little too hard at that. "What are you laughing at, alien?" Connie kidded, and we all started teasing each other. When we were done with our fun, I headed to the bathroom to brush my teeth, and Onacona came with me. Once we were inside, Onacona took off her long-sleeved shirt, leaving just her tank top, and showed me her arms. I marveled. There wasn't a bruise or a scratch on them. No signs of surgery left, no fading or discolored skin, or scars.

"She healed me," was all Onacona said, and I cried tears of joy at the gift given to my friend.

We left the bathroom, and Onacona proudly walked back into the room without long sleeves on. After we all settled into our sleeping bags. I spoke. "We have a Wotan Witch, a Shaman healer, a Volva Stitch Witch, and an Astral

Witch. I think we must be the best superheroes ever." I joked and not, and they all agreed.

Chater Eleven, Beasts and Bones

We all woke up with the sun, each of us with a fire in our bellies. None of us truly knowing what will be asked of us, but we rose fully united in the cause. "We need to find someone who can teach us spells or how to scry," Connie bade.

"I don't know where we can do that. I don't have any money to pay a teacher at The Pondering Pixie either. They have fees for any teaching they do." Shelly sighed.

"Actually, I may know a person from there that can help. Maybe even two. If we call The Pondering Pixie and talk to Priestess Singing Rock, she might help us out." I plotted, remembering my conversation from last week.

"Who's going to drive us there?" Onacona asked, trying to work out the detail.

"I may have an idea about that too, but we'll have to stop

by my place to grab a number. Also, last week when I was there, the priestess had mentioned they were going to do a short class on scrying in black mirrors." I said, thinking this may be perfect.

We quickly dressed and headed up the stairs to grab some breakfast. Shelly's Mom greeted us in the kitchen. "Good morning, ladies. What are your plans today?" She smiled then Shelly answered her Mom.

"Well, after we eat, we plan on walking to Jamie's house to grab a phone number so we can contact some witches and learn spells." My jaw dropped, and I thought to myself, "Are we allowed to tell our parents that?"

Shelly's Mom laughed. "OK, darling, that sounds like fun. Just be home in time for dinner."

I exhaled, thinking. "Of course, she wouldn't believe us. I doubt anyone outside our circle would." I still felt awkward after the conversation and tip-toed my way around the kitchen. After breakfast, we packed up and got ready to go.

Since it was daylight now, we had to take the long way to my house. Hopping fences and cutting through yards would get us into trouble. After walking down, a couple roads, we came upon the field that Evan and I found the dog in. I started telling my friend the story about how we found the pup when the shiny object I left in the hole flashed in my mind.

"Hey, do you all mind if we stop for a minute at the hole, I saw something in it when I was digging the dog out and was wondering if it was still there? It probably won't be, but I'd like to see." I asked.

"We are on a mission here to get phone numbers," Connie appealed.

"Come on, it will only take a minute. I remember exactly where the hole is." I tried to persuade her.

"Fine, but if you can't find it, let's not spend all day digging in the mud and miss our opportunity to scry." Connie agreed.

"What did it look like?" Onacona asked.

"I didn't get a good look, but it was black and shiny and barely showing through the dirt. It's probably nothing, but I'm curious," I answered.

"Ha-ha, since you say it's nothing, it will be something." Shelly mocked.

"And you love me for that," I teased and blew a kiss at her.

"You got me there." She grinned. We entered the field, and I led the way.

We reached the hole, and it was muddier than the last time I had been there, and it stunk. "That smells like something died in there," Onacona lurched.

"Are you really going into that pit?" Connie squirmed, holding her nose.

"I'll be fine as long as spiders don't crawl into my ear." I teased and started to undress, and I saw Connie playing with her ear like she was trying to get it out. "Sorry Connie, I won't mention the spider again," I felt bad.

"Good, I'd like to forget it is in there," She groaned.

Once I was down to my training bra and panties, I reached my legs into the hole. "Ewe, the mud is slimy and spiny," I wined, disgusted by the mush between my toes.

"You don't have to do this now," Onacona deterred.

"Yes, I do. I don't know why but I do." I explained, then lowered myself into the hole. I had to wait several moments for my eyes to adjust. Then I remembered I had a "hand light, rune thing," and I stretched my hand out and nothing. I closed my eyes and concentrated. "Sally, how do I get this thing to work?" I asked my Bluestocking. "I didn't get the response I was hoping for. Instead, I heard her reply, "Hurry!" I opened my eyes, and my hand was glowing, lighting the inside of the crevice.

I was disgusted to find I wasn't kneeling in the mud. I was kneeling in a carcass! My impulse was to leap out of the hole, but my Bluestocking hadn't said run. She said, "hurry." I held my hand out in front of me and restrained my need to vomit. I looked to the spot where I had seen the object before, and a huge half-decomposed skull sat in its place. "Of course," I moaned. "You all are going to want to stand back for a minute!" I yelled up while restraining the need to puke, and I heard them move. I grabbed the huge head in my arms, then twisted it, let it drop with a thud, then used my knee to crack the spine and yanked and bent it some more until it came loose with loud crack and pop. The sounds alone made me dry heave. I lifted it above my body, used my legs to thrust it out of the hole, and then vomited. I heard the girls let out screams.

"What the heck, Jamie!" Shelly yelled into the hole. I didn't respond in fear that more vomit would come out if I opened my mouth again. I held my breath the best I could and clawed at the dirt.

"What kind of beast is this?" I heard Onacona say.

"Who cares, No don't touch. You're touching it, really, Onacona?" I heard Connie groan, disgusted.

I held my hand over the spot, and I saw what I was

looking for. A sharp bit poking out of the dirt. I dug around it, trying to pry it free. When the earth around me started to tremble.

"You feel that?" Connie asked. "Jamie, get out of there!" She yelled. I didn't stop; I dug faster and faster. Then I pried my finger under the object and popped it free. I gripped the thing in my hand just as a loud hiss echoed through the hole.

"Get out of there NOW!" My friends yelled. Not wanting to find out what it was, I stood ready to leap free, but my foot slipped in the slick bile of the decaying creature, and I fell. Then It was too late. The sound of heavy breathing came rushing towards me. Fear began to wash over me as it grew louder and closer. I extended my hand out in front of me as I tried to push myself up with the other, and I could see a giant beast erupting through the dirt. My amulet exploded, orange light circled me, and the beast bounced back. I started flailing my arms, panicking, then six hands gripped me, ripped me from the hole, and dragged me away from it.

I was back in the sun, and the shaft rumbled. I scrambled to my feet, and we all fled across the field. None of us looking back until we landed on the road.

"I told you it was going to be a big deal," Shelly scorned.

"What was that? Did you see it?" Connie queried.

"It was a giant beast of some kind, like a badger but much bigger, luckily my amulet lit up just before it reached me and stopped it from hurting me," I said with a shaky voice.

"Really, what did your amulet shield look like?" Onacona asked, interested, and I looked at her, and to my horror, she was still holding the half-rotted head.

"Oh, for the love, Onacona, why are you holding that nasty thing?" I snorted.

"I want to know what kind of creature it is. So, I'm taking it home." She commented as if it was normal. I looked at it. It was huge and definitely not like anything I had ever seen. It was bigger than the moose skull I found when I went camping with my grandpa a couple of years earlier. The parts of flesh still attached looked like it had been clawed by something even larger and was leathery like a gorilla's face. In fact, the whole thing looked similar to a gorilla except for two long tusk-like teeth protruding from its lower jaw.

"So, what did it look like?" Onacona puzzled.

"What?" I asked.

"Your amulet when it lit up." She reiterated.

"Oh, it wrapped around me like a cocoon and had a spiral on it in front of me," I answered.

"That's cool," She noted.

"You could've been killed by whatever that was, especially if it killed whatever this is!" Connie barked.

"I know, but Sally told me to hurry, not to leave, so I hurried," I said in my defense.

"Good to know, so if Cordelia ever tells me to hurry, I know to run instead!" Connie blustered.

"So, what did you find?" Shelly inquired with a hint of fear in her tone.

"This," I uncurled my finger to take my first real look at the thing I had been clenching onto. Everyone stopped and looked.

"It's a spearhead," Shelly noted first. It was long, sharp, smooth, and made from some sort of black stone.

"That's it?" Connie rasped.

"Well, it has to be important, or Sally wouldn't have told me to hurry," I defended. A car started driving towards us, and I suddenly realized I hadn't stopped to put my clothes back on. Embarrassed, I dove behind a bush, and Onacona joined me with the head. The car drove past, and Connie threw my clothes at me. I quickly slipped them on.

Then she threw a towel. "This would've been useful before I put my clothes on." I hollered to her.

"It's not for you. It's for the head! You don't get luxuries." Connie yelled back, and I rolled my eyes. Onacona wrapped the head in it, and we joined the other two back out on the road.

We started to walk, and I slapped Connie on the arm and taunted her, "Jerk face."

She laughed and pinched me. "That's for scaring me," She countered.

"Thank you all for saving me back there," I commented sincerely.

"Like we would let you die," Shelly winked at me, and we continued walking towards my house.

We arrived at Onacona's house first, and we slipped into her backyard to put the head in her bunny freezer so we could have time to figure out what to do with it. Just as we reached the freezer, Dawn stepped out of the hawk hut and saw us.

He walked towards us, and we all stiffened. "Hi, sweetie. How are you feeling?" Dawn greeted Onacona, and I knew it was code for how are your arms.

"I feel great!" Onacona smiled brightly.

"What's that you're holding?" He looked puzzled as a piece of rotted flesh plopped onto the ground from under the towel. I held my breath, knowing we were caught.

"We found it in the big field on our way back from Shelly's house," Onacona paused, and she set it on top of the freezer, and the sheer weight made a thudding sound when it landed. "I don't know what it is. That's why I brought it back here." Onacona explained.

Dawn moved in closer and said, "Well, show it to me, then maybe I can help." Onacona lifted the towel, and Dawn's face dropped, and we all stood in silence. "You found this in the field?" He questioned with an utter look of disbelief written across his face.

"Yes." I squeaked. "No, it can't be, well maybe, it looks like an Ogre," He whispered, and I couldn't tell if he was kidding. He stepped forward and poked it.

"Not to be disrespectful, but does everyone in your family touch dead things?" Connie gaged and looked sick.

They both answered, "Yes." Connie eyeballed them both with a look if uncertainty.

"I guess you should finish putting it in the freezer, and I'll take some samples to work and have them tested to see what kind of animal this is," Dawn commented. Onacona lifted the head, and I opened the freezer, and she set it in it.

"Onacona, I'm going to run home and shower before we

go," I stopped, realizing that I had just revealed our plan.

"Go where? I think Onacona has probably done enough running around considering the week she had," Dawn stated.

"But we." I started, and Onacona cut me off.

"Go shower, Jamie. You need it, and I need to talk to my Dad. I'll come let you know what is decided after we are done," Onacona looked at her Dad, relaying some unspoken understanding. Then walked towards the balcony stairs, and he followed.

Connie, Shelly, and I walked into my house, and I was surprised to find it empty. I walked into the kitchen, and there was a note on the counter for me. It read, "We are running errands and won't be back until late. Make yourself some dinner, love Mom." I was relieved I didn't have to come up with excuses for being gone all day. "Make yourselves at home," I said and ran for fresh clothes and the shower. When I was done, I emptied the pockets of my dirty clothes into my clean ones and then hid them in the hamper, so my Mom wouldn't question why they were so smelly. Then I continued down the hall and found Shelly, Onacona, Connie, and Dawn sitting in my living room.

Memories of the night Onacona spilled her secrets

flashed in my mind, and I was instantly worried. "What's going on?" I muttered.

"I was just telling Connie and Shelly that my Dad is divorcing Sheryl, and she won't be around anymore," Onacona answered, and I sighed in relief. "Also, I told my Dad everything." She added pleasantly.

I instantly thought that was code for, "She did not," so I just nodded and spoke, "Neat." Not wanting to give anything away.

"Are you girls ready to go?" Dawn invited. "Go where?" I asked, confused.

"The Pondering Pixie, My Dad said he would take us," Onacona remarked pleasantly.

"Sure, should I make us all some sandwiches before we go in case, we get hungry?" I offered.

"Sounds good," Connie responded, and I quickly walked to the kitchen. A feeling of dread started to creep over me. "If he really knew what was going on, there was no way he would let Onacona hang out with us anymore. In fact, they might move altogether."

"Jamie, do you mind if I have a word with you in private? It will just be for a moment," Dawn summoned, just as I had gotten all the ingredients out. My heart plummeted into my stomach. "Help. I mean sure." I answered. Connie and Shelly gave me worried looks as I headed back into the living room. I knew they were thinking what I was thinking.

"Onacona, you can stay," Dawn stated as she got up to leave. I could feel tears welling up in my eyes. "So Onacona tells me you are all going on a spiritual journey and exploring realm walking. That last night she met her guide, and that's how her arms were healed. Is that true?" He asked, and I nodded.

"First off, I don't know how I am going to explain this to her doctors. Maybe I will tell them I used an ancient tribal remedy. White people love that. I do use cold bacon grease and tobacco leaf to heal my animal's scars," Dawn reflected.

"Bacon grease?" I questioned, confused.

"Yes, an animal's hair will grow back white where a scar has formed. If you shave the white off and put the cold bacon grease with tobacco on it, the hair grows back the color it originally was. Yup, that's what I'll tell them," Dawn looked pleased with his plan. "The next thing I wanted to say is, I think it's great you girls are doing this. Every person is meant to have a tribe, and Onacona hasn't had many opportunities to experience what that's like, and now she gets too." He finished.

"Onacona mustn't have told him everything. He's being way too positive. "I wondered and felt a bit relieved. "Thank you, Dawn. I appreciate you saying that, and I needed Onacona more than she needed me," I replied and believed it.

Connie hollered to us from the kitchen, "I have the sandwiches ready. We should eat them on the road." I put my shoes on, and we all headed to Dawn's truck. The truck had one long bench seat in the front of it, with no back seat. So, we had to sit on each other's laps as we drove. We bounced up and down while trying to chew. Connie and I were on the bottom, hoping the ones on top of us didn't have to fart. However, we didn't have to ask a stranger to give us a ride which was my original plan, so this was much better. In summer, we would be able to ride in the bed of the truck, and that would be more comfortable.

When we arrived at The Pondering Pixie, Dawn let us know that he had to collect a new skylight for the hawk's shed and would be back shortly to join us. The rest of us rushed inside, just in time to hear Priestess Singing Rock announce that the scrying class would start in fifteen minutes. I was relieved we had a few moments to discuss what was told to Dawn. I turned to Onacona. "What did you tell your

Dad? I felt put on the spot and was scared he wouldn't let us hang out together anymore, and if that happened, I would die," I snapped.

"Ya, that sucked!" Connie chimed in.

"Sorry, I had to tell him something. I had an Ogre head in my hands, and then he wanted to check my arms to see how I was. I didn't have time to tell you." Onacona pled in her defense.

"Wait, what happened to your arms?" Connie asked, confused, and Onacona went pale.

"That's none of your business," Onacona said, and even I was surprised by her tone.

"So, you told Jamie, and after everything we have been through, you don't trust or like Shelly and me enough to let us in on your little secret?" Connie scolded. I felt instantly angry at Connie's accusations and inability to respect Onacona's wish to not share.

So, I stepped in. "Hold on just a moment, Connie. You are taking this way too personally, and it really has nothing to do with you. I only know because." I got interrupted by Onacona.

"No, Connie is right. I don't trust her and Shelly as much. Since kindergarten, I have been going to school with you two, and neither of you ever talked to me until Jamie came along. So why should I have to share every personal thing about my life with you?" Onacona stormed off in one direction, then Connie and Shelly stormed off in another direction with looks of anger and shame. I stood still awkwardly, wondering what had just happened and if it was fixable.

"Awe, you look like you could use a couple moments in the meditation room to collect yourself, am I right?" a voice from behind me spoke. So, I turned and a lady I recognized from the last class was standing behind me. She was plain and smiled politely.

"I guess," I agreed.

"Right this way." She said as she turned and walked towards a closed door. As we started across the store, I felt a shiver go up my spine, and I glanced up at the lady in front of me, and for a fraction of a second, I swore I saw her eye twist backward in its socket to watch me.

I took another step then the feeling of "something was wrong" overpowered me, and I couldn't ignore it.

"On the other hand, I should go find my friends and talk this out before class," I lied and turned. She grabbed my arm before I could run and started to drag me towards the door.

"Let me go!" I yelled, and I tugged at her fingers, but they wouldn't budge. I looked quickly around the shop, and everyone was frozen in place. Not from shock, either. Everyone was paused in mid-motion, frozen in time. "Connie, Shelly, Onacona!" I screamed and gathered my balance, then spun and elbowed my abductor right in the gut as hard as I could. The blow didn't affect her. Instead, it had knocked me down, but my arm had twisted itself free in the struggle.

I took advantage of the opportunity and started to scramble to my feet. When I was grabbed around the waist and lifted off the floor, I started kicking my legs and squirming as much as possible while prying at fingers that were now unnaturally large. In my struggle, I was able to turn myself around and face the now creature that was previously a woman. Its jaws had disengaged, and its head was tilted back. Its teeth were jagged, sharp, and brown. I screamed in horror. As it raised me over its mouth and dropped me into it.

I slid over its tongue, past the teeth, and landed in a pile of mush. I could feel its muscles squeezing me like a snake squeezes a rat. I heard my friends screaming my name in the distance and the crashing of objects. Hot fluids started to burn my body. The pressure and pulses of the restricting muscles made me feel like I was disintegrating. I couldn't feel my legs. I wanted to scream in pain but didn't want the fluids to enter my mouth. In desperation, I used what strength I had and started to squirm. "You have to fight," I told myself. I could feel the creature moving, and I knew my time was limited as I desperately needed air. I heard a popping sound, and the muscles loosened around me. I slid my hands into what was left of my pocket and found the spearhead. I grabbed it tightly and drug it the muscles wrapped around me, and I heard the beast whale in pain.

The sound was terrible a guttural. The muscles started to push me, jolt me back and forth, and I began to move up its throat. I held tightly to the blade and continued dragging it up the insides of the beast as it attempted to vomit me up. My head reached its mouth, and I gasped for air. I heard Connie scream, "Get its necklace!" Afraid the beast would snap me in half with its teeth, I dug the spear into the ridges of its throat to stop myself from coming up any further. Its hands started thrashing at my head, and I could feel chunks of my hair and skin out being ripped out.

I didn't care. The pain was so intense all over my body that my scalp was the least of my worries. I also knew death would greet me soon as I felt my body dying. "At least this way, the beast could choke on me, and we would die together." I thought as I lost feeling in all parts of me.

"Now!" I heard Shelly scream. I heard a clink as something fell to the floor. My hand erupted with white light, and my amulet burst with an orange glow as my shield enveloped me, and the beast exploded. I tumbled to the floor. I didn't try to move; I couldn't. I tried to inhale, but it was too hard. My head started to spin. I opened my eyes but could only see with one. I looked around, and my friend's feet were around me. I saw the priestess running towards me, other people were fleeing from the store, then everything went dark.

Chapter Twelve, Healing Realms

I woke up to a mix of sweet smells, lavender, honeysuckle, incense, lemongrass, and tobacco. I opened my eyes and saw long flowing strips of vibrantly colored fabric hanging from the ceiling and swaying in the wind. "Am I dead?" I asked the universe.

"She's awake!" I heard Onacona yell, and she ran to me and wrapped her arms around my neck. "Where are we? What happened? What was that thing!?" I asked, wondering If what I was remembering was real.

"Just wait a minute. We all will explain everything," Onacona comforted me and started to adjust something on my head.

I looked at my body, and I was completely covered in maple leaves from head to foot. "What am I wearing?" I felt completely caught off guard.

"We will explain everything once we are all here,"

Onacona said again. I started to pull leaves from my face.

"Don't touch those, you're not all the way healed yet," Onacona insisted and stuck it back to my face. I looked at Onacona, and she seemed happy, so I knew at the very least I was safe. A warm, gentle breeze softly surrounded me, and the sheets of fabric swayed with it.

"That's nice," I thought to myself. Then I remembered it was autumn. "The wind should be cold." My eyes widened, and I became more alert. I looked past my feet. The room opened to a beautiful meadow with all kinds of flowers in bloom with a forest along its edge, and I swore I could hear the lull of the ocean just beyond. I thought to myself. "Yup, we are all dead, and this is the afterlife." The surroundings were enchanting, and it felt like the perfect place. "All that missing is unicorns and fairies." I imagined as I gazed at the view. Suddenly, little fluttering movements caught my attention, and little winged creatures started skipping from flower to flower. Then a unicorn stepped out of the forest. "Holy cow! Look fairies and unicorns!" I blurted out.

"I figured you to be more of a dragon person," Connie said, and I looked at her.

Shelly was standing next to her and spoke, "Ooh, I need fairies too."

"OK, will someone please tell me what happened already? Are we all dead?" I questioned and raised my leafy arms in the air, then gave them a shake.

"We aren't dead. We are in your pocket realm." A woman I didn't notice before said and stepped around a piece of fabric.

"Sally? What? If I'm not dead, how come you're solid? What's a pocket realm?" I pinched myself, and the pain from it was worse than it was supposed to be. "Ouch, pinches hurt worse when you're dead. I wasn't expecting that." I rubbed the top of my leaves to soothe the pain.

Sally cringed and took my hand, "OK, don't do that and calm down. Just listen for a moment. A pocket realm is a place that you create between worlds. It reflects what you want to see. Priestess Singing Rock sent you and your friend here to give you time to heal from the calsake attack. You were inside her for too long, and her venom had eaten away most of your skin. Unfortunately, one of your eyes had slid onto your cheek. You were lucky your organs didn't spill out, or else you would've died." Sally took a breath, and I erupted.

"WHAT! MY EYEBALL FELL OUT OF MY HEAD! YOU! You told me to be calm, but I was eaten by a monster! Oh, I'm done. I'm not doing this anymore!" I crossed my arms, and the leaves on them crunched and poked me. "Also, what is with the leaves?! I feel like a dang fool?!" I snapped and was sure I looked like one too.

Onacona jumped in and said, "I can explain the leaves. I put them on you. The maple helps to regrow the skin." I shook my head and raised my hand to stop anyone else from talking. I had to think all of this just raised more questions for me.

I took a deep breath and ranted, "OK, I'm freaking out, so I need someone to tell me from start to finish what happened, so I can wrap my head around it." Sally began to speak, and I interrupted her. "Not from you! You started with detached eyeballs. Connie, will you explain it all for me?"

"OK, well, we had just had our argument in the store. Shelly and I went into the meeting room and closed the door to cool off before class started, and Onacona was in the restroom. Then we heard you yell for us, so we tried to run to you, but the doors wouldn't budge. Then Shelly started to chant, guided by her Bluestocking, and the door started opening a little bit at a time as if our magic was being blocked. I started chanting with her, and we got it open wide enough for us to squeeze through. We ran to the restroom and did it again to get Onacona out. Then we ran to the storefront just as you. Um, were swallowed." Connie shuddered then continued, "I grabbed a cauldron from the sale's rack and hocked it at the creature, and It told us we were too late and started tried to leave. Then I somehow summoned fire, and it blocked it from going out the door. Then I started throwing more cauldrons at it. Shelly and Onacona were chanting and throwing items at it.

I tried to get the fire to burn the Calsake, but its amulet lit up and blocked it. Then Shelly started to shoot little dark balls of energy at it without success. So, she encircled it with starlight, and it stopped it from fleeing. The monster started to push through the magic we threw at it, and I knew we had to remove the necklace to do any real damage to it. So, I yelled to remove the necklace, and then Onacona walked towards it. Her eyes started to glow with blue light, and with each step she took, the building would wobble. The creature screamed and looked like it was going to be sick. So, I yelled out again to "grab the amulet." Onacona reached for it, but the calsake sent her flying back with the swipe of its hand. Shelly used dark matter to catch her. Then the beast started ripping parts of you from its mouth, and I was horrified. So, I grabbed a cheap wand off the shelf and leaped towards it and slid it under the chain and popped it off. Once the amulet hit the ground, the creature exploded." Connie paused to think.

Shelly chimed in, "You forgot to tell her that you lept like a giant frog across the store at it." Connie glared at Shelly.

"That wasn't pertinent information! Anyways, when the Calsake died, its spell was broken, and everyone started running when they saw the mess. When I saw you, I thought you were gone, but Onacona lifted you with her magic, and The priestess gave us stones and told us to clap or slap them, so we did, and mist surrounded us. Then we were here, and our Bluestockings were all here rushing to help. Onacona and Catori laid you down right away. They started washing you with milk and honey and working their healing magic on you. Mine rushed me to my pocket realm where there is a witch kitchen, and we concocted a paste to hold your eye in its socket. Oh, I had to touch your eye. That was awful, and Shelly went with Vega to collect energy to help speed the healing. Once we got all our ingredients together, Onacona started to paint you with them and place the leaves on you. Once she was done, you became more stable, and it turned into a waiting game," Connie paused.

"How long have I been out?" I asked, still trying to soak

it all in.

Connie continued, "time works differently here, so a couple months here but minutes in the real world. Let me finish before you ask any more questions, so I don't get mixed up. I'm almost done. Shelly, our Bluestockings, and I had to mix potions and leap through the time gaps to find everyone that saw the beast and erase their memory of it. The spell and the potions were hard and complex. Finding the people was easy, though, since they didn't have time to get very far due to the time differences. We have stayed here to learn and be here for you when you wake up. We each have our own pocket realm, and they are all attached to each other so we can walk through doors into each other's realms. Our Bluestockings set them up this way for us. The priestess had the portal stones because her Bluestocking had talked to ours, and she was going to introduce us to these realms after class, but it didn't go as planned. These stones are for us to keep. I'm done now. You can ask away." Connie finished.

"Sally, where were you when I was healing?" I asked everyone, but she was mentioned.

"I." She paused and looked sad, then an ugly, horrible-looking old crone walked in and put her hand on Sally's shoulder. I guessed it was Cordelia. Sally took a deep breath and continued. "I couldn't stand to see you like that, so I tracked where the calsake had come from, and I killed the others I found. They don't belong in your world, and I had never dealt with them before. I should've done the research first. I shouldn't have killed them the way I did," Sally stopped, and shame was on her face.

"What, your sad you killed them? You should be proud! One ate me!" I barked, confused. I was relieved to find out they were all dead. Sally sat down next to my feet and looked at the crone.

Cordelia spoke, "the calsakes were misplaced here unwillingly by The Lion's Gate. They are magical creatures and generally peaceful. They were thrust into this world while working a spell to close The Gate. You see child, in their world, people grow on trees. They aren't like people here. They are lifeless and eaten like fruit once ripe." Cordelia made a plucking motion with her hand like she had just plucked an apple off a branch, and I cringed. "So, they were shocked to find people alive here and have been starving, trying to find a way home. The one that attacked you had been going there under a glamor spell to try and find a portal back to her world. The scent of magic on you must have made it impossible for her to resist any longer, and she lost control. So, before you judge her too harshly, just imagine what you would do if you were displaced into an unfamiliar world and your food was walking and talking. Would you starve yourself and your friends for weeks, or would you find one and try to eat it?" Cordelia hissed, and the room went silent.

"I feel bad for her friends, but not for her! I would never eat anything I could talk to," I snapped. "I would kill myself first," I thought. I spoke again, "Sally, you were protecting humanity and me. You didn't know, you saw a threat, and you saw what it did to me. I would've done the same if I was in your place and able. What did you do after that?" I finished.

Sally swallowed, "I learned what I had done and had to report it to Odin and Freya. They pardoned me and had me leave to speak to the gatekeeper of your world, and I found him dead. I reported back again, and they sent teams to different worlds to see the status of their keepers. Now, I am tracking and trapping beasts that don't belong here and trying to return them to where they do belong, but who knows how many have been misplaced? Who knows who had the gatekeeper killed and who knows what they are planning?" She finished.

"When you all were fighting the calsake, how were you able to use magic?" I asked my friends.

"When I saw you get swallowed, it erupted from me as if it had always been there, buried until I really needed it," Shelly answered. Then a beautiful woman walked in behind her, and by the way, she glittered. I knew it must be Vega.

Then she spoke to me, "We were going to teach you slowly over time how to access your magic, but to save you, we had to unlock it in them, and they handled themselves beautifully with it." She smiled and stroked Shelly's hair.

Then Onacona spoke. "It was the same for me with my magic, except when I walked towards her, part of me could see all her pain, and I wanted to heal her. Then I saw your heartbeat fading inside of her, and I saw the spearhead lodged into her, and I knew the greatest kindness I could do was to put her out of her misery."

Then Connie, "it just poured from me too. I'm guessing this old hag had something to do with it." Connie chuckled, and she sounded like a witch. Cordelia tossed a pile of mud at her. "Hey!" Connie protested then smiled, and whispered, "It was worth it." and winked at me.

"Thank you all for saving me and putting yourself in harm's way for me. I am so grateful to each of you. I don't know how to repay you." I held my breath while fighting back tears. Then another beautiful woman walked in, with a crown of antlers on her head, and I knew that must be Catori.

She smiled at me then spoke. "We need to let Jamie rest. Onacona go and collect more leaves to redress Jamie's wounds. Connie, you get her a sleeping potion. She needs to heal completely before we exhaust her any further." Onacona and Connie left, and Shelly sat next to me.

"You relax. When you're all better, I am going to take you ice skating on Saturn's rings," Shelly sparkled, and then Connie came back in, rubbed an ointment under my nose, and I floated off to sleep.

Chapter Thirteen, Entering Asgard

"Wake up Jamie, It's time," I heard Sally summon me. I opened my eyes to find Sally standing next to me.

"Time for what? Breakfast?" I grumbled with a groggy voice.

"Time for that and so much more," Sally answered. I scanned my realm, and no one else was there. A dragon was trotting past my balcony, and I shook my head, not knowing if I should be embarrassed or pleased with the sight of it. Sally looked at it and eyeballed me.

"Where is Connie, Shelly, and Onacona?" I asked.

"Oh, they are training with their primary forces. You need to get caught up. They have been diligently training nonstop for about three months now. While you just lie there like a lump on a log with all sorts of obscenities frolicking around in your garden," Sally teased, and I blushed, wondering what other thing I had manifested while slumbering. I looked at my body to see if I was still covered in leaves. Instead, I was wearing a brown leather bodysuit with intricate engravings of vines, a red tank top, and I could feel that my hair pulled back into a stiff hair glove.

"How? Who dressed me?" I remarked, confused about my new ensemble.

"I did, and you are far from fully dressed. Now chop-chop. We only have a week before you have to get back to the shop to meet Dawn," Sally said and clapped her hands at me.

I sat up and felt wobbly and unmotivated. "I don't think I'm up for this," I groaned.

"You will be," Sally whispered under her breath.

"What was that?" I asked, unsure if I heard her correctly.

"You will feel better after eating. Come with me," She stood up, and I walked with her into another room. Things in the room started to shift, and I thought I was fainting. Then a kitchen manifested, and I marveled at the magic. Sally walked to the oven with mitts on and pulled out a plate with sliced apples and pineapple and then a bowl of oatmeal, and everything was ready to eat.

"You know this isn't how a real kitchen works, right?" I

taunted sarcastically.

"Who's to say your kitchen is real?" Sally teased back.

"You got me there. I'm pretty sure at this point I belong in an institution." I joked, uncertain of anything anymore.

"Come on now, self-doubt serves no purpose. Push those thoughts aside and eat," Sally insisted, and I started stuffing my face. The fruit tasted sweeter and more intoxicating than any other fruit I have ever eaten before. My body felt stronger, and I started feeling renewed.

"This is the best fruit I have ever had," I smiled while chewing.

"Well, the Gods and Goddesses will be pleased to hear that. You can tell them yourself tonight. It's from their personal gardens," Sally informed with a grin knowing full well she had just dropped a bomb on me.

I choked, "No, I can't meet them. That's way too much pressure. What if they don't approve of me? Do they know my thoughts? Should I worship them when I see them or offer them a gift?" I panicked while continuing to fill my mouth with the otherworldly food.

"Ha, I knew that would get your attention. I can't get you up to speed here. I have to take you to Asgard to learn magic and how to fight from the very best! You don't have to bring any gifts unless you want something in exchange. Also, please don't worship them. They hate that. You would only embarrass yourself and them. They only require honesty and effort. Treat them like family, and you'll be fine," Sally briefed.

"My family and I constantly fight," I said, thinking of how that would look in Asgard.

Sally snapped her fingers and said, "Come on, Jamie, focus, treat them like your friends then."

I shook my head, wondering how I had gotten here. "What now?" I asked.

Sally smiled, "Let's get you dressed."

We stood, and the room started to shift again. When it stopped, I was staring at sheaths and weapons and magical tools and my arrowhead. "I need you to clear your mind and choose a few items that you are the most drawn to," Sally instructed, and I closed my eyes, letting go of my expectations. I walked around the tables and shelves of items. I stopped at a pair of semi-circled knives with dragons carved from metal as the handles. The sides of the blades were golden in color.

I picked them up, and the eyes of the dragons glowed. "These," I said while examining them.

"Good choice," Sally applauded, then walked to me and

wrapped a belt around my waist. "Attach them to this, then select your next items," I looked at the belt. It matched my outfit perfectly and had a pouch that fit the blades with a pocket for other items.

I began to walk again and stopped at my arrowhead. "This too," I told her, and Sally nodded. Then I stopped at a pocket watch. I picked it up and wondered why I would need it? I opened it, and it seemed rather normal, except it wasn't working. I went to put it down but couldn't bring myself to, so I slipped it into my pocket and moved on to select a little box and a slingshot. "I think that's it," I grinned, proud of my selection.

"Well done, Jamie. Now let's continue to the bridge." Sally smiled wildly.

"What bridge?" I asked suspiciously.

"The Rainbow Bridge to Asgard, or as we call it, Bifrost," Sally revealed.

"Where is that?" I studied her intensely.

"We will have to step into the mortal world but have to make haste to not waste time. When you see the bridge, run for it. It's constantly moving to avoid unwanted attention. Be fast. If I make it and you don't use the stone to come back here, and I will meet up with you another time." Sally instructed.

"OK, run for the bridge. Do I need to activate it somehow? I thought people just fell through rainbows?" I pondered.

"People who don't approach the rainbows with pure intentions can't catch them. Where do you think the pot of gold at the end of the rainbow came from? It's to test people. Everyone can tell rainbows have magic, so they always chase them, wanting gold or riches. Once you appreciate it for its beauty, you will find they are easier to catch," Sally explained to me.

"Huh, that's crazy. Who would've thought?" I said, amused that something as silly as a bit of money could distract the world from experiencing a priceless wonder for centuries.

"OK, ready yourself it's time on three, one, two, three!" Sally said and put her hand on my shoulder.

The mist swallowed me, and I got ready. As soon as I saw sunlight and the rainbow, I looked for the Bifrost. Once I had it in view, I sprinted for it. I wanted to stop and see where I was, but unable, I hurdled over rocks and fallen branches pushing as hard as I could and just when I thought I wouldn't catch it. The rainbow began to slow, and I pushed harder, forcing my feet to move faster. I ran between a couple trees and saw a ledge.

"Great," I thought to myself. I ran down a little incline and leaped for the rainbow. For a split second, I thought I was going to miss it. Then I was being pulled up faster than lightning, surrounded by all the colors. I was pulled past the clouds, the sky breached, and I soared through the gap.

Then slammed onto a beach. "Dang it, I got sand in my mouth." I cursed to myself while sweeping my face clean from the sand. "The last thing I want to do is meet a bunch of Goddesses and Gods with filth on me." Once I was satisfied that the sand was off of me, I looked around and took in the most beautiful scenery one could ever imagine. Large ships sat on crystal clear waters lining the beach as far as I could see. Souls stepped from them and embraced their loved ones already there who were waiting or returning to welcome them. They walked smiling and laughing into the forest, vanishing through golden archways. I looked over the forest and saw a city with architecture like nothing I had ever seen before, a mix of shining metals and earth intertwined. As if the ground itself had moved rock and wood to create the beautiful structures. Pillars of many metals stood proudly at the entrances. The rooftops made from aquamarine looked like the sky blessed it from above.

There was a flowered archway with a giant stone etched with runes standing next to it and a golden road leading into the forest near where I stood. It didn't glow or pulse like the ones the spirits entered. "This one must be for me." I approached it and stopped before entering and took a second look around. "Where is Sally?" I wondered. I took another step and passed through the gate into the woods. I took but a few more steps when the forest vanished. I found myself standing in front of two massive white Clydesdale's.

"Hey, you never called me," A voice said.

I moved to the side of the gigantic horse and saw the boy I had met sitting atop one of the beautiful steeds. "Oden?" I sputtered, confused.

"Yes. You never called why?" I looked into his piercing blue eyes and felt a bit guilty.

"I didn't have a reason to," I wavered.

"You didn't have a reason, or you didn't want to?" He asked again.

"Why does it matter?" I questioned, feeling like something was off.

"Ride with me," he offered, and extended a hand to the beautiful steed that didn't have a rider.

"To where?" I hesitated. I felt like I knew him, but not as Oden from the store. I couldn't place it though, I just knew something was wrong.

"I'll take you to where you need to go." He promised.

"Why should I trust you?" I felt uneasy and started to walk past him. He moved his horse to block me.

"Really, it's faster to ride," he hinted with a smile, and something just didn't sit right with me. I didn't feel threatened. In fact, I was sure I could trust him with my life, then I figured out what it was.

"I don't want to ride with you because you are lying to me about who you really are," I clamored firmly. Oden smiled, and light sparkled around him, and he changed into a young teen about thirteen or fourteen. His eyes changed from light blue to deep green, and his hair changed from short to long, and he wore an orange tunic with a rope necklace with a bone hanging from it.

"Very good detecting deception. That was your first test," He said.

"What's your true name?" I asked. "I am Hermodr. I was asked to bring you to where you need to be," he explained.

"Where is Sally?" I retorted, wondering why she wasn't leading me through Asgard.

"She is with the Valkyries preparing for your lessons there," Hermodr advised.

"How do I get onto the horse?" I asked, looking at its bareback and the beauty standing much taller than me.

Hermodr whistled, and the horse knelt. I swallowed and hopped onto its back. The horse stood with grace, and it followed behind Hermodr as we rode up a hill. At the top of it sat a little stone cottage next to some trees. "This is our first stop. You must face what's behind that door to get to where you need to go," Hermodr said cryptically.

"We didn't get very far, to begin with. I could've walked," I delayed, not amused that it was clear I had a series of challenges to follow.

"Go on. You don't want to keep these ones waiting. They are known to be patient," he urged with a smile that seemed phony.

"Fine," I protested and jumped to the ground. My heart started to pound in my chest as I approached the door. The cottage felt much larger now that I was standing next to it. I reached for the oddly shaped mushroom knob and twisted it. I stepped inside and looked around. A cauldron was hanging in a fireplace, a large wolf pelt was on the floor, and a table stood with three items on it. A frog, a spider, and a bat.

"Hello," I called out and walked to the cauldron. Something was bubbling in it. Something incomplete. "Am I supposed to add one of these to the cauldron?" I hollered and waited. No response.

A clock appeared on the wall and started ticking loudly. Tick, tock, tick, tock. "Alright, I get the message. What are you trying to make?" I bayed, not wanting to choose the wrong thing. The clock grew louder. I looked in the cauldron again, then at the table, and none of the creatures displayed on it felt right. "I'm not adding one of these," I yelled over the sound of the clock, and the clock grew even louder. I went to the potion again, and the sent was familiar, like clean laundry and a home-cooked meal. It smelt like home. I took in the rest of the house, and it felt bare like it needed love, as if it needed a personal touch to make it a home. I chewed off a fingernail and dropped it into the pot, and the clock stopped. Everything went silent. I started to worry I had made the wrong choice. I wondered what would happen to me if I chose incorrectly? Then I began to walk to the door, not wanting to play this game any longer. I opened the door and stepped through it right back into the same room as before. The only thing that had changed was this time two women were standing before me.

"You followed your instincts to find what you needed, then you doubted yourself," One of the women sputtered.

"I don't think she's ready, sister." The other women hissed.

"That's yet to be seen, sister," The first woman countered. The room started to spin, then I was sitting on a dragon overlooking a forest. My eyes zoomed in past the tops of the trees to the earth below, and I saw a man in a leather loincloth and fur boots stomping and dancing around a wicked fire. I was thrust from the dragon and flew towards the earth. I whistled like Hermodr had and landed on a white horse, and I fled from the man and the fire, coaxing the horse to run faster, faster. We ran through a vast forest around bends and over hills until we reached a cliff's edge. I climbed off the horse, but still, the pounding feet like a drum were beckoning me back. The sound felt like an ancient curse pulling at me, wanting me to slip into its trap. I leaped from the edge, and the dragon swooped down and caught me. We flew through a canyon until the stomping was gone, and a door opened in front of us, the dragon veered to miss it, and I tumbled from the dragons back into the cottage room.

"You see, sister, she did not hesitate when it mattered most. She did the only thing one can do when threatened with a generational curse, and because of it, her line won't suffer the consequences." The woman uttered.

"Wait, was that real? Are you actually putting me in danger? Did I just ride a dragon?" I questioned, getting fed up but also a bit excited.

"She is but a girl, of course. She fled from a strange man in a dark forest. I am not convinced," The second woman discouraged.

The room began to spin, and I shook my head and demanded, "Enough of this," but it was too late. I was sitting in a car, no I was driving a car. I tried to slam on the breaks, but the car went faster. Another vehicle was moving towards me in their own lane. The road was narrow, just two lanes, with deep ditches running along both sides of it. There was nowhere to go or turn. I tightened my grip on the steering wheel, knowing something terrible might happen. I checked the speedometer. It read ninety miles per hour! "Oh, no," I whimpered to myself, my stomach tied in knots. I tried tapping the break again, nothing. Just as the other car was but feet away, an old man on a bicycle rode right out in front of me!

I quickly looked to the opposite side of the road, and into the other vehicle needing to swerve. I saw the faces of two females, a woman, and her daughter next to her, both looking horrified. I instantly knew if I veered into their lane, I would kill them and me, and if I drove into the ditch, I would kill him and me. He was too close. That staying straight and killing him would be the least number of lives lost. So, I chose not to swerve. Still, not wanting to hurt anyone, I blasted the horn. The old man threw himself from the bike into the ditch, right as the other car sped past me, while I instantaneously hit the bike, sending it hurling through the air. I looked into the rear-view mirror and saw the other vehicle stopping to help him. Luckily, he was already on his feet, brushing himself off. "Wow, I must look like a real jerk," I deduced aloud as my heart was pounding. I looked forward again to find a giant crater opening on the road, and I fell into it and landed in the cottage.

"Was that really necessary?!" I rasped. The woman didn't speak, just pointed to the front door. I moved quickly to it to avoid another horrible situation. I found Hermodr sitting on his horse eating an apple.

"Back so soon? I figured you would want to live with the two sisters. In fact, I think they want a daughter of their own. You are a bit shifty. I'm sure you would fit right in," Hermodr teased, smiling.

"Ha-ha, very funny I am never going in there again!" I pledged as I mounted the horse needing to put distance between me and the sisters.

"That pleasant, huh? Well, the next stop will be a breeze for you then. Let's get a move on," Hermodr pushed. I let out a sigh and turned my horse to follow him.

I rode with Hermodr through a forest for about ten minutes and into an enchanting garden filled with exotic flowers, many of which I had never seen before. Their scents were intoxicating and breathtaking. We walked past some giant shrubs into a clearing with a large pool surrounded by four women on each side of it, all dressed in white hooded cloaks. Each holding swords in front of them, standing neatly like chess pieces on a game board. They stood motionless like statues staring into the water as we approached them. Then Hermodr stopped, and my horse came to a halt. "What do I do now?" I whispered to Hermodr.

"Why are you whispering? You know they can hear a fart from a mile away. It's kind of their thing," Hermodr bantered.

"Nice, Hermodr. Way to make things even more awkward," I rolled my eyes.

"My pleasure." He responded, and my horse knelt, and I slid off of it. I stood for a moment, and no one moved. I raised an eyebrow and turned to look at Hermodr. He shrugged his shoulders, and I rolled my eyes. I turned back around, and a woman was standing nose to nose with me. I jumped back, startled.

"Come on, does everyone here have to be so dramatic?" My heart pounded. I started to ask if it was some sort of introduction competition. Before I could open my mouth, the woman pointed at me, and I went flying over her head and crashed into the water.

I stood up and could hear Hermodr laughing. I wanted to tell him to stick it but stifled the urge, not wanting to be sent flying again. I looked around, and the women started to walk towards me, closing in on me. I wondered if I was supposed to fight them then a woman spoke, "lay. We will protect you, dear one." Her voice was inviting and warm, so I nodded and laid on my back to float my ears dipping below the surface. It was peaceful, and the waters smelt like roses and fresh rain. "Close your eyes," The woman instructed, and her voice wasn't muffled as I would expect. I closed my eyes, I felt safe and confident. Then, I felt my body rising from the waters. I heard the sounds of wind rushing, and the smell turned from roses to fresh snow and the burning of pine. I felt my body lower, and I was placed on my feet.

I opened my eyes, and I was standing between fire and ice. Both towered over me in their majesty and power. I could feel the energy of both pouring into my body, and it filled me with strength. My skin started to glow and pulse. "Choose one," I heard the same woman's voice in my head. It wasn't much of a decision. I already knew in my very core which one I belonged to. I turned to the fire and walked into it. It danced a sacred dance around me. It was playful, forgiving, and treacherous. I closed my eyes, embracing it all, the good and the bad. A wisp of flame entered into my chest, and I felt my heart open and burn with passion. Then I felt my body lowering again, and the smell of rain and roses filled my senses. I opened my eyes, and the women embraced me. "You are one of us, a Wotan Witch! Accepted by the sacred fire, your abilities now will begin unlocking. Use them with wisdom. You are free to roam anywhere in this kingdom, welcome sister," One of the women said.

"Thank you," I smiled not sure what it all meant. I looked at Hermodr, and he was smiling too. In fact, he looked proud.

Once I said my goodbyes, I walked to Hermodr, and he mentioned, "You must be something special the last thousand souls to enter the fire were burned into nothing." Hermodr eyeballed me as if he had something more to say. I waited, then he grinned wickedly, and said, "let's go meet my Dad. He's just lo." Hermodr fumbled on his words.

"He just what?" I asked surprised he fumbled when it was obvious there was going to be some sort of punch line.

"I mean, he is going to love you." Hermodr corrected himself.

I was curious about what he was going to say before he caught himself, and I didn't trust his smile anymore, but deep down, I trusted he wouldn't harm me, so I asked, "Who's your Dad?"

"Odin," Hermodr said plainly, and my horse knelt.

"Wait, I know Balder, Thor, Vidarr, and Vali are Odin's sons. Why haven't I heard of you?" I asked politely, not meaning to sound disrespectful.

"Believe it or not, I am. I'm lesser known among earthly dwellers, though Frigga is my mother and Odin, my father. I am just less dramatic than my siblings. Even as such, my deeds have tilted me as a great hero. However, I don't feel the need to seek attention. I find quieter ways of helping," Hermodr clarified.

"You think you're less dramatic?" I teased, laughing while riding next to him.

"Are you making fun of me? Huh, and here I thought you would be more worried about meeting Odin?" Hermodr mused.

"You said, he's going to love me. So, what should I be worried about?" I kidded. This place felt like home, and I realized I was nervous at times but not afraid.

"I heard about your attack. Have you fully healed?" Hermodr asked, and I thought I heard a bit of worry and anger in his voice.

"How did you hear about that all the way from here?" I pondered, curious about how he kept knowing little details about my life. Like the boy Oden I had met, and that I never called him, now this?

"I like to peek at mortals to see what sorts of mischiefs they get themselves into," Hermodr brushed it off, but his tone wasn't convincing enough to completely sell it.

"All mortals? Or just me?" I dared to ask. He looked at me, and I could tell he was withholding something, and it looked like it was hurting him to do so. Not wanting to cause him pain, I changed the topic. "Never mind, I am healed, thanks for asking. So, Hermodr, do you live with Odin and Frigga or with someone else?" I wondered if the children of Gods still needed to be raised like earthly kids. I looked at all the elaborate homes lining the streets we were riding on.

"I haven't lived with my parents for a thousand years, and I'm currently living alone. Catch," he tossed me an apple. "You need to keep yourself nourished," he instructed, and I gave him a nod and ate my apple. We arrived at a tall castle with giant silver and golden pillars. The pillars had carvings of battles and births, and I could see it told a story of the Gods, their families, and their deeds. It was beautiful to behold. I walked with Hermodr upstairs made of stone and noticed little fossils in them. The doors stood about six stories high, made from giant logs and had runes carved into them. "Are you ready?" Hermodr asked kindly.

"Does it matter? We have come this far. I can't turn back now." I took a deep breath, and Hermodr touched a series of runes on the door, and they opened.

We stepped into a giant hall with a large open fireplace burning in the center of it. The fire burned blue, but the heat was more comforting than intense. Many doors lined the room. A large, spiraled staircase at the back of the room was carved from bone and led endlessly upwards to other levels. There was a series of pictures adorning the walls in elaborate frames and sculptures placed perfectly throughout. The dragon sculpture especially caught my attention. It was beautifully carved and looked like the dragon that I had ridden. "This place is amazing. I love the dragon," I complimented.

"I knew that was going to be your favorite piece," Hermodr commented. Then a door swung open, and Sally busted through it and stormed towards us.

"Hi Jamie, I need you to go to the staircase and touch its railing. It will take you to a room. There will be a bath, get cleaned up, and put on the dress on the bed. I'll be up to get you shortly," She instructed me while glaring at Hermodr.

"What's going on?" I asked the tension between the two was obvious.

"Nothing dear, I heard you had an eventful day. I hope Hermodr was well mannered," Sally snarled.

"He was. Why wouldn't he be?" I pushed, looking at the two of them, eyeballing each other.

"I was just making sure," Sally reassured me through gritted teeth.

"What's wrong? Where have you been?" I demanded.

"I was all tied up, so I couldn't meet you. Just go get dressed, please I need to speak to Hermodr alone." She mumbled at me, and I gasped and took off walking towards the stairs. Sally began talking to Hermodr in a low voice once

I had reached the fireplace. I couldn't make out what was being said, just that the tone was serious, and I really wanted to know why. I thought of how the Wotan witches at the pool had said I was one of them. Then how Hermodr had said, they could hear a fart from a mile away. "I wonder?" I thought and closed my eyes, focusing on my hearing. I felt a slight popping in my ears then I could hear everything. This place was bustling with people. I could hear the clanking of dishes, laughter, footsteps. I focused on Sally and Hermodr, making sure to not look back. It worked; I could listen to them.

"I had to tie you up. I wanted to spend time with her," Hermodr told Sally.

"You know what you did is forbidden! You could've jeopardized everything, you stupid fool!" Sally growled.

"Your just mad because I caught you off guard," Hermodr rebutted.

"Want to try again?" Sally challenged.

"You know she entered the fire and is now a full Wotan Witch," Hermodr boasted.

"Yes, I have been informed. I am proud that she passed all the tests. She did beautifully. Wait. Why did you mention that?" Sally paused, concerned.

"I think she has figured out how to hear us," Hermodr guessed, almost laughing, and I realized I had stopped. I quickly started walking again, keeping my eyes locked on the stairs.

"Great, thanks a lot, and change out of that ridiculous glamor." I heard Sally mumble.

"My pleasure, wait, what?" Hermodr sounded confused. I heard a groan. I turned to see Hermodr rubbing his cheek, looking bewildered, then I placed my hand on the stair railing, and everyone vanished.

Chapter Fourteen, The Choice

The mist cleared, and a new room came into view. "My room," I spoke aloud. There was a tall bed with a plain-looking green dress atop it and matching shoes on the floor. A vanity with a small chair and large mirror was placed near a bathtub. A dresser stood opposite me next to a couple large windows. I walked to them and looked out. I could see all of Asgard to the ocean. "Beautiful," I gasped and etched a love heart on the window. I walked to the bath, and the smell of sweet perfumes emanated from it. I undressed and hopped in the water, and it felt like silk against my skin. I relaxed fully into it and let my head slip under the surface and blew bubbles with my mouth.

I soaked for as long as I could and only got out once I had to relieve myself. I put on my dress and moved to the vanity. Atop it was a hairbrush. I started to comb through the tangles in my hair. I paused when Sally walked into the room with another woman. She was beautiful and slender, dressed immaculately, and moved with grace. "This is Phoebe. She is going to get you ready," Sally introduced us.

"Nice to meet you," I greeted her politely, and Phoebe walked over to me and pulled a comb from her pocket.

"Nice to meet you too. This won't hurt a bit." Phoebe told me. She ran the comb through my hair once, and it was instantly dried and smooth. Then, little strands started to lift, twist, and fold until a series of braids and curls had formed. The braids wrapped around behind my head neatly, and the ringlets rested on my shoulders.

"Wow, I wish I could do this at home," I remarked, pleased with how beautiful it was. After my hair was finished moving, Phoebe placed little flowers neatly into my braids. When she was done, I marveled at her work and felt prettier than I ever had before.

"Now, let's see that dress," Phoebe requested. I stood and turned to face her. She stared at it for a moment, lost in concentration. Then she slipped her hair behind her ears, and they had little points at the tops of them. She was stunning herself.

"You're really beautiful," I complimented.

"I know," she smiled and took out a sewing needle and some green thread from her pocket. Phoebe then started to sow into my sleeve, and the thread started weaving in and out rapidly. The dress began to change around me. The lower half fanned out, and the top lowered around my shoulders while the waist came inwards. Then vines and flowers began to appear on my dress, and I was in awe of her magic.

"You are really talented. Do you work here often?" I asked.

"Not in the sense you are thinking of. The Goddesses give me golden apples in exchange for my services. They are precious to my people as we are unable to grow them where I'm from. I come and go as I please. It is a fair trade, so we are equals in our views," Phoebe explained. I stood silent while the artist did her work. When the needle stopped, Phoebe announced, "OK, I am finished with your dress, now let's see your shoes."

I slipped my shoes on, and Phoebe sowed into them, turning them into beaded pieces of art with golden vines leading from my toes upwards until they wrapped around my legs. They were also extremely comfortable, "I could sleep in them. Which I always thought was impossible with pretty things. I promise to never get these dirty," I complemented while admiring them.

Phoebe let out a chuckle, "My clothes never get dirty, fade, burn or tear. So, you can do what you please in them." She stepped back and her crystal clear eyes took me in.

"She looks perfect. Thank you, Phoebe." Sally said graciously.

"You are welcome. May the wind be at your back until we meet again," Phoebe gave a single nod and touched the railing leaving before I got the chance to thank her.

"I want to see," I begged Sally, only able to reflect on half of me in the vanity mirror.

"Just touch the mirror, and it will extend," Sally instructed, and I did the table vanished, and the mirror now stood at full length. I cupped my hands over my mouth and giggled at my beauty and felt confident in my appearance. For the first time ever, and there was freedom to it. My amulet matched the colors of the flowers on my gown. Not a hair was out of place.

"Alright, stop fawning over yourself, and let's get going. Unless you want to keep all of the Aesir waiting?" Sally mocked at me as I swayed my dress back and forth.

"Wait, all of the Aesir? Hermodr said I'd only be meeting

his Dad?" My confidence vanished, knowing full well that meant all the Gods and Goddesses and peoples of Asgard.

"Well, a couple might have other things to do, but yes, the majority will be there," Sally denoted.

"Why?!" I whimpered, terrified wanting to wish myself into a corner.

"Because you are a full Wotan Witch now, something that wasn't supposed to have happened until after this lifetime. A new Wotan Witch is only selected if one of the witches dies a final death. It's been thousands of years since Asgard has had a full thirteen. Hundreds of thousands have tried to fill the role in the past, and all have perished in the fire or the ice. That is why I was so cross with Hermodr. He put you in danger!" Sally said fiercely.

It dawned on me that Hermodr had mentioned people died in the ritual. "Wait, I thought he was joking about everyone who died in there because the ritual was so easy! I thought I could trust him! I felt a sort of big brother bond with him, and he betrayed me?!" I ranted, furious, and started to storm towards the staircase so I could hunt him down and beat the life out of him.

"Wait!" Sally jumped in my way. "I shouldn't say this, but in his defense, you can trust him. After you met with the two sisters. He was beyond certain you were the one the fire and ice were waiting for. The Two Sister laid out a test you were meant to take and were expected to fail. Then you would go on to a battle test and begin training. Since you didn't fail, he took you to the sacred waters. He wouldn't have brought you there if he didn't believe in you."

"I don't care if he believed in me! I blindly followed him trusting my instincts. They failed me too! How dare he assume just because he peeks in on me from time to time that he has the right to make that sort of decision on my behalf? I don't know what this title means. I'm not ready for anything so important that it claimed thousands of lives!" I growled, furious, and tried to push past her. She held me back, then I felt a pain in my neck, so I tilted my head to the side and popped it. I felt blood racing through my arms, and I broke free from Sally's grip with ease.

"Ouch! Jamie, you need to get yourself under control now!" Sally demanded, jumping in my way again but I shoved her aside, and she crashed into the wall. I barely noticed what I had done. I was lost in anger, consumed by it.

Sally burst forward, then slapped me, and I snapped out of it. "What happened? Did I hurt you? I'm so sorry!" I apologized in shock and horror. Sally began chanting, and I could see her shoulder start to mend.

"You have many powers now. Learning to control them is going to take president. Odin is going to have a serious conversation with you tonight. So, to keep you from losing control downstairs at the party, I think I need to tell you something about Hermodr. Sit." Sally pointed, and a beautiful bench manifested in the room.

"What about Hermodr?" I asked as calmly as possible, and for a moment, Sally looked scared of me. I felt guilty for that and buried my rage. "I am really sorry I hurt you. It wasn't my intention at all," I atoned softly.

"It's alright. I've healed already," Sally forgave me and showed me her shoulder. "I am not supposed to say this as it may interfere with your current life's journey, but I think I have to. At least I will tell you what bits I can, and Odin will have to go over everything else with you." Sally whispered.

"I don't want to get you into trouble," I said, concerned for her.

"Just don't repeat what I say. Agreed?" Sally proposed, and I accepted her offer. "You were right to feel a bond with Hermodr." Sally paused and looked around, making sure we were alone. So, I whispered to her, "Is he my cousin, brother, a best friend here, work colleague, don't tell me he is my boss?" Sally shushed me then told me to concentrate my hearing on her. I shut my eyes, and my ears popped, and I could hear her hair moving and her muscles tightening as she walked to me. "I hear you," I said in a soft voice.

"Hermodr was, and sort of is, your spouse," Sally's voice echoed in my head.

"You didn't have to yell!" I snapped, then swallowed, and my ears adjusted back to normal again.

"I didn't. I barely whispered it.

"Hermodr is my spouse? That's gross! I'm eleven. I can't have a, you know what, and even if I did, I'm pretty sure I wouldn't let him make decisions for me!" I said as softly as I could muster.

"It is true you wouldn't, and of course, there wouldn't be anything romantic until you returned here. Earthly partners are temporary unless a pair decides to go together, but most don't risk it because it complicates things." Sally explained.

"I'm still going to let him know I'm not happy about him putting me in harm's way without my consent. I'll keep everything else a secret as promised." I reassured Sally.

"I wouldn't expect anything less from you in any lifetime," Sally chuckled.

"Am I the same person in each lifetime?" I asked

curiously.

"No, our circumstances change us each time. However, your core traits seem too always be there. In every life, you choose compassion over cruelty. You are always loyal, even at your own expense, and you are always brave when it comes to protecting others, but not always when it comes to yourself. If I can teach you one thing, it would be for you to know that you are worthy of your own love and protection too." Sally leaned over and kissed me on the head. I heard a raven's caw, and Sally stood. "It's time." She motioned, and we walked to the staircase and touched the railing.

We settled in front of a pair of giant double doors, and I reached for its troll face knob. "Wait," Sally said, and I froze. "Wait for the signal. Everyone here is obsessed with their elaborate introductions. It's because we all know each other, and it takes traveling to make new acquaintances. We rarely get the opportunity to introduce ourselves. So, expect a lot of creative introductions tonight," Sally warned. She snapped and started to shimmer. Then she was dressed in a beautiful, tight orange gown with gray lace just below her chest. It had one long sleeve with lace and jewels swirling down its fabric. Her hair was half pulled up, the other half flowing with curls. A lace and Ammonite fossil hairpin was placed perfectly in the folds of her hair. "I wanted to match you tonight," Sally winked at me.

A single raven cawed, and the doors opened, just as a huge murder of ravens went swarming past us into the great room then spiraled upwards, leaving through various portals in the beautiful turquoise ceiling. A horn bellowed, and a booming voice filled the room and announced, "As every sky must have its stars, as every warrior has their scars, every beginning has its end before it can begin again. We have waited thousands of years, long past the shedding of our tears. The twelve Wotan Witches are now complete as Jamie makes them whole as number thirteen." The man thrust his hand at me, and I looked in wonder at all the beautiful people and creatures standing in front of me, expanding for what looked to be miles, and I felt big and small at the same time. Everyone raised their hands to their hearts as if they were cupping them. I didn't know what to do, so I curtsied like I had been taught during the summers I had spent in etiquette school.

The audience started to eyeball each other with looks of confusion, I figured I must have done it wrong, and I could feel myself blush. Sally took my hand, and we walked down a couple steps onto the main floor, and twelve women

288

dressed immaculately walked to me. The same twelve that had been at the pool. They stood in front of me, and I ever so slightly whispered to them. "Am I supposed to do something? Why are they all still staring at me?" One of the women stepped forward, and I popped my ears. "Announce we will now perform the witch's dance. Our magic will make sure you don't falter," The woman instructed. I nodded and swallowed my embarrassment and focused on my voice. Then as loudly as I could, I announced. "WE WILL NOW PERFORM THE WITCH'S DANCE," my voice carried on magic all the way to the end of the hall and every being heard.

The sea of people took a step back, making room, and my right arm, lifted on its own just in time to catch a sword. Then everyone started to hum, and I turned to face the people standing behind me. I knelt and thrust the blade into the ground. The humming began to pulse, and I could feel my magic awaken. I leaped from my location onto the sword's hilt, then back rolled off it. Landing in a kneeling position, I kept my head down then a drum started to beat. I tossed my hair back and rose with my claws out while I hissed furiously with my mouth. I swooped my leg around me and turned to face the witches twelve. We locked hands and thrust them side to side while letting our bodies follow as a woman began singing from behind, her tune wild, her song otherworldly. The thirteen of us unlinked and linked our hands again, we rolled our heads, and the sacred fire sparked from within. The fire from us moved into the center of our circle. We released our hands and danced around it wild and spiritual. I felt my magic rising within me, and I stopped. I opened my hands at my sides, let my head fall back. I rose from the floor. I felt energy resounding through all of my pours. The woman finished her song, then the drumming faded, and when the humming slowed, I drifted back to where I started. Then the crowd roared with excitement.

The twelve Wotan Witches circled me, and one whispered, "we support whatever you decide. We have waited thousands of years for you. A few more will not offend us." When she was done, I looked at her.

"What decision?" I asked. The women parted, and a man about my father's age, tall in stature, muscular with long blond hair with one ice-blue eye and a golden eye patch over the other, approached me. He had two large Ravens perched on his shoulders. His gaze locked onto mine, and the next thing I knew, I was sitting in an armchair in an endless library with Odin seated across from me and a fireplace was crackling at to our side.

"Hello Jamie, I am Odin. You are in my library. All my sacred knowledge is stored in these books. Choose one. It is a gift," Odin said and gestured with his hand towards his sea of books. I gaped at them and felt like nothing more than a blip in a universe.

"Oh, nice to meet you. Thank you. How much time do I have? This could take me forever," I gasped, overwhelmed but pleased.

"Yes, time, you have as long as you wish." He noted in a voice that was soft but powerful.

"Is this all just your knowledge, or is it every book ever written in every world?" I asked as I stood and started looking.

"My dear, this is just my wisdom. I have another library with every book ever written," Odin had a sparkle in his eye as if he were amused at my wonder.

"Have you read all of them? I couldn't imagine doing that. I read one book from the sixties on meditation, and I wanted to gag at all the nasty stuff written in it." I gabbed, then straightened up, remembering who I was talking to. "Oh, sorry, I shouldn't have said that to you," I quickly apologized, and he laughed.

"I think I know which one you're talking about." He snapped his fingers, and a book appeared in them. "Is this it?" He asked, amused. I walked to him and looked at it and blushed.

"Yes, that is it," I acknowledged hesitantly, wishing I would've kept my mouth quiet.

"Ha-ha, it is an amusing piece of work," He chuckled, then in a poof, it was gone. I started to walk down a long hall, and I looked at Odin. He stood and walked next to me.

"What's on your mind, Jamie?" He questioned while looking at me inquisitively.

"What am I supposed to do? Is finding this book some sort of test? It isn't a secret that you are known to be the God of wisdom, and I've read some of what you went through to gain that knowledge. I mean, I literally have all the knowledge in the universe in front of me, and I have to choose one book. I don't mean to sound ungrateful. I am. This is the best gift anyone has ever offered me, but at the same time. You have to know how tempting it is to want to read more of them, if not somehow all of them," I looked at him, hoping he understood what I meant and didn't take offense.

"Very good, Jamie. That is the purpose of this. No, it's

not a test. It's about making hard choices and the struggle to do so. Like the book, I have another other hard decision for you to make. You can choose to stay and begin your training with the Wotan Witches, change into your true form, and resume your true life here. However, that would mean leaving your family and friends on earth behind. Or you can choose to stay in your current life and return after fully living it. I want you to consider that if you decide to return to earth, you, your family, and your friends will all eventually grow apart in time as nothing in earthly life is permanent. However, If you choose to stay. You will not gain the wisdom your current life offers, and you will not experience the journeys you were intended to take. I only offer this because your end goal is achieved. I would nurture bringing you here now and to have you stay. To protect you from the hardships you will face in earthly life. However, in doing that, I would rob the earth of your protection and kindness, and it would greatly alter many lives. Had you not entered the pool. This would have been a different meeting." Odin finished with a look of compassion written on his face.

I thought about what he had just offered, and my heart ached. I wanted so badly to be done with the beatings at home, the pain, the pressure of living up to my parent's expectations of me, and how soul-crushing it is. I wanted to be done with the unfairness, betrayals, and toil that is life. Yet, I don't want to leave my sibling behind or my friends to suffer alone without me. I didn't want to leave my parents to mourn the loss of a child. Despite it all, I love them. This place, though. It feels like home, and I ached to stay. I loved that it was full of beauty, adventure, security, and magic.

"How does one go back to the way things were after gaining this kind of knowledge?" I asked Odin.

He looked at me and said softly, "You learn to hide it, and earth has a way of making you forget from moment to moment as well."

I sniffled, trying to hold back tears, thinking I would never see Waddles again or Onacona. We kept walking and walking, and I kept bouncing back and forth between the two choices. "Do I have to decide now?" I asked and looked up into Odin's face.

"You know in your heart what you are going to do. Delay in speaking it will only cause you to needlessly suffer longer. You can take time to consider it, needless to say, or you can say your truth now and move forward with your decision and have peace in your heart," Odin looked at me without judgment. I knew his words were true, and I knew he would accept my decision without lecturing me, no matter what It was.

I mustered up some courage, and in the most absolute tone I could manage, I replied, "I've decided to go back and live out my life as I was meant to, despite it all. I hate saying it. I know things would be better here, but I don't have it in me to abandon the people I love and care about." As soon as I finished, I felt sickened by it.

Odin put his hand on my shoulder and softly said, "You will always have a home here, and no matter how deep life cuts you. How you bleed and how you need to heal. You never have to second guess this. It is my oath to you." I let the tears stream down my face. No one had ever offered me this kind of love and compassion before, and it moved me. I wrapped my arms around him. He reached down and collected me with his giant hands and gave me a healing hug that I so desperately needed.

After he set me back down, he gave me a gentle pat on the shoulder. I turned to the bookcase, and a book with a pair of dragons on it caught my attention. I pulled it from the shelf and announced, "this is the one."

He looked at it and responded, "wise decision, I will have it delivered to your room. It is time for you to go back out and enjoy your celebration." I gave Odin another quick hug. Then he gave a single nod, and I was back at the party in the very same spot surrounded by the very same people. The only thing different was Odin wasn't standing in front of me anymore.

"You decided wisely, and we honor you for that," One of the Witches said.

"Thank you, it wasn't easy. What are your names? You know me, but if we are all a pack, I think I should know yours as well." I asked.

"We dear are not a pack. We are your coven, and I am Afridh." Afridh said. Then the another stepped up to me. "I am Ella," she nodded, then they each took turns. Next was Agatha, then Agnes, Adliza, Abela, Acilia, Ebba, Agata, Edela, Etta, and Adelixa.

"It's a pleasure to meet all of you," I greeted kindly, trying to store all those names in my head. "So, what now?" I asked.

"Now, you eat, dance, and walk proudly amongst your peers, for you have earned your place amongst us all," Abela stated.

I looked around at all the beautiful adults. "I don't feel like I did anything. I don't know why the fire chose me?" I felt touched by her kind words but majorly out of place.

"That's simply because you don't remember," Etta said.

Then Agata spoke, "Do you remember when you saw yourself the night you rose in the circle cast with your friends, in the hollow house?"

I thought for a moment, then the memory of the night in the abandoned house popped into my mind and my journey to my higher self. "Yes, I do." I nodded, and I pictured that woman standing proudly amongst all these beautiful beings. "She would fit right in here," I mentioned, remembering how whole I'd felt in her presence.

"You felt complete when you were with her, did you not?" Agata questioned.

"I did. I didn't want to leave because it was so, I was so, whole. When I was with her." I said, unable to fully explain the immense peace I had felt.

"She is you. You traveled deep inside yourself that eve and Eisa reached out and touched you. You felt fulfilled because you are the final piece. You need not suffer any more lives or deaths beyond this. You have effectuated thousands of journeys for wisdom and experience. All you need is within you. This is the reason why the fire chose you. All things burn within you. So yes, your place is here, and your toil is fleeting as is a single breath." Agata's kindness wrapped around me like a blanket.

"So, Eisa and I make a whole, and she is in me, so she is experiencing all of this too, so I'm not stealing her party, right?" I rambled, not wanting to be a glory hog.

"No dear, you are one with Eisa," Agnes said smiling.

"Well then, let's go enjoy our party. This is going to break my head. How did my Grandpa know to call me Eisa? The clever old sap." I sputtered on, trying to wrap my head around it. While my coven and I walked proudly into the crowd.

We took about three steps, then Loki appeared in front of me in a poof while riding an Ogre to introduce himself as it rained glitter. After chatting for a moment. We walked about two more steps, and a man jumped from the ceiling, landing right in front of us, introducing himself as Magni, son of Thor. A few more steps and a tidal wave came crashing for us, but the water turned to snow before impact, and a Goddess named Irpa introduced herself. Gesture after Gesture. Then a boy about my age approached me and asked if I wanted food. I said "yes," and he handed me an apple, then I kicked him in the shin, thinking it was Hermodr, it was not. I apologized profusely, and he graciously accepted my apology but quickly exited.

After hours of introductions and I had more than apples for food. The ceiling changed from sunlight to starlight, and a male vocalist began singing softly. I stood silently and watched as the masses toke up partners and began to slow dance. I told my coven that I wanted to go outside and headed to the balcony to sit and rest my feet for a while. They nodded then moved to the dance floor with their partners. Once I exited, I looked at the balcony to find a spot to settle down in. The landing extended the full length of the hall with multiple doors so people could access it. I spotted a bench to my left and made my way to it and sat.

I took in a deep breath and closed my eyes as a breeze surrounded me. It was soft and comforting. It smelt nice, like fresh snow had just fallen. I began thinking of my friends and wondered how they were doing and what they were up to, and if their realms pulled at them like this one beckons me. I felt safe here, appreciated, and I imagined this was what it is supposed to feel like at home. The truth is, at home, I constantly worry and fear that I will upset my parents somehow and get a beating or yelled at or have a random item thrown at me. "Did I make the right decision to go back?" I wondered. Either way, I had made my choice, and I had to honor it. I began to watch the starlight dance on the ocean off in the distance, and one star in particular shown extra brightly. After a while, the sound of gentle footsteps coming from behind me captured my curiosity.

I turned to look, and a stunning woman about my mother's age approached me. She wore a long metallic white dress with a golden belt adorned with wings, her eyes and hair were the color of the sun, and she moved with courtliness. Everything on her seemed to match. She smiled at me, and I could feel love pouring from her. "May I?" She asked and pointed to the seat next to me.

"Of course," I answered with a nod and tried not to stare.

"It's a wonderful night, is it not?" She reflected.

I nodded. "Probably the best I've ever experienced," I commented softly.

"This is one of my favorite places to look out over Asgard. Though I normally sit there." The lady pointed, and I looked further down the balcony, and a beautiful throne sat with rams carved on the sides on its base and cats at the top. I swallowed.

"Are you Frigga?" I asked, unsure how I should behave around the queen goddess of Asgard.

"I am. I wanted to formally meet you. I know you have

learned much tonight, and you are exhausted. So, I will not keep you for but a moment. However, I do wish to give you a gift for your journey in claiming the keys, so listen closely." Frigga instructed, then her eyes began glowing. "Before you, a path will unfold, and through darkness and shadows you must go, until you reach a pillar glowing with purple light, there, you will be greeted with hardship and strife. Many you'll need to keep it at bay, as you alone go the rest of the way," Frigga's eyes dimmed and returned to normal, and she put her hand on my shoulder. "Remember to fight fearing not death, for this is where you will return in the end," she finished, then stood up to go back to the party.

I reached out gently, taking her wrist in my hands. "Wait," I pled.

"Yes?" Frigga answered and sat back down. I didn't know if it was the love, I was feeling from her or if she had persuaded me with magic, but I had to say what I was feeling to her.

"At my home on earth, whenever things are going good. I am always nervous, waiting for the other shoe to drop because I know it won't last, and nothing is worse than being caught off guard, which still happens a lot. So, I never fully get to trust, and I never get to fully relax. I don't think anyone should have to feel that way. Especially in a place that is supposed to be safe. So, will you please tell Hermodr I forgive him? I don't like that he tricked me into completing my journey before I was meant to and that I had to make the decision I had to make because of it. Still, if he didn't do what he did, I wouldn't be at this party, and I wouldn't be talking to you now, and I wouldn't have been able to feel all of this. So, I forgive him and, on some level, am grateful. I would tell him myself, but I have a feeling he's been hiding from me," I expressed sincerely, and I meant it.

Frigga gave me a small smile of appreciation, but there was a look of sadness on her face. She took my hands in hers. "Thank you for saying that. He will appreciate it, as for the other. I mustn't interfere. However, I will arrange with Sally for you to come here more often, to train," Frigga determined kindly and, while giving me a sly look, then stood.

"I wouldn't ask you to interfere. Please don't think I would. I know better." I blurted out before she could go, worried she thought I implied that.

"I only spoke aloud only to remind myself," Frigga reassured me, then gave me another sly look and continued, "It was lovely to meet you, Jamie. I must return to the celebration now. Odin wishes to dance," She walked around me and headed back into the celebration. I thought to myself a moment longer. Then I, too, stood to rejoin the party. Once inside, I studied the scenery and people around me. I wanted to always remember this all of it.

I noticed two people walking towards me out of the corner of my eye, and I thought to myself, "Great, I wonder how this introduction is going to play out?" I turned my head slightly to try to sneak a better look, and I realized it was the two sisters. "Oh boy! I know how this introduction is going to go. I'm going to get thrown from a dragon or die in a car wreck," I panicked and turned to make my escape and ran straight into Hermodr.

"Care to dance?" He asked, a little too smug for my taste.

"No, I don't dance," I tried to walk past him and he shifted.

He looked over my shoulder towards the two sisters, then back at me, "OK, as you wish," he said and started to turn. I could hear them approaching.

"Wait," I moaned with irritation and grabbed him by the arm. He shifted to stand next to me and looked at me, grinning, and I rolled my eyes. He stuck out his elbow, and I took it, and we moved near others who were dancing. The music felt too slow all of a sudden, and then Hermodr turned to face me. He placed his hand on my back. I rolled my eyes again, then, just as we were about to start dancing, a drum started echoing rapidly. Then some kind of wind instrument joined in with a tune matching it, and the vocalist started singing a shanty. I stepped back and busted out into a funky dance with the music shaking my butt and wiggling my shoulders. Hermodr watched me with a look of shock and horror strewn across his face. Then I knew. I had won.

After a couple more, fast songs, and satisfied that I had completely humiliated Hermodr. I decided I was done for the night. I was beyond exhausted, so I thanked Hermodr for the dances. Then I made my way back to the staircase and put my hand on the rail, which returned me to my room. I plopped down on my bed. My dress was so comfortable that I didn't bother taking it off. Though a nightgown was laid out at the foot of my bed. My bed felt how I imagined laying on clouds would feel if I could lay on them, and before I could yawn, I fell asleep.

Chapter Fifteen, Myth and Magic

I lunged from my bed, barely landing on my feet, startled by a trumpet blasting next to my head. "What the! Why!?" I cursed, angry and confused. Sally was sitting at the foot of my bed.

"I thought this is how you earth-dwellers like to be awakened on training days.

"No! It is definitely not! The only people who wake up to that horrible sound are the ones that sign up to!" I snarled while trying to put my heart back in my chest.

"Well, it seems to be effective anyhow. Now get dressed and meet me down in the dining hall," Sally instructed.

"Where's the dining hall?" I asked. When you enter the great hall, just take the fourth door to the left.

"Fourth door to the left, gotcha," I replied.

"Your clothes for today are just over there." Sally pointed

to a lounge under a window that wasn't previously there. I nodded, and she left.

I went to the sofa and lifted a dress from the top of the pile. "Ewe, what the heck is this?" I scrutinized while looking at a frumpy dress that resembled my grandmother's moo moo. "Ugh," I groaned, then slipped off my pretty dress from the night before and marveled at how there wasn't a wrinkle or crease on it. Nor the smell of body odor. Then I slipped on the garment and lifted the next. "This one I can live with," I thought as I looked at the blue-green hooded cloak. I put it on and then looked at the bench. "Oh, this is nasty. I'm not wearing this!" I nearly gagged as I gaped at a skull hat. "I wonder what type of poor beast you were," I muttered and then poked it and shrunk back. I turned, leaving it where it was, and headed to the spiral staircase.

I found the hall and sat next to Sally. She was waiting for me chewing on an apple. Then a plate appeared in front of me with two apples on it. "OK, I have to ask. I love apples and all, and these ones are especially delicious, but why is everyone and everything here feeding me apples?" I put one in my mouth and chewed.

"They are the sacred fruit from Idunn's garden. They give us eternal life, heal our wounds, nourish our magic, among many other things. They are sacred in almost every tradition," Sally explained.

"I spat mine out. "I don't want to live forever. Not until I come here for good, at least," I protested as I pictured myself as a vampire watching all my children and children's children fade away.

"Don't be silly, your mortal. They keep you alive while you're in an immortal realm, and you don't push out the sacred food! You need to eat it all. It's a gift," Sally insisted, and I looked at the chunks on my plate and cringed. "You do know when you slice an apple through the midpoint between the bottom and the top, it reveals a star hidden in it? Apples are powerful magic all in themselves," She chatted.

"That's neat when I'm done. Do I get to learn how to battle monsters or what now?" I inquired, curious about how the day would go.

"No, monster battles today, but that does remind me," Sally mentioned, then paused and snapped, and the giant skull hat materialized on my head.

"Gross! I am not walking around with dead things on my head!" I protested as I tore it off, then tossed it onto the table. I stood up and walked towards the door. "So, where are we going?" I probed. Today you start with learning rune basics with the Wotan witches," Sally answered.

"That sounds so great," I enthused and quickened my stride. I knew most of the runes already from books I had read. Learning to do magic with them was one of my dreams. I had never had anyone who could teach me before. Once we got outside, two horses stood waiting, and I mounted mine. We road through the streets of Asgard, and I took in the hustle and bustle of the city. Beautiful people eating and sipping drinks at tables along the route. They played games and sat reading books. I overheard bits and pieces of what was being said. It was wonderful, tales about adventures past and adventures yet to come, of romance and heartache, trials, and triumphs. "You know Sally, the people here aren't all that different from the ones on earth, at least not in personality. Except for the ones walking around naked. I've never seen that on earth," I mentioned.

"Well, we are, and we aren't. You'll learn as you get to know the place better. After we cleared the streets, we headed into some woods then we raced the horses through deer paths until we reached the edge of a large circle made of stone and bones.

"This is where I leave you. Enjoy," Sally quipped.

"Wait, alone? I thought I would be learning with the

Wotan Witches today?" I gave her a confused look.

Sally hopped off her horse. "Your right. There isn't anyone here? We better look around," Sally confounded and motioned for me to join her. So, I hopped down.

"Wouldn't it be quicker to look for them on horse?" Before I could say "Back," Sally snapped her fingers, and the horrible skull was on my head, then she shoved me into the circle.

I stumbled, then caught myself, and twelve women burst into laughter. I looked at them and around at the cabin-style hut that was as big as a barn. It seemed cozy and welcoming, with a cauldron brewing in the corner next to a stone fireplace. "Ella, it looks like you owe Sally the tongue of a paralimore," Adelixa said.

"Welcome Jamie, this is our sacred space. Only Wotan witched may enter here," Abela greeted me.

"Thank you. I am really excited to be here," I responded and removed the skull from my head, and they all started laughing again. "OK, what's going on?" I pressed, feeling like the tail end of a joke.

"In every form, you have never liked to wear the symbol of your power. Ella wagered Sally that she wouldn't be able to wheedle you through the circle door with it on your head.

Ella muddled up. Now she has to produce the tongue of a paralimore," Agnes explained.

"I have two questions. Why was that horrible thing before it became my helmet? My symbol of power? Also, since I don't have a thesaurus with me, is there a way I get one or twenty? So, I can better understand words like Wheedle, paralimore, and muddle?" I asked as politely as possible.

Acilia answered. "Your skullcap is all that remains of your very first body, the first you who embarked on a quest for growth and knowledge. As for the other, Acilia approached me, took my head in her hands, and pressed her thumbs into my cheeks. Then chanted. "Open maw where words thus flow, so you may natter what you do not know." Then she cupped my ears, and the wind made my eardrums shake. "Ears to hear the subtle cues of words lost and words new, make the knowledge twist and stew, as they settle into you," Acilia finished and let go of my head. I bent forward in pain, struck down by a stinging In my head. I started to dry heave from the agony. My nose started bleeding, and I was sure the spell had gone wrong. Then Acilia wiped the blood from me and etched an X onto a rock, and the pain stopped.

"That, my dear, was your first lesson with runes. The rune I drew was the Rune Gebo. It means "a gift for a gift." It is a core value in working with magic, energy, or any entity, really. You have to sacrifice something to gain something. What happened here was you asked for better understanding, and when you didn't make an offering in exchange, you felt the imbalance. When I put your blood on the stone and sealed it with the rune Gebo, it put things back into balance." Acilia explained.

"Does it always have to be blood?" I wondered if I would need to cut myself like all the witches in the movies do.

"No dear, not at all, it can be a lock of hair, fingernail clippings, food, mead, a kind gesture towards a stranger, frog eyes, and so on. These are all acceptable. I only used your blood because it was already coming from you, though blood magic is very powerful," She paused.

Edela took my hand and led me towards an armchair covered in furs situated next to a large table covered in bottles, candles, rune stones, and many other items. "People often ask for things and do nothing, then are disappointed at the empty results. They expect the gift to just happen, but to manifest, you must act, and to receive, you must return the favor. If you look at it from a basic level, a scholar trades time, study, and money to gain wisdom and title. Once the title is received, they don't automatically become rich or gainfully employed. They must find a person searching for their skills and title, then offer them time and wisdom in exchange for money both get and give. It is a partnership, as it is with all magic. Do you understand?" Edela asked.

"Yes, you don't own magic, and magic doesn't own you. It's give and take in equal balance. Does magic always answer one's call?" I asked, curious if I could give a finger for a million bucks.

Edela chuckled as if she could hear my thoughts. "No dear, magic picks and chooses. It has to work around your life agreements. Each soul agrees to the life they will live before being born. Each life is like a spider's web. It's woven with many paths, twists, and turns. You make decisions as you go and weave around your web; however, it is a spiral in a circle, so, by nature, you will always end up at the center when it is meant to be. You choose your web so you can gain wisdom and experience where you need it. Because true knowledge only comes from experience. Therefore, magic can't change everything you wish it to. A person meant to be a popper can't just become rich by magic if it isn't woven. That doesn't mean you shouldn't take care of the popper since their web may intertwine with yours or someone you care about. They may hold a key lesson you are meant to learn," Edela paused and looked at me as if she could see the wheels turning in my head trying to catch up.

"Can someone fail at life?" I asked, thinking of all the horrible people I see in the five o clock news. "Certainly, my dear, say one was given wealth, and their life purpose was to overcome greed, and then they refused to help when the opportunities arose. When they die, they will have achieved nothing, so, therefore, their soul hasn't grown, and it becomes a life wasted. Or worse, say one was meant to overcome temptation but instead gave in to their wickedness and harmed another. In that instance, said person would lose a portion of their soul. Then should they repeat those actions, they lose more and more, and that, my dear, is where the term "soulless" comes from," I thought about what Onacona had said and what she called them, devoroc." I gasped, and Edela continued, "When a soulless person passes away, it's not just one life they have to make up for. They have to scratch their way to the surface again to start repairing the damage they did."

"That means they get reborn as blobfish or bot fly," Afridh interrupted, and I was startled.

Edela smiled then continued. "Witches live by a code, we

give a gift for a gift, we protect those weaker than us, We maintain balance. We do as we please as long as it doesn't interfere with someone else's web," Edela patted me, then got up and walked across the room.

Then Afrid sat next to me. "I can taste your question. Go ahead and ask it. You don't have to worry about judgment here," Afrid offered.

"What happens to the chunks of souls from the bad people, the ones that go missing?" I asked, guessing I already knew from the night in the van and the terrible screams I had heard. "Yes, good question, they try to hide in the dead realm or the resting realm, and some are devoured by others. Some are recycled by the soul retrievers and placed in the eccotomb to be turned into stones. The rest, if they have any sort of intelligence, go about spreading fear and hate. People love to be offended and become angry, so they feed their energy into it, giving them the power to spread their evil," Afrid answered.

"One more, if everyone returns somewhere after they die, then what about the good ghosts? Why are they still around?" I asked, trying to put it together.

"Souls have to transition, you see. It takes nine months to enter the world and takes time to leave it as well. That way, they can say their goodbyes and guide their loved ones through the pain of their loss. Let them know it's OK. Some have loved ones who are more vulnerable than others, so that soul may choose to stick around longer to provide extra comfort. Then some stick around and wait to go with their loved ones when they go. The point is some stick around. Now that you have a good idea of what comes, let's move on to the Rune Asa or Ansuz the God Rune," Afrid concluded.

We spent the rest of the morning going over the majority of the other runes in length. Each sister witch took turns guiding me in deep meditations. They shared with me the feelings, images, and stories of how the runes came to be. Their meanings, and what power each rune possesses. They taught me to read the runes fully. To not just read the runes that fell face up but how they fell into place was important too. If they landed in a circle, it might mean fertility, or if they landed in the shape of an arrow, you are headed in a certain direction. We kept going deeper and deeper. "The Seer showed Odin Ymir, the empty earth. The sons of Burr lifted the land from the sea. The Aesir then moved the sun and stars and arranged the universe to be day and night. That is how the earth came to be.

While sitting in Asgard, Odin looked over all the worlds and wanted to know the mysteries hidden from his sight, so he sacrificed his own eye on his spear Gungar and threw it in the well Mimir, then hung for nine days and nights from Yggdrasil the tree of life. Thus, he was gifted the knowledge of the runes and all the secrets of the worlds," Agnes imparted. I felt bound to Odin and marveled at his courage with his sacrifices to attain the sacred knowledge and his nobility for sharing what he learned. I figured the next time I saw him, I'd pat him on the back and say. "Thanks, I owe you one."

"Ready to eat, Jamie?" Agatha asked.

"Let me guess apples?" I responded.

"Not quite what I had in mind," Agnes remarked.

"Oh good, don't get me wrong, I really like the apples, but some variety would be nice," I answered politely.

"Good, next lesson the rune Uruz, a witch is never reliant on another's services. A witch must know how to hunt," Agatha remarked, and I raised an eyebrow.

"hunt what? Actually, just no, thank you," I returned.

Nothing sounded worse.

"If you don't hunt, our training here is over. I cannot teach what the hunt will. This you must learn from experience. It is vital!" Agatha drilled me firmly.

I thought hard about it. Hunting wasn't in my nature, but the fate of worlds relied on me closing The Gate, and I needed to be trained. "Fine, what do I have to hunt?" I mumbled in agreement.

"We will hunt a Urus of Alfheimr. The wild bulls of the elf realm. You know they once lived on earth," Agnes informed.

"Alfheimr?! The light Elf realm?" I bellowed in excitement.

"Yes, the light elf realm, we will be in the wilds, so the chances of you meeting an elf are dim. We aren't going there to dine at one of their elaborate cafes." Agnes briefed me.

"Am I wearing this? I don't know how to hunt, let alone a bull? Don't they just graze in a pasture? Won't it be unfair?" I questioned, not wanting to sacrifice anything placid.

"It will be a fair hunt, and you must do it to learn why the Uruz earned their name on a rune," Agnes grinned wickedly, then snapped, and my belt with my chosen weapons appeared around my hips. Along with pants on my legs and the moo moo tucked into them.

The twelve cast their runes, and it was decided that Agata, Agnes, and Etta would come with me on the hunt. The others seemed disappointed that they weren't chosen to go. Agata, Agnes, and Etta snapped their fingers and quivers appeared strapped over their shoulders, and blades at their hips appeared. Agnes took my hand and led me to the boiling cauldron where Etta and Agata stood. "Are you ready?" Etta asked.

"For what? Boiling cauldron sauce?" I teased, not really wanting to know what was in it. The bubbles were as thick as slime, with a mucus quality and the same yellow color of a newborn baby's poo.

"Today, we travel by cauldron," Etta winked.

"Gross! Why do I always have to get all dirty? That looks hot, and I have no desire to get burned. Can't I just slap my stone?" I complained.

"Not for this journey, you can't. Now take my hand and repeat after me." Agata extended her palm, and the four of us clasped hands, then Etta dropped a silver hair into the cauldron and spoke. "Spiral, spin, turn and twist, open a path through your mist, into Alfheimr we must go to sow the seeds we must sow." The cauldron rumbled then we all joined in. "Spiral, spin, turn and twist, open a path through your mist, into Alfheimr we must go to sow the seeds we must sow." The cauldron flew from the floor onto the wall in front of us and began spinning. The substance inside it began twisting like a tornado extending inwards far past the length of the cauldron. "Spiral, spin, turn and twist, open a path through your mist, into Alfheimr we must go to sow the seeds we must sow." The cauldron grew, and the spiral of yellow goo turned into a golden tunnel, and we stepped into it together. The goo wrapped around us and pulled us as fast as lightning to Alfheimr.

We landed on a mountain top, the cauldron settling next to us. I looked from a cliff's edge over a vast forest of golden leafy trees with turquoise rivers and waterfalls. "Whoa, this is majestic," I sighed. The forest seemed never-ending, stretching as far as the eye could see. I turned around to look at Agata, Agnes, and Etta to see their expressions and learn what we would do next and found them running away from me. Into the golden forest resting beyond. "Hey, wait!" I yelled and took off after them. "Come on, I thought you were going to tell me how to hunt!" I shouted after them trying to catch up. I ran deeper into the wood for several minutes, with them staying a good distance ahead of me. "Can we stop running now?!" I huffed. Then they quickened on hand

and foot, bounding as if they were wild deer fleeing from a bear, their knees bent backward powering their hurtles away from me. "Well, that was weird," I spoke aloud. I looked around, and I realized I didn't know how to get back to the cauldron. "Great, I'm lost now! Thanks a lot!" I shouted and started walking.

The forest smells were sweet like perfume, and the ground was soft covered in short golden grass and white wildflowers. I noticed nothing seemed bothered, no broken sticks or twigs, no fallen leaves. "This is the cleanest forest ever. Do you see this?" I yelled, hoping I would get some sort of response to where Agata, Agnes, and Etta went. I kept walking, and my tummy growled. "Shut up, you, you got us into this mess. I should've asked for an apple," I babbled irritated at the situation. Then I heard a bird in the distance. I looked around, wondering where the sound had come from since it was the first sound, I had heard since entering the forest. I stilled and listened, then it dawned on me. "Oh, right, I can summon sonic listening now." I popped my ears, and I could hear the bones creaking in its wings.

I cast my gaze to where the sound came from, and I focused my sight. A tiny speck off in the distance at the top of the trees moved. "What kind of bird is that? I focused harder and walked towards it to try and get a better look. I squinted my eyes, and they popped. "Ouch," I whimpered and looked to the ground and rubbed them. Once I dropped my hands, I could see the tiny hairs on the blades of grass, and the pollen settled on a flower's petal. The colors were more vibrant and complex. I looked up. "Whoa!" I could see through miles and miles of forest. I cast my eyes to the bird, and it came into view. It wasn't a bird at all. I wasn't sure what it was. The best I could describe the creature was as a flying fennec fox. "Aren't you precious," I garbled towards its adorable, pointed face. My tummy growled again. "Fine, this bull better not be adorable," I scrutinized silently, still unsure how I was going to do this deed.

I closed my eyes and focused on listening. Then sounds of fluttering heartbeats all throughout the forest surrounded me. I looked towards the sounds. The woods were full of life, from insects to wolves with white coats, possums, white deer, and many unfamiliar creatures. In the distance, I could see some large boulders protruding from the ground, and I heard a grunt from behind them. "I bet that's you," I whispered to myself. I started walking towards it, and I gazed down the path. It was too far to travel just on suspicion. Then I heard a clank like a huff hitting a stone.

"That has to be my bull," I determined and raced through the woods. I ran for about twenty minutes, twisting my way around trees, rocks, berry bushes, up and down little hills, and the boulders were still far off in the distance. I wondered how Agata, Agnes, and Etta could jump, run, leap, and bound. Like they had, away from me, and if I could do that too. I put my hand on the ground and kicked with my legs. Nothing happened other than me kissing the dirt. I tried again and again with no results. Feeling like a fool, I started to jog again, locked onto the sound of the beast. The temperature around me seemed to adjust with my movement, so I never broke a sweat. Then I saw the head of the bull emerge from behind the boulder. Its head was massive like a bison, with horns as long and thick as my legs. It turned and started to trot off in the opposite direction.

"No, no, don't you dare!" I cursed and sped up as fast as I could go. It started to get further and further away. "Come on!" I cried out and pushed myself as hard as I could up and incline, lept from the top, and then soared about thirty feet. "Yes! Yes!" I cried in relief and hurtled again, finally gaining on the Urus. I lept and ran, getting closer and closer. I was about a hundred yards away when I jumped again, hitting some branches, and the leaves rustled. The massive bull stopped, turned around, and faced me. I froze and gaped at its sheer size. Its enormous body stood taller than Dawn's truck and much taller than me.

"Oh boy. Agata, Agnes, and Etta, where are you? I could really use your bow and arrows right about now!" I shouted. The beast stomped and started to charge me. For a moment, I admired it. It wasn't going to run away from me, its predator. It would rather face me and fight than be chased down and die.

The bull lowered its head, aiming its horns towards my chest. My instincts to survive kicked in, and I reached for my belt and retrieved my curved knives. I stood ready, and when it was an arm's length away, I jumped, landing on its back. The bull bucked, and I tumbled off of it, hitting the ground. The beast turned to face me again, and I rolled onto my feet. We circled around each other sizing each other up. It lashed its huff against the ground, and it charged. I spun away from its horns, and the bull turned and kicked with his hind legs knocking the knives from my hands, sending me flying towards a tree. I put my arms out in front of me to try and lessen the blow. When I collided with the tree, my arms stopped me, absorbing the force of impacts, and my legs curled under me. I used them to spring from the tree and twisted my body, landing on my hands and feet upon the ground. The bull was already rushing towards me. I lept at him, landing with my feet on the broad side of his horns, and jumped off. His face hit the dirt, and he fumbled. I took the opportunity and dove for my knives. When I turned, the bull was but inches away, his horn aimed at my abdomen, ready to impale me. I swiped down with my knife, and his right horn fell to the earth.

The beast knocked me upwards with its snout taking my foot into its maw. I folded over on its head, slamming onto the boney ridge. It felt like hitting cement. It rushed us forward, bulldozing my legs into a tree, and I cried out in pain, and I lost my grip on one of my knives, and it tumbled to the ground. I grabbed onto the remaining knife with both hands while the bull backed up so it could charge again, and I started thrusting the blade downwards. The bull cried out in pain, loosening its hold on my foot, but before I could move it, It rammed us into the tree again. I flung backward, crashing into the tree. Things went hazy for a brief moment. The bull snorted blood running down its neck and stomped again. He tilted his head to one side, lowered his remaining horn aiming it at me, and charged. I rolled to my left and onto my feet, spun to face his side, and with all my strength, I brought the blade down on the bull's neck again, and again, blood splattered on my face, and I stopped once I heard the crack of his spine. The bull fell to the earth, its breathing labored. I backed away from it, limping. I choked back a sob as my heart pounded in my chest.

"Well done, Jamie, now you must thank him for what he taught you here, for his contest and his life, then you must end his pain," Agata said softly. I nodded, not wanting to see the bull suffer. I grabbed the spearhead from my belt and crouched next to the bull's head. I put my hand on its neck and softly stroked it. "Thank you for teaching me to see, to hunt, to use my legs and arms, and to fight. Thank you for teaching me to have courage and to not flee. Thank you for the life you have lost to me." The bull looked at me, and I saw peace in his eyes, and I didn't fully understand it. I took my spearhead and thrust it down into the bull's temple, then let the tears stream down my cheeks.

Agata, Agnes, and Etta knelt next to me, "Now I'll share with you why this needed to be and what must be done, work, don't talk or question for we must hurry. Start removing the hide." Etta imparted. Agata, Agnes, and I went to work neatly slicing and pulling at the hide in silence. Etta then proceeded to tell us a tale "A long time ago, A bull and a cow were in love the cow became full with calves, and the bull was proud. The bull went to a fro telling all the world of his good fortune. Then on his walk home, he found himself being followed by a hunter. The hunter was old and frail, so the bull ran instead of fighting. The bull thought it wasn't worth the bloodshed, and this fight would be too easy. That this hunter posed no real threat. So, the bull ran over hills and through a valley. In his mind, he was leading the hunter away from his love, his family. Once he was sure he was safe, he changed course to return to his consort.

When the bull arrived at his meadow, his cow was nowhere to be seen. Then the smell of her blood drifted to him, carried in on a breeze. He ran to help her following the sent. Then when he reached the place of its origin, all that was left was her hoofs, heart, and the fetuses of his descendants. The bull, in agony, screamed a mighty scream that shook fate awake. Then, in his pain, the bull consumed what was left of his family's remains. He ate the hoofs and heart of his beloved and the babes that were meant to be. So that he may carry them with him and never forget how he had failed his family. Fate, intrigued and touched by the bull's actions, came to the bull, and asked what he would change, and it would be granted. Fate imagined the bull would ask for the lives of his family to be spared. However, having felt the deepest of pains possible, the bull wanted to ensure this could never happen again.

So, the bull told fate that only through a fight fought hard and true could a bull be found worthy of a cow's love, then together would start a family anew. Overcome with grief and rage, the bull jumped and pinned fate down, then told her there and then that he never wants a cow to suffer in agony or pain or be murdered again. Fate, angry at the bull's betrayal, granted the bull his request but with different terms to settle the debt. Fate wielded her magic throughout all the world that no more were calves or cows from the womb would be born, but rather through a sacrifice and the loss of a bull's hide in a battle fought hard and true and with pride. Only then the bull could be reborn with his family anew, and from there on, the cow and calves would forever be hidden from the hunter's view." Etta finished, and my heart hurt, but at the same time, I felt relief that maybe something good would come from this.

Together we finished pulling the hide from the bull's carcass and folded it in half, then we placed it neatly on the ground folded in half. "Now, what do we do?" I queried.

"We need to clean it," Agnes answered.

"Ewe gross." I thought to myself but started to cut despite my own resistance. Once done, we placed the entrails inside the pelt, and everyone stilled. The blood, entrails, and the hide began to mix, then the fur started to move.

"Jamie, take out your box from your belt," Agata advised me, and I did. I looked at the little box. It had a small latch that locked the top closed when turned. Other than that, It was ordinary, and I wondered what use it could have in this situation. "Now, place the box on the carcass and open it, hurry," Agata instructed, and I did what she asked. Then to my amazement, the carcass shrunk until it was small enough to place in the box. I grabbed the tiny body with my fingertips, put it in the box, and put it back on my belt, and Agata nodded in approval.

"Get ready to run," Agata warned as the pelt started to tremble and move.

"I don't know that I can run. I think I may have sprained or broken something in the fight," I told her. The three looked at each other, then Agnes and Etta each took one of my arms in their hands. The pelt rose, and a bull, a cow, and two calves lept out from under the hide. The Witches thrust upwards, taking me with them, and I looked down as the cow and the calves faded from my view while the bull frolicked around as if he was playing with them.

We landed next to the cauldron and chanted, "Spiral, spin, turn and twist, open a path through your mist, from where we came, we now must return to share all the knowledge we have learned." Once we arrived back to the safety of the Witches hut, we stepped outside. Tables and lanterns were set up neatly in rows, with barrels of mead and candles decorating the area and it looked beautiful. A large fire pit with a spit was prepared. My coven stood lined up and asked me to remove the bull from my box. I took it out, set it next to the spit, and watched it grow back to its enormous size.

"You must now take the horn and remove it," Edela told me, and I took a blade from my belt and swiped downwards, cutting it cleanly off. Then Edela handed me a satchel. I opened it, and there was some polish, beeswax, and a stone in it.

"What do you want me to do with it?" I asked.

"Use the stone to soften the rough edges of the horn and polish it, then seal it with the wax. Tonight, you tell your story while you drink from it. I collected the horn, then my leg buckled, and I fell.

"Well, ladies, I don't think I am going to be up to telling

stories tonight," I remarked, disappointed while rubbing my leg.

Adelixa swept me up in her arms, "we will have you good as new in no time." She reassured me and then took me into the hut.

I removed everything but my cloak and slid my legs out to examine them. They were covered in bruises and lesions. Some of the cuts were deep enough to scar, and I thought, "Mom would be stitching these if I were home." I hadn't even realized I had bled until now. I just knew that they hurt. Adelixa mixed herbs and plants then rubbed ointments into my leg, and they went numb, then she proceeded to pop the bones in them.

"Did they break anything?" I asked.

"No, they just got displaced. I'm excited to hear the story of your hunt tonight. You see, killing the Urus is the perfect example of balance. He wished for a family, then faced you and sacrificed everything to gain it. In doing so, he proved he deserved it. He didn't lay down and hope it would happen. He did what he had to, and when it was over, he got his heart's wish.

Like the bull, you, on the other hand, put yourself in great danger and suffered blood and pain, which you set aside and fought through. You also set aside your stubbornness for the opportunity to gain wisdom so you can defend your friends and family. You sacrificed for knowledge. That is courage most don't have. So, tonight when you share your deeds, don't hold back, don't lessen your words with modesty. That way, others can gain wisdom from what you have learned," Adelixa finished with her sentiment and started replacing the gashes with new skin. I stopped her at one of the cuts.

"Don't heal this one. It's shaped like the Uruz rune. I want to keep it and have it scar. That way, I can share it when I tell my story. So, I can always remember today," I said, looking at it with pride. Adelixa nodded and moved on to heal the rest of my lacerations. I pulled out my stone and got to work on my horn.

Later that night, under the stars, I stood on a table and acted out my fight with the bull and told my story amongst many of the people from Asgard. I held up my horn with pride and drank apple juice from it. After I was done, everyone cheered. When I sat down and ate the meat that I had provided. Others started to share their stories and boasted about their adventures and great hunts, and I cheered for them too. We laughed together at our failures during our quests and shared what knowledge we gained from those lessons. When the last story was told, Odin approached me to bid me good night. "I patted him on the back and said, "thanks, man, I owe you," and he erupted in laughter, knowing I knew of his great deeds. He nodded, then disappeared into the night. After I said my thank yous and goodbyes, I mounted my horse and headed back to the castle.

Chapter Sixteen, Tumbles and Fumbles

Sally had collected me from my room earlier than usual to start some basic defense lessons. She promised they would only last a few hours until lunch at most, and then I could do more studies with my coven. When we reached the training field, four of my coven sisters were already there, ready to train, and two giant men stood next to them. We started with a jog, and Sally, Adliza, Abela, Acilia, and Ebba stayed by me the whole way. I asked the adults If I could practice shifting into the running form I had taken during the hunt, and everyone thought it was a good idea. Then instructed me that changing forms is called skiftende.

At first, I made a joke of myself hoping, bucking, and kicking in the dirt, but after about fifteen tries, I managed it successfully. For my upper half to shift, I just had to pop my neck. For the lower half to skiftende, I had to focus on my destination and jump. After I was successful, as many times as I had failed, I was confident that I had it down. Then we moved on to fighting, and Sally showed me some tricks to maneuvering my curved knives. I told Sally the lesson was a day late, considering my fumbles with the bull. After about three hours of lunging, swipes, and strokes, practicing rolling to my feet, and blocking. Sally said I was OK to rest, so I moved to the edge of the field and sat, then watched the men strike at each other using chains as whips.

Ebba came and sat next to me and handed me a jug of water, and I gulped it down. "Jamie, have you started trying to control your light of Gebo?" Ebba asked. I looked at my hand and the mark resembling the rune Sol, and I completely forgot about it.

"No, I haven't thought about it. The light only seems to work when I'm in or near something that wants to harm me and around supernatural events. Since I have been here, it hasn't turned on," I answered, and she smiled at me.

"Are you curious why Adliza, Abela, Acilia, and I are all here with you?" Ebba glanced at the field, and I looked around.

"Not really. You are training me," I answered.

"If we were merely training you to use weapons, Sally or

one of the weapon masters here would be more than qualified for that. Us witches are here to make sure your magic stays in your control and to teach you how to maintain that control," Ebba briefed.

"Oh, am I dangerous?" I questioned, thinking about the other night when I accidentally knocked Sally against a wall.

"Dangerous yes, malevolent no. However, you have gained many new powers. As you grow, more will manifest, and knowing how to control those powers will keep you from having mishaps. We will start with your light. It is triggered by your basic instincts to ward off threats." Ebba informed me.

"Should I make an offering to use it," I asked, not completely sure?

"No, this isn't the same as working a spell or where you have to ask for magic to assist you. What you are doing here is working with the magic inside of you, the magic you were born with, and the magic given to you when you stood between the fire and the ice," Ebba explained. Then she called for Adliza to come to me, and she walked across the field.

"Jamie, I need you to remove your amulet for this," Adliza informed me, and I took it off and handed it to her, and she slipped it in her pocket.

"Why?" I queried, feeling exposed without my necklace.

"Ebba is going to wield some of her magic at you. You need to get your hand to shine and stop her magic from making contact with you. Your amulet will work as a shield, and we need your light to do that," Adliza coached me.

"I can't. My hand blasted light at a creature when I was in a crevice in the ground. Also, when the calsake swallowed me. Then it worked as a flashlight for a moment as well. I don't know how to make it a shield. It seems to barely make any light at all, or it explodes with light," I explained. not wanting to hurt anyone accidentally. Adliza nodded at Abela, Acilia and they walked over to Ebba.

"Don't worry about hurting anyone Abela, Acilia will shield to keep that from happening. Come with me," Adliza instructed, and we walked into the field facing the other three witches with a good amount of distance between us.

"I want you to close your eyes. Place your palms facing upwards. Now feel the light coming from your core and move it to your hand. Picture it as a small flame. No, no smaller than that!" Adliza raised her voice, and it startled me. I opened my eyes, and my light rocketing upwards well past the top of the trees.

"Oh shoot, I'm sorry," I apologized and closed my hand.

"What were you picturing?" Adliza asked.

"I was picturing a candle's flame," I answered, and her eyes grew wide, and it was the first time I had seen any of the Wotan witches rattled.

"Well, you did well extinguishing it. You wait here. I'll be right back," Adliza instructed. I looked at Ebba, Abela, and Acilia and they all looked bewildered too. Then I looked at Sally, who was on the other side of the field, laughing hysterically and giving me the thumbs up. I shrugged my shoulders at her, not fully understanding what was going on, and she just kept on laughing. I rolled my eyes. Then a little portal opened up next to me, and the rest of my coven was there.

They formed a line next to Ebba, and Adliza came back over to me. "What is all this about?" I questioned Adliza.

She answered, "Oh, you don't need to worry about it. Now, let's start again. Close your eyes, face your palms upwards, and take a deep calming breath. Now picture a tiny spark of light. TINY! SMALLER THAN A SLIVER. Alright, that is excellent. Now imagine it making a shield around you. NO PICTURE IT MAKING A TEACUP IN FRONT OF YOU!" Adliza spoke frantically, and it startled me again. I opened my eyes and saw what was happening, and my light was around me like a house rather than a shield, and it had knocked Adliza down.

I quickly closed my hand and ran to her. "Are you OK? I'm so sorry I didn't mean for this to happen," I apologized again and offered a hand to help her up.

"It's alright, dear. These things happen when we train with our active powers. How do you suppose we work with your light? The meditation isn't performing as I imagined," Adliza bid. I thought about it for a minute.

"Well, I suppose it is my power, maybe it's visual, and the thought of having anyone wielding power at me makes me nervous. So, maybe it is trying to protect me at the same level my anxiety is at?" I mulled over what the problem could be. "Can I have a moment alone in the field instead of having a wall of adults standing across from me?" I asked while working out the details in my head.

"That sounds wise." Adliza nodded and motioned for the others to move from the field. They sat at the far end of the area near a barrier, and Sally and the two men joined them, and they all stared at me! "Well, that's not helpful," I thought to myself. I turned my back to them and opened my hand. "OK, light, I need you to make a shield," I reached it out in front of me, and nothing happened. "Hand light go!" I commanded and thrust my hand out in front of me. I peeked over my shoulder, and about four more people had joined the others. "Well, that's just great, you stupid hand. You sent up a beacon, and now all of Asgard is going to watch me make a twit of myself!" I whispered and slapped my hand. Then I heard laughing from right behind me, and I spun around to find Hermodr had snuck up on me.

"Great, what do you want? Besides to laugh at me?" I asked.

"I saw that you were putting on a show and decided to come and watch. Also, fair warning about a hundred more is on their way. That whole section over there is about to be full," Hermodr pointed to the area Sally and my coven were sitting.

"Oh, that's just great! Everyone gets to watch me scold myself for not being able to summon my own power. I'm useless," I felt defeated and dropped my hands.

"Useless never, dramatic, obviously. Watching you make a fool of yourself will be the best entertainment we've all had in a while," Hermodr teased.

"Ha. Ha., Very funny! Why are you here? Also, why do you pretend to be around my age? I know you're older. I heard you and Sally talking about it in the hall, don't you think that's creepy? Because I sure do!" I scowled, taking myself loathing out on him.

"Don't you think it's creepy that you look so young?! Anyhow, this was my age when we first met? Also, I am unable to change back while you're here. I've tried. We are," Hermodr stumbled on his words, then continued, "Friends, and since we are such good friends, whenever were close, our friend bond makes me take a form like yours to try and make us better friends. If you don't like it, take it up with the friend goddess, numskull!" Hermodr barked.

"What a load of bull, ha, friend Goddess? Really! Sally is my friend, and she isn't my age. I'm not an idiot, You, self-involved, overconfident fathead!" I ridiculed in an attempt to return an insult.

"I'm an overconfident, fathead?! Well, if I'm an overconfident fathead, you're a spineless bonehead! Bonehead!" Hermodr sneered and zapped me in the shoulder with his magic. The electricity pulsed through me, and I shook.

My mouth dropped open "How dare you?! Who do you think you are?!" I growled and walked towards him with my fists up, and he shocked me again, harder this time, and it knocked me off my feet. I stood up and raced towards him, and he sent a bolt of electricity at me again, making me face plant. I spat dirt out of my mouth and let the rage consume me. I stood and met him, I raised my hand, and the light blasted from me. He countered it with his magic. It crackled, hissed, and roared. He moved and knocked our two streams downwards, and they rippled through the earth's surface, tearing a path across the entire field, sending the people who were standing tumbling to the ground. "Oops," I whispered, feeling bad about what we did.

"Very good, bonehead, now make it a sword and let's have a real fight," Hermodr challenged.

"I can't shape it," I replied.

"Sure, you can. Stop over thinking it and just do it!" He instructed, and I started to think about it, and he whacked me with the broad side of an electric sword, and I convulsed.

"Really! That hurts!" I yelled a Hermodr, and he smacked me with his sword again, and I tremored. He threw his sword and sent it looping in the air, then he caught its hilt and swung it at me again, and I raised my arm to protect myself, and his blade struck mine. The light and electricity sent sparks flying. I lunged to my feet and forward to attack, and our swords met, he stepped closer to me, and the blades hissed. I jumped back and thrust again with the point forward, and he knocked it away with ease. Then he twirled gracefully and slapped me on the butt with his sword, and the current rippled through me while he walked backward laughing. I grunted and turned my light into a ball and threw it at him. He maneuvered, and it flew past him and hit the dirt, sending chunks of soil flying. I made another ball and sent it flying, and he transformed his sword into a baseball bat and swung. The ball came flying back at me, it hit me in the shoulder, and I went plummeting backward on impact.

"Are you even trying?" Hermodr mocked. I fashioned my light into a pebble and took out my slingshot aimed and shot it. It hit Hermodr right in his gut, and he fell forward to the ground and didn't move.

"No, oh no, what have I done?!" I ran to Hermodr and rolled him onto his back. "Hermodr, Hermodr, are you OK?" I pleaded and started to shake him. "Hermodr, please don't be dead. Please, no, no. SOMEBODY HELP HIM!" I screamed, and tears welled up in my eyes. I looked at all the people watching, confused why they weren't here helping him. I looked at Sally and saw she was laughing, and I knew he was pranking me. I turned back to Hermodr, and he grabbed my head, rolled me to the ground, then mounted me.

I bent my legs and bucked, and he tumbled over me. We went back and forth, then he pinned my hands behind me and sat on my back. I cursed at myself for getting caught, "stupid, stupid, how could you let him get the upper hand," I tapped out, and he let my hands go, but he didn't get up.

"You did exceptionally well for your first day, Eisa, I mean Jamie. You have no technique when it comes to swordplay." I interrupted him.

"Gee, thanks! I've only practiced with a sword, how many times. Uh, NEVER!" I lashed out.

"Steady girl, you didn't let me finish," Hermodr started, but I cut him off again.

"Will you get off of me?" I growled and started to squirm.

"Only if you promise to let me finish talking." Hermodr posed, and I hesitated, then accepted,

"Fine." He moved off and sat next to me. I got up and started to brush myself off, but my clothes were clean. So, I situated myself next to him.

"What I was going to say is you didn't know how to use a sword, but you were able to fashion one. You were able to create balls and then even a tiny pebble. That is really impressive for one's first day. Not only could you make them, but you also wielded them with control, and they didn't lose shape once. All you needed was to stop trying to control and overthink it. You witches like to plan and overthink everything. An active power doesn't work like that. Your magic is an extension of yourself like an arm. You don't tell your arm where to move. You just move it. Now make a shield," Hermodr charged. I put up my hand, and a small shield formed in front of it. I looked at it, then closed my hand, and it went away.

"You didn't have to shock me so much. You know that really hurt," I joked.

"You didn't have to shoot me with a light pebble," Hermodr teased, and I lightly punched him in the shoulder.

"You were fine, wait, how were you fine?" I asked.

"I'm a God," he boasted and raised his hands.

I rolled my eyes, "Well, God or not. I'm glad you're OK. You really had me going there for a minute," I sincerely spoke and gave a slight smile.

"I know it was hilarious! You actually screamed for help!" Hermodr erupted in laughter. I popped my neck and felt my arm grow stronger, and I punched him in his shoulder and sent him flying for about three yards before face planting into the earth. The crowd of people broke out into laughter, and I stood up and walked towards them to see what Sally the

Wotan Witches had in store for me next.

Sally and the witches praised me for how I did on the field. Especially for the bit where I punched Hermodr, we ate apples for lunch, and Sally left on Valkyrie business. All of the Wotan witches left through a portal except for Ebba and me. We headed back to the sacred circle on horseback. "Why couldn't I go through the portal?" I asked Ebba.

"Portals can be tricky if you aren't committed to where you want to go. You can get torn in half. For example, if you wanted to go to the circle, however, you wanted to go to your room as well. The portal will do what you wish and send you both places. It can get a bit messy, so we won't jump into that one just yet," Ebba winked.

"What about when we traveled through the cauldron or the stone that takes me to my pocket realm?" I questioned.

"The cauldron portal worked because of the spell you chanted, it was specific, and we used a hair of an elf for a bond. The stone comes from your pocket realm, and it wishes to go home, so when you slap it, you wake it up, and it goes home taking you with it. Then when you slap it again to leave, it wakes up and realizes you aren't supposed to be there and puts you back." Ebba explained.

"Great, now I feel bad about having my stone and slapping it. Does my stone have a name?" I smirked.

Ebba shook her head and trotted ahead of me, then shouted back. "You should ask it."

When I reached the circle, Ebba and all the Wotan witches were standing in a row waiting for me. I felt a bit nervous at the sight of them. They seemed more focused and in tune with each other than their normal racing around, joking, and making potions. They were dressed in brown cloaks, each holding a different item. An apple, a bunch of beets, shears, chalk, a drum, a bowl, a bunch of lavender and chamomile flowers, a mirror, a small hammer, a horn, an egg, and a cup of ink with a nail in it. "What are we doing today? If it involves me eating beets, just let me know now so I can mentally prepare," I teased while looking at them suspiciously.

"Come with us. Today we begin by the river," Afridh motioned for me to follow her and turned, walking slowly away from the circle. Everyone else stood waiting, so I fell in line behind her, and then they settled into line behind me one by one. We walked through the woods in silence, and I took in the smells of honeysuckle and pine. It was a bit warmer than normal. Either that or I was on edge, waiting for something to go wrong. "I wonder if they were mad at me for shooting light at Hermodr. After all, when I shot him, I didn't know it wouldn't hurt him. I hoped it would just knock him down, but I didn't know. "I'm probably going to get disqualified and thrown out of the Wotan Witch's Coven. If so, I deserve it," I worried silently and decided that whatever fate met me at the river. I would accept it and thank them for all they have taught me.

We arrived at the edge of the river, and a makeshift bed on an alter with a pillow lay on the bank. Torches were lit on either side of the bed, and a raging campfire with a cauldron sat closer to the edge of the water. I looked nervously around and wondered. "When witches get thrown out of a coven, do they get sacrificed? They never said what had happened to the other witch that had died before me?" Everyone behind me stopped but Afridh, who continued to the water's edge.

"Sit with me," She spoke softly and sat. I scooted next to her and looked down at my knees, waiting for my scolding. "Today, we work to release your inner pain and cleanse you. To prepare you for your linking," Afridh versed softly with a tinge of sorrow, and I began to question, but she paused me. "All things will be made known. Just listen."

I nodded in silence, and Afridh continued, "look at the reflections in the waters, stare deeply into them, don't look away. Watch them change," She paused, and I did as she asked, and the reflections did indeed start to shift, and I saw people from my life hustling down sidewalks either to work or school. It looked like a normal day of life. Then I saw an old man trip falling to the pavement and people rushed by him. No one stopped or asked if he was alright. The old man got up, looked around with hurt and anger on his face, then continued on his way.

"Most in your world have lost their basic instinct to recognize that we are all connected. Everyone who passed the fallen man forgot that he is their brother. That his pain matters, they were more concerned about hurrying to where they were going. One will ignore another's pain, feeling it is normal. Then when one is in pain, they are outraged when they find they are alone in it themselves. Said person then often inflicts pain on others to feel connected. Therein lies the disconnect. Jamie, when you get hurt by your parents, it is not your fault. It is due to their lack of empathy and connection because they have forgotten that kindness and love heal and teach. Not making others experience the pain and emptiness they feel," Afridh paused, and I started to tremble, and I tried to hold back my tears.

"Don't hold back. Let it out. Think of every time you were hit over the head, every time you were knocked down, every time they whipped you, every time they threw things at you, and every time they told you that you weren't enough, weren't worthy. Bring it to the surface, feel it." I broke down. I started to sob. I heard footsteps behind me but didn't turn, hiding my shame.

Ella leaned over next to me, placed the beets on my lap, and spoke, "take these to the cauldron and boil them. At the same time, you summon all your pain." I went to the cauldron and dropped them in and let my tears fall. As they boiled, the water changed to red.

Then Agnes stroked my cheek, handed me a bowl, stood next to me, and spoke, "strain the beets into the bowl and boil it down into a paste." I did as she told me to, and my pain turned to anger as I stood waiting for it to thicken. Then the sound of steady drumming sounded, and my heartbeat pounded in time with it. Agnes looked into the bowl and instructed me further, "Now put the bottom of the bowl in the river and cool it."

I knelt at the river, the drum still pounding. My anger and embarrassment started to surface, and I realized I was angry at myself for feeling vulnerable. I slammed my hand into the bowl and covered it in the thick red ink, and then wiped it down my face. "scream, force that pain and rage out, get rid of it! Speak your truth free and unburden yourself from it!" Agnes challenged hastily. The drumming grew louder and more rapid. The years of abuse, fear and hiding raced through my brain. I plunged my fist through the water, hitting the sand below, and screamed. The twelve Wotan witches screamed with me. I sat upright on my feet then started to release the words that needed to be spoken with my cries.

The witches continued their screams as if shielding me from the embarrassment of it and letting me know I wasn't facing this alone. "HOW COULD YOU! YOU ARE ALL I HAVE, AND I CAN'T TRUST YOU! STOP HURTING ME! I AM SMALLER THAN YOU! I deserve better. I AM WORTHY OF KINDNESS AND LOVE! STOP, BECAUSE OF YOU, I HAVE HATED AND DOUBTED MYSELF! IT IS YOU I SHOULD HATE AND DOUBT! Not me," I curled back into a ball and wept. The others fell silent with me. When I sat up, Agatha handed me the apple and told me to eat it. I did, and I could feel its magic mending my shattered heart, then she motioned for me to go to the bed.

I walked to it and laid down. Ebba stood next to me, used the shears to cut a small braid of my hair from behind my ear, and handed it to Adliza, who wrapped it around the egg and placed it next to me. Acilia started to cover me in the lavender and chamomile buds.

Abela spoke as she did, "Close your eyes and fill the space the pain used to be, fill it with courage, kindness, friendship, and self-love," She paused, and I thought of all the good times. I pictured the joy I felt while camping with my family, my grandparents talking to me on their front porch, Waddle's belly laughs, the fireflies, and all the beauty I had seen and experienced with my friends and while in Asgard. Then Abela continued with a chant.

"We cleanse your spirit and set you free no longer alone in burden will you be. We summon to you goodness, courage, honor, and peace, then with lavender and chamomile we bind love to Jamie." She said it thrice, and I sat up and inhaled deeply as if it was my first ever breath. I felt amazing and free. "The cleansing is complete!" Abela bellowed then witches howled in Joy.

Ella sat next to me and handed me the mirror, and spoke,

"now we perform the linking. Look into the mirror and stare into your eyes, for in you the chosen symbol lies." I stared into my own eyes and cleared my head of any thoughts or questions. My face turned to a blur, then disappeared, and white mist rolled past my gaze. Then three triangles floated into view, each linking three planets one to another, then the three triangles interlinked, connecting all nine worlds. All life in them was intertwined. The creatures, the trees, the rivers, the soil, and the people all were one. "All things are connected," I whispered, recognizing the deeper meaning of what I was looking at. Then I announced its name, "I see the Valknut!" and put the mirror down.

Etta sat by my legs facing me with the ink and skinny nail, and Edela, with the small hammer, sat at my side and took my right arm into her lap. "We must imprint the symbol on you now for the linking to work," Edela studied my wrist. I looked at the nail, ink, and hammer and realized they meant to tattoo me.

"Stop! You can't tattoo me. My parents will have my head and will skin me to remove it! It's not normal on earth for someone my age to have a tattoo," I withdrew my arm.

Etta smiled and spoke, "Jamie, the gading mark will remain invisible to the mortal's eye until you come of age and wish it to be seen. The gading mark is your link to Asgard and to us. If you need help, you need only to trace the outline clockwise, and we will come to you and help you. Or if you trace it counterclockwise, it will bring you to us, and when you tap the center, it will return you home." I looked at Etta and nodded and gave her my hand back and braced. She began etching the tattoo. I cringed with the first poke, but after that, nothing.

When she was finished, I marveled at her work. My skin had barely bled, and there was almost no swelling. "That wasn't so bad," I thought.

Agata walked over to me, handed me the chalk, and told me, "Now draw my symbol on the egg." I did as she asked, then she continued, "now bury the egg and the braided hair into the earth and say an incantation. Do this as your offering."

I nodded and walked to the woods and dug a little hole. I gently put the egg and my hair in it and covered it, then drew the rune Gebo over it in the dirt and let the words for my offering come to me. "I feel the magic stirring around and bid you to allow, linking the Wotan witches to me. Ignite my gading mark so that it may be. I offer you here part of me and abundance in an egg so that we may make this trade." I looked at my wrist. It glowed briefly then settled, completely healed.

I turned to the witches. Adelixa walked to me and handed me my horn then stated, "drink, and it will be done." I took the horn and drank the honeyed water, and we walked back to the hut. Once we arrived, Adelixa told me to go back to the castle and read the book Odin gave me, and I bid everyone good night and took my leave.

When I got to my room, I took a bath first, and a set of clothes had materialized. They were laid out for me with a robe when I got out of the water, and I slipped into them. Then plopped down on the bed, I opened my book with the pair of dragons, and my heart skipped a beat. It was a book about every type of key.

Chapter Seventeen, The Key to Going Home

The book had tale after tale of keys. I realized very few keys actually belonged to locks or doors, but rather can be, love, a latch, a turning point in someone's story, or a hand, a button. In one instance, it mentioned a marble being sent through a hole to trigger a lock. It could be a series of numbers or fire. There were so many possibilities. The book didn't narrow my search down to a specific key but made me realize that a key could be more than a piece of tin, and to learn how to lock The Gate would mean I would have to know who unlocked it and what kind of key they used. "I have to get those diaries from the abandoned house from Shelly! I have three more days here. Maybe I can send Sally to fetch it or narrow down what kind of key it is with the Wotan Witches. I wonder what time it is on earth. I know it's supposed to be just a few minutes, and if I risk leaving, I wouldn't have time to finish my training. I still have so much more to learn." I walked to my belt and pulled out my watch to see what time it was.

"The watch still isn't moving. I wonder if the battery is dead?" I pondered as I looked at it. I continued trying to mull over a plan in my mind to contact Onacona, Shelly, and Connie and to get the papers and books so we could figure out what type of keys we were looking for and try to at least get this part of the puzzle done. Still, I also wanted to stay and learn more, and the Wotan witches would be a great source of information to help us solve this. "I can't just sit and do nothing," I decided and headed to the staircase and touched it. I walked into the great hall, and the twelve Wotan Witches were standing in it waiting for me. "Hey, I need your help in figuring out what and how many keys for The Lion's we need," I advised as I approached them.

I knew they didn't all just show up to say hi. I knew they were planning something, but that had to wait. This was more important. "Jamie, it's time," Agnes said.

"Time for what? To figure out what each key is? Yes, I agree. Let's find the keys," I pushed, not willing to accept another ritual at this time.

"Jamie, it's time for you to rejoin your friends and share what you have learned. It's time for you to go," Edela said with almost a whisper.

"No, I can't. I'm still horrible at fighting, and I feel like if I work with you all on this, we can figure it out a lot quicker. Plus, I don't want to leave. My room makes my bed for me and gives me clothes that don't get dirty, and I love you all." I burst into tears and rushed to Agatha and hugged her. Then started grabbing at the others to pull them into my hug, and they closed in around me. I knew in my heart that Edela had spoken the truth. I needed to close The Gate.

"There is one more thing we want to give you before you go," Acilia offered.

"No, please don't, I don't have anything to give to you, and if there is one thing I have learned since being here is that there is a balance to uphold. A gift for a gift." I wept, feeling already so indebted to everyone here.

"Well, it's not really a gift. I am returning your amulet to you. We just tweaked it a bit. I give it back to you confident that you won't misuse it," Afridh mused and slipped it over my head.

"Oh, right, I gave it to you earlier today. What did you do with it? It doesn't look any different." I asked while looking it over carefully.

"Tap the center of the spiral," Ella instructed. I did, and a puddle formed in front of me.

"Gee, thank you so much. This will come in really handy when it's hot outside." I smiled my best, thank you smile while completely confused by it. The Wotan Witches laughed and laughed.

"Is this a prank? I put my hands on my hips and tapped my foot.

"Having you here has been the best gift we have had in a really long time. Your energy reminded us of what it was to once be young. Watching you has made us laugh. It was priceless when Agata shared her memories with all of us of you bucking when you were trying to skiftende while hunting the bull. Ha-ha." Adelixa roared with laughter.

"You all saw that?" I felt humiliated and blushed.

"What Adelixa is trying to say is you restored and returned us to our formal power. With that power, we were able to make a portal for you. Therefore, a trade was accomplished," Ebba expressed.

"Really a portal? How awesome! Oh, wait, I'm already torn. I want to stay here and go to my friends and China. If I enter it, I will surely die," I rambled and took a step back from the puddle.

"This portal is controlled by your voice and mind alone.

You tell it where you want to go, and it will take you there as long as it is in the same realm. You must use your gading mark to travel here. There are but two rules for using this portal, firstly never try and jump to another world or realm with it. Secondly, only magically blessed individuals may travel through it with you. Mortal often will take what isn't there's, and since only you can command it, they may try to take you too to own its power. Eventually, mortals will figure out how to make portals. Showing them this one will greatly alter the course of nature and the lives of the people involved. Otherwise, enjoy China for us. The Yuan Gardens are beautiful this time of year," Adliza winked.

"Thank you all so much. I am going to annoy the crap out of you with my gading mark. Just so you know," I teased. We hugged, and I returned to my room to find my items already packed. I lifted my suitcase and then headed back to the hall to locate Sally.

When I entered the great hall, Odin, Frigga, and Hermodr were there. I turned to Odin and Frigga and politely said, "Thank you all so much for your support, for helping me, for welcoming me into your beautiful home, for the party. Well, for everything, really. It all means so much to me. I wish there was a way to repay you for your kindness.

Odin smiled then responded, "You and I will have a less straining conversation one of these days. I look forward to the time we get to meet again."

I nodded and gave the muscular beast a hug. Then I looked at Frigga, and she knelt to my height and hugged me and whispered in my ear, "don't forget what I said, don't fear death." I nodded.

I looked at Hermodr, "How's the arm?" Odin and Frigga both started laughing.

"How's your swordsmanship?" Hermodr retorted.

"Why does that matter? I don't plan on getting into any mid-evil battles soon," I rebutted.

Odin and Frigga turned and started walking towards a door, and I watched them as they went.

"Now there's a beautiful couple," I thought. I looked a Hermodr and rolled my eyes, "Well, I'll see you soon," I smiled, and he nodded and looked sad. I took a few more steps and realized I couldn't leave it that way, so I looked over my shoulder and said, "Hermodr, thanks for all your help too. Next time I come back and have some time, maybe you could teach me how to use a sword."

He turned and looked at me, "It would be my pleasure." I nodded and walked out the front door.

Sally stood waiting for me on the steps, "Alright, you ready?" I looked at the castle then at her.

"No!" I mourned and started to sob. Sally came to me and wrapped me in her arms, and I tucked my face into her sleeve. I felt a soft burst of wind, I pulled back and I was in my pocket realm. I dropped my bag and took in the room around me. I went to the landing and changed the outside to look like Asgard and whispered, "My heart will always be there."

I heard footsteps behind me, and I turned to find Onacona, Connie, and Shelly standing there, all with arms open wide. I rushed to them, and we embraced. "So, how was your trip to Asgard? Your back early?" Onacona noticed.

"It was absolutely magical," I told them everything I had learned. I showed them my new tattoo, and told them about my party, the Wotan Witches, the hunt, about my portal, and the book. Then I asked, "So how have you all been? What have you been up to?" They looked at each other and giggled. "What?" I asked.

"Well, where do I start? I had to spend my first-month training in the bogland of the world Vinjinkler, and let me tell you, it stunk so bad! I was tasked with finding a three-eyed toad called a hupshocter, and I searched all through the mud and the yuck before I bumped into one's leg," Connie paused and rolled her eyes. "Let's just say it wasn't pleased that I needed its eye for my crystal ball. I don't think I had ever flown so far as I did when that toad kicked me! After a long fight, I finally retrieved its eye. Then I had to learn to use it by licking the toad's corpse." Connie dry heaved.

I thought, "there's the Connie I know."

She continued, "Then I was tasked to find magic broomweed in the windswept world of the Fargoret people, and they are downright nasty, the whole lot of them! They were extremely religious. They worshiped the "almighty" Emgor, and being a witch was the ultimate crime. They chased me with torches and spears! Those silly people, here I am trying to save all the worlds, but would they listen? Nope. Then when I finally found the stupid broomweed. I had to make a broom from it and learn how to fly! Let's just say after I hit the first bump, I tossed out the wooden handle and replaced it teeter-totter seat and bar. I had to learn to read curses and what to do to undo them. That brings me to

Shelly Because if I go over everything that has happened over the past couple of months, I'll just be talking for next three days. Why don't you go Shelly," Connie huffed and shook her head?

Shelly began, "I can't wait to spend a few days with you! I have really missed you. To think, if I hadn't met you, we wouldn't be here. The past few months were the best, so fun! I helped realign a new solar system. I winked at you the night you were sitting outside with Frigga. She winked back at me. I got close to The Lion's Gate and tossed as much power at it as possible, but it sent it hurling back at me, and I ended up really far away. If I didn't have my stone, I think I would've been lost forever.

Then, Vega and I discovered that The Lion's Gate was opened a long time ago. The tale of how, was hidden in our world when the proud Khnum broke through The Gate to enter earth and rule over all the lands. Then Khonsu, a hunter from Khnum's home planet, came and dragged him back and ended the tyranny. Still, other beings used the rift to travel here for thousands of years before it was closed. So, Vega and I traveled to try and find out how The Gate was opened the first time and what the keys were, that were used back then to close it. I went to Konhnsu, the planet Khnum came from. To see if I could get any clues, but the planet was in ruin.

I did manage to find one thing though. In one of the old museums in a shattered display case named after Khnum, it had a picture of a bull horned alien man beast then this, I think it's a map." Shelly handed me a stone tablet with what looked like a layout of pyramids spread over our earth. It had little markings on the contents. I recognized some of the places from geography in school and having to memorize all the countries for class. The triangles were etched on Mexico, throughout South America, Egypt, Italy, Cambodia, Iraq, Indonesia, Rome, Antarctica, and more.

"Can I hang on to this? Also, really great find." I praised Shelly, and she smiled.

"Oh, I can go on forever about how wonderful the sky is but, I should give Onacona a turn." Shelly winked at Onacona, and she nodded.

Onacona swallowed and said, "I went to the Wilnoc World and met all the great healers from all sorts of worlds. I learned how to wield magic to end and begin life. I learned how to listen to one's soul, and I have a sisterhood there too. We walked through the resting spirit realms of different worlds to collect the devoroc. The twisted soulless."

Onacona paused and looked worried, "The ghost realms are a mess right now. The devoroc are entering new life in the waiting realm where they shouldn't be, and from what I can tell, it has been happening for a while. Then when they are in the wombs of their host's mothers, they pass from the baby to the Mom, and then, when the adults lock in love, they mostly move to the males and rest in them, twisting them.

I have learned how to spot when they are in someone or infecting a ghost. My Stepmom was infested with one." Onacona paused.

I asked, "So what she did wasn't really her fault?"

Onacona looked at me, "It was her fault you have to be twisted on some level, to begin with, and they feed into those desires and make them more appealing. The people are still in control. They just have heightened impulses. We have to close The Gate. So, we can banish them to the eccotomb where they will be devoured and turned into gravel. So, we can end the infestation. They are especially attracted to power, so they infect our leaders, and the people meant to protect us," Onacona shivered and had horror in her eyes.

"OK, we need a plan, Connie. Why don't you send Cordelia to secure the books we collected from the abandoned house? We should start there and see if any of the locations on this map are tied to anything in those journals. People don't just accidentally open The Lion's Gate. Someone had to organize this." I paused to think of what else we should do. "After that, I think we need to go back to the first abandoned house to collect the books and papers we left behind. Then we need to investigate the other abandoned houses around the school as well. Connie and I will take point when we go there since we have fought off beasts and survived. Onacona, if we come across any ghosts, you tell us if they are good or bad. Shelly, you have a ridiculous amount of power, and since you found the map. Maybe you could see if you can't find out who did this, but first the journals and the books," I said, ready to go.

"Wait, what about our families and School?" Connie asked. I thought.

"We need a plan for that too. Maybe we can find a way to be gone four days tops? If we can hop back and forth between the pocket realms, we can buy ourselves time that way. I mean, fifteen minutes on earth is about three months here, right?" I submitted, then tried to figure out how we could convince our parents to let us be gone longer.

"I know. Let's go back to The Pondering Pixie, meet my Dad, slip him into the meeting room, and then meet back at your pocket realm. He will think we are in the restroom, and then we will find your parents and tell them we are having another sleepover that will buy us another earth day and night. After we will tell my Dad we are staying at Shelly's, ride home with him and slip back into this realm, Then tell Shelly's parents she is staying at my place. If we hop back and forth, we can use as little earthly time as possible," Onacona suggested.

"That might work. How do we get all our parents to agree?" I asked, coming up empty-handed and everyone looked stumped. "Well, we can try," I felt doubtful that I would get a yes. "Connie, you go summon Cordelia, and I'll tell Sally what we are planning," I entailed as I made my way to the other room.

After Cordelia left to collect the journals and I had Sally standing watch, we slapped our stones and found ourselves in the Pondering Pixie. Everything looked back to normal, all the people from before were still there chatting and shopping as if nothing had happened. The priestess looked relieved to see I was OK, and I gave her a smile. The store entrance bell rang, and Dawn stepped in.

Onacona ran to him and wrapped her arms around him, and said, "I missed you, Dad."

Dawn chuckled and patted her head, "I've only been gone a few minutes."

Onacona's eyes widened, and she giggled, "let me show you to the meeting room. Then I'm going to run to the toilet." Onacona looked at us, and we clapped our stones and returned to my pocket realm.

I asked Connie, "Can you use your crystal ball and see where my parents are at?" She nodded and entered into her pocket realm, then came back with a giant fluid-filled eye. "Oh, Conny that's gross, I don't even want to think of what the rest of this creature looked like," I sneered as I looked at it.

"No, you really don't," Connie quipped. She gazed deeply into the large red pupil and started sliding her hands around it, and somehow the thing was still sticky. It didn't seem to bother her.

"Huh, didn't she shame Onacona for carrying the Ogre's head? I guess she's grown." I thought as I watched her.

She let out a croak, and stood, "They're at the dollar theater."

Cordelia popped in with the journals. "You mortals live in the worst filth," Cordelia huffed.

"Ya right! I've seen the inside of your hut. You have body

parts in jars," Connie retorted with her hands on her hips.

"Here are your books. I'll be in my bog getting the human body soil and germs off of me. Next time you need me to fetch something, send me somewhere outside, not an indoor cesspool," Cordelia wined.

Connie muttered, "Unbelievable. My house is spotless. Hers looks like a hoarder's den."

We pulled out the journal and opened it and started reading. "I had a strange dream last night that an Ogre entered my tent and took the schematics of my ground-penetrating radar results for the work we've been doing, it seemed unshakably realistic, and when I went to collect them today, they seemed wrinkled and warn. Just odd. That aside, we located a unique etching on the walls in one of the tombs. That we established with the radar. It has the star consultation, Leo, when the sun and Sirius are aligned, creating what's known as The Lion's Gate. For an astronomical event, these take place frequently, once every year around the beginning of August, to be exact. So, finding out the significance will be a journey on its own." We looked at each other with raised brows. "Does it say where the dig was?" Connie asked, and I started flipping through the pages and reading. "No, it just says Z.U.I. when he is referring to its location. I answered. I looked at the stone map.

"That doesn't narrow it down enough. We need to go through that room again. See if we can't find an old airplane ticket or something. I bet the last letter 'I' stands for the country. Still, if you look here on the map, there are pyramids in Iraq, Iran, Indonesia, and India. That's too many places to search. We need to investigate the other houses as well. There might be something hidden in one of them, a clue," I slapped the journal closed, annoyed.

"Wait, the three houses make a triangle, and our school sits in the middle. Most of the staff is unnaturally rude. Pyramids are triangles, it all has to mean something. Also, whatever growled at us from the other house may have been what killed the Ogre. It all has to be connected," Shelly added. We all sat perplexed.

Onacona walked in. "Are we ready? We need to make this quick she motioned.

I looked at Connie, "Are my parent's still there?" She looked into the eye again and answered, "yes, and your Mom is in the bathroom, so perfect timing." We slapped our stones, and it returned us to the Pondering Pixie.

"Oops, I guess the stone returns us where we woke it up last? Are you all ready to try my portal for the first time ever?" I offered a bit nervously. We all went into the bathroom, and I tapped my stone and said, "Dollar theater bathroom." The puddle formed in front of us, and I hopped in first. I landed in the bathroom in a stall and quickly shut the stall door, then the others popped in behind me. I placed a finger over my lips to let them know not to talk about jumping through a portal. I heard a toilet flush, and I exited and went to the sink to pretended to wash my hands, and my Mom walked out.

"Oh, hi, Mom, what a coincidence," I greeted with a smile and gave her a hug.

"Oh Jamie, what a surprise, what are you doing here?" She looked at me "Oh child, what on earth are you wearing?" My Mom scowled. I looked down and realized I was in leather overalls and a white tank top and my belt.

"Oh, ya, I forgot I was still wearing this. We were playing dress-up at Shelly's house.

"Are those real knives?" My Mom puzzled, and I stepped back.

"No, they are realistic replicas," I lied and started blushing.

"Why on earth would Shelly's parents allow you to wear fake weapons in public, and it's way too cold to be running around in a tank top!?" My Mom grilled.

"Um, can I have another hug?" I gave her my puppy dog look.

"Don't try and butter me up. I have half a mind to drive you home right now. Good lord child!" My Mom scolded with a look of disappointment on her face. I started thinking of what I could say. Then Shelly walked out.

"Hi, Mrs. Eriksen, sorry about what Jamie's wearing. We were playing outside with our coats on, and then my Mom offered to bring us here. We were so excited we forgot to change. My Mom didn't notice it with her coat on," Shelly fibbed. My Mom started to blush for questioning her Mom in front of her. It was something parents just didn't do.

Then Connie walked out and added, "We left our coats on our chairs to save our spot in the movie. Hurry up, Onacona. We don't want to miss any of the good parts."

Then Onacona walked out, "Hi Mrs. Eriksen, I was wondering if you would allow Jamie to stay the night at Shelly's again. My Dad said I could, and I need her help with some of homework that I'm trying to catch up on, and with some other things." Onacona looked at her arms, and my Mom turned to mush.

"Alright, dear. Jamie, I want you home at a decent time

tomorrow, hear me?" My Mom instructed.

"Yes, Mom," I nodded, and we walked out of the bathroom and around the corner, then I quietly opened my portal and spoke, "My house," We all hopped in and landed in my bedroom. The girls quickly made their way to the phone to call their parents as we had planned. I stayed back and looked at my room. It seemed so small now and unwelcoming. I sat on my bed, and it felt uncomfortable, unlike the soft beds in Asgard or my pocket realm. It was weird, but it didn't feel like my room. It was as if I didn't belong there anymore. I walked down the hall and looked into my sibling's rooms, and they too felt like something foreign, something that wasn't home anymore, just a distant memory. It would be hard to adapt back to this life after having a peek into a better one.

I slipped into my parent's room next and pictured all the times I had to lean over the bed and pull down my pants for a whipping. "Never again!" I mumbled to myself. I walked to the kitchen, and the girls had made their calls, and it was all arranged.

"We have the rest of the day and the night and tomorrow together," Connie announced.

"If it all works out like we want it to, we could have

months, possibly a year, until we have to return," I blurted out with a smile, and everyone else faces dropped at the idea. So, I shrugged, "We ready?" I looked around, and everyone nodded. I tapped my amulet and said, "Pondering Pixie." The puddle opened, and we hopped in. We landed in the toilet stall and made our way into the meeting room, and the lesson was about to start. "Oh no, we didn't plan to have to stay for this," I whispered to Onacona, and she looked away from everyone in the room. I saw blue light coming from around her eyes, and the ground started to rumble, and then it stopped.

Everyone in the room gasped, "Was that an earthquake?" Then the room filled with chatter.

"I think it was. We better cancel class so I can check the store and make sure everything is in place and that there isn't any gas leaking," Priestess Singing Rock announced.

"That's really strange. I don't think that's ever happened here. That's too bad, girls looks like we have to go home," Dawn said, and we each gave an "oh shucks or oh darn" in response, then headed off to his truck. On the drive home, Onacona asked her Dad if she could stay the night at Shelly's again, and he reluctantly agreed. When we pulled up to their house Onacona gave her Dad another long hug, then we headed to the nearest bush and clapped our stones.

Chapter Eighteen, Travel Abroad

We arrived back in my pocket realm. I opened the door to the room that had been a kitchen and said, "Before we do anything else, let's eat." I focused on the fanciest restaurant I had ever been to, and the bare room turned into its dining hall.

"Good choice," Shelly looked pleased.

"Well, I'll have the lobster ravioli and chilled prawns," I spoke, and it materialized in front of me.

"Oh, I'll have the crab cock tale and clam chowder," Shelly requested.

"I'll have the crab legs and blackened salmon," Onacona chimed in. We turned to Connie, and she looked troubled.

"What?" I asked.

"I hate seafood." She uttered displeased.

"Connie, we are in a magic realm. You can order

whatever you want," I taunted her.

"Oh, right, I'll have a Hawaiian pizza with curly fries and a large side of ranch dressing," Connie ordered then we all dug into our meals.

"This is so much better than apples," I thought as I ate my lobster ravioli. When we were done. We headed back to my room.

"OK, before we go back to the abandoned house, let's go through all the papers we have here and make sure we aren't missing anything," I suggested. We read through everything carefully. Most only stated the duties of the people at the site and how the machinery functioned. Then a passage caught my attention. "Listen to this!" I motioned to everyone and started to read.

"Somehow, today, during routine mapping and marking of the east tunnel, The crew and I all became overly exhausted, and within minutes we all fell unconscious. We awoke hours later and immediately left. Several tests were run to check the air quality of the chamber. However, everything came back normal. When we got the, go ahead we went back into the tunnel, just a few feet further down from where we fell. I found a door we hadn't noticed previously. Upon entering the room, we found a large alter with a stand. Whatever was in the stand will remain a mystery as it was gone. However, the markings on the alter depicted three symbols. On one side of the altar, I saw three drawings and on the other three more. The first was a ghost, the second was a falling star, and the third marking is yet to be deciphered. On the other side is a depiction of the ancient God Khnum, the bull-horned God. Which is odd since we aren't in Egypt. Then It depicts him trapping souls or spirits in a gate to keep it open. The third is a depiction of Khnum traveling through The Gate by what looks like a rocket ship. Which would be impossible because the Sumerian civilization is the most ancient civilization known to mankind."

I took a breath "Listen, the first three have to represent the keys, three keys, we need three! The other three must be what he did to keep The Gate open, but not only that. Don't you think it's odd that we thoroughly searched the whole abandoned house, but upon entering the most important room, we, all suddenly, became too tired to search it thoroughly? It was the only room untouched in the whole house as if everyone who attempted to explore it became too tired to bother with it. Just like the researchers all fell asleep in the tunnel. I don't think this can be a coincidence!" I determined feeling that someone cast a spell to keep people out.

"I think you're right; let's go to my pocket realm. I have an awake potion I can make; maybe it will counteract whatever is making everyone sleepy," Connie got up and started walking towards the side door.

"I think the Sumerian Civilization is a huge clue to where the pyramid is. I need to ask Catori if she knows where they lived. Onacona's eyes glowed blue, and Catori appeared. "Yes, you needed me?" Catori smiled at Onacona. Where did the Sumerian people live?

"The Sumatrans? That was long ago. If I have my Earth geography correct, they lived in what is now Iraq and Iran. Why?" Catori asked.

"No time to explain we are on a mission. Thank you." Onacona said and walked past her.

"If a specific fallen star is a key, that is going to be really difficult to find. There are thousands of starts falling every night, and if it hit the earth, it can be deep within an ocean," Shelly added, and we all paused.

"Maybe we should just focus on the first key, for the moment then, and we can see if that gives us any clues to where the fallen star might be. If we need a ghost, I'm sure Onacona can help us find one. However, it will probably be a specific ghost as well. So, let's just focus on that. We need to look at the alter and see if anything is missing from the journals. We should head out to see if we can narrow down our location. There are lots of pyramids still in Iraq and Iran, and every time we leave the pocket realm, time turns against us," I rambled on, mostly thinking out loud.

When we entered Connie's pocket realm, I was shocked to find a mix of boy band posters and name-brand clothing mixed with magical objects, a book of spells, a cauldron, and a shelf full of bottles filled with spices, things, and herbs. "Let me just look here," Connie pulled out a large leather-bound book and started scrolling through the pages. I noticed that I couldn't see the outside of Connie's room, and my curiosity was sparked, so I walked to where it should be, and I reached out my arm, and it went through the wall. I stepped through and found all the boys from the poster walking around, holding flowers. I stuck my head back through the wall.

"Really, Connie?" I teased. She instantly went red.

"What are you doing?! I put the wall up because I couldn't make them go away!" Connie argued.

"Sure, you did," I teased while lifting my eyebrows.

"Oh, I have to see this." Shelly mused and began walking

towards me.

"Oh, you haven't seen this. Get prepared to be thrilled," I winked.

Onacona eyeballed us and tried to stay put, but curiosity got the best of her, and she walked through the wall to join us. Connie came running behind her to stop her. Once Connie stepped through, all the guys started bringing her the flowers. Then some started offering her plates with food.

"Connie, you clever girl," Shelly chirped as she took in the singers.

"Oh, dear," Connie blushed.

"Yup, this is a total accident. That's why they only come to you, right?" I snickered.

Connie picked up a caramel square from one of the plates and popped it in her mouth. "A girl can dream, right? In fact, it was one of your dreams that made me think of it, and I wasn't really into the unicorns," She explained with a grin, and we all burst into laughter. I blushed.

"What did I dream?" I dared to ask, hoping it wasn't too bad.

"Oh, about some hottie maybe a bit older than us with long hair always wearing an orange tunic and necklace with a bone on it.' Connie made kissing motions with her mouth.

"What the! I dreamed of Hermodr?!" I thought.

"So, who is he?" Shelly tittered, and I began to blush.

"No one." I lied.

"If it was really no one, then you would've said, I don't know, so spill," Onacona called my bluff, and I looked at her.

"Really? Now you chime in," I glared, only she could call my bluff.

"That wasn't an answer," Onacona pushed.

"He's someone I just met in Asgard. I don't know how I dreamed about him. I didn't know him yet." I argued.

"Ooooh, Jamie has a boyfriend." Shelly snickered.

"I do not!" I protested.

"Then tell us who he is?" Connie grinned. Loving that the attention was off of her.

"He's a jerk and." I stopped, but it was too late, and I knew what was coming.

"And" Onacona was grinning and loving this way too much.

"Fine, his name is Hermodr, and he's the son of Odin and Frigga, and apparently we used to be, or still are? I don't know. It's weird to think about. My higher self who is inside me, he's, her husband!" I spat in disgust, and Connie's mouth opened so wide her candy fell out.

"No way! That is so weird," Shelly gaped.

"You're telling me I had to dance with him at my party, anyhow. Can we please get back on task?" I pleaded, and we went back into the main room. Connie started pulling items from her shelf.

"So, did you kiss him?" Onacona asked quietly.

"Gross not in a million years." I made a gagging motion.

"If I ask my bluestocking, do you think she will tell me if I have a husband out there?" Shelly whispered.

"No, don't ask. I wasn't supposed to find out. Sally had to tell me because I began to hate him," I explained.

"So, you don't hate him?" Onacona raised her eyebrow.

"No, I don't hate him. I just don't like him. Can we please change the topic?" I growled.

"Come help me find all the parts to this potion," Connie ordered as she started to line up bottles, and I was relieved that there was something else to concentrate on.

"Sure, what do you need?" I asked.

"Love because it's a looovee potion," Connie mocked, and everyone erupted into laughter, and I started to blush again.

"Haa Haa. Connie, I bet your cosmic husband is out there right now, shaking his head at all your boyfriends. Mine said he checks in on me," I snapped, and Connie's eyes widened as she dropped her ladle, and Shelly and Onacona started to roar. Then Connie handed me a couple bottles.

"Here, put these in the mix." She instructed, and I moved to the cauldron. After the potion was made and things had settled down. We hunkered together.

"OK, we will end up where we clapped our stones last, and then I will open a portal to the abandoned house. We go straight to the fourth room and grab as many items as possible. Then we run outside and clap our stones, so we don't end up back inside when we leave here again. Got it?" I asked, and everyone shook their heads.

Connie passed out Dixie cups with bubbling brown goo in them and said, "Drink up."

I lifted the cup and gagged. "Oh yuck, I don't think I can. Can't we add chocolate or something to it first?" I asked.

"Oh, just plug your nose and pop it down in one gulp," Connie rolled her eyes, and I plugged my nose and chugged the bubbling goo.

* * *

"Ready?" I asked, and we clapped our stones, and when the mist cleared, we were in the bushes we left from. I tapped my amulet and said, "abandoned house." The puddle formed in front of us, and we jumped in. We landed in the living room and ran to the back room. I swung open the door, and we entered and started shoving items into plastic bags, grabbing anything that could be a clue.

We heard a crash, and the house shook. We all froze. "Was that you, Onacona?" I asked.

"No," She answered.

"OK, you keep grabbing stuff. I'll look check the hall," I volunteered, and everyone rushed. Shelly started opening drawers on the desk as I crept to the door and looked into the hall, and the house shook again.

"There's a locked compartment in the desk. I can't get it open," Shelly called out. Loud stomping was coming down the hall, but I couldn't see anything.

"Blast magic at it!" I yelled and slammed the door shut as the steps quickened.

"Oh right," Shelly hummed.

"Hurry up! Something is coming!" I pleaded, then the knob started to twist, and I grabbed it. Then something pushed against the door, and I leaned against it. I began to slide forwards, so I popped my neck and Skiftende as the force was too much for my mortal strength to hold.

"Hurry!" I cried out. Then the house began shaking violently, and the door burst from its hinges sending me hurdling across the room with it. I hit the desk knocking it over. My ears rang from hitting my head. Through blurry vision, I saw my friends standing in front of me blasting their magic at a giant ape-like creature, hair coving most of its body except its face and bald chest, which had spiral carved into its very skin deflecting their powers. I rolled to my side to get up, and an envelope taped to the bottom of the desk caught my attention. I grabbed it quickly and tucked it into my belt pocket, and my watch fell out. I grabbed it to put it back in and noticed it was ticking. "It wasn't ticking in Asgard or my pocket realm. Or was it?" I thought. I pulled the knob to stop it, and the house stopped shaking, and everyone rocked and fumbled and stopped for a moment, confuse. I tucked it into my pocket and then retrieved my knives. I ran around my friends, my amulet shielding me, and I tripped right when I was about to attack, my arms flew down, and my knife cut the toes off of the creature.

It howled in pain and started to weep. "My toes, you cut

off my toes," It bellowed in a gruff and deep tone. I quickly got up and stood ready to fight, and it wailed some more.

"You can speak," I asked.

The creature looked surprised. "You understand me?" It managed to get out.

"You're speaking English, so of course I can," I answered.

"No, I am speaking in Garlock, the language of the of my people." The creature answered. I looked at my friends, and they all looked puzzled.

"He's speaking English, right?" I questioned.

"No, you are speaking whatever he is. How are you doing that?" Connie asked.

"How am I?" I thought and remembered the spell the Wotan Witches cast on me. "Oh, it must be a spell my coven cast on me," I whispered, and the creature moaned again, and everyone flinched.

"What does it want?" Onacona asked, so I turned and reflected on how the journal said that an Ogre took his schematics.

"Why did you attack us, and why did you take the original owner of this house, schematics from the pyramid?" I asked.

"I didn't attack you. Most people can't see me. I remembered you from the night of the storm and thought you were back to collect something you left behind when I heard you taking more. I was only trying to scare you away. How do you know about the pyramid, and why are you stealing from Jacob?" The creature asked.

"I asked you first," I replied.

"I can't talk about that, please I need help. I can't walk like this," the creature pleaded.

"If we help you and put your toes back on, will you agree to take us to someone who can tell us about the pyramid?" I proposed.

"I can't do that," he cried.

"Well, enjoy being toe-less," I turned to my friends and opened the portal.

The creature gasped, "Witches."

I turned around, "Yes, we are, and we are powerful too. Do you want your toes back on or not?" I posed the question again.

He didn't budge, so I lifted my foot to jump in, then he cried out, "Wait!" I smiled a wicked smile and turned.

"So, we have a deal then?" I looked at him, and he nodded. I closed the portal.

"Onacona, can you heal him?" I asked.

"Yes, but are you sure?" She questioned, looking uneasy about getting close to giant.

"Yes, he's agreed that if we heal him, he'll take us to see someone who can tell us about the pyramid," I reassured her. Onacona gave the nod and moved towards the creature. He recoiled when she got close. "She's not going to hurt you. She's going to help you. Do you have a name?" I asked the creature.

"Yes, I am Buttercup," Buttercup said, and I barked out a laugh on accident.

"Oh, sorry, I got a tickle. It's a witch thing, so why Buttercup?" I figured it would be Brutus or Basher, not Buttercup.

"It's the term humans use for our flower of masculinity, and the sound of it demands respect and emanates with power," Buttercup preached with pride. I fought hard against the urge to laugh.

"Can I start?" Onacona bid.

"My friend is going to start healing you now," I translated, and he nodded.

"Buttercup is ready for you to start," I told Onacona, and she paused and gave me a blank stare and then choked back a laugh.

"What's so funny?" Buttercup questioned as Onacona lifted one of his toes and started to wield her blue light around it.

"She has to laugh to get her powers flowing." I lied. He nodded, and Shelly whispered, is that really his name?

"Yes, it's a masculine name and demands respect and emanates with power," I chuckled back, and she and Connie both snorted, trying to contain their laughter.

"I have the toes reattached. I just need some powdered capers and algae to numb the pain and seal the wounds," Onacona announced.

"I'll get it," Connie offered and clapped her stone and vanished.

"Where did the other witch go? This isn't a trap, is it?" The Ogre roared.

"She went to collect some items to dress your wound. The toes are reattached. Also, speaking of traps, if you double-cross us, be warned I am a Wotan witch, and I can summon my whole coven in an instant, and they will slaughter you all to protect us! "I threatened.

"Me, double-cross you? Are you serious? It's humans that can't be trusted. Why do you think we stay hidden? Your kind is the monsters," Buttercup spat.

"That may be true for humans, but we are witches, and we only harm in self-defense or to eat," I retorted.

"Ya, and are you feeling hungry?" Buttercup asked and bared his teeth.

"We don't eat creatures we can talk to," I explained.

"All creatures can talk. You should know that if you are who you say you are," Buttercup made his point, and I was stumped, besides the bull, who had to die for his family to be born, I didn't see anyone in Asgard eat meat, and I felt shame.

"You have my word as a Wotan Witch that no harm will befall you or your kind unless it's in self-defense," I promised sincerely, and Buttercup nodded, accepting it.

Connie popped back in and handed Onacona the algae and powdered capers, and Onacona finished mending his wounds.

"Awe, that feels better. Tell your friend thank you." The Ogre said.

"Can he walk on it? I asked Onacona.

"Yes, It's just the skin that needs to mend completely. The tendons, muscles, and bones are healed. Skin, eyes, and hair take longer. Tell him to leave it on for two weeks. After that, he won't even have a scar." Onacona instructed and stood.

I repeated it to Buttercup, and he stood. "We did our part. Now it's your turn." I persisted.

"Alright, I'll take you to my land realm but don't be surprised if my kind finds you repulsive because you are." Buttercup cautioned.

"Well, thanks for the warning and the compliment," I smirked. Then translated for my friend.

"Do you think you can recreate the spell so we can understand him too?" Onacona asked.

"Hum, maybe. I can try. I think I remember it," I answered.

"Yes! Please do!" Shelly begged.

"I want it too," Connie added.

"OK, let me think," I said. Then I asked Buttercup to wait a moment, and he sat in the hall squished between the walls with his head bent at the ceiling, and I wondered how he managed to fit at all.

I thought hard about the spell and approached Connie. "Wait, why do I have to go first?" She protested.

"Because you wouldn't flavor the sludge," I mused. She rolled her eyes, and I took her head in my hands and pressed my thumbs into her cheeks. Then chanted. "Open maw where words thus flow, so you may natter what you do not know." Then I cupped her ears, and she flinched. "Ears to hear the subtle cues of words lost and words new, make the knowledge twist and stew, as they settle into you." I stepped back, and Connie cried out in pain and grabbed her head and vomited. Then her nose began to bleed, and I wiped it on my hand and drew a Gebo rune with it on the floor.

"That hurt!" Connie barked.

"Well, magic gifts come at a cost," I responded.

"Well, did it work?" Shelly asked.

"Hey, buttercup," I called.

"What?" He grumbled. I looked at Connie, and she nodded.

"Oh me, next," Shelly stepped up, and I repeated the spell, and she cried as she vomited. Then I looked at Onacona, and her face was pale.

"Well, your next, let's get on with it," I stated.

"I think I'll pay magic first," She said and lifted a pair of scissors from the ground and cut two locks of hair and laid them in an X pattern on the floor. "Ok, I'm ready," Onacona closed her eyes, and I did the spell. When it was done, she opened them and normally stood without pain.

"Don't tell me that worked," Connie grumbled.

Onacona called out, "We are ready to go now, Buttercup."

"Finally," He groaned and walked hunched over down the hall. We looked at Onacona.

"I understood him perfectly well. Thank you, Jamie," Onacona smiled.

"Son of a." Shelly, Connie, and I mumbled, and we walked down the hall following Buttercup.

When we got outside and into the yard, Buttercup instructed us, "Stand Back, this will get a bit shaky."

"Speaking of shaky, how come nothing is moving, look a bird is literally frozen in mid-air?" Connie questioned.

Everyone stopped and looked around. "That's my doing," I mentioned. "I wasn't sure since we were in the house, but I had a feeling. We didn't have enough time for all of this and, the watch from my belt look fell out, I pilled the tiny nob out, and everything to test it and it appears it worked.

"Whoa, that's awesome!" Shelly studied the watch.

"Hey, when Cordelia showed me the magical tools, I was about to pick up a watch, but I went for a magic wand instead. I wish I got the watch," Connie stammered.

"Why? A magic wand sounds awesome," I wondered.

"It's not. It's just a pretty stick that does nothing. Cordelia added it as a prank," Connie cursed under her breath.

"Oh, darn." I sighed, then the earth began to rumble, and the ground started to open beneath us. We stepped back, and a tunnel started to form.

Then Buttercup spoke, "This way," and he hopped in the hole.

"So that's why the house shook." Then I summoned my light, to use as a torch, and hopped in behind him, and Connie, Onacona, and Shelly hopped in behind me, and the earth closed up behind us.

I checked looked at my watch, and pushed the nob in but it didn't tick, so I knew we were in another realm. I slipped it in my pocket and followed Buttercup through a series of massive tunnels. As we went further and further, the tunnels opened wider and wider with markings and drawings covering the walls, and a story unfolded. It looked like the Ogres, and other creatures lived with humans at some point and got along. Then people started to read or talk and then they forgot how to communicate with other beings. Then the humans began hunting them to extinction, pictures of families dwindling until they were all gone. Next, a great storm blew snow over all the world. "The ice age," I believed.

The Ogres and other creatures I didn't recognize moved

to another realm saving what was left of them. Then they prospered in unity, only surfacing to gather things they needed from earth or to heal its forests.

"Buttercup, do these tunnels only lead to earth and your world?" I asked to pass the time as we walked past more drawings.

"No, not just your realm, other realms too. We know where to access them when we need to. Other realms are a secret from flesh-eaters, so don't ask how to get there," Buttercup mentioned.

I nodded to myself. "You know I got eaten once, your right, it is a horrible way to die," I said, and Buttercup stopped and looked at me.

"You are ugly but intact. Did the beast that ate you poop you out whole?"

"Not exactly. Let's just say Onacona healed me as well." I smiled at Onacona. He grunted, and we continued to walk.

"I'm curious were you alive when these paintings were made?" I asked as we passed some more depicting a journey of a creature to the fairy world.

"Some yes, some no," Buttercup answered.

"Where you around when your kind lived with humans?" Connie queried.

"No, that was before my time," Buttercup responded.

"Buttercup, you protect that room that Jacob worked in. Why?" I asked.

"To keep secrets for the foul beast," was all Buttercup said. We turned down another tunnel and approached a gigantic door the size of a ship, and the Ogre stopped.

"You stay with me and no eat anything unless I say so," Buttercup postulated.

"I agree." I spoke

"I promise," Onacona added,

"I swear," Connie affirmed.

"You have my word," Shelly vowed. Then the Ogre touched the door in several places, etched a symbol with his finger, and whistled a tune. Then the giant door became liquid.

"Follow me," Buttercup directed, and we followed him through the door.

Chapter Nineteen, Gaiagoblins

We stepped into what resembled a city, except the homes and offices were carved from stone or made from holes in hollow trees instead of buildings. The bridges were natural archways, and the water flowing beneath was clear as glass, but what really caught my attention was all the creatures that strolled down the streets. Some were human-like, only with huge gaping eyes and long slender noses. They were my height or a bit taller, with very lean bodies. Then there were short human-like beings who looked like garden gnomes with long rounded noses and bulging eyes wearing cloaks. There were fluffy creatures about the size of a German shepherd. They had furry faces that came abruptly to a point with beady eyes, and they spoke normally with the other. There was also short toad and pig-like creatures that walked upright and had two small horns atop their head, and of course, there were other Ogres, and the city was bustling. "Stay close." Buttercup motioned, and we started to follow him.

"This place is amazing. Look at all these inhabitants. It's like being in a fairy tale?" I whispered to my friends.

"Ya, I've been weirder places. This place seems nice compared to the boglands." Connie rattled.

"I saw spirits like this, but I haven't been anywhere like this before," Onacona inserted.

"This place is fabulous! I wish I had a camera and five roles film!" Shelly observed excitedly, and I nodded in agreement.

We stayed close to Buttercup as we walked to keep from drawing attention to ourselves, but it didn't take long before a toad-like being gasped, "What in the world are those creatures?"

I looked, and he was pointing at us. "We are witches," I said with a smile.

"Witches, you say. You look a lot like," His eyes grew wide, and he fled. After he was a safe distance away, I could hear him shouting, "The tales are true! The foul face flesh-eaters are real. Come and see!" I smiled, thinking people would have something similar to say about his face.

"Foul faces? Does he own a mirror?" Connie mumbled, and Buttercup groaned, so we all clinched our jaws.

"What are they doing here? Where did they come from?" I heard the creatures disputing.

"Great, this is how it started in Fargoret. First, they question, then they try to poison you, then they chase you with torches." Connie growled.

I smiled, "Some time you're going to have to tell me all the details of the places you have been or, better yet, take me there." I snuck a peek behind me, and a large crowd was following a good distance behind us.

"Sure, I'll take you, then they'll have someone else to throw rocks at sounds like a really great bonding opportunity," Connie snickered, and Shelly, Onacona, and I giggled.

We turned a corner, and large boulders were perturbing from the earth shaped similarly to a castle but crooked and twisted. "This is it. I'll take you inside to meet the one who can answer your question," Buttercup announced. We walked through a vast hall and into a massive empty room except for a throne made from vines sitting atop a platform. Two large doors closed behind us before the crowd had a chance to enter.

"Wilfred! Wilfred! I brought people from the Monster realm here to talk to you." Buttercup bellowed.

"Wilfred, it must be an old man, and it's not very formal for a castle," I whispered to my friends, and they nodded. Then the sound of soft feet echoed in the room.

"Coming." A woman's voice rang out, and we looked at each other again. One of the skinny human-like creatures entered the room. She had thin, stringy hair, those giant gaping eyes, and a long slender nose. She wore a crooked golden crown and black cloak. She sat on the throne and greeted us, "I'm Wilfred, ruler of the Gaiagoblin realm. Why have you come here?" She asked directly but pleasantly.

"We need to know what the artifact was that was taken by an Ogre in a pyramid, and where the pyramid is located, and anything else you can tell us about the three keys to close Lion's The Gate we are on a mission to restore balance," I asked hoping that revealing this wouldn't be used against us.

"I see, and if I tell you, what do I get?" Wilfred questioned, and I thought.

"I can cast a spell so you can understand any language in any universes," I offered.

"Hum, that could be useful, but I don't travel much these days. What else do you have to bargain with?" She studied us as I studied her.

"I healed Buttercup's toes, isn't that enough?" Onacona asked.

"Yes, you healed them in an agreement that he took you to someone who could give you answers, and I can. He fulfilled the terms of the arrangement. Now, what do you have to offer me?" Wilfred bade. I gripped my box and was ready to offer it, but before I could.

"I have a magic wand. It doesn't do anything, but it's beautiful, and someone with your beauty should have pretty things," Connie offered and pulled a jeweled wand out from the inside of her coat. It was beautiful and had a pink crystal adorning the top.

I admired it and thought, "I would've picked it too if I had been offered it." Connie lifted it up, and the queen's eyes fixated on it. Her blue tongue swiped at her lips, and she bent forward, almost standing.

"Now there's a trade! I accept! Buttercup, bring me the wand!" The queen demanded, and Connie handed it to Buttercup, and he took it to the queen. Wilfred's greedy fingers clawed at it, then she opened a hole in the earth and dropped it in. After she sat and looked at us.

"I have long wanted to obtain the wand of an Orgat.

How come it doesn't work?! Did you clean the Orgat's ear, and your wish failed?" Wilfred taunted.

"What?! That wand grants you a wish?!" Connie's mouth fell open, and I knew what she was thinking because I was thinking it too. We could've wished The Lion's Gate closed. It took all my strength not to argue with the queen and try to convince her to give it back. However, I knew it would be hopeless. If there was a chance to barter, she wouldn't have hidden it away. She did that encase we fought her for it. She knew that we didn't know what Connie possessed. I was furious, but I held my tongue. If we put up a fight, we would lose all hope of receiving what we came here to learn. I looked at Connie and could tell she was about to yell and throw something at the queen. So, I put my hand on her shoulder and shook my head.

"Wilfred, you have your half of the trade. Now you must respect our arrangement and honor the terms set forth," I insisted firmly but respectfully, trying to sound as much like my Dad did in court as possible.

"Yes, ask your questions," Wilfred agreed with a slight look of surprise.

"First, where is the pyramid, and what is its human name?" I knew to be specific this time.

"The pyramid you speak of is Ziggurat of Ur in Iraq," Wilfred answered.

"Who opened The Gate?" I questioned.

"The devoroc opened The Gate!" Wilfred spat, and Onacona's face contorted with fear and curiosity.

"How? They are incomplete. I know only spirits can travel through The Gate, but how are bits of twisted energy able to force The Gate to stay open?" Onacona questioned.

"It happened by chance when two foul pieces from the same being's lost soul collided and became one, and it became more powerful. So, it sought out its other missing parts, knowing its earthly master wasn't done inflicting his cruelty. Once all of its counterparts united, it formed into a monstrosity, the likes of which I had never seen before. However, in taking that form, he, at the time, unknowingly trapped himself in the spirit plane. Fore, a fully formed beast can't enter into a mother's womb and be born. So, for a time, all he could do was haunt your earth's physical plane, and he did in an attempt to learn how to cross the threshold and live.

Then in his journey, he began to recognize other pieces of devoroc that once belonged together and started matching them until an army of devoroc monsters was made, but an army wasn't enough. They still didn't have life, a world, or the ability to enter the physical realm and walk in the sunlight! So, the beast, not quite dead and not quite alive, went to The Lion's Gate when it opened and asked if he could travel through it. The Gate, not knowing what he was but seeing the death in him, allowed it, but only if he returned. Then the creature agreed and traveled. He saw magic in all the worlds and knew he might find a way to live in a physical plane if he had time to learn it! Then in an ancient, ruined world, he found a story of a being who forced The Gate to stay open. So, he decided he would do that to travel as he pleased and gain his knowledge. In one of his journeys through The Lion's Gate, he found a single devoroc had followed him, and he tossed it aside, and it collided with a waiting soul on its way to birth and stuck. Curious by this, the beast followed it. The devoroc's death was hidden by new birth's light and able to infest the soul and inter the mother's womb giving him a foothold in the physical plane.

The beast then released as many bits of devoroc as possible so they could do his bidding and infest the hierarchy's and compel them to enable their constituents to do their acts of horror! Then more and more would become soulless until all would be his to rule. Beware, the beast is cunning. He leaves enough devoroc behind to cover up his trail, not wanting to unveil himself until he obtains enough power to walk fully in any of the living planes of existence and rule all the realms." Wilfred paused, and my heart had dropped into the pit of my stomach.

"I have to tell the Wotan Witches and Asgard, no one is safe as long as The Gate is opened," I thought.

"How did he keep The Lions Gate open?" I didn't want to know, I wanted to hide, but I had to ask.

"By trapping the Obvojen Dusa in the opening of The Gate, 'The good souls.' keep The Lion Gate from trying to close, then the beast stole the keys. Hiding one in a waiting soul. The Lion's Gate has to be locked to stay closed. However, The Lion won't allow anything to close it, as long as the pure souls are trapped. They must be freed! Fore, the Lion is incapable of determining the greater good and won't risk one soul for another. Once they are released, you can enter as the first key. No more devoroc will be able to enter the waiting spirits, but to set all things right, you must fully close The Lion's Gate," The queen looked at me, and I got a strange feeling that she was saying I was the first key?

"What was the relic taken from the tomb, and what was its purpose? You must want to close The Gate, or you wouldn't have sent Buttercup after it." I questioned, hoping I was right.

"The relic allows you to gain access to The Gate. It's not much to look at. It resembles a spearhead. I had it and intended to claim the first key for myself. However, the Ogre I sent on the mission to collect the key and drag it to The Gate was killed, and the item was lost," Wilfred scowled, and I felt my face go pale. I looked away from my friends so they wouldn't see my fear.

"How come mortals can't see you?" I dared to ask.

"Only a true witch or magically awakened being can see us, or once a ward has been removed. Otherwise, mortals tend to eat us!" She bellowed.

"My light of Sol had awakened that night in the storm. That's why I didn't see the Ogre when I freed the dog that day and didn't realize I was actually digging in a carcass and not dirt. The dog was pinned under it, and it hadn't rained in months. When I removed the Ogre's head, it was severed from the ward. That's why Dawn could see it," I started piecing together the events in my mind, and I realized that magic had been nearer to me for longer than it seemed. I was being watched that day, being hunted, and why I was chosen for this task became clearer.

"How do we find the second key?" I requested.

"The second key was taken by the Original devoroc monster and is hidden from my sight.

"Do we have to have all three keys before we attempt to close The Gate, or do we place them in one in at a time?" I asked.

"One at a time, Flesh Eater! I want The Gate closed, so I will warn you, you have time for one more question, stay here longer than that, and you won't reach the passage to your world in time. When our sunsets, any lips that have tasted flesh turn to stone. It is how we keep ourselves safe from you!" Wilfred giggled, and my friends and I squirmed.

"OK, what is the Third Key?" I felt like that was the most important of the question I had left.

"The third key is a particular golden web of destiny. Now run!" Wilfred spat, and I turned on my heels with my friends next to me.

We threw open the doors to the stone castle and took to the street in a sprint. The sun was on the horizon and disappearing quickly. The crowds dispersed with terrified creatures scattering, screaming, "The flesh-eaters are going to eat us!" doors started slamming closed, and creatures were collecting their young.

"We aren't going to eat you!" I shrieked as I sprinted.

I heard a voice in the distance cry out, "Don't trust them! That's what they all say." I ran, refusing to shift as I watched the sun slide down further the horizon. I wouldn't leave my friends behind. If the sun disappeared before we made it, I would vanish with them. I closed my eyes for a brief moment to seal my oath, and when I opened them, Connie was bounding off like a frog in the distance at great speed, Shelly at her side using dark matter to carry her. Onacona was just a few feet behind me. I wanted to clap my stone but didn't want to end up back here accidentally in the middle of the night.

"I wonder," I tapped my amulet as I ran and said, "tunnel to my world," and the puddle formed. I grabbed Onacona's hand, and we jumped in. We landed in front of the giant door, and it was solid. Connie and Shelly reached us, and I opened my portal again, hoping the tunnel's inside was in the same realm. We jumped in and landed in the tunnel just on the other side of the door. I was relieved until I realized being in the same realm meant we could still turn to stone. "Run, we aren't safe yet!" I yelled, and we ran, winding our way through the tunnels.

I didn't dare use my amulet again since Buttercup had said these tunnels traveled through many realms. Feeling as if death was at my heels, I popped my neck and lept, then shifted. I picked Onacona up, put her on my back, and bounded at full speed Connie and Shelly at my side. When we reached the spot we entered, Shelly blasted it with her starlight, and it tore a hole through the earth, and the realm divided above us. Connie lept out, and Shelly glided up with ease, then Onacona and I bounded out from the hole. I landed on the ground and shifted back. Then sat. I pulled my watch out and froze the earth, so we could breathe and not be bothered. We all sat in silence for several moments, and something in the house rumbled, and we ignored it overwhelmed with everything else.

"We need to go to our pocket realms now and tell our Bluestocking's everything. I need to summon the Wotan Witches and make sure they warn Asgard and protect it!" I finally spoke, and the door to the abandoned house opened, and a long-twisted arm reached from the door and started extending towards us. I shot light at it, and it shattered. "Go! Now!" I cried to my friends, startled by how it broke, and we slapped our stones and landed in my pocket realm.

"How was it able to move when the world was frozen?" Shelly asked.

"He is learning magic, so he knows how to block against

it too, and since it reached for us, we no longer have the element of surprise. He knows we're coming! Also, the way his arm crumbled. In my vision, the night we stayed in that house, his hands were like green smoke and mist. He's getting closer to figuring out how to cross the threshold! He's starting to materialize in our plane! What do the three houses have to do with it? Never mind, we don't have time for that. Go to your realms. We need to report what we have learned!" I ordered, and everyone ran for the door leading out of my room.

I traced my tattoo, and the Wotan Witches appeared next to me dressed for battle with skull helmets on their heads. "What is it, Jamie?" Agatha asked. They all look confused to find themselves in my pocket realm.

"Can you read my mind?! You all read each other's minds, and Sally and I have communicated in my head before. Can you do It with me? I learned a lot, and I don't want to leave anything out," I spoke frantically.

"Yes, we can," Ebba stepped forward and put her hand on my head, and my eyes rolled back into my mind, and the events of the day began to replay. I forced my mind to fast forward to the part where we met Wilfred. I allowed them to see my thoughts during the conversation to know my reasoning for leaving the wand and to let them know that I was the first key. When Edda let go, all the Witches stood with great concern written on their faces.

"Wilfred must be infested to know this much, to have such detail, but still she was fighting it trying to help. Adliza, Abela, Etta collect Loki. His Jotunn blood will allow access to their world and go fetch the wand. We can't let the master devoroc wish himself into existence. If you get caught, promise to give the wand back after The Gate is sealed. Ella and Etta, go check for infested souls in Asgard, Afrid you set up protection wards. Agata, go inform Odin to gather an army in case we don't get the wand in time," Ebba instructed. Everyone with a task vanished immediately without question.

"Good work getting all that information, Jamie, and for freezing time to see where Wilfred hid the wand. She's normally much kinder," Ebba praised.

"I knew something was off, and I couldn't reach it, or I would've stolen it back," I told Ebba, and she nodded. "About the other thing, you all knew, didn't you?" I questioned, not able to say it. "All that talk about death and telling me not to fear death, and only spirits can enter The

Gate, I have to die, don't I?" I asked, and Edela approached me.

"At first, we didn't know, Hermodr knew, that's why he tricked you and us at the pool. He knew if we were linked that even if you got lost in The Gate, we could use that link to bring you back to us. The Valknut is especially powerful, as it is Odin's chosen connection to his soldiers so they can find their way to him even in death," Edela answered.

"How did Hermodr know?" I asked, feeling like a fool that I ever mistrusted him. He was protecting me.

"He was watching over you and when he saw an Ogre put a dog in the hole to lure you into its trap. Hermodr fought the Ogre and made it tell him why it was after you. He then kept the secret so he could trick you into the pool. That night in the empty house, he called to Eisa to awaken your magic. The devoroc felt his pull and tried to thwart his plan because they recognized you as the first key. Hermodr didn't know what the creature was. He wanted to figure it out, so he went through Odin's libraries and came up empty-handed. The Ogre only told him you were the spirit key. He didn't mention the devoroc. We were only made aware the night after you performed the witch's dance. That is why we quickly focused on training you and making you ready to link. You were so timid when you arrived, we had to strengthen your self-esteem. That is why we performed the wild hunt as we did. Without proper training, so you could prove to yourself that you are capable of great things," Edela put her arm around me.

"Can I come back, or is this it for this life?" I questioned.

"It will be this life, willingly sacrificed, that forges the bond for creating the key. So, it will be the end to this particular life," Edela lowered her head, but still, I didn't mourn.

"Can I say goodbye to my family?" I inquired, concerned for their sorrow, and need for closure.

"That wouldn't be wise. The devoroc now know you are aware of them and that you remain seeking to close The Lion's Gate. They will use their influence to coerce dangerous people to seek after you, to stop you, and if you return, you will put your family in danger. The devoroc will try and use anyone you love to get to you," Edela warned softly, and picturing being a lost girl in the newspaper and my family pleading for my return, made my eyes well up.

"Odin said I would have more hard choices and sacrifices and to make. I figured he meant when I was an adult," I sniffled. Then I thought of Onacona, Shelly, and Connie, and

I sobbed.

"Will I get to see my friends after?" I asked.

"That is yet to be seen. I truly don't know. When you die and come to Asgard, you will become Eisa, and this life will be but a drop of water in an Ocean. Jamie, this is still your decision to make," Edela reminded me and started braiding my hair.

"Of course, I have to do it, but if I find a way to not die, will you still let me be a Wotan Witch?" I asked as plots formed in my mind.

"You will always be a Wotan Witch, and whatever you decide and whatever you choose, that will never change. Even if it was just, you and Eisa was gone, the fire and ice chose you, and they are the very first essence of life. You are us, and we are you," Edela reassured me.

"Why am I the key? There has to be something else we don't know?" I asked,

"We aren't sure, although we think it has to do with your blood link to Asteria," Adelix chimed in, and I thought of what my GG had said.

"Don't forget my roots. Asteria will be more precious than gold," I thought for a moment, then looked at all the Wotan Witches, "You have to make everyone promise not to tell my friend's that I am going to die, or they will quit. I need them, and you there when I enter the passage to The Gate and claim the that I am the first key," I professed. Edela, Ebba, Agatha, Agnes, Acilia, Ebba, Edela, and Adelix put their fists to their chests and pounded three times in agreement, honor, and trust.

Sally stormed in wearing full battle attire, "We enter The Lion's Gate tomorrow evening. We must move soon. The devoroc monsters have formed a line at The Gate to stop all travel, while a faction is headed towards Wilnoc, to steal the powers of the realm walkers and to kill the healers!"

I panicked, "No! No!" I ran to the door and jumped into Onacona's pocket realm to warn her not to go, but it was too late. She had left to warn them.

"She's gone!" I shouted to witches then jumped into Shelly's pocket realm. I lingered for a moment and noticed everything was either made of glass or overly fluffy, and it was all pink, except for a tiny golden star. I fixated on it. It was no bigger than a speck of dust. I picked it up and closed my hand around it. The room seemed empty, and my head started to spin. I cried out, "Shelly!" where was she? "No, come on," I couldn't have two missing friends.

"Coming, I'm in the bath," Shelly responded, annoyed,

but it was a welcome sound. She stepped into the room in a fluffy pink robe and pink glass slippers with little bunny ears on the toes. I blinked to regain focus. "Shelly, Onacona has gone to Wilnoc to warn the healers, and there is an army of devoroc monsters headed there now!" My voice trembled, and her mouth dropped open.

"What do you need me to do?" Shelly dropped her robe and was fully dressed in a bodysuit that glittered like starlight.

I blinked again, "I don't know. If they are warded against magic, then throwing power at them won't help. Can you arrange a couple stars or planets in their way to buy us time? Asgard is readying an army, and we can't enter The Gate until tomorrow night." I plotted as fast as I could.

"I will arrange a whole universe in their path, full of creatures that like to eat gross things, that should buy us enough time, and have Connie send Wilnoc a message to warn them that they are coming. I have to go now for this to work," Shelly turned, then stopped. "Wait, you're entering The Lion's Gate tomorrow? You have the first key?!" She smiled with excitement.

"Yes, the Wotan Witches knew exactly who it was once I gave them all the details," I lied as little as possible.

"That's great!" Shelly ran, hugged me, and kissed my

cheek then shot off like a shooting star. I then turned and ran to Connie's pocket realm.

"Connie!" I yelled as I burst through the door, and she didn't startle. She just continued stirring something in her Cauldron.

"I know what you're planning already. I saw what everyone was saying and doing in the toad's eye. You just sent Shelly away. WHY!?" Connie pled.

"I didn't want to but protecting Wilnoc and Onacona is more important to me, then, than going on a wild goose chase after a goddess who may or may not know a way to help me," I stumbled on my words. Then looked around.

"Did you cast an honesty spell on me?" I questioned while tapping my foot.

"Yes, I did. I didn't want to hear you lie to me too. I can read spiderwebs and see your fate, and just a minute ago, there were two paths! One where you met the Goddess Asteria and one where you didn't," Connie pulled no punches.

"Let me guess, sure there were two paths, but both lead to the middle of the web, to ultimately my death, right? If I did meet Asteria, it wouldn't change that outcome. The only path forward is for me to live on in Eisa. As her, I will still be able to help find the keys! That's all that matters!" I struck back.

"Yes, you died in both paths, but you came back as Jamie in one and as Eisa in the other!" Connie erupted into tears.

I walked to her and hugged her. "Connie, why is your pretty face leaking? If I had to choose again, I would choose the same path. It's a whole world of healers versus me. I'm a girl who is blessed with people who love me, and now I have a chance to do right by them. I'm going to do it. Part of me feels like I was meant to die when the calsake ate me, but all of you, my friends, put your safety aside and battled it. Your friendship and love saved me already and gave me a precious gift. More time with you and the gift of getting to see you hop like a frog in the Gaiagoblin world, but Connie, I love you, and now that you are a Volva or a Stitch Witch, I need you to do something for me?" I asked.

"What?" Connie raised her eyes to look at me. "Actually, a few things, one, don't tell Onacona what's going to happen to me. It will be too hard for me to say goodbye to her. Secondly, I need two potions, the first to borrow something, I don't have the power to glamor yet. If I look like the devoroc monsters, I figure I can slip past them and free the souls once in The Gate. Also, I need a calling card and to borrow something," I handed Connie a few locks of my hair and the tiny golden star, then spent the next several minutes whispering my plot into Connie's ear. When I was done, she looked at me with a raised brow. Then reluctantly agreed to help me, and I returned to my room. When I got back, the Wotan Witches had left, and only Sally remained.

"Oh, come on, I can't say goodbye to you too. I've had enough," I wined.

"No, it's not that, anyways I've seen you die plenty of times before, so I'll spare you the tears. Though it will be your most interesting death, also your final one. Going out in a blaze of glory. Boom," Sally made an exploding motion with her hands.

"Alright, this isn't helping. So, besides this death, what was my second most interesting one?" I joked, and Sally thought.

"The time you got decapitated by a grogjocker," Sally laughed.

"Decapitated, I thought that was a fairly normal ending to any woman in the Crusades?" I joked.

"Well, you see, it's all about how you got decapitated that made it spectacular. Grogjocker are giant stone creatures, and you were asleep when one's rumbling awoke you, you sat up just as it was sitting down, and your head went right up." I cut Sally off before she could finish.

"OK, that's enough of that story. Anyhow, I think I'd like to try and get some sleep before tomorrow," I told her.

"OK, I'll be in tomorrow after a briefing to ready you. Make sure you eat. We will need you strong," Sally instructed.

"No apples?" I looked at her and smiled.

"No, no apples this time," She winked then departed. I climbed into bed and pulled my blanket around my neck and sat planning my day.

About an hour went by, then Connie popped in. "I have the two potions. The second one was especially difficult to make, then I remembered where I could get the extra ingredient, Shelly's room," Connie handed me two bottles. One looked like tar and the other like starlight.

"Let me guess, they both taste like dog crap?" I asked as I studied them.

"Yup," Connie said proudly, then she curled up with me on the bed, and we drifted off to sleep.

Chapter Twenty, Asteria

I started floating away from my body, rising through the abyss, past all the realms into a land of fire and starlight. I landed on glass earth, and dust that looked like glitter in the shape of tiny stars floated away slowly. I studied my surroundings with care, I didn't feel at home, like I had in Asgard, but it felt familiar all the same. The landscape was wild and beautiful. The hills were iridescent glass, and the sun reflected rainbows all around me. Then a woman dressed in a glittering white gown with long hair the color of frost in late fall with a star on her forehead started to walk to me.

"I see you made your choice Wotan Witch," the woman spoke.

"Well, when you snooze, you lose, goddess of the stars," I sassed.

"How were you able to obtain my golden essence for

your potion? You have never been here?" Asteria asked, and I thought of how my GG had said, "She would be more precious than gold." Then, when I saw a little golden star in Shelly's room, It called to me like a distant thought. Then I knew that sometime while I had slumbered, Shelly had visited this place, and a single piece of glitter followed her home.

"You are the Goddess of the stars, yet when there is a breach in your realm, you do nothing to correct it? Why?" I demanded. Ignoring her question. She was supposed to help me. She was my ancestor, too, the roots of my mother's line.

"Wars no longer concern me, nor does your species," she blustered.

"Fine, then I guess we're done here. I'll leave," I growled and started to walk away.

"You will not drink that potion!" Asteria roared, and the glass around me clanked like wind chimes.

"It's a harmless potion. I'm only borrowing your powers. They'll return when I die," I remarked over my shoulder.

"You will not leave me defenseless or use my powers against!" Asteria stumbled on her words, and the glass began cracking.

I turned to face her, "You leave me no choice! When I was in Gaiagoblin and saw the etchings on the walls of the ancient passageway, I saw a beautiful woman with a star on her head. In love with a tyrant, Bull horned God. So, I knew instantly that you were useless. That you were corrupted and helping Khnum. That he had to be the one who opened The Gate with your help! Then Wilfred confirmed my suspicions! I knew that only a beast that had crossed the divide before would figure out how to do it again, even when his soul was torn into a million pieces! Even if it took him four thousand years! The hunger to rule and enslave mankind was something he or you could easily render up! I knew Wilfred was lying when she said everything happened by chance. I know, enough that everything that happened couldn't all a coincidence!" I paused and took a step closer.

"After I saw those paintings, I also knew that you put Shelly on the path to Khnum and led her to the world Konhnsu to find that map so we would spend forever looking in all the pyramids. I knew you infected Wilfred, which is why Buttercup was so desperate to get us out of that house. Even if it meant taking us to his realm, but guess what? The Gaiagoblins are stronger than you think and warned us to leave before we died. Had we attacked them and killed them, we would be doing you a favor. We would be silencing the only being who knew what you did! Then we wouldn't have heard about the setting sun and would have died there! AM I RIGHT?!" I spat.

Asteria clapped slowly and stepped closer, her magic wrapping around me. "You may have figured out some of it, but you're in my realm. I pulled you here. I can snuff you out and return you to stars. Then when I'm done with you, I'll order Shelly here and finish her too. I have waited four thousand years to reunite with Khnum permanently in the living world. He has found a way to free us both from our exile, and we will rule the earth again, and nothing will get in our way! When I take up my throne as Goddess of the world the first thing, I'm going to do is wipe out your entire pathetic little line." Asteria clung to me, and I could feel my body suffocating.

"Stop!" I tried to squirm, but the goddesses grip was too tight. "Stop, I have something you want to hear. Something that would be useful to you." Asteria loosened her grip enough for me to talk, and I felt my body breathing.

"What? Could you offer me?" Asteria growled.

"The next time you're exiled for four thousand years, spend that time evolving instead of pinning over what was lost!" I mocked her. S

he wrapped her powers around me violently, then

whispered, "I made sure the first key was hidden in my line so I could always track it. Now that you're dying, I will hold onto it myself. The first key is a song of life and death that can only be sung by the dying. Since part of you is regrettably from me, I knew where to find you and the key. It would've been too obvious if I had it here when The Gate first opened. Wilfred came looking for it, so I infected her and ordered Wilfred to fetch it and keep it hidden for us. Then she sent that silly Ogre who tried to trap you and failed. Khnum and I knew we would eventually need it after we were done to cast out all who refused to worship us and to keep them from coming back and being born again," Asteria pulled my head back and raised her arm over my mouth as if she was going to remove the key from my throat. I closed my eyes and braced.

Then I felt her magic loosen its hold, and I blasted her with my light and knocked her down.

"HOW DARE YOU! Wait, how? You're a spirit!" She driveled as she struggled to her feet unable to use her powers.

"The thing about my light, it's ancient rune and god seed magic, and it works in every realm," I strutted. I turned, and a huge blast of starlight erupted from Shelly, and the Goddess shattered.

"Thanks, Shelly," I smiled. I knew I couldn't challenge a goddess in a magic fight and live.

"For what?! You're going to die tomorrow anyhow," Shelly scolded.

"So, Connie told you?" I cringed.

"Yes, and it's not OK!" Shelly began to cry, and I went to her to hug her, but she fell through me.

"Um, let's talk about this tomorrow, can you send me back to my body, then use the Goddesses powers to make it even more difficult than you already have on Khnum's army headed to Wilnoc? Maybe if they can block your magic just throw a planet on them and squish them or something? Then you can come to my room, and we will talk about my death," I proposed.

"You can bet we are going to talk about! I won't allow it!" Shelly spat and blasted me back to my body, and I kinda felt bad for the devoroc army. I hadn't seen Shelly that angry before and with all that power.

"Well, that army is in for a treat." I thought, and I opened my eyes.

"So, how was it?" Connie asked.

"The Goddess is shattered, literally. Shelly was not

happy. You did that on purpose, didn't you?" I studied Connie's face as she held her breath, then gasped.

"Yes, she can be so ditsy, and I wanted her to be ready for a fight," Connie admitted, and I shook my head.

"Oh, there was no fight. Shelly annihilated Asteria. Warning, never tick Shelly off." I laughed.

"Oh, and good job with the potion! You are quite an amazing witch," I smiled.

"Ya, I added a bit of stardust and frog eye slime into it so Asteria would know for sure that I was planning to steal her powers, but your hair was a nice touch to let her know. It was doing it at your bidding," Connie boasted, and I gagged.

"You better never let that slip around, Shelly. if she finds out she drank frog eye slime, she will kill you too," I joked.

"True," Connie said with a slight look of concern.

"So, any word from Onacona yet? Why hasn't she slapped her stone and come back? I asked.

Connie shook her head, "I don't know. I'm guessing she's refusing to leave the other healers until she knows they're all safe, and she couldn't possibly bring a whole world of people here," Connie puzzled.

"No, something isn't right. She would at least pop in and give us and update then pop out again?" My gut started churning. "Can you see her in your hupshocter?" I asked.

"Ya, I don't see why not. Let's go try," Connie stood and started walking to her room. I followed behind, hoping I was wrong, and Connie was right. Once we entered, Connie began to stroke the giant eye and looked into its red pupil. "I see, Wilnoc is under attack! The devoroc are already there! The ones Shelly's stalling must be a distraction! I found Onacona, she's hurt, she lost her stone, Oh no!" Connie cried, "A devoroc is approaching her!" Connie stood,

"Quickly do you know how we can portal there?" I implored.

Connie shook her head, "no."

I traced my finger over my Valknut, and seven of the Wotan Witches appeared. "Where is everyone?" I asked rapidly.

"The others are expelling devoroc from Asgard and preparing for battle," Agata advised.

"I need a portal to Wilnoc now! They are under attack!" I demanded.

"You can't. You can die," I cut Agata off.

"There's no time for that, and there is nowhere else I

want to be! Onacona is in trouble! I can do this!" I pleaded. Agata gave a single nod and opened a portal, and I jumped in with Connie right behind me.

I landed in carnage and bile. The healers were getting slaughtered, and the devoroc were using little bottles to collect their powers. I studied the horrors around me. The ground was covered in dead bodies, blood, and the screams were deafening. The giant creatures were twisted with cruelty, taking pleasure with their killing, inflicting as much pain as they liked. When bits of their souls tried to flee from the horror, the beasts would scoop them up and return them to their hollow bellies. I stood shocked at their horrific features. Their faces looked like rotted torn shreds of flesh wrapped carelessly around their incomplete heads. Where their eyes should be instead were gaping pockets of tissue as if they were plucked from them. Their mouths opened from their throats under their chins and let out echoes of satisfaction. The skin reminded me of roadkill and glowed a filthy dark green. "This is a massacre," I muttered. Then fear struck me, and I yelled, "Onacona," I tried to sound over the screams of pain from the realm walkers and the laughter and war cries of the devoroc.

"I think she's this way. It looks familiar," Connie

bellowed, and I shifted as we raced over the rubble and the slain. I summoned my sight and hearing and began searching for signs of Onacona. I could hear Ebba and the other six Wotan Witches who followed me slaying the beasts behind me, and the cries of the beasts were a welcome sound.

Ella caught up to me, "We were able to remove the wards from the ones we cut down, by removing their heads, the symbol is imprinted in their ear. However, they're able to reform. We haven't figured out how to stop them yet, but once they take shape, we are able to trap them,"

I looked at Ella, "Thanks for letting me know, try and focus on removing as many wards as possible," I instructed, we nodded in understanding then raced opposite ways.

"Connie, remove as many devoroc ears as possible while we search," I yelled. Connie bounded from the earth onto a devoroc, smashed it onto the ground, then used her toe to slice off its head, then swiped again removing the ear. Then she lept to the next and the next, and I thought, "Impressive." I pulled out my knives and raced to meet her, chopping, and cutting with each lunge while filtering through the sounds to find Onacona.

After we cut through a line of devoroc, Connie and I paused while they reformed. "Are we close?" I begged, starting to fear the worst.

"Onacona has to be around here. I remember that house," Connie puzzled while pointing to a structure nearby.

I cried out again, "Onacona!" Then a whimper for help had me turning and running away from the battle towards an open field with a forest on the other side. I focused my hearing and locked on to Onacona.

"Jamie," I heard her rasp.

"This way, Connie!" I called out as I turned sharply to jump through a thicket of trees and into a clearing. I flew into a rage at the sight of a devoroc dragging Onacona by her hair. Her eyes were glowing, and I could see her attempting to command it to the eccotomb. The devoroc's ward thwarted her attempts. I let out a growl I didn't know I was capable of. With it, my focus turned from Onacona to the beast. My bounds quickened towards the creature, and I lept and landed on its back, my maw disengaged as I clenched my teeth on its head and ripped it off. Then I bit again and swallowed its ear. I stole a look at Onacona, and Connie was helping her get up.

I turned back towards the beast, and its parts began to swirl, and the monster started to form again. I took out my slingshot and began shooting it with light. The beast screamed in agony, and I hit it again and again. Then I saw a single piece of it trying to float back to its master, so I steady aim and shot it with a light pebble, turning it into a stone. I halted for a moment, surprised at what had just happened, then I realized what I had to do.

I closed my eyes and cleared my head and pictured a little house of light around me. I took a deep breath in and pictured the light growing into a two-story house. Then I imagined all the witches and healers safe inside my home and the devoroc outside. The sounds of screams and the shaking of the earth broke my concentration, and I opened my eyes, and Eisa was standing in front of me. She smiled, and I felt that powerful, overwhelming peace again, the peace I had felt that night in the abandoned house. I felt that wholeness. I felt complete. She put her hand on my shoulder, and she whispered, "You found your power," Then she folded back into me, and I put my hand over my heart. The place I felt her, and the light returned to me, and I extinguished it.

"Why are you standing there looking all peaceful, Jamie? You only turned killed the beasts that already had their wards removed. There are still plenty more, oh, and they're headed this way," Connie looked at me with her mouth open while pointing through the trees at a massive army of devoroc racing frantically for us. "Go be peaceful on those ones now. I'll wait here with Onacona," She scoffed.

I turned to look at Onacona. I handed her my pebble, "Go back to the pocket realm. I can't focus if you're in danger. I will meet you there!" I spoke and then bounded off towards the army running at me.

My amulet encased me with its brilliant orange glow, and I stopped about a football field's length away from the charging beasts. I turned back for a second and looked. Onacona and Connie were gone. "Good, I thought. I saw the Wotan Witches ripping the beast's ears off as they charged me. The Wotan's were ferocious in their attacks, yielding nothing as they lept from creature to creature. Their bodies vaulting and moving so quickly the monsters had no time to react. I bent down and picked up a pebble and tossed it up and down to taunt the devoroc, to make them keep their focus on me while my coven did their work. The ground started to move as they started to approach. Closer and closer. "Steady girl," I said to myself. I swallowed, hoping they couldn't scent the fear on me or see it on my face. I pushed back my instinct to bolt and reflected on my training.

"Don't overthink it. Your magic is an extension of you. Like an arm, you, don't tell your arm to move. You just move it," Hermodr's words played in my head. "Fear is useless. The only thing that keeps you from being great is you," I whispered under my breath. When Khnum's army was but feet away, and the devoroc monster's claws were thrashing so closely, I could feel the bursts of air on my face. I reached my arms wide and bore my claws and hissed as my light burst from me, creating an enclosure around beasts, I commanded a full dome overhead, so they had nowhere to flee. Then I started pulling my hands closed, willing the bubble to grow smaller and smaller. The screams of the devoroc shattered my heightened hearing, and I could feel my ears bleeding. I ignored my pain and focused, smaller, and smaller, pulling my hands closer and closer together. Everything went silent and, the beasts trashed in their trap and started to climb on top of each other and betray one another, trying to force more space, and the ones tossed into the light turned to small stones and fell to the earth. I pulled my hand closer and closer until they met, and I clasped my hands closed. I looked over the sea of pebbles, then at the Wotan Witches walking on them towards me while dropping ears onto the rocks.

Then Adliza started to point at me while mouthing something, but I couldn't make out what it was. So, I began to walk towards her and then she started bounding for me, they all did, then I realized they weren't looking and me anymore but behind me. I spun around just as a claw swiped at my face, and Acilia bounded over me as I fell back to flee, and she tackled the monster and ripped off its head. I blasted it with my light and turned it into a stone. Then Abela took my head into her hands and wiped off some of the blood. Then she licked my blood off one of her fingers then rammed it into my ear, and I thought my head was going to explode. I dry heaved at the feeling, then my ears popped, and sound came rushing back in.

"That was too close. We need to get Jamie back. We go to The Gate soon," Agate spoke.

"Agreed. Still, some of us need to stay behind and help finish off any remaining devoroc, and the healers can send them to the eccotomb. Jamie, can you clap your stone?" Agata asked.

"No, I gave it to Onacona," I replied, and the witches looked at each other with concern.

"Where do you want to be?" Acilia asked.

"I don't know. The bath in my room in Asgard or with Eisa?" I said, doubtful.

Ebba opened a portal and hopped through, then a few

minutes later, she popped back and handed me a stone. I looked at it, and it wasn't my stone. I had studied my rock.

"This isn't my stone," I noted and started to shift, readying for a fight, thinking Ebba was tainted with a devoroc.

"No, but it's a stone from your pocket realm. I just collected another," Ebba explained.

"Oh, whew, that makes sense. I didn't realize. You mean I could've had multiple stones at all the different places I wanted to pop in and out of?" I shook my head and took the stone and clapped it.

I entered my pocket realm, and it was full of injured healers. My room was changed into a hospital of sorts with beds lining the walls. Onacona and Connie had brought back as many wounded as possible. I looked over the hordes of people and beings and found Onacona. She was carrying a giant creature that looked almost alien, just heavier to a bed. Working her magic to reattach a leg as she limped, ignoring her own injury. "Onacona, what can I do to help?" I offered.

"The ones outside are infected. Can you gently use your light to heal them? I'm busy tending to the injured and can't get to them," She asked.

"Sure, I'll give it a go," I accepted and walked outside.

The infested healers were sitting cross-legged meditating, keeping the devoroc at bay. They looked so peaceful I felt a bit awkward approaching them. So, I went to a girl who looked younger than me first, "Hey sweetie, I'm going to use my light to help you," I stated softly.

She opened her eyes, and one popped out towards me, and she spoke, "Who are you calling sweetie, food?" I jumped back.

"Onacona, this one's a calsake!" I yelled, as my shield went up, and I raised my hand.

Onacona came running to me, "don't hurt her! Remember they're not bad, she's just infected." Onacona looked at it empathetically.

"Ya well, that's easy for you to say you didn't get eaten by one. You fix it, and I'll work on another," I backed away slowly, then walked to a large man and tapped my finger on his arm. He nodded without saying anything, so I allowed my light to ripple through him. Then a little ball of green mist fled from him. I hit it with a harder blast, and it turned to stone.

The man breathed, "Thank you, now I must help with the healing," he rushed past me into what used to be my room.

"You're welcome," I muttered after he was gone.

Then I moved to the next one and the next one. When I

was done, I conjured trays of fruit and started feeding the people in beds. I hesitantly handed the calsake a pear, and she shifted it into a lifeless human and tore off its arm and ate it. I shuttered, the insides looked like any other fruit, so I tried to remind myself, "It's just a person-like pear." Still, I made sure to put distance between us.

A portal opened, and Sally stepped into the room, "It's time," was all she said, all she needed to say, and I nodded.

Chapter Twenty Ones, The Lion's Gate

"Onacona, will you come with me to the entryway of The Gate?" I asked, and she looked at me.

"I'm going in with you," She said, confused.

"No, I have to go in alone. My light will protect me and me alone in there.

She looked at me sideways, "Are you sure?" She questioned.

"I'm sure," I answered. Then Connie and Shelly walked into the room, both with eyes swollen.

"We all go to war together then?" I said, then a hand landed on my shoulder, and I turned, and all twelve Wotan Witches were there.

"We all go together," They all said in unison.

I looked at Sally, "What can we expect?"

She looked at me with worry in her eyes, "The Khnum

army is much larger than imagined. Odin's army is there fighting at the entrance already, along with the Valkyries and other Gods and Goddesses. They are trying to clear a path to get you into The Lion's Gate. However, we don't know how many devoroc lay beyond the archway.

"What does the entrance look like?" I asked, wanting to confirm what I was looking for.

"It's made of stone and cloaked in shadows and darkness," Sally answered.

I thought of what Frigga said, "Wait, that's wrong, that's a trap, they are hoping I go in alone! Frigga told me something the night of the dance," I swallowed. "She said, before you, a path will unfold, and through darkness and shadows you must go, until you reach a pillar glowing with purple light, there, you will be greeted with hardship and strife. Many you'll need to keep it at bay, as you alone go the rest of the way." You see, you have to go with me through the darkness, then I alone go through the purple light," I said, and everyone's eyes grew wide.

I knelt and tied a purple band around Onacona's ankle. "This is so everyone can recognize Onacona," I explained.

Then I handed Onacona the bottle Connie had made for me yesterday. "This will make you look like one of the devoroc monsters, drink it, and when we get to the battlefield, pretend to chase us into the entrance. Once inside, we will battle, aim to remove the ears of the devoroc. Then with your powers, send them to the eccotomb so they can be turned to stone." Next, I turned to Shelly, and I saw a faint star-forming on her forehead. "Shelly, do you still have all the powers of the Goddess Asteria?" I asked.

"I do, actually. How strong was that potion you made, Connie?" Shelly inquired.

"It's not the potion, after you killed Asteria, the powers had nowhere to go, and I couldn't think of anyone more right for the position of Goddess of the stars than you. After I enter the archway, I need you to keep any devoroc from following me, so I can get to the purple light and release the souls and call upon the first key, the one hidden inside of me. Connie, when I free the souls, I will need you to remove any curses or wards so they can be freed and add wards to keep the devoroc from coming in behind me to just steal the key again. Sally, how many Valkyries can be spared? Whatever is behind the dark wall will expect the Wotan Witches to be with me, but not a brigade of Valkyries," I finished.

"Wait, you killed Asteria? Why?" Sally asked.

"Oh right, I didn't tell you. Also, I didn't kill her. Shelly did. Anyhow that's a long story," I blushed.

"So, give me the compact version," Sally raised a brow.

"Just look in my head so we can get this over with," I exhaled theatrically. After Sally and the Wotan Witches read my mind and saw what I saw, I could see the wheels turning.

"You are acting more like Eisa already. I don't know of any child able to concoct what you have. It's almost like your merging even now," Sally stated while studying me.

Onacona blurted out, "What does that mean?"

I stomped on Sally's foot. "Ouch! What was that for?" Sally moaned.

"You go round up Valkyries, and we will meet you on the battlefield. We will be the ones running from a devoroc with a purple tie around her foot. Find a way to make sure no one attacks Onacona, alright!" I demanded.

Sally nodded, "You sound just like Eisa," I threw a ball of light at Sally, and she vanished into a portal.

"Why are you merging with Eisa already or at all?! You're going to be alright, right?" Onacona demanded.

"Can we talk about this after today?" I pled.

"That's not fair, Jamie. You have to tell her." Connie appealed, and Shelly nodded in agreement. I looked at Onacona, and I could tell she was getting ready to scold me, so I spoke before she could, "We are all changing. Shelly is a Goddess now and already is starting to look older. I mean, look at her. She has heels on. Connie too, I think only a real Volva could make potions the way Connie has. We have delved in too deeply. I don't see any of us returning to the way things used to be. I don't think we can be who we used to be. I prefer this world, and I know that things this great don't come without immense sacrifice. It's a choice we all need to make for ourselves. Besides Sally, when was the last time Catori, Cordelia, or Vega were here without being summoned? Onacona, we are drifting apart, and it's not all bad. I know your sisterhood is calling to you the way the stars call to Shelly, and we have all seen Connie go from not wanting to hold a hawk to battling beasts without fear. Accepting change is just part of growing up. I know, if we fight it and go back, we would all be miserable, at least I know I would. I accept that change isn't perfect, and it can't be controlled, that it's often violent and painful. Still, we are coming out the other side better, wiser, kinder, and I would like to think fulfilled. I have to die in order to become who I am meant to be, and it's my choice, just like my birth was, and I will be there with you when we find the other keys. I may look different, but it will still be me. Sally told me once that my key attributes have always been the same in every life, and I believe I have loved you in all of them and will love you still after it. Please don't be mad, I'm scared, and I need you there with me until my final descent," I poured my heart out and said all I could and hoped she would understand.

Onacona stood crying, attempting to find words, and I looked at her and could tell she too was growing. Accepting that birth and death are equally meaningful, beautiful, bloody, and painful, as are light and darkness. I started to feel the song in my soul and knew it was time. "It's time. We need to go now," I whispered, and Onacona ran to me and wrapped me in her arms and healed me. I turned to the Wotan Witches for the portal and found them all sobbing too. "Really, you too?" I sighed and rolled my eyes. Edela opened the portal, and Onacona began to shift into a devoroc. I skiftended and summoned my sight and hearing, then jumped into it.

I found myself in a pit of death and rage that seemed endless. War cries sounded as far off as I could hear. The Asgardians, men, and women battling continuous lines of devoroc monsters, removing ears, and using their powers to turn them into pebbles. I saw women with wings fighting fiercely against the hoards. I looked across the fields, straining my sight for miles, and saw a devoroc that was massive, towering over the others with long steer-like horns protruding from his head. His face was better formed and more defined than the others, shaped more like a bull than a human. "Khnum," I whispered under my breath. He was watching the battle while heavily protected from the fight. "Coward," I thought. I could see him searching through the destruction and bodies. His head started to turn in my direction, and I crouched. "That fight is for another day," I contemplated while I peered through the people and waited for his head to move again before I stood.

The Wotan Witches and my friends landed beside me. "It's this way! Come now!" I heard Sally's voice in my head, and a map formed in my thoughts.

"Follow me!" I took off bounding, weaving in and out of devoroc monsters and soldiers locked in battle. I removed ears as I went, and as I got closer to the darkness, winged women started swooping down, clearing the monsters from out of our way. I looked back, and Onacona was chasing behind us. The plan seemed to be working as other devoroc who turned their attention to us turned away when they saw her perusing us. "Good," I thought. We rounded a bend, and I came to a halt as three rows of devoroc stood guarding and watching at the dark archway. The Wotan Witches lept over me and made quick work of the beasts, and an army of Valkyries landed behind me. I looked at one of the beautiful, winged women, her sword covered in green blood, "Sally? You got your wings?!" I cheered and felt so proud of her. She winked at me then placed herself in front of me.

The sound of a horn bellowing through the air and caught me by surprise. I turned to look. Khnum had spotted us and was ordering his minions to storm us. Shock and anger formed on his face. "Yup, I have a battalion of Valkyries and witches, so take that," I thought. It was too late for them. The Asgardians held them back, meeting them step for step. The Valkyries formed a circle around Onacona, Sally, Connie, Shelly, and me. My friends stood to my right as we marched to the darkness. Then, the Wotan Witches fell into place by my left.

"Whatever is beyond that door, we will face it together," Asteria whispered. My hearing caught it over the sounds of thrashing and magic. The Valkyries in front of me vanished into darkness first, ten at a time, and when I stepped up to its threshold, I peered into the pitch.

It felt horrible, cold, and empty, hands reached from the darkness, pulling at me, cries of death and despair pleading to me for help, begging me to join them, calling for me.

Wanting to claim me. I lifted my hand and blasted them back. Now scared of what horrors were waiting for me beyond the darkness. My instincts told me to flee, but I knew this was a fight I couldn't run from. The song inside me urged me to continue. So, I summoned my courage, and with my friends and my coven standing next to me, I entered the darkness to return the first key.

My eyes adjusted quickly to the dim red light and hundreds upon hundreds of devoroc stood battling Valkyries in a long cavern. More Valkyries flew past me overhead as they entered in from behind. Their strength was amazing. They showed no fear, almost as if they welcomed the challenge. They were brutal with their attack. Shelly sent dark matter tumbling at the void after the last of the Valkyries had entered. She formed a wall with it to keep any more devoroc from entering. There were too many, though. I began blasting my light, only affecting the ones that had lost their ears. Onacona joined in combat, her rage unleashing as she swiped at their ears with her claws then banished them. Shelly joined in and moved boulders, crushing them then blasting them with her starlight as she went. Connie lept from one to other, sending fires down their throats, then ripping their ears off, leaving them to burn from within. I took up my knives and bounded for the monsters, the Wotan Witches next to me. I caught the first one off guard, sliced its head off, and then turned it into a pebble. The second one swiped at my amulet, and I fell back trying to protect it. The creature jumped on me and tore at my flesh. I screamed at the pain, as Abela drove her sword through its head. I forced my legs under me, then drove my knives upwards as another lept for me, slicing through its core, ripping it in half as its blood and entrails rained down on me. I heard the next one approaching from my side, and I spun and cut off its ear and banished it. More grouped together and started to close in on us. "Go! we will hold them off!" Agnes called out and the Wotan Witches formed a line behind me.

I turned as the next came at me, and I lept straight up as it dove for my midsection with its talons thrashing for me. I landed on its back and sliced off a section of its face in my attempt to remove its ear. More green putrid blood splattered on me. I sent another burst of light through the cavern to prevent any devoroc from reforming, and I started to push my way through the rabble. I hit the ground and started to crawl between devoroc legs, and I felt so little and insignificant. Still, I understood my task and knew I had to find the purple pillars. I couldn't see any purple light, and creature after creature clawed at me, just as others stepped on me or kicked me. I tried my best to sneak past unseen because I knew even with all my powers, I wouldn't make it very far if I tried to battle my way through.

Then the sound of a familiar woman's voice cried out to me, "Help, help, Free us." I crawled to a boulder and snuck behind it and stilled so I could focus on it and remember. "Who is that? I know I've heard that voice before. I know I have." I thought, and I thought.

Then a man called out, "please help us, please if you can't save us all, please just save my wife, her name is Cynthia, and she shouldn't be here. It's my fault she's trapped."

Then it clicked, "It's Jacob, the old owner of the abandoned house. Cynthia must have gotten caught and trapped here with him." I still wondered what he knew and why Khnum or Wilfred never just tore the house down, no one would miss It, and that would ensure all the secrets remained hidden. I wondered why they never took everything from that room themselves. I thought of Buttercup coming into the room, and then I recollected that little envelope I found taped under the desk. I reached into my belt and pulled out the letter. I quickly opened the envelope and unfolded the piece of paper and read it.

"I can't take this anymore. I was mystified by the magic world, and now he killed my wife! My Cynthia! Then took my beloved Jenny. Khnum's chains couldn't contain Neter. He grew to be too powerful! I have to end this! Eventually, he will have come back here, and I will finish him myself or die trying! Asteria won't even bring Neter to her world. She won't even touch her own son. I have to find my Jenny, she's all I have left. I only hope she's still alive. Whoever finds this, Khnum and Asteria aren't your greatest threats. Neter is." I put the letter down. "Really, this isn't enough?" I thought.

Then I heard a sound above me and looked up to find a devoroc crouching over me. I tried to leap away, as the monster swiped, ripping my amulet off of my chest. I hit the wall then bounded forward and ran. I couldn't go back for it. There was no way as a hoard of devoroc gathered and focused their hunt on me. I bounded, for where the cries echoed from, and started to hurdle towards them, but the devoroc were on my heels. I turned and swiped with my blades taking the closest ones out as others raced closer. I turned and ran down a tunnel, and a devoroc lept from the darkness. I attempted a blow, but he moved away swiftly, and I missed. He lept for me, and I backed up and blasted light at him, but it had no effect. I rolled away before he landed on me barely making it.

I got to my feet, and I stared at him and hissed as I stepped backwards towards the sounds of the trapped spirits. The devoroc charged at me, and I ducked and spun, cutting into his shins. He roared in pain, and I backed up again. The devoroc crawled towards me, roaring and streaking, and other devoroc were closing in with their attention fixed on me. "Crap, crap." I turned and ran down a lengthy cavern, racing to the pleas for help using my hand as a touch. I could hear the rushing thuds of feet behind me and knew I had to be quick. I came to a fork in the tunnels and called out, "where are you." The pleas sounded louder pointing me in the right direction. I willed a ball of light to move slowly down the opposite tunnel hoping the devoroc would be thrown off and follow it. I dimmed my light and pushed myself to move faster and faster. Then a faint purple glow started to reflect on the walls, and I knew I was close. I heard the devoroc behind me. There were fewer of them. "They must have split up," I thought. I pushed myself to run even harder and I stormed into a cavern with two giant pillars of purpled light.

I willed myself to stop myself at the sight of the souls standing in between the purple pillars that arched at the top, trapped behind a barrier of gray smoke, and guarding them was seven devoroc. "How do I free you?" I cried out as the devoroc charged me. I bounded up the wall, hoisted myself off it, and took the head off one of the devoroc. I blasted light while another devoroc tore into my back. I could feel my blood gushing out of my body, and I screamed out in pain.

"The knife on the demon! It cuts through the barrier," One of the spirits answered. I twisted, and another devoroc dug his claws through the lining of my rib cage. I swiped down with my knives, separating its arm while I thrust upwards with the other, removing its ear and blasted it with light. I summoned a light shield around me and pushed the beasts back. I pulled the severed arm from my side and cried with the pain. The remaining five were driving through my shield, with my dying strength weakening me.

I spotted the one with the knife and willed my powers to push the others away. I raised my blades and let the devoroc enter my space. It growled, as I tried to focus. My sight was growing dim. "Not yet" I told myself and the devoroc lept for me. I pushed it back with my light inching my way to the souls and the purple Gate. My legs began to tremble, and the other four started to close in. "Just a little closer," I urged myself while struggling to breathe. The devoroc with the knife started to grunt and push and paw his way towards me and when we were at the very edge of the prison. I let my shield down and ducked.

The devoroc bounded over me, slamming into one another, and I reached for the knife as they were overhead and pulled it free. I rolled to the barrier and thrust it in. The spirits started to turn to wisps of smoke, and with what strength I had left, I used it to run forward to the purple archway. I pulled out my spearhead and drove it into my gut. I fell forwards onto my knees and tumbled through The Lion's Gate.

I landed on my side onto what felt like clouds. Letting my tear streamed down my face, and with my dying breath I let the song slip from me.

"Into life, we choose to go, to find our paths and to grow, through toil and pain, knowledge we gain, and in the end, we return again.

Only the mothers magic can reach through the realms and summon to them their infant kin.

They pay the price, the blood sacrifice, to bring forth life. It's the sacred dance we enter in when we choose to be born again. We learn as we grow, experiencing it all. We learn to walk, and we learn to crawl. We are meant to heal, love and to share, help and care, mend and repair. To be wild and free, to seek out beauty. The magic within calls to us. Let it remind us we are more then we see.

For when we fall for a moment, we stay behind to say goodbye, to help our loved ones mourn and to cry, and to nudge them to move on with their lives. We enter to The Lion's Gate with a song to return us from where we came, and all we take are the deeds of our journey and the wisdom we gained.

Chapter Twenty Two, The Beginning

I opened my eyes and found myself in a meadow. I heard traffic from a distance and turned. I blinked. Then I was at the roadside. I looked around, "Where am I? What happened?" everything was hazy. I saw a building in the distance and closed my eyes, then I was at it. "I know this place. I'm in Missouri." I thought of my GG, and I was at her front porch. I stood silent and watched her stuff tobacco into her pipe and strike a match.

"GG, what happened? Where am I?" I called out, and she startled, losing her grip on her smoke, and it hit the ground. She began screaming in pain and shaking. I was confused as to why, as her pipe hadn't burned her. I moved closer and put my hand on her shoulder. "GG, are you hurt?" I asked.

She looked at me with tears running down her cheeks.

"My child, my dear, my love, you're dead! My grand baby is dead!" She screamed in agony and began rocking.

"I am, oh yes, I remember now. GG, I'm OK now. The pain is gone; I'm safe. I love you GG, thank you for always being there for me. You gave me hope, joy, and pride. I thank you for that. I have to go now. I love you." I turned, and she bent forward and sobbed into her elbow.

I thought of my Mom and Dad, then I was with them, and their movie was just getting out. I whispered to my mother, "thank you for giving me life, for giving me a family, and for protecting me the best you could. Thank you for your kindness." Then I went to my father, "thank you for doing the best you could, for always being there when I needed you the most. For taking me camping and fishing. I love you." I brushed my Mom's hand as I went to turn from my parents, and her face dropped, and she lost hold of her bag, and it spilled to the ground.

She turned to my father, "Shawn, something is wrong, something happened to Jamie!"

My dad looked at her with an eyebrow raised, "Tracy, what are you talking about? Pick up your purse. Jamie is fine." My dad rolled his eyes.

Then I kissed Evan on the cheek, and he shivered. "I love

you, Evan, behave and take care of Mom and Dad. They will need you to be patient with them while they grieve."

I approached Neil. He pointed at me and said, "Look, Momma, Jamie." He giggled and waved, and I waved back and blew him a kiss, and both my parent's faces went pale. They began to panic and rush towards the car. I moved to Noora as she followed behind them. I noticed a bit of dark energy in her, so I blasted my light at it, and a stone fell to the earth. Noora took a deep breath in, and Neil collected the stone. "Look, Mama Jamie made a rock," he spoke and smiled.

"We should go find Jamie now!" Noora quickened her stride, and then I moved to Waddles, and I stroked his cheek and kissed him.

"I promise to always look out for you, sweet baby," I smiled and left.

Then I thought of my Grandpa, and I was with him. "I love you, Grandpa," I uttered, and he looked around. I turned and found my Grandma sitting on the couch next to him. "Grandma! What are you doing here?" I asked as she had died a few years earlier.

"Oh, sweet Jamie, I check on him every day. He, and my children were the best of my life, and oh how I love him. I decided to wait until I return to myself. So, I can go with him when his time comes, but you shouldn't." She said, and I went to her, and we embraced. "I am so proud of you Jamie, you were so brave." My Memaw whispered.

"I'm proud of you too, Memaw. Thank you for making me feel important and for loving me," I responded. Then I went to my Grandpa and kissed his cheek, and a picture of me on the wall began to glow. I moved towards it, and when I was next to it, it fell to the ground, and I stepped into it.

I stood facing Eisa, and she smiled at me. I felt the wholeness and absolute love and completeness that I longed for. Eisa extended her hand to me, and I took it. We turned and walked through The Lion's Gate, and there was no devoroc to be seen, and I saw new life untainted flowing towards the earth. I looked at Eisa, knowing my task was fulfilled, and she bent down and hugged me, and I whispered to her, "help my friends." Eisa looked at me and nodded, then I allowed myself to fold into her, and we became Eisa.

I emerged from the pillars fully formed into womanhood. I extended my knives. I ran for the devoroc who had hurt Jamie, and I slashed them into ribbons. I sent out a title wave of light, and it reverberated through the caves. The ground rumbled. I bolted through the tunnels slicing and cutting down any devoroc that crossed me. I entered the main cavern and took in the scene. The battle was done, and the remaining devoroc were attempting aimlessly to escape. Onacona had embraced her powers and was dispelling the last of them with a mere tune. While at the same time, she simultaneously healed the injured Valkyries and witches.

Shelly's star had fully developed on her head, and she used her starlight to enchant the archway, and the darkness was gone. Connie worked using her fire to etch wards in the caverns to keep any further devoroc from entering. I looked at them, amazed. They had fully accepted their journeys and stood nearly as tall as me.

I looked to the twelve Wotan Witches, and they saw me, and I bowed my head to them. I lowered my blades and walked to the center of the room, and I announced, "Jamie has sealed The First Key into The Lions Gate, and no more devoroc are infecting new life! They are once again locked out of The Lion's Gate and the resting realm. All thank Jamie for her sacrifice." The room went silent, and everyone raised their hands to their hearts to show respect. Then the Valkyries turned to rejoin the fight beyond the archway.

Connie, Shelly, and Onacona walked to me, and I offered, "Let me help you finish closing The Lion's gate. I know, your friendships meant everything to Jamie, and I hope over time that you will accept me as your friend as well. I know it will be strange for you as now I am Eisa, but It would honor me if you allowed me to help." Jamie's friends looked at me with tears on their cheeks.

"You kinda look like her, only old. I don't know, it's hard to accept you. I don't know you. I feel like you killed Jamie. I'm mad at you." Connie spoke softly. I lowered my head, part of me felt like somehow, I had killed her.

Shelly stepped forward and put her arms around me, and said, "not that long ago, I was cowering against a wall on a playground with no hope as the meanest girls I had ever met threatened to abuse me. I felt like this was simply life. I didn't know it then, but I was broken and wouldn't have protected myself when they attacked. Then Jamie and Onacona came charging over and rescued me. Somehow, they scarred off the mean girls. Jamie didn't know me and had nothing to gain by helping me, but still, she did. I know you're not Jamie, but if she is in you, even if it is just a drop. I owe it to Jamie to give you the same chance she gave me," Shelly stepped away, and I remembered that event, and I felt like I had lived it. It was different than the mere memories of my other lives. Those felt like a dream.

Onacona studied me with her honey-colored eyes, and somehow, I knew she was about to speak. I put up my hand to stop her from talking. "Wait! I, I am still merging with Jamie. I feel her more than the others. I think she's. She's becoming more prevalent." I fell forward to my knees, my head throbbing from within. Then all of Jamie's experiences, thoughts, and memories filled me, as if they were my own.

"What's happening?" Onacona cried out and raced to me and put her healing hand on my back. The twelve Wotan Witches encircled us and started to chant. I felt fire and ice moving inside of me pulling Jamie to the surface. I didn't want to push her back, she was so brave for a little girl, so I allowed her to rise. My bones started to break, my body contorted, and my bones began to mend. The pain was excruciating, and I thought I was dying. I sobbed through the pain then Jamie became half of who I am. The tension eased and settled. I raised myself to a seated position.

"What was that? I thought I fell, I did fall, I'm still Eisa, right? No, not just Eisa. I'm Jamie too? I don't know what's going on?" I looked at the Wotan Witches and my friends. Onacona's eyes were wide.

"You have successfully entirely merged into your true self. The noblest identities of all your past lives have now rested on the surface and have formed you as you are meant to be. You now reflect both sides of Jamie and Eisa in balance. It will take you time to adapt. Let's go home to Asgard so you can rest," Agata spoke, and I nodded.

I looked at my friends, and they looked confused but hopeful. "Hey, when you're done using my pocked realm as a hospital, let me know so we can hang out," I offered. Then I felt a tap on my shoulder. I turned, and Sally was standing there.

"You're not leaving without me and this," Sally handed me my amulet.

"Thank you," I smiled and placed it around my neck.

"You look like a dang teenage, Eisa. I better not have to deal with you sneaking out at night to meet boys," Sally joked and rolled her eyes.

"Whatever, Mom," I teased, then stopped with the thought of boys as a portal opened. "Wait, you're not taking me to Hermodr, are you? I gaped, terrified at the idea.

"Not unless you wish it," Adliza answered. I searched my heart, and a portion of me did want to run to him, but the other part recoiled at the thought. "No, I think my feelings for him are going to take some time for me to fully understand. I'm not ready to play house with him," I decided honestly.

Adliza nodded.

I turned back one last time to look at my friends, and Onacona ran to me and hugged me. Then Connie and Shelly came over, and I hugged them. "I'll see you all soon," I whispered and let go. Then Abela and Sally put their hands around my shoulders, and we stepped into the portal and returned to Asgard.

The End

of book one, Jamie and The Lion's Gate, The First Key.

Thank you for reading.

Book two: Jamie and The Lion's Gate, The Second Key (In progress to be released in 2022)

Author's Notes

Jamie and The Lion's Gate

Is dedicated to my children, my heart.

A special thank you to all my readers.

Thank you to those who supported me through this

process.

Thank you,

Mom, Sally, Odin, Piper and Phoebe

Thank you to my Models

Piper, Katy, Phoebe and Cavalier

What was your first experience with something not explained? Something that touched the core of your soul so profoundly it altered your path forever and led you on a journey away from mainstream life? For as long as I can remember, supernatural experiences have taken place in my life at key moments and have greatly shaped who I am.

When we are young, our families play the biggest role in shaping who they would like us to be. As we grow, we ultimately choose our own paths. My true journey, my chosen path, started the first time I heard a voice that wasn't there. I was just about four or five years old, still too young to attend school. It was well into the night, and I awoke to a loud commotion in my house, so I climbed from my bed and walked to the door to see what was happening. I reached for the knob to open it when a woman's voice clearly demanded: "Amie don't." There was no mistaking that voice. I ran back to my bed, climbed up the side of it, and looked at the top bunk where my older sister lay fast asleep. I wondered how it didn't wake her. The tone of the mysterious female's voice had a tinge of panic, and it wasn't muffled or a whisper. I quickly lowered myself to my bed, pulled the covers over my head, and reluctantly drifted off to sleep. I told my Mom and sister about it the next day, but neither had any idea where it came from. My Mom believed me and said, "It must be someone watching out for you." Even today, I can still hear that voice as clear as if I had just heard it and wonder what would've happened had I not listened to it. "Amie, don't" I wonder if those two words saved my life? This experience is why I never closed off to the belief that something else was out there. It is why I couldn't because this happened, and there was no mistaking it.

I have experienced many paranormal and supernatural events throughout my existence and I know it seems odd. However, I have developed to a point in my life where it seems more strange to continue on pretending it doesn't happen. These events have brought curiosity, joy and wonder to me when I need it the most and yes sometimes a bit of fear too. I also wanted to reflect on some of the difficulties my friends and I faced during the era. In particularly the few tragically lost to suicide. I have a allot of good memories in Idaho and love the mountains and the beauty and freedom they provided me with. I haven't visited the area in years so my writing is in no way reflective to how the state is now. The book is based in the early 1990s, 30 years ago. To my friends who still live there thank you for making the world a kinder place. I love each of you.

This novel has a few of my paranormal experienced in it, not all of them. I am happy to share more if asked. The Characters in Jamie and The Lion's Gate are made up and do not depict, anyone one unique individual, though it does reflect some similar to life experiences. I will list them below. This book is fictional.

For updates on my upcoming work follow me on Facebook @jamieandthelionsgate

- Old owner of our house showing up to fistfight my Dad for having it painted.
- Strange man throwing trash at me the same day I found his dog stuck in the earth.
- The sleep over in the RV. The shaking, the game, The crazy voice on the CB radio and muffled screams. All of it.
- The spearhead was inspired by a spearhead that

magically appeared on my birthday. In the middle of nowhere in my car. When no other adult was anywhere near me.(I still have it.)

- The school teacher setting me up, and my Mom going to town on the principal and the teacher being forced to take a sabbatical after. (That principal never did call my parents again.)

- The brown dress and getting into a fist fight to rescue a friend. (we were all scrappy girls in those days we had to be to survive.)

- Raven at my window.(Not in Idaho)

- Meeting my higher self and the feeling of wholeness it provided me.(Not in Boise.)

- The ritual by the river is based on real events.

- Scrying for past lives. Done it allot makes for a great evening with friends, the book details how to do it.

- Having seen a few creatures I can't explain.(some of the Gaiagoblin creatures are based on those.)

- The dreams and the cloaked man with yellow eyes. (I went into detail about it on FB)

- The three abandoned houses did sit in a triangle around the school.(My next school after we moved again was on Elm Street across form a grave yard.)

- Being stranded during a blizzard. Was based on an event when I was stranded in a blizzard. (different area of Idaho.)

- The calsake was inspired by the time I was invited to a meeting that turned out to be a cult event. (I explain it on FB)

- The talk with Odin and the tattoo was inspired by a Maori traditional healing I under went. Which was amazing. You bring all you struggles to the surface, share your story. The healer uses smoke, herbs and energy to remove the pain from you. Then you get a beating to become stronger then what hurt you, so it can't hurt you again. Then etch a tattoo on you to tell your story. (I felt the healing energy and it felt amazing and I felt free after. Yes it took a couple days for the bruising to go away. Still 100% worth it.)

I'm probably leaving some out, and I will add more in the next books yet to come. May you be safe and love your children. Soon they will be adults too.

Made in the USA
Las Vegas, NV
25 October 2021